THIS TIME FOREVER BOOK 3

CHASING
Forever

KELLY JENSEN

I0563575

RIPTIDE PUBLISHING

Riptide Publishing
PO Box 1537
Burnsville, NC 28714
www.riptidepublishing.com

Chasing Forever

Cover art: Natasha Snow, natashasnowdesigns.com
Editor: Carole-ann Galloway
Layout: L.C. Chase, lcchase.com/design.htm

ISBN: 978-1-62649-843-3

First edition
December, 2018

Also available in ebook:
ISBN: 978-1-62649-842-6

THIS TIME FOREVER BOOK 3

CHASING
Forever

KELLY JENSEN

RIPTIDE
PUBLISHING

For Brian

As you grow older, you will discover that you have two hands, one for helping yourself, the other for helping others.
— Sam Levenson

TABLE OF
Contents

CHAPTER 1

Malcolm Montgomery loved Morristown. Anyone who thought New Jersey was a shithole hadn't ventured far enough west. Or south. Or east. In fact, they probably hadn't left the turnpike, breezing past the ports without stopping at Ikea. Maybe they'd been stranded on the wrong side of the Ben Franklin Bridge at 4 a.m. or they'd heard the horror stories about Newark, despite phrases like *urban renewal.*

Morristown, though . . . Morristown was Small Town America on a grand scale, and still only forty-five commuter minutes from New York City. Fringed by farms and centered by Morristown Green, the town had everything a body could need, including the Colonial, a bar that had survived urban rethinking, beautification, a five-minute spell of popularity when they built the hotel across the street, and the casual indifference of a lifelong patronage.

The Colonial was where the locals drank. It was named for the high school football team, and trimmed with decades of memorabilia. Mal's father had drunk there, though thankfully didn't anymore. His father would fit into the daytime crowd, but the after-hours patrons would be a little too rowdy for him. Tonight, they seemed a little too rowdy for Mal, and the brilliant idea he'd had two hours before—that a beer or two and some lively conversation would somehow alleviate the weight of the past five months—had faded to a dull buzz in the back of his head.

But he loved the Colonial. It was a permanent pin on the board of this town. It wouldn't win any awards for décor or service, unless you liked looking at photos, newspaper clippings, and pennants; a healthy dose of sarcasm; and hot wings that weren't particularly hot. The place had always been there for him, though, and the barstools were pretty comfortable.

"'Nother one?"

Mal nudged his empty glass through a beery puddle. "Sure." He'd had a coaster. Bits of it clung to his fingers, rolled into pills. The rest spread out beneath his feet like bird food.

Leo Green, great-grandson of Bernard Green, founder of this faded collection of wood and brass on the north side of Morristown Green (no correlation), dropped a fresh cardboard coaster onto the bar and topped it with a foaming glass of porter.

"Want to close out your tab?" Leo asked, voice tinged with something that might be pity, might be hope. Probably hope. It was, after all, Christmas Eve, and he had a man to get home to.

"Not yet. I'm still not having a good time."

On cue, "Jingle Bell Rock" straddled the airwaves, climbing over the mild flutter of conversation floating through the bar. Everyone else seemed to be having a good time. Drinking, talking, planning, maybe getting ready to go out and party or go home and party. All except the couple at the table behind him: Brian Kenway and a woman Mal didn't recognize.

Glancing over his shoulder, Mal took another peek at the pair. They made a striking couple; Brian with golden-blond hair, paler at the temples, and maybe blue eyes—Mal had never gotten close enough to confirm the exact color. He'd wanted to, but he and Brian moved in different circles. Brian's companion had the look that fashion magazines would describe as *gamine*. Chin-length hair, dark and glossy. Wide, dark eyes.

The frowns they leveled at each other over several empty glasses marred their beauty somewhat, though.

Turning back around, Mal asked, "Why don't you have any live music?"

"Because I don't want to be open past ten."

"The Pig and the Frog have live acts tonight."

"Maybe you should go drink there."

"Too noisy."

Leo flipped open the dishwasher behind the bar and spoke through a wispy cloud of steam. "No pleasing some people."

"Ever think of changing your name to the Slothful Sloth?"

"You complaining about the service?"

"Nope. Just the crowd."

Shaking his head, Leo slid two clean glasses onto a shelf with maybe a little more force than necessary. After the clinking stopped, he said, "Seriously, Mal, you're pissing me off."

Mal dug out a grin. "Good. You can join me in my pity party."

Leo sighed, but smiled. "When do you go back to work?"

Grin fading, Mal ran his palm down the length of his left thigh. He wasn't sure if the ache in his bones was real or not, but he felt it all hours of the day. Sometimes at night too. His right leg—that was a whole different story and often required something stronger than beer. But not tonight. Tonight he had to drive, because gone were the days when he could rely on the mile-long walk home to sober him up.

"January second." He reached for his beer.

Leo picked up the glass he kept under the bar. Tonight, the inch of liquor was a few shades darker than Leo's brown skin. Mal had given up guessing what Leo drank after he began to suspect Leo changed it whenever he got it right. Leo lifted his glass in a toast. "To January second."

"Just because I'm going back to work doesn't mean I'm going to stop decorating your bar on a Friday night."

"Let a man have his dreams."

"Asshole."

Leo clinked his glass to Mal's. "Back at you."

"So what are your plans for the holidays?"

"You're looking at them."

"Kelsey in town for a while?" Kelsey, Leo's husband, was an artist. He traveled six months of the year, exhibiting and gathering inspiration for his next show.

"Yeah. At least until Feb."

"Nice."

"What about you?" Leo sounded interested and he would be. They'd gone to high school together and had both landed back in Morristown before it was cool to be gay. Still wasn't . . . totally. But they got by. Quietly.

"Donny is hosting this year," Mal said. "We're all due at noon to open presents and admire the inaugural wrecking of his new kitchen."

"That fuckwit finally finished your brother's kitchen?"

"Donny threatened to sue if it wasn't done by Christmas."

Leo made a show of checking his watch. "It only took them eight months."

"I told him not to use that guy. He shoulda used my guy."

"Isn't there some family relationship or . . ." Leo trailed off as the voices behind them rose. His brows arched up. He nodded, tight dreads bouncing, and Mal turned.

As Mal watched, a scowl spread across Brian's face, an expression Mal hadn't seen on him before. Brian more often wore a laconic smile—and usually at one of the other bars in town. In fact, the last time Mal had seen him had been at the Pig on the one night a month they hosted Miss Bacon and Friends. Unfortunate name, but Mal always enjoyed the show. Miss Bacon was another Morristown High alumni, five years after him and Leo, and didn't care if Morristown was cool with the gay thing or the drag-queen thing.

Brian's companion stood, shaking her head. Brian said something.

She slapped him. The sharp *crack* of her palm meeting his skin split apart Frank Sinatra's dulcet tones as the entire bar took in a breath.

Brian didn't cup his cheek. He didn't scowl or rock back. Nor did he speak. No defensive words parted his lips, no apology. He just sat there, stone-faced and . . . handsome . . . and watched as the woman collected her coat and purse. She rummaged for a minute before pulling out a folded bill that she let flutter to the table. Brian's expression soured a little, as though her leaving money offended him. Then he watched her go, along with everyone else in the bar.

When all eyes turned back to him, Brian stood, seemed to wrestle with the appropriate mind-set for a moment—at least, that was how it appeared to Mal. As though he couldn't quite decide if he was pissed, amused, sad, or indifferent. Then, jawline hardening over a squaring of admirably wide shoulders, Brian stalked toward the door.

Apparently, the show was over or taking a commercial break. So everyone in the bar did what everyone usually did while the ads played. They got another drink, visited the restroom, and occasionally glanced back at the screen. In this instance, the table where Brian's jacket still hugged the shoulders of one chair.

Mal didn't need a refill, so he pushed his glasses back up his nose and waited out the pause, letting Leo serve other customers, then tipped his head in the direction of the abandoned table. "I've seen him around. Didn't think he was straight or into women."

In Mal's fantasies, he definitely wasn't.

"He's not. Or I didn't think he was. He's in here pretty regularly on Thursdays." Pickup night. "And never takes women home. So unless he's climbed the fence, which, granted, some folks do when they're bored . . ." Leo held out his hands. "I don't fucking know. So long as he pays his bill, I don't care, either."

"A regular on Thursdays?"

So much for that idea, not that Mal had entertained it for long. He'd indulged in a daydream or two (or four), but he knew Brian was way out of his league. Usually dressed in a suit, or the remnants of one, except to Miss Bacon's shows, when he dressed to impress. And he always had someone by his side, which was why Mal had never bothered approaching him.

"Not your type," Leo confirmed.

"Yeah? Who do you think is my type?"

"I dunno. Someone quiet and bookish like you. Don't you gaming nerds have conventions or something? Go get yourself one of them guys."

Been there, done that, twice—once with a guy out on the West Coast who only ever answered to the name Aether Flameshadow. Online relationships weren't his thing. After being single for so long, Mal was starting to wonder if relationships were his thing.

Leo interrupted his train of thought with, "Maybe another professor."

"I'm a high school teacher."

"And Brian Kenway is a player."

Mal wasn't surprised that Leo knew Brian's name. Leo knew everyone in Morristown.

The door opened with a rush of cold air, and Brian reentered the bar, pausing only to stamp a little snow from his shoes, before eyeing the assembled patronage, all tuned back in to his channel, and giving them a short salute. Everyone went back to their business as he collected his jacket, his bill, his empty glass, and approached the bar.

Mal straightened in his seat, not wanting to appear too slumped over his beer. He thought about pushing his fingers through his hair, then remembered he didn't have hair anymore. Well, he did, but it was a lot shorter than it used to be. Grayer, too. He nudged his crutches deeper into the shadowy nook he'd tucked them into and then tried putting one elbow on the bar, wincing when it slipped through the beer puddle, nearly landing him face-first on the varnished wood. The scent of hops and old French fries wafted up to meet him before a warm hand caught his shoulder.

The pressure on his shoulder was enough to wake some of the old athletic reflex—whatever hadn't abandoned him on the side of Lake Road last August—and jerk Mal back to an upright position in front of an extremely well-made face.

"Thanks," Mal muttered and wondered if his cheeks were as warm as they felt.

Brian squeezed his shoulder. "See, it's not all bad."

"What's that?"

"Right when you think your life is about to do a body slide along the length of the bar, someone comes along and stops everything."

Mal blinked questioningly at the man in front of him, the man who did have blue eyes, he now saw. Four shades bluer than Mal's own washed-out denim color. And the sort of handsomeness that wasn't a mask. Attractiveness was ingrained in every line of Brian's face. From the easy laugh lines cornering his mouth and eyes, to the way his brows refused to curl against nature, but still managed to look rugged. His nose was long and straight, but pointed a little sideways, as if it'd been broken at some point. Of course, that only made him more interesting. His hair wasn't all blond, just mostly, the paler strands at his temples only serving to highlight the fact that Brian had been designed by nature to age well.

Brian's mouth tilted upward, slightly. A smile or possibly an amused smirk.

Mal cleared his throat. Reached for his glass. Then decided to go for it. He stuck out his hand. "Mal Montgomery and I have no idea what you're talking about."

For a moment, it seemed as though Brian might take offense. Then he tipped his head back and laughed—quietly and not for long enough to embarrass himself or Mal. He gripped Mal's hand in a solid shake. "Brian Kenway."

"I know." *Whoops.*

Brian's eyebrows did not jump up. Instead, he widened his smile. "My reputation precedes me."

"Something like that."

"Leo been gossiping about me again?"

"We were wondering what happened to your *friend*," Leo said.

Brian flipped one hand carelessly in the direction of the door. "I was an asshole. She'll forgive me tomorrow. Or maybe the day after that."

Okay, then. "So…" Mal moved his mouth a couple more times, but no words came out. What the heck? He had a doctorate in medieval and premodern European history, an area that did, on occasion, dip into language studies. "Want a beer?" he finally managed.

Grinning, Brian draped his jacket over one stool and sat on the other. Right next to Mal. "Sure. What are we drinking?"

"Snowdrift Vanilla Porter." That had been a serious question, right? One he was supposed to answer.

Brian nodded toward Leo, who got busy fitting another glass under the tap. Brian waited until he had his glass before lifting it for a toast. "What should we drink to?"

Mal picked up his glass. "Health."

They clinked and sipped. Brian appeared to savor the beer before swallowing, humming, and then licking his lips with a long, slow swipe of his tongue. "Tasty."

It wasn't that original a line, but it shot straight to Mal's cock, along with the imaginary press of that tongue, to stir the slumbering beast. Not so much he had to shift on the stool, but enough to feel a little like Rip Van Winkle waking to a new world.

"So, what have you heard about me?" Brian asked.

"Huh?"

"What nonsense has Leo been filling your ears with?"

"Oh, um . . ." Mal had never been a good flirt—he didn't have the gene for it. Or the knack. Or enough opportunity to practice.

Generally, he was much wittier online, especially when he knew what he was talking about. "Ah . . ." Had he tried that sound yet? "Thursday nights. We talked about Thursday nights."

"How come I've never seen you in here on a Thursday?"

Because I'm a high school teacher didn't seem like the right answer. Neither did an explanation about his legs. "I've been busy."

Brian smiled again, a boyish grin that suited his face. Made him look mischievous and even sorta cute, if you could get away with calling a good-looking guy cute. "What do you do?"

Okay, Mal knew how to handle this one. Short answer, not long. And make it sexy. "Right now, I split my time between . . ." So much easier online. "I play video games."

"For a living?"

"No. I'm on leave from what I do for a living."

"Now we're getting somewhere. Is this an administrative kind of leave? Did you do something naughty, Malcolm?"

"No one calls me Malcolm"—except his father and only when they were going to have a talk—"and no, I did not. What about you?" Mal let his gaze slide left to the fading pink mark on Brian's cheek.

Brian returned one of his rascal grins. "Recently, offending my best friend and business partner. It's a tough job, but someone's got to do it."

Leo appeared in the middle of them, or as middle as he could get with a foot of bar in the way. "Ready to settle your tab, Professor?"

Brian's eyebrows danced again. "Professor?"

"It's a joke and . . ." Mal couldn't do a sideways glance when facing someone, and he didn't know how to do coy, either. Another guy would know where to go from here. A less awkward man might simply ask if Brian was interested in taking this elsewhere. Not Mal. Not his thing, the fact his cock still tingled notwithstanding. Brian was a fantasy, not reality.

Besides, what did he have to offer a man like Brian Kenway? Now, in particular. He couldn't get to his knees. Heck, he could barely walk. Sex was probably completely out of the question, even if Brian wasn't put off by the first two facts.

"You seem to be doing a lot of thinking over there, Professor," Brian said, his tone quiet. "Can I offer a suggestion?"

Mal shook his head and the sharp movement failed to throw off his descending gloom. He felt in his pocket for his wallet. "No. I'm good. Leo, I think I'll settle up."

Brian seemed to wrestle with his mind-set again, and fascinated, Mal watched, now employing a sideways look as he counted the bills in his wallet. By the time he'd laid his cash on the bar, Brian Kenway had obviously decided how to react.

He smiled. Offered a gracious dip of his chin. "I'll wish you a happy holidays, then." Brian turned to Leo, gave him the same smile, same little nod. Then he laid a hundred-dollar bill on the bar. "On me."

He swept his jacket off the other stool and swung it over his shoulders in a gesture that, if Mal tried to emulate it, would result in him collecting every glass along the length of the bar and sweeping them to the floor. And then Brian was gone, the Colonial falling silent once more as though someone had clicked the remote, pausing the show in the middle of the final scene.

CHAPTER 2

Brian didn't hate Morristown. More, he struggled against what he perceived as the pull of a small town that kept sucking him back in. He did like the center. He lived there and worked there. Drank there and fucked there. The center of Morristown was like an island in the middle of quicksand. He was comfortable there, and safe. But he often felt as though he were cut off from the rest of the world by an inward tide. Every time he struck out, he became mired by a curious sense of inertia.

Take what had happened at the Colonial tonight. The professor was a nice-looking guy and the law of averages usually meant the nice-looking guy should end up in Brian's bed. Or at least in the restroom for a quick exchange of lustful intent. But right when Brian seemed to be crossing that divide, leaving his island, the quicksand had yanked him back. Along with a little help from Malcolm Montgomery.

Just as well. Mal wasn't his type. Too bookish. Too educated. Too nice. Mal's shy and slightly awkward manner probably only seemed endearing in the moment—cheeks flushed, glasses catching the light. In the morning, he'd be even more obviously not Brian's type. Too serious. Too put together.

Mal's smile, though. It'd been a while since another man's smile had made Brian's gut clench.

Hunching his shoulders and turning his jacket up around his ears, Brian angled southward through Morristown Green, taking the path that would lead him to the other side of the island, to Dumont Place, and along there to King Street and the condominium he called home.

Brian disliked living on King Street. The name reminded him too much of Charlie King, the current partner of his ex, Simon. Brian and

Simon had been together for twelve years before Charlie . . . Well, it hadn't been quite like that. Actually, it hadn't been like that at all. Brian had been the one to move out, thinking it was the only way to let Simon know how much he needed him. Who'd have guessed leaving would mean the end? Like, the real end. Not Brian, but then, he obviously had no idea how to do a relationship, despite years of practice.

So he'd moved into one of his stable of condos on King Street. That was how they'd been sold to him, as a fucking stable, even though the architecture was so far from farm-like, a horse would probably take offense. Regardless, he'd claimed the one he'd never managed to rent, and settled into his post-relationship funk, which, so far, alternated between two states: an unsettling likeness to being in a relationship because nothing had changed, and a deep loneliness that echoed so loudly, he was convinced Simon and Charlie could hear it all the way across the Delaware River in their cozy farmhouse (that horses would probably line up to be next to) in Bethlehem, Pennsylvania.

The cold had started to edge in on Brian's mood by the time he reached the end of Dumont Place, numbing him. The couple of Manhattans he'd drunk at the bar had boiled away in his bloodstream, and only the taste of the beer he'd had at the end lingered on his tongue.

He should call Vanessa and apologize for being an asshole. Shuffling a hand in his jacket pocket, he eased his phone out and woke the display. Ten thirty. He was walking home from a bar at ten fucking thirty. Vanessa was likely still on her way back to Newark, and he doubted she'd take a call from him tonight, anyway.

Brian crossed Pine, started up King Place, which would become King Street, and made plans, once again, to sell his *stable* and find somewhere else to live. Somewhere off the island.

The condos were a package of four, all facing different directions to give the illusion of privacy. The roof structure helped, making each "home" seem like a separate dwelling. The shared parking lot was more convenient than fourth wall breaking, and if you were social, which Brian was, being able to sit out the back and converse with the neighbors could be pleasant.

The architecture was that odd mixture of country and cape that often popped up in western New Jersey. It was blandly East Coast, with sloped roofs, dormers, a porch, and neat, cream-colored vinyl siding. They were pretty houses, each with a postage-stamp sized front garden, complete with a path and flowered border. Brian couldn't take credit for his own garden; he paid someone to look after it.

He pushed open the cute gate in the adorable white picket fence and trudged up the perfect path lined with snow-covered shrubs. After stomping his feet on the stairs leading up to the porch to knock away any trace of snow that hadn't been meticulously swept from the path, he dug into his pocket for his keys. The jingle echoed like a cold bell, metal on the verge of cracking, as he slid the right key home and turned the lock. Brian pushed inside, already lifting his chin in anticipation of the warmth that would bathe his face, and stopped as air nearly as cold as outside fluttered across his cheeks.

His first thought was that he'd left a window open, but Brian never opened his windows. Even in good weather. He suspected his housekeeper did sometimes. Either that or she had an air freshener that made the place smell like she had.

The cold breeze was coming from the kitchen end of the long hall and did not abate when Brian shut the front door. He kept his jacket on as he paced the length of the condo to the frigid and moonlit kitchen. Glass crunched under his feet, spilling out in a rough circle from a pane over the handle of the back door.

Feeling for the warm rectangle of his phone, Brian turned a quick circle. The kitchen looked about the same as he'd left it: clean and uncluttered. All the knife handles were sticking out of the block on the counter and the microwave blinked the time at him from over the range. He retreated to the hallway, breath puffing in little clouds in front of his face, passed the closed door of the downstairs powder room, and ducked his head into the dining room he'd repurposed into a home office. At first glance, his stuff seemed to be where it should be. The laptop on the desk, the TV on the console across from there, the frames on the wall—though why anyone would steal a photo, an architectural print, or award with his name on it confounded him. Likewise, the few things he kept in the glass cabinet opposite the door all seemed to be in attendance.

Brian pulled out his phone as he crossed the hall to the living room. He'd dialed a nine and a one but not the second one when he saw the figure on the couch. Whoever it was had taken the blanket from the back, and the other blanket from the love seat and had both tucked so tight, Brian couldn't be sure the shape was human. He knew, though. He also knew the need that wrapped a person so tight, not even a finger stuck out. Nothing to show, nothing to lose. He knew what it was like to be that cold, that afraid, and that lost.

Why this kid—and it had to be a kid, that was the only thing that made sense—had chosen his house made no sense. He rarely dropped into the youth centers in Newark managed by the Smart Foundation. His name was on the stationery, but he was Vanessa's *quiet* partner. He wrote letters and checks. That was their agreement.

Tucking his phone into his pocket, Brian approached the couch with a heavy step. He was surprised when the figure didn't move. The kid should have been up and over the back by now, eyeing him with a mixture of hope and distrust, maybe a good portion of disdain, and even a little loathing.

He didn't have a dead body on his couch, did he?

So far, he'd had a pretty crap night. Vanessa had lost patience with him, which was rare—they'd been friends forever. Then the professor had proved immune to his charms.

Now this.

Brian sat down on the love seat, putting him at a ninety-degree angle to the sofa, and considered his options. Calling 911 still felt like a good choice. The kid had broken into his house and was using his blankets. But nothing seemed to have been stolen, and with it being Christmas Eve, the kid would be stuck in a cell for a couple of days, or one of those holding tanks, the transitional homes where screenwriters collected plotlines for their TV dramas and still managed to get it wrong.

Shuffling closer to the sofa, Brian grabbed a fold of blanket and tugged.

The body didn't move.

He tugged harder and the body groaned, the sound so small and feeble that Brian reached for more blanket. He peeled it away from the kid's face and the odor of unwashed skin and clothes drifted up.

Brian let go to switch on the lamp set in the corner of the sofa and love seat.

The reaction was instant. The boy screwed up his pale face and burrowed back into his nest, hiding all but his shocking blue hair and the ring at the top of one ear. A second later, that disappeared too, leaving a single wisp of hair.

"Hey." Brian tugged the blanket away again, exposing the boy's face. His skin had a porcelain quality to it, fine and almost translucent, a tracery of veins apparent near his ear, the hollows of his cheeks without color, his lips almost blue. And he wasn't wearing lipstick. The kid was cold.

Really, really cold.

"Listen, I don't care who you are or why you're here, but if we don't get you warmed up, and real soon, we're both going to have more to deal with than some broken glass and a police report."

Brian plucked the blanket away, exposing the shoulder of the boy's coat—wool, not down, and fashionable rather than functional. Beneath, he wore a sweater, the round neck stretched to show the T-shirt beneath. Clothing enough for a quick walk home from the Colonial. Not for whatever this kid had been doing—which, judging by the smell of him, had been at least a week of outdoor living.

A funk Brian had never quite forgotten, even if he hadn't been able to smell it on himself after the second week . . .

The boy opened his eyes, also blue, and cringed, pulling the blanket around his shoulders. "You're going to call the police?" His voice was soft and high. Not girlish, just not quite settled into adulthood. Or shy. Could be that.

"I haven't decided yet."

Pale brows crooked together, drawing Brian's attention to the fact that they were blond, which accounted for the shocking shade of his hair. Blond hair loved color.

"C'mon. I can offer you a shower and warm clothes while we wash the rat's nest you're sleeping in. Some food and you'll feel halfway decent. Then we'll talk about what we're going to do." Brian kept his voice and tone quiet and all of the options open. He didn't want the boy to run. Didn't particularly want him hanging around, either, in case his friends figured this was a safe place to park their flea-ridden asses. But he could offer one night.

The boy looked at him for about half a minute, his reaction time likely more affected by the cold than a need to think things through. He probably hadn't been living rough for long. He didn't seem wary or frightened enough.

Finally, he asked, "Don't you want to know who I am?"

"That can wait until you're clean and warm, I think."

A quick nod and the kid started pushing out of his nest. Once he was standing, Brian guessed the boy was fourteen or so. He was small enough to be twelve, but he stood with the attitude of someone resigned to being slight. Someone who'd decided he'd always be on the lighter side of normal, with ghostlike skin and huge eyes. A boy who'd dyed his hair blue and pierced his ears all the way around because, what-the-fuck-ever, he was already weird.

Brian collected the blankets and nodded toward the hall. "Upstairs. I'm leaving the kitchen door unlocked. You know the way out if you want to leave."

"Why would I want to leave?"

Kid definitely hadn't been doing this for long.

Brian directed him to the guest bathroom. "Towels in the linen closet there, soap and shampoo in the tub. Pull the little thing up to get the water coming out of the showerhead and use as much hot water as you like. Dump your clothes outside the door before you get in. I'm going to put them in the washer. You'll find some sweats right here when you're done. Okay?"

The boy gave him a wide-eyed nod. "Okay."

"You like cheese?"

"What?"

"Can you eat cheese?"

"No. I'm, um, lactose intolerant."

Of course he was, because being on his own wasn't hard enough. "How about some soup, then. Tomato? Chicken noodle?"

"Tomato. Thank you."

"Okay. Give me your clothes. You stink." He didn't mean to be harsh, but he also kinda did. While he wanted to make the kid feel safe, he also knew the kid would feel better when he was clean and warm.

More open and more receptive. If he'd been taking care of himself for much longer than a couple of weeks, Brian's tactics wouldn't work, but he'd already proven that he was fluffy as a newborn chick.

The bathroom door closed, and Brian heard the shower curtain rings rattle. He paused in the upstairs hallway to dump his armful of blankets outside the closet housing his washer and dryer, then went to find something small enough for his guest to wear. His sweats would all be too long, but the kid wasn't going anywhere. He also grabbed a long-sleeve T-shirt, a hoodie that was too small but still had sentimental value, and a thick pair of socks.

The boy's clothes were in the hallway as requested. Brian exchanged them for the clean ones. The coat was dry-clean only, so he stuck it on a hanger over the dryer. It would get aired out, at least. The rest, he shoved into the machine before setting the selector to antibacterial. Then he went to inspect his soup collection.

A cold wind met him at the bottom of the stairs. "Goddamn it." First, he needed a piece of cardboard and a roll of duct tape.

Brian had a can of rustic tomato (whatever the hell that was) heating on the range when the boy appeared in the kitchen, his already slight figure swamped by Brian's clothes. His cheeks were pink, though, and his lips had lost their blue tinge. He also looked tired, as though he'd fall over if he had to stand up for too long. Indicating a stool on the other side of the island he used as a dining area, Brian set him up with soup, toast, and a glass of water. He put a multivitamin next to the glass.

"Feel better?"

The kid nodded. "Yeah."

"Okay. How about we get to know each other a little bit?"

Again, the almost requisite panic failed to register in those wide blue eyes.

"I'm Josh," the boy said. "Joshua Kenway."

Kenway? Brian arched a quizzical eyebrow.

"I'm your nephew. Ellen's son? You are my Uncle Brian, aren't you?"

CHAPTER 3

"Uncle Mal, Uncle Mal!"

Unlike the accident that had wrecked his legs, Mal could see this one coming. He braced one crutch against the brick step, digging the rubber tip into a groove as his niece and nephew crashed into him and for a bare second, he thought he'd be okay. Then he was tipping backward, crutch falling away, leaving one arm free to flail while the sky wheeled overhead. The time before he hit the ground seemed endless. Flashes of memory assaulted him—the sensation of flying, bright lights, voices out of nowhere, and fear. His recollection of the accident didn't always coincide with what had actually happened, but the moment the car had hit him, that sudden and sharp impact, would always be remembered as fear.

A strong arm caught him around the back of the shoulders. Mal slipped sideways a little, his braced leg sliding across the bricks, but the anticipated smack of hard concrete didn't happen.

"Hey! Hey, I've got you," his rescuer said.

Donny hauled Mal upright and the wrench in his knee sent a flare of pain up and down his right leg. Swallowing a yell, Mal concentrated on keeping a hold of his remaining crutch—though it might have been better to let it go. His right shoulder wasn't happy, and all he needed was to rip open multiple old injuries. But Donny held him steady and stood there, arm still around Mal's shoulders, until Mal offered him a nod.

"How're we doing?" Donny asked.

Rather than admit that a curl of fear still lingered in his gut and that everything hurt, Mal tried for a smile that felt more like a grimace. "I'm good."

His niece chose that moment to burst into tears.

Christmas Day was off to a great start.

Arriving at the scene of averted disaster, his mother pushed through the struggling mess of Donny and kids, and immediately echoed Mal's expression, lips thinning as she shook her head. Like it was his fault he was standing there with a leg brace, one crutch, and various aching body parts. At least he was wearing a coat?

"You okay?" she asked, frown softening.

"Yeah, Ma. I'm okay."

She pulled her bawling granddaughter into a hug. "See, Uncle Mal's just fine."

If only she knew.

Mal jerked his chin toward his car. "I've got some stuff in the car." He made to turn and she stopped him.

"No, no. You go on inside." After pushing him toward the door, she started organizing the children, directing each of them toward a task. Didn't matter whose house it was, his mom was in charge of logistics.

A short while later, Mal found himself on the couch in the family room, braced leg propped up on an ottoman and a steaming mug of hot chocolate cupped between his hands. He bent forward to inhale the aroma and winced. Spiked hot chocolate. "What's in this?"

"Whiskey," Donny answered, sitting next to him on the couch, a similar mug in hand. "How's the leg?"

"Which one?" Mal leaned forward to massage the left, which had started to ache, and for a moment, emotional fatigue threatened to overwhelm him. God, he was sick of being sore, of being less able, worried, broken, afraid of falling. Of feeling old before his time. Tired of wondering if he'd ever run the Patriots' Path again. Complete another section of the Appalachian Trail.

He didn't want to think about running a marathon. He generally saved those thoughts for when he was really depressed.

Beside him, Donny looked on quietly, as he sometimes did, almost certainly deciding between comfort and motivation. "You'll be steady come springtime," he finally said.

Motivation it was.

Mal tried to find the right mood, the right response, and took a slug of his doctored hot chocolate instead. And coughed and spluttered. "Jesus. How much whiskey did you put in this?"

"Enough to make sure you had a good day."

"I need to be able to drive home."

"You live three blocks away. I think we can manage something. Or you can stay."

Instantly, Mal drew in. Not go home? "Lois is expecting me."

Donny laughed. "You do realize Lois is a cat?"

"Humph."

"Finish your hot chocolate and I might let you come play in my new kitchen."

Mal did as he was told because it was easier to let go. He didn't want to be the guy who cried on Christmas Day, and he did love his family, even if every one of them but him shared the same naively optimistic philosophy: everyone was going to live long, trouble-free lives, that a setback was merely a reminder that life needed to be lived, and that everything could be fixed by a shot of whiskey.

His niece and nephew both gave him socks for Christmas, to keep his feet warm until springtime. His parents gave him a gift card to REI, where he never shopped because their cheapest hiking gear was too expensive. They meant well.

"For springtime," his mom said, ever optimistic.

"Thanks, Mom."

Donny gave him a bottle of whiskey. "It's actually from Scotland."

Studying the label, which proudly proclaimed the bottle as *The Finest Scotch Whisky*, Mal said, "I'd hope so."

"No, I mean I ordered it special, doofus. Can't get it here."

"Thanks, Donny. That was real nice of you." And it was.

Donny's wife, Rachel, gave him a new trail guide for Northeastern Pennsylvania. "For springtime," she said as well.

Blinking away tears, Mal nodded and pretended deep interest in the survey-quality maps until the focus shifted from him to someone else.

Food happened, more whiskey happened, wine too, and Mal forgot his melancholy mood. He even started to believe he might be using the trail guide come spring. Or by summer at the latest.

His shoulder had stopped throbbing and his left leg, the one he'd broken, had gone pleasantly numb. His knee sent an occasional *ping* from beneath the massive dark brace enclosing most of his right leg, letting him know it was there. He'd managed to hobble from the table to the couch without using his crutches, but now his bladder was reminding him he'd had more than a bit to drink, and a trip to the bathroom was going to require aid, especially as his head had started to wander tipsy paths.

"Need a hand?" his dad asked.

"Yeah. I want to get down the hall. Can you get my crutches?"

"You can lean on me. I'm heading that way."

Rather than argue—not even sure why he wanted to—Mal levered himself back to his feet and limped alongside his father to the hall bathroom. After Mal took care of business, his father said, "Wait here," and took his turn.

Were they going to have some sort of father-son bonding moment in Donny's drafty hallway?

"So how are you doing?" his dad said, emerging from the bathroom a minute later.

Yes. Yes, they were.

"You know how it is."

"No, I don't. That's why I'm asking. You don't look so good, Malcolm. I mean, you're healthy enough to pacify your mother, but you're quiet and snippy."

"A car hit me, Dad. And left me on the side of the road with a lot of broken bones and one seriously messed-up knee." Three torn ligaments. All the important ones. The most important so beyond fubar, he'd had to have surgery. Hence the big, obnoxious brace. "If this graft doesn't take, I'm fucked."

His dad's eyebrows rose up at the curse, but he didn't comment.

Mal bowled on, "And I was lying there for twenty minutes before anyone saw me." He'd been knocked unconscious, which in retrospect had been a blessing. It had been an ugly leg break. Three different places. "Now I don't know if I'll ever walk properly again, let alone hike, and you know that's my sanity check every summer. Forget ever running another marathon. Coaching the track team." Then there was his love life, the lack of which he would prefer not to discuss with his father. "So, no, I'm not doing super fantastic, but I'm okay. I'm trying to live the family philosophy."

His father winced at that. "What can I do?"

"Stop asking if I'm okay." *And get me another whiskey. Or cut me off.* Mal felt as though he was in that place where the day could teeter into disaster or oblivion and couldn't quite decide which direction to go. And he didn't know why he was suddenly so angry. "I'm sorry," he mumbled. "I didn't mean to snap."

His father gripped his shoulder. "Are you seeing anyone?"

Nope. Not going there. "Why?"

"Because I care. I'm worried and I'd like to know if there's someone else worrying. Someone looking out for you."

Brian's handsome face teased the periphery of Mal's thoughts. He gave his head a quick shake. "No, there's not."

"Why not? It's been years since you and Noah broke up."

Seven, not that Mal was counting.

"You know your mom's friend, Daphne? Her son—"

"God, Dad, no." Mal held up one hand and stopped just short of making a warding symbol. "I don't need you guys to set me up. Jesus, the last date Mom set up was the absolute worst."

His dad tried, unsuccessfully, to stifle a chuckle. They'd all enjoyed that story.

The son of another of his mother's friends had been told Mal was interested in history and hiking and so had decided a trip to Gettysburg would make a great first date. Fantastic idea, in theory, until the date's car had broken down halfway and he hadn't had any roadside assistance. Mal had had to call his. After the car was towed and they'd been dropped off at a rental place, the date had discovered he'd left his wallet in his car. Mal had rented them a car and paid for the lunch on the way home too, because he hadn't been going to tempt fate any further, despite the date's insistence they could still salvage the weekend. That was when Mal had learned that a room had been booked and the date had wanted to surprise him with an overnight, on a first date.

So not his thing.

Putting away a smile, his dad clasped Mal's shoulder. "I wish I could say the word and make everything right for you. I hate seeing you unhappy."

"I'm happy, Dad. Deep down, under all this current misery, I'm very content, okay?" As content as he could be, having spent his fiftieth birthday recovering from the first of several surgeries that, so far, had only made him feel older. At least he'd had Donny at his side, turning fifty eight minutes after he did.

He'd always have Donny.

After dessert, when Mal was on a stool in the kitchen, pretending to dry the dishes Donny kept stacking in the rack beside him, Donny said, "Leo called me last night."

"Yeah?"

"Said he was worried about you."

"Seriously? I just had Dad corner me in the hallway."

"I know. He was our elected official."

"Jesus, Donny." Yep, he'd always have his brother.

"Leo said that prick Kenway was sniffing around you at the bar last night."

Cheeks flushing, Mal said, "And what business is that of Leo's? Or yours?"

"I know Kenway. Sort of. Through his clients." Donny worked with their father in real estate. "I made the mistake of calling him when I wanted quotes on my kitchen, and he not so politely informed me that if I wanted twenty kitchens, and the houses around them, he could help me. Apparently construction managers only consult on large projects."

"Heh."

"Yeah. And then he gave me the number for the idiot that took eight months to finish the job."

Yikes. "Ah."

"I don't like the way he does business."

"Are you actually warning me off this guy?"

"Which guy?" Rachel had wandered into the kitchen.

"Brian Kenway."

"Oh, I know him!" She turned to Mal. "Are you and Brian a thing?"

"What? No. And Donny's doing his best to make sure we're not." Which only made Brian more attractive, of course, in a whiskey-addled, you're-not-the-boss-of-me kind of way.

"Why not? He's a lovely guy. Handsome too!"

"How do you know him?" Donny asked.

"He's on the board for the Smart Kids Foundation." Rachel worked at the high school as well, as a guidance counselor.

"So he gives money to disadvantaged kids. Bully for him."

"He does a lot more than that. He's the one who reviews the scholarship applications and he writes to every one of the recipients after graduation to congratulate them. I've seen those letters, Donny. They're on file."

"It's easy to write a nice letter," Donny said.

"Why don't you like him?"

Not currently a part of the conversation, Mal watched as husband and wife sized each other up as if to determine whether the argument was worth it. Then Donny turned to him. "Leo says he's a player, and I didn't like his attitude on the phone. I've seen him at work too—he's ruthless. The fact he has a soft spot for kids doesn't make him nice. He's not your type, okay?"

"Did Leo forget to tell you I blew him off?" Mal said.

"You what?" Donny choked.

Rachel had gone bright red.

"Oh for God's sake. I turned him down. Not . . ." Mal waved a hand.

Rachel recovered first. "He really is handsome. I'd—"

"Jesus, Rach." Donny looked as though he wished he were still choking.

Meanwhile, Mal was letting his tired and drunken thoughts amble down the hallway of the Colonial, toward the bathroom, where he had never taken a guy, but had stumbled over a few. He wasn't the sort to get to his knees in a public place, and with whiskey rushing through his veins, Rachel giggling to one side of him, and Donny spluttering into the sink, he couldn't help but wonder if that was part of his problem.

Even before ending up with two broken legs, he hadn't exactly been living life to the fullest, had he? He made it seem like he did. But fantasizing about sucking a guy off in public and doing it were two very different things.

Was he too old to try something new? To actually get out there and do what he said he would? And was Brian Kenway the guy to try that with?

Maybe.

Maybe? *Way to be assertive, Mal.*

Sighing, he pushed off the stool and limped away in search of the whiskey bottle.

CHAPTER 4

B rian listened to his sister's voice mail prompt for the fifth time before hanging up. He hadn't heard Ellen's voice in over thirty years, and the flattened cheer of her asking him to leave a message pulled at memories he'd worked hard to suppress: a moment of simultaneous joy and horror, and the day that had changed the course of his life forever. The eighteen or so months that had followed his unprepared tumble into living somewhere other than home.

Did she ever wonder what had happened to him?

Shaking off the creep of thoughts he'd rather not entertain, Brian dialed her number again. If she'd listened to his first four messages, she knew who was calling, why, and what he thought of her in as much detail as the message time had allowed. His sixth call went to voice mail. With a growl, Brian threw his phone toward the end of the bed.

Loneliness often poked at him, but this morning the feeling seemed stronger, even though he had a guest. Brian wanted to roll over, bury his head under one pillow, hug another one, and tug the quilt over his head. Bed was warm and the world was cold. But after he got up, it would be obvious that he'd left only one dent in the bed. No one waited to welcome him back inside the cozy huddle of blankets and pillows. That had been the best part about being in a relationship. Sex was awesome, but sharing a bed through the night and into cold winter mornings was more intimate. Having someone to talk to, even if there were parts of his self he couldn't share.

Could he have told Simon why having Josh here had him so off-balance? Brian glanced at the stack of pillows next to him. Would he have been able to share the coincidence of him and his nephew having a family expiration date of fourteen years?

Groaning, Brian pulled the quilt over his head. Simon was as much a specter of his past as Ellen. He'd managed to stop thinking about his sister. Obviously he needed some practice excising happier memories.

"Uncle Brian?"

Brian flipped the quilt back and looked at the ghost hovering in the doorway. Josh's hair seemed even bluer in the filtered daylight pushing through the drawn blind. His skin more pale, and his cheeks more gaunt. The jut of his Adam's apple extra prominent. What a gawky kid. Cute, though, in a not-quite-as-offbeat-as-he-wanted-to-be way.

"What's up?"

"Can I, um, get something to eat?"

"You're asking now? Why not break another window?"

Josh rocked back, face furrowing with frown lines that were too deep for a fourteen-year-old.

"Sorry." Brian pushed his quilt down far enough to indicate he was getting up. "I'm not a morning person." Usually, he was. Or used to be. He poked his legs out over the side of the bed and half sat, half rolled out of bed. "Careful when you go downstairs. I swept last night, but didn't vacuum. You were out and I didn't want to wake you." And now he sounded like a grandmother. Speaking of whom, "Why aren't you at your grandmother's?"

Eyes widening, Josh shook his head. "She, um, doesn't like me."

"Huh. Well, she didn't have much time for me, either." Except to stuff a twenty in his hand and tell him to get lost.

"Is it true you left when you were fourteen?"

Brian grunted. "Runs in the family, doesn't it?"

He slipped his feet into slippers that he hated and treasured at the same time. A gift from Simon, they were the ugliest footwear imaginable: a moccasin-type thing with tassels. But the Sherpa lining hugged his feet and kept his toes warm. He grabbed a sweatshirt from the end of the bed, dislodging his phone, and pulled it on over his bare chest. The phone got tucked into the pocket of his sleep pants. Josh hovered, watching everything as though Brian getting out of bed was a lesson in how someone should get organized in the morning.

He moved aside when Brian waved him through the door, and waited for Brian to pass him and lead the way downstairs.

Brian scowled at the cardboard taped over the lower pane in the kitchen door. His crude patch seemed to be working, though. No arctic breezes trailed down the hallway and his kitchen was sunny and warm.

Why did it have to be sunny?

"So, what do you like?" Brian opened his freezer. "I've got bread. We could do French toast. Hmm, I think there are some frozen waffles down here somewhere. Or if you're in the mood for eggs, we could do that. Anything else you can't eat?"

"I, um, don't eat meat. Like, a vegetarian?"

"Like a vegetarian or an actual vegetarian? And why don't you eat meat? Is that why you're so pale? You look ill."

Getting all frowny again, Josh slid behind the big island and claimed the same stool he'd used last night. "I don't like the idea of animals suffering."

"Suffering is a part of life."

No answer.

"Do you eat eggs?"

"Yes."

"Even though they're baby chickens?"

A smile cornered Josh's small mouth. "Mm-hmm."

So he had some spunk. "Eggs without cheese coming up. Want an English muffin or something on the side? Can you eat butter? Never mind, this crap I use isn't real butter anyway. Why don't you go get the vacuum? I've got a handheld thing in the closet in the hall."

Josh did as he was told, and Brian scrambled up a pile of eggs, whisking them through a puddle of "butter" because the boy was way too skinny. Brian toasted muffins, pulled jelly out of the fridge. Poured a couple glasses of juice and put on a pot of coffee.

They ate in a companionable silence, Brian feeling weird because he had someone in his house, but also . . . because he didn't mind. Not yet. It was nice to have company, even if that company didn't eat meat and didn't talk much.

He picked up his cup of coffee, circling his hands around the warm mug. "So, tell me again what you were doing wandering around

Morristown last night?" So far, all he'd gotten out of Josh was that his mom had kicked him out about a week ago—he didn't ask why because fuck—and after his friend's father found him camping out in their basement, Josh had wandered Newark for two days before catching a train to Morristown. He'd gotten lost twice between the station and Brian's house, which considering the station was literally at the end of King Street, was somewhat baffling. "How did you know where I lived?"

"I looked you up. White pages dot com."

"Huh. And you came here because . . ."

Josh bit his lips together and studied his plate.

Brian took a sip of his coffee. "Honestly, I'm surprised you know who I am. I was pretty sure your mom and grandparents had struck my name from the family bible or whatever."

Josh gave him a sideways glance. "They don't talk about you much. Mostly it's a 'don't want to end up like Brian' kind of thing."

If only they knew.

"Awesome. And did you end up like me?"

Eyes filling with tears, Josh blinked at his plate. He sniffed and turned his head away, lifting one hand to scrub at his cheek with his sleeve. Brian let him be. He didn't know how to comfort a kid, and if he were sitting at the kitchen counter of a virtual stranger, crying, he'd want to be left alone until he pulled himself together. Damn if the boy . . . young man? What was fourteen? Painful, that's what it was. Fourteen sucked, whether or not you met the status quo.

"How did they find out?" Brian asked when the cheek rubbing had stopped.

Josh talked to his plate. "I told them."

"Ah." Brian lifted a hand and dropped it. "I'm sorry, Josh. Your mom can be a bitch, okay? But she's your mom. I'm sure she'll get over it."

"No, you don't understand." Josh's voice was thick with tears yet to be shed. "She kicked me out. Gave me fifty bucks and pushed me out the door."

A cold shiver sidled down the back of Brian's neck, pinching his shoulders together. "She . . . what?"

"She said she won't have a gay son and told me to leave."

"It's 2018 for Christ's sake."

Eyes still wet, still tragic, Josh gave a big shrug and then seemed to collapse toward the counter. Brian let him fold—he had other shit to do, like stabbing the Redial button on his phone.

The call went to voice mail.

Brian was off the stool by then, pacing near the kitchen door. "You fucking bitch," he hissed into the phone. "You really think kicking your son out of the house because he is who he is is acceptable behavior? You don't deserve to have kids. You're poison." Gasping for breath, he glanced up to find Josh staring at him in horror. "Fuck you, Ellen. Is this because of me? Do you still hate me that much? You know what? You all deserve each other. Don't call me back because I don't want to hear your excuses. Just come get your son and make this right." He ended the call and dropped his phone onto the counter.

"You're sending me back?"

"You can't stay here. I'm not . . . I can't . . . I'm the bad example, okay? The whole family hates me."

"They hate me too!"

"I cannot believe this is still a thing." Brian paced back past the door, looking down when something snapped beneath his ugly slipper. "Missed a piece." He bent to pick it out of the rubber sole and angled toward the trash can where he paused, one foot depressing the peddle, his hand hovering over the open lid. "Why did you tell them?"

"My sister said I should."

"You have a sister?"

"And a younger brother."

"Are you the oldest?"

Josh nodded.

"What's your dad like. Can you talk to him?"

"He left when I was four."

"Not going to ask why."

Another hint of a smile touched Josh's face.

"What about your other aunts and uncles? There were five of us."

The smile fell away.

"Finish your breakfast. I'm going to make some more calls."

"Why can't I stay with you?" Josh's eyebrows were crooked together in genuine question.

"You don't even know me, Josh. I could be a degenerate. I *am* an asshole. I also don't have time for a kid. I work. Long hours. I'm away a lot, and I don't live the sort of life a kid should follow."

Rather than cry, Josh seemed to harden under the assault. His mouth closed, his chin jutted forward, and his shoulders fell back a little. It was heartening to see, that he wasn't completely soft. Then again, how could he be if he'd been raised by Ellen? If his sister had turned out anything like their father, and it sounded as though she had, Josh probably hadn't had the most pleasant childhood. He'd have been too different from the get-go.

Scraping his fingers against his palm, Brian thought about doing the comforting-touch thing, fought against the urge, and finally compromised with a quick squeeze to Josh's shoulder. "Finish up. We'll go somewhere and do something this afternoon, okay?"

Josh ducked his shoulder out from beneath Brian's hand and turned back to his breakfast.

Brian left the kitchen and went into his home office, phone out, a call already going through.

"It's way too early for you to be calling to apologize for last night," Vanessa said as she answered.

"I'm not apologizing yet."

"Brian—"

"Wait, no . . ." He sighed. "I am. Okay. It was first thing on my to-do list today. I was even going to call last night, but figured you'd still be driving."

Vanessa huffed through the phone. "Is there a palm print on your cheek?"

Brian reached for his cheek and an image of Josh scrubbing his face while he tried not to cry had him stopping with his fingers at his jaw. He dropped his hand and made a fist. "No."

"There should be."

"I know."

"So why are you calling?"

"My nephew showed up last night."

"You have a nephew?"

"Two of them, apparently. Probably more. I did have four siblings." Brian glanced at the small collection of pictures hanging on the wall behind his desk, all of them him doing stuff with people who weren't his family.

"How did he find you? Why?"

"Google or something, and Ellen kicked him out."

"Oh my God."

"I know."

"You have Ellen's son there? What does he look like?"

"He has blue hair. Listen, Ness, I need a favor."

"I still don't have my apology."

"Are you sorry you slapped me?" Brian managed to touch his cheek this time, where he rubbed at an imaginary mark.

"No! God, you are so infuriating."

"You love me."

"Actually, not right now I don't."

"Ness—"

"No. Don't. Tell me what you need."

"Somewhere for Josh to stay while I sort shit with his mom."

Vanessa said nothing for a beat, then: "You're going to go see Ellen?"

"If she won't take my calls, yeah."

"How do you have her number?"

"Josh's phone." Which was cheap and cracked and shouldn't even work. Maybe he'd get Josh a new phone before he— "So, do you have any suggestions?"

"Are you asking me to take him?"

"No." *Maybe?* "Doesn't the Smart Foundation have a house in Newark?"

"It's not a great place, Brian. I mean, it's better than being on the streets, but the kids there are sad. If Josh can go home, it'd be a better option."

Brian nudged away his own memories of *sad* places. "What if he can't go home?"

"Why can't he stay with you?"

"Me? I'm not the right guy for this."

"No, of course not. You're just the money man. Put him in one of your properties, then. Pay the bills."

"He's only fourteen."

"I don't know what to tell you, Bri. It's not as if he has nowhere to go. You have a large family. Surely someone else can take him in."

"I guess I'll start making calls."

"Maybe wait until tomorrow. It is Christmas, in case you've forgotten."

"Ness?"

"Mmm?"

"I'm sorry, okay? I shouldn't have said what I did. I . . ." An oily and uncomfortable feeling surged around Brian's gut. "I'm an asshole."

"You can't hide behind that forever, you know."

"Why not? I'm forty-eight, single, and all my friends and exes are happy and together and getting married. Seems like this is the perfect time to be bitter and maybe feel sorry for myself."

"Way to be a friend there."

"You don't want me to be your man of honor or whatever the hell it is you want me to do."

"But I do. We've been friends since we were sixteen years old. Who else is going to stand there with me? Who else knows me well enough to not insist I have a hundred fucking bridesmaids all dressed in some frothy shade of purple? Or drag me out to a strip club the night before."

Brian felt an evil grin corner his mouth. "We're totally doing the strip club."

"If it's tasteful—"

"It's the future, Ness. You can have any wedding you want."

"If it's the future, why are kids still being kicked out of their homes for being gay?"

Brian's mouth turned downward, the motion making him feel old. And sad. "Point."

"Well, you do need a project. Something to help you get over Simon."

Brian looked at his picture wall again, specifically at the single remaining photo of him and Simon on vacation in Spain. The one he hadn't been able to pack away. "I'm over Simon. It's been two years."

"Mm-hmm. So, are you going to be my man of honor?"

"Do I have to wear purple?"

"God, no. But we should coordinate." Vanessa's tone held laughter.

"So when is this disaster happening?"

"Were you even listening to me last night?"

"Of course not. I was sitting there feeling sorry for myself and hating you at the same time."

"Brian." Vanessa sounded exasperated.

"Hmm?"

"You should keep Josh around for a bit. I think it'd be good for you."

"I really don't know why you'd think that. I'm not the sort of person who takes in strays and then keeps them forever. I see a dog sniffing around my yard and I'm already yelling at it to get off my lawn."

A soft cough pulled his attention from the vista of gray slush and sad trees outside the front window. Josh stood in the doorway of the den, covering his mouth as he coughed again. The distress pinching his face obviously wasn't related to the seizure of his lungs.

"I gotta go. Talk to you soon." Brian clicked off, dropped his phone, and chased his snuffling nephew back toward the kitchen.

CHAPTER 5

Mal hissed as one of Satan's servants pushed his heel toward his thigh, bending his right knee at what felt like an unnatural angle. The physical therapist let his leg go, her practiced fingers digging into the side of his swollen knee for a few seconds before encouraging him to bend the leg again. Mal concentrated on not swearing, which meant hissing again.

"Experiencing a lot of pain, hon?" the therapist asked. Her name might be Amanda. He usually had someone else, but with the holidays, his regular therapist was on vacation.

"I'm fine," Mal said, the tightness of his words probably indicating how not fine he was.

"Don't worry, I'll hook you up later." She winked.

Too relieved she'd let his leg straighten to wonder whether she was flirting or offering him illicit drugs, Mal bent forward to massage his knee. The right side was still numb, and the left felt like it belonged to someone else. After his near fall on Christmas Day, it was even more sore, swollen to twice its usual size, and mottled with bruises. The staples had only been removed a week ago, and the scars were ugly. All in all, the abused joint didn't much resemble a knee.

Amanda returned with her laptop balanced on one arm. "Okay, let's see. Looks like you've been using one of the red bands."

Red had recently been demoted from favorite color.

Amanda retrieved a resistance band and instructed him in the painful art of flexing, pushing, and generally wearing out any muscle and/or tendon in his leg not recently stitched back into place. It hurt. It always hurt. Mal pushed through the pain as he always did, letting the counts float through his head. He lost track now and again as his thoughts tore free of stinging reality to pass back over Christmas Day—which, in retrospect, might have been his most depressing performance yet. He shouldn't have had that much to drink. His whole family seemed to think he was ready to call it quits.

Just a couple of broken legs. That was all.

Amanda tugged the band from his fingers. "Okay, now let's do some leg lifts." Her cool hands slid beneath his calf to add support as he corralled his thigh muscles and instructed them to lift.

Again, his thoughts wandered. This time to the discussion about Brian. He could picture the guy being an ass to his brother. Brian seemed the type. Recommending an incompetent tradesman was a dick move, though, and didn't seem to fit what he knew of Brian. Reputation would be important to a guy like him.

"Can you go a little higher?" Amanda asked.

Grunting, Mal lifted his leg a little higher. A burning sensation traveled along the back of his leg, and when he considered the effort it took to swing this foot in front of the other one, he wanted to cry.

"Okay, let's turn you out sideways."

Mal hated this exercise. After turning so that both legs dangled over the edge of the table, he had to tuck his "good" leg under the bad one and lift both. He always imagined slipping off the table, his new ligament tearing before it had a chance to become his replacement ACL. The idea of having to endure surgery all over again made his stomach clench. Maybe not ever being able to walk properly? His vision started to swim.

"You doing okay, hon?"

No, he wasn't. Gritting his teeth, Mal forced a smile. "Just . . . sore. I nearly fell on Christmas Day." He didn't mention how much it had cost him to stay upright, even without his brother's steady arm. How his knee had throbbed since, and the strain in his shoulder.

"I wish you'd said something when you first came in. That's probably why the joint is so swollen. How's your pain?" Her neat eyebrows scrunched toward the middle of her forehead as she studied the laptop again. "What have you been taking?"

"Advil."

"Mm-hmm." She nodded. "How many times a day?"

"Ah . . . only at night."

She shook her head. "Maybe try taking one right before PT. And with the swelling you have, definitely every day. The pain doesn't make you stronger, Mal."

Don't I know it.

"Listen, I know it's hard to find that balance between using your knee and allowing it to heal, but you really need to watch that you're not doing too much. It could set you back. When's your next appointment with your surgeon?"

And on it went. Same routine, different day. The hope he would make a full recovery clashing against the warning he might not. Admonishment and sympathy. And beneath it all, the cold and slimy fear that this was it. That this was as good as it got.

Then it was time for the only part of physical therapy he could say he enjoyed: the cold compress. Leaning into the upraised back of the work table, Mal reached for his phone, then decided to close his eyes instead. He was too tired to surf all the happy-happy-joy-joy of Facebook. Amanda arranged the icy cuff around his knee, activated it, and thankfully left him in peace.

Mal drifted more than wandered, not letting his thoughts snag anywhere for too long—though Brian continued to feature now and again. He wasn't sure why, beyond the fact that the guy was good-looking, charming, and not his usual type. He allowed the beginning of a fantasy, the same old one, where he'd followed Brian home. Where hope had triumphed over fear—until the question of what to do with his crutches poked a hole in his daydream. Depression wallowed in, thick and heavy.

Oh, for Christ's sake, Montgomery. Stop with the pity party.

He'd been down this road before and he'd recovered before. Not enough to save a promising football career, but enough to live a good life. A great life, all of which would resume January second.

Had he been this depressed after wrecking his shoulder? Probably. What he did remember was the enormity of having to rethink his direction in life. Thankfully, that wasn't an issue this time.

He *would* be going back to work. He would walk again.

Until then, he'd content himself with furry cuddles from Lois, and a few more fantasies about Brian Kenway.

As she always did, Lois greeted Mal at the door, somehow managing not to trip him, despite needing to wend her way around his crutches, between both legs and then around the left, her tail trailing up to his knee.

"Hey, sweetness," Mal crooned, wishing he could bend to stroke her sinuous back, ending with the little tug to her tail she seemed to enjoy. Once they got settled on the couch, he'd give her the full attention she deserved as his most loyal companion, his best friend with fur.

With a distinctive chirrup, Lois led the way to the kitchen, which wasn't far. Mal lived in an updated split-level ranch, and he'd never been so happy to exist in a space with four steps up and a few more down instead of full flights of stairs. If he lived in Donny's house, he'd have broken his neck twice by now. Of course, Donny had practically moved in here with him after he'd been released from the hospital, both times. Mal had had a pretty bad concussion right after the initial accident and hadn't been able to walk at all after the surgery on his broken leg. If he thought his life was limited now, he only had to think back a few months. The most recent surgery to repair his ACL hadn't been as traumatic, but again Donny had been here, and the one to pet Lois, feed her, clean her litter tray, and watch her frolic among the falling leaves.

His kitchen wasn't as fancy as Donny's, but it had been completed on schedule and suited the open-plan feel of his house. Light flooded the space, spilling in from tall windows lining the kitchen side to meet the more muted ambience illuminating the large bay window on the living side. His couch beckoned beneath a warm blanket of sunlight.

Lois was on the island counter, wandering back and forth, leaving a trail of loud purrs. Her food and water bowls were perched at one end, making it easy for him to feed her.

Mal fed Lois and gave her the sort of petting she sometimes tolerated while she ate, laughing as she turned to nip at his hand.

"I know, I know. You're eating. Hurry up, sweetness. I need a cuddle on the couch."

Then, leaving her to it, he began the arduous process of taking a shower. After navigating the short flight of stairs to his bedroom, Mal stripped, tossed his leg brace onto the bed, and hobbled to the bathroom. With every step, he imagined his knee buckling. While he waited for the water to heat, he deliberately thought about nothing. Thought about nothing as he sat on the plastic chair Donny had gotten for him, and turned his face toward the spray. Thought about nothing as he soaped up, his back twinging as he reached here and there, his head throbbing, his body one large ache.

Thought about nothing as he washed his junk.

Definitely didn't think about the fact he hadn't jerked off in months.

Ignored the subtler ache in his balls.

Thought about the trail guide his sister-in-law had given him for Christmas.

Thought about a man he shouldn't spend so much time thinking about, and stroked the appendage he'd paid too little attention to for far too long.

He hardened quickly, his cheeks heating with a mixture of shame and arousal. Brian would never have to know. He climaxed quickly and efficiently, guilt stripping most of the sensuality away. But as he sat waiting for the shower to rinse him a second time, he felt calmer than he had in a stupidly long while. More together. More . . . human.

CHAPTER 6

E llen's house was typical of Newark: crowded by its neighbors and slightly depressed by that fact. The block on Summer Avenue—sullied by dirty snow and grimy cars—was otherwise neat and orderly, with all the houses being in decent repair. It reminded Brian of . . . not home. Of the house he'd grown up in. Three stories of narrow functionality, packed with his cop father, hairdresser mother, and four brothers and sisters.

"Told you she wouldn't be here," Josh said from his slump in the front passenger seat. He'd all but stated his mother was psychic and never around when she needed to be, unless it was to kick her son out into the street.

Brian had the idea she was in there and not answering, though. "You're sure you don't have a key?"

Josh rolled his eyes. "No, I don't have a key. If I had a key, we wouldn't be here."

"That makes no sense."

"I'd have gone back to get my stuff and then . . ." Josh waved a hand through the air, as though the rest of his sentence should be obvious.

Brian suppressed a sigh. They could break in, but he'd left his criminal days far, far behind him. Also, he should be setting a good example for Josh. Sitting in a car outside the house of the woman who'd thrown Josh out probably wasn't doing that. He was showing Josh what he didn't have anymore. Likely wouldn't ever have.

Had he really thought Ellen would answer the door? Take Josh back? She'd kicked her own kid out of the house the week before. With fifty bucks. Nothing else but what he was wearing and a piece of shit phone.

Shaking off an unwelcome feeling of déjà vu, Brian muttered, "God, what a bitch." He probably shouldn't be saying that, either.

Josh grunted in agreement before saying, "So, can we go now?"

Brian pulled out his phone and opened the map screen again. "Where did you say Will lived?" He didn't have a clear memory of his much younger brother, but had a vague feeling he might be the most sympathetic of his remaining siblings.

"I don't want to go to Uncle Will's. He's a cop like grandpa and has been calling me a delinquent since I was nine."

Scratch that. "What about—"

"None of them want me, okay? That's why I ended up out in Hicksville with you." Josh reached for the door handle. "You know what? Forget it. I'll go live in the shed out back."

Brian squashed more unwelcome memories—helped along by the persistent cough Josh had had since Christmas Day. Josh tried to hold it back, but the cough won out, forcing a horrible bark from his throat.

He'd die in that damn shed.

"Josh, wait." Gripping the wheel, Brian gave himself a stern talking to. *This is your nephew. Hell, this is* you *thirtysomething years ago. Be the one who makes a difference in his life.* "We'll figure this out, okay?"

Brian peered through the window again, ducking to take in the whole shape of Ellen's house. Then, sighing once more, he put the car in gear and pulled out into the street.

"Tell me about your dad," Brian invited as he navigated his way back to Interstate 78.

"I told you all I know. He left when I was four."

"And they weren't married?" Yay for double standards. Unwed mothers were fine. But not gay sons. "Where did your mom get the money for that house?"

"I don't know. She works and she has boyfriends. Maybe they help her out."

"What does she do?"

"She's the branch manager at City Savings and Loan."

Brian tried to picture Ellen in a suit and failed.

"How come you don't know what she does?" Josh asked.

"Did you miss the part about having to look me up on Google? I'm officially disowned."

"Why'nt you change your name, then?"

Good question.

Brian merged with traffic onto the interstate, then glanced over at Josh's ragged attire. "We need to go shopping. Get you something else to wear."

"Fine."

He took the exit to Short Hills Mall and circled the sprawling lot twice before finding a spot where he judged his car would be safe from door dings and teenagers with sharp objects. Josh peered through the windows with narrowed eyes the entire time.

"What?" Brian finally asked.

"I'm going to be the only person in this mall with blue hair."

"And whose fault is that?"

Grumbling, Josh pushed open his door and practically threw himself under an oncoming car. Brian managed to get around the hood and collar him in time, yanking him back. "Jesus Christ! Watch where you're going."

"Like you care." Cough, cough.

Fuck. My. Life.

The mall was busy, as any self-respecting mall would be the week after Christmas, and Josh did indeed stand out, but not because he had blue hair. It was his attitude, which Brian had taken as typical teenager. Weren't they all defensive and rude and waifish? Not according to the clientele of an upscale mall in New Jersey. The teenagers sprinkled throughout the mall looked and acted like models in a photo shoot.

Brian blended well with his dark, fitted denim—skinny jeans for the nearly fifty-year-old—a heavy button-down shirt and fine-gauge cotton sweater. He knew the soft blue of his sweater brought out the color of his eyes and flattered his skin tone and hair. And he knew his ass looked good in the jeans. It should. He'd done thirty minutes of squats and lunges before getting dressed that morning.

Josh, in his wool coat and baggy jeans, wasn't underdressed. He was overdressed, and his furtive manner gave the impression he was ready to smuggle out half of every store in his pockets. Brian should have asked him to leave the coat in the car.

It was enlightening to watch Josh's reaction to the mall and its stores. Brian recognized a lot of himself—all those years ago, and in fleeting instances now as Josh wavered between interest and a disdain that might be fueled by the knowledge he could never afford to wear *that*.

Brian paused outside a row of stores designed to dress the young and said, "So, we should get you at least one more pair of jeans. A couple of shirts. A sweater? Socks and underwear." He indicated the worn black shit kickers taking up more floor space than Josh's feet probably warranted. "And shoes."

"What's wrong with my shoes?"

"Nothing. But you can't wear them every day."

"Why not?"

Because shit kickers don't go with everything, Brian had been about to say. But who was he to judge? Also, he was a self-confessed shoe whore who never wore the same pair twice in one week if his outfit didn't demand it. Glancing down at the deep burgundy ankle boots he'd put on with his jeans, Brian pursed his lips. "How about a pair of sneakers?"

"All the better for running." Josh's upper lip curled in a sardonic manner before he nodded toward a store across the way. "How about there?"

The store was Brian's worst nightmare. Unlike the places on their side of the walkway—neat, color coordinated, and playing bland, contemporary music to bland, contemporary shoppers—the store on the other side was black on black on black, with streaks of purple graffiti and a window display of clothes that had surely been rescued from donation bins across the country.

"I don't see any Giants' gear in there," Brian said, referring to the hoodie Josh wore under his coat.

Rolling his eyes, Josh started across the mall. Brian followed.

Several hundred dollars later, Josh had two new outfits, only one of which bore rips and tears not rendered by excessive wear.

Tucking his credit card back into his wallet, Brian said, "I cannot believe we paid eighty bucks for a ripped pair of jeans."

"You paid it, not me. Can we get something to eat?"

The food court was another adventure. Being lactose intolerant, vegetarian, and turned off by the texture of most vegetables—including beans—meant the only option was sushi. Apparently Josh's version of vegetarianism included raw fish.

"So you're a pescatarian."

Josh shrugged. "Sometimes."

Brian hated sushi. The very idea of it turned his stomach. He also harbored a lingering suspicion that anyone who ate it was either riddled with intestinal worms or about to expire from mercury poisoning. Josh inhaled thirty bucks' worth, his cough never interfering with the slurping of rice and raw flesh.

Gross.

They picked up sneakers (black with a black logo), sweats (dark gray, thankfully not already distressed in any way), and a purple sweatshirt with a skull and crossbones across the back. Brian was exhausted by the time they turned toward the car. But when they were passing the cell phone booth in the center of the mall, he called out, "Hold up."

Josh looked up with a bored expression, as if he weren't holding most of Brian's weekly wage from string handles looped around his wrists. "What?"

"Let's get you a phone."

"I have a phone."

"Who's paying the bill on that one?"

Josh scowled. "Whatever. If she cancels it, I'll live."

"What if I need to call you?"

"When? After you've found me some other place to crash? No, thanks." Josh turned away.

"Don't you have any friends you'd like to stay in touch with?"

Under the wool coat, Josh's slim shoulders hitched up and down. A shrug? Did that mean no?

"What about your brother and sister?"

"I'm pretty sure Ava has moved into my room by now, and Liam is just like Uncle Will."

Assuming Liam was short for William, apparently well named, then. "You could try calling your mom."

Josh spun around, his bags flaring out in an arc of expensive rainbows. "Why? She doesn't want to hear from me."

"She's . . ." *Mad* wasn't the right word. *Mad* didn't kick a kid out onto the street. *Deluded* might be better, but . . . "She'll think things through. Ellen isn't stupid. She has to know—"

"You don't get it." Josh's lower lip quivered. "I can't go back. She won't take me back, and even if she did, I wouldn't go. You didn't hear what she said. She said I was unnatural and that God had no place in His world for people like me."

Brian shuddered inwardly as more unwelcome memories rolled through him. His father speaking in low, biting tones. His sister screaming. His mother looking on, expressionless.

He glanced around at the audience he and Josh had managed to attract—gazes averting as he met them, the not-so-subtle open mouths—and lifted his chin. Put away the past.

He'd long ago decided not to be ashamed of who he was. Of whom he loved.

"None of that is true," he said, his tone inviting no argument. "God made you as you are, Josh."

Also aware of their audience, Josh flung himself into a turn and stalked off. Brian strode after him and resisted the urge to reach for his collar. Again. How did one rally a recalcitrant child? Leashes were only for pets and toddlers, weren't they?

"Josh."

Josh kept moving until they were back at the doors they'd entered by. There, he turned, stony-faced, and lifted his chin. Then a fit of coughing caught him, and Brian experienced an odd urge to hug the kid, this lost little boy. Brian's chest was constricting and hurting and whispering secrets he didn't want to hear. Josh wouldn't thank him for a hug, though. Brian remembered enough about fourteen to appreciate that. So he stood there, feeling all kinds of useless, until Josh had stopped coughing.

Eyes red from the effort, Josh finally looked up. "Can we go?"

"Yeah, we can go."

CHAPTER 7

M al checked his watch. "Shouldn't you be going?"

Brian Kenway hadn't made an appearance at the Colonial tonight, and probably wouldn't. But just in case he did, Mal needed the stool next to him free. So they could . . . chat. Yeah, chat.

"Long as I'm home to kiss Rach at midnight, we're all good," Donny said.

"Didn't you guys go somewhere nice last year?"

"You implying my place isn't all that?" Leo said, appearing suddenly on his side of the bar. He eyed their glasses. "Drink up. I've got a mortgage to pay."

"Love this place," Donny said. "Don't know why we ever go anywhere else."

Snorting, Mal picked up his glass and drained the swirl of nearly flat beer at the bottom. "I'll take another."

"Coke for me," Donny said, pushing his glass across. "I've got to drive soon."

"Seriously, you should go now. Not like I don't have any experience holding up my end of the bar."

"True that," Leo put in, sliding a fresh glass through the beery puddle left by the last one. As usual, Mal's coaster littered the floor at his feet.

Donny checked his watch. "Kids are all into it this year. That's why we didn't go out. They're old enough to want to stay up until midnight."

"Then go be with them. Leo will look after me."

"No, I won't." Leo moved off to *not* look after another patron, and Mal caught a glimpse of golden-blond hair at the other end of the bar.

Refusing to let his breath catch in his throat, Mal pushed air outward and turned his attention back to Donny. "Go. I'm fine. It's the last day of the year, meaning I made it through the holiday season without offing myself. Your shift is done."

"Not funny."

"I'm not as depressed as you all seem to think I am. Not being able to walk well yet is getting me down some, that's all. Don't you ever feel old and useless? Add a pair of crutches to that."

"I could have come out tonight because I wanted to drink a beer with my brother. Ever think of that?"

"You're drinking Coke."

"Don't be an ass." As always, Donny sounded patient, but in his place, Mal would rather be drinking beer. And sitting with someone he could kiss at midnight.

"Go home, Donny. Thank you, love you, appreciate you spending time with me on New Year's Eve. Now go home and kiss your wife and kids, okay?"

"Yeah, okay. You good for a—"

"I'll be fine to drive. Stop worrying. I'm the older brother, remember?"

"By eight minutes, dickhead."

"Every minute counts."

Donny dropped a kiss to his forehead—a gesture borrowed from their father, and not often used. Right then, though, it meant everything. Mal gripped his brother's shoulder, the twin who wasn't even a near copy, but nonetheless occupied half of his heart. "Thanks, Donny."

"Happy New Year."

Donny exchanged a few more un-pleasantries with Leo and left. The crowd near the door shifted as he pushed through, and Mal glanced toward the end of the bar, leaning out a little to see if—

"Looking for me?" Warmth pressed gently against Mal's back, wrapping around him with the scent of cardamom and oranges, wool, and the musky odor of male.

Mal hunched forward a little, and the pressure against his back eased as Brian drew away, angling sideways to sit on the stool Donny had abandoned. Brian hadn't shaved, and the white-blond stubble only made him more attractive, giving the lower half of his face a well-defined edge. His blue eyes flashed with humor and maybe one more drink than the hour required. He had a glass in one hand, a puddle of dark liquid clinging to the bottom.

"Fancy meeting you here," Brian said.

Mal rolled his eyes. "You're going to have to try harder than that."

Brian grinned. "How about: I was hoping you might be here?"

Warmth moved across Mal's back again, the remembered feel of Brian right there—a flush following in its wake. He worked against ducking his chin, against the shyness he'd combated his entire life. "I've heard you're trouble, Kenway."

"Good. Means I don't have to warn you off."

"Does that work?"

"You wouldn't believe how well."

"Everyone loves a bad boy."

Chuckling, Brian lifted his glass as if in a toast. He drained the last of his drink and set it on the bar. "What about you?"

"Hmm?"

"Love a bad boy?"

"I like *men*."

"Oh, nice!"

Mal found himself grinning. "Are we keeping score?"

"If so, you're ahead by two. Keep it up and you might get a prize."

Whatever flirting mojo Mal had gained from his last beer failed him then. Either that, or the quick flash of what his prize might be—a fantasy that needed more than a few seconds at the bar to properly unfold—robbed him of words. He cleared his throat, gave in to the chin dip, and pretended interest in his drink.

The scent of Christmas oranges invaded his space again as Brian leaned in. "Thinking about what you want?" he asked.

If Mal turned his head slightly, they'd be inches apart. Correction: their mouths would be inches apart. He kept his gaze stubbornly forward. "What are you talking about?"

"I think you know exactly what I'm talking about."

Thankfully, Brian leaned away. He raised his glass toward Leo, who nodded from the other end of the bar. Mal took a long draft of his beer. He immediately felt it when Brian turned his attention back to him.

"Is your friend coming back?" Brian asked.

"Who?"

"The guy you were with just now."

"What? Oh, no, that was my brother."

"You two seem pretty close."

"We're twins."

"You don't look much alike, though."

Relieved the conversation had turned toward the mundane, Mal sat back a little. His right leg, trapped beneath the bar by the brace, shot a small protest up the back of his thigh, and his knee throbbed in warning. PT had been hard that morning. He should have his legs elevated, but figured he had all night—after he'd seen midnight come and go—to prop them up. Most of tomorrow too.

"We didn't come from the same egg," he told Brian. "So we're more like brothers, I guess." Except they weren't. They'd shared that space for nine months and the proximity still seemed to surround them, even fifty years later. "When my hair was longer, the resemblance was easier to see. Our eyes are the same color."

Brian nodded, accepted a fresh glass from Leo, and held it up. "What are we drinking to?"

Mal raised his beer. "Family."

What might have been a wince crossed Brian's perfect features before he smiled, echoing the word softly before taking a sip.

Figuring family might not be a safe subject—and it often wasn't for gay men—Mal nodded toward Brian's glass. "What are you drinking?"

"It's a Manhattan. Whiskey, vermouth, bitters. Should have a cherry and I make them with a twist of orange peel, but Leo's doing the best he can."

"I heard that!" Leo called from his end of the bar.

Mal laughed. "I could never drink cocktails."

"Have you tried?"

"Once or twice."

"It's a tolerance thing. Anything you do for long enough gets easier." One blond eyebrow arched up and down as Brian sipped at his drink.

Mal grinned at the suggestion of only the good Lord knew what. "I'll keep that in mind." He tried for an eyebrow raise.

Brian grinned. "Now you're getting it."

"Getting what?"

"How to flirt."

"I think I was doing okay before."

"Oh, you were. Up by two, remember?"

"So it's a game?"

"Sure. That's what we're doing here, isn't it? Playing a game?"

Mal's smile slipped a little. He shrugged. "I dunno. I mostly come here to drink. Because, you know, it's a bar."

"Right. But it's also a well-known gay bar."

"So that immediately means I'm here to hook up?"

"It's not Thursday night," Brian said.

"I don't follow."

"And it's cute that you don't." Brian's gaze dipped down, and Mal felt the weight of all that attention on his mouth—along with the press of teeth over his lower lip. *Whoops.* He quickly rearranged his lips so there was no biting. No chewing.

Brian continued to study him.

"Stop looking at my mouth."

"How does it make you feel?"

"Uncomfortable," Mal admitted.

"But in a good way?"

Mal swallowed. "Not sure."

"I think you are."

Mal leaned back a little, putting some distance between them. He rubbed a hand over his head, feeling the warmth of his scalp. The dampness of his short hair. He was sweating and off-balance. His dick wasn't suffering the same uncertainty, though. Not wanting to adjust his pants, he rubbed a palm along his left thigh, easing an ache that might or might not be there.

Watching Brian sip his drink, Mal got the sense they were on pause, but that the break would be over very soon. And that he had to be the one to press Play, Rewind, or Stop. Brian obviously liked to flirt and didn't mind unsettling his partner. He also seemed to know when to take a breath—and Mal could appreciate that. Did appreciate it. It made Brian seem less the asshole his brother and Leo had made him out to be.

"So, what do you do?" Mal asked, deciding to reengage at a lower speed.

Brian responded with a quick smile, as if to say, *Okay, we can do this*, and lowered his drink. "I'm in construction. Management."

"Where you don't get your hands dirty."

This time, Brian's smile was wider. "I wouldn't say that. I'm a pretty hands-on kind of guy."

"I can imagine."

"What about you, Professor?"

"You remembered that."

"I don't forget much. So, are you? A professor?"

"No, though I do have a PhD." Why had he felt compelled to share that fact?

Brian didn't appear put off. "I can't imagine wanting to know so much about just one thing that I'd study it for that long."

"Yeah? You come across as pretty tenacious."

"Oh, I am, when it's something I want."

"Imagine you really, really want to know the origins of modern language."

Brian visibly shuddered. "Uh, no. How about if I imagine I really, really want to know what your mouth tastes like."

Wow. "You don't need to go to college for that."

"You're making me work for it, though."

He was, and he was enjoying it. Brian almost made it easy. He led confidently and didn't seem to mind waiting for Mal to catch up. Like now. He was looking at Mal's mouth again, but not in a weighty way. His gaze flicked up now and then, and the grin he wore had a lackadaisical quality to it, as though he didn't mind if this particular gambit didn't pay off.

Mal checked the time. What the heck—it was New Year's Eve and he should get kissed.

Brian followed his gaze, clearly checking the time for himself. "Want to wait for midnight?"

"No." Because . . . "I'm not very good at this." *Okay, that's enough. Stop talking now.*

"You're doing fine."

"There're probably a dozen other guys in this bar who would give their left nut to talk to you. Why are you bothering with me?"

"Why would you ask a question like that?"

"Because you unsettle me."

"But in a good way."

Brian smiled, and Mal let his lips curve upward in response—because Brian was right. Heck, yeah, he was uncomfortable and it wasn't because his legs ached. Or the creeping fatigue from PT. The knowledge that even getting to the bathroom was a journey he had to plan. He wondered, then, if he should grab his crutch, pull it out of the shadow of the bar, and show it to Brian, and quickly realized that if he did, he'd be making another excuse. Besides, he didn't want to have sex with Brian tonight.

Actually, he did.

But he wasn't going to have sex with Brian tonight. Brian Kenway obviously enjoyed playing games and much as Mal suspected he'd enjoy a night in Brian's bed, he knew it would probably be a one-off thing. No one put this much intensity into friendship. Brian saw him as a hookup. Nothing more.

Mal didn't do hookups. Since his breakup with Noah, he'd preferred loneliness to the sharp disappointment of connection and separation, or the simple fact that people so often weren't who he thought they were in the light of day.

He glanced at the clock over the bar. "Three minutes."

Brian showed him another grin, this one not at all lazy. "Need some practice puckering up?"

"Fuck you." Resisting the urge to stretch his lips, lick them, get all loose and ready for a kiss, Mal laughed. Then licked his lips, damn it.

Brian chuckled softly and raised his glass for another sip. He did it slowly, as though knowing Mal would watch him swallow and wonder what the drink would taste like on his lips. His tongue.

"Want a taste?" Brian asked, offering him the glass.

Mal accepted the glass and took a quick sip. The drink was strong and his head spun lightly. Putting it aside, he licked his lips again, tasting bourbon and something sharper, drier. Vermouth? The bitters touched his tongue last, a tangy aftertaste, and he could imagine how well an orange peel would go with the drink.

He was wondering how Brian managed to smell like oranges when the countdown began.

"Ten, nine, eight . . ."

Brian hadn't leaned in. Should he do it?

"Seven, six, five . . ."

Should he take his glasses off?

"Four, three . . ."

What if he missed?

"Two . . ."

What if the kiss landed on Brian's cheek or nose or—

"One!"

Oranges, cardamom, cinnamon, and musk. Warmth whispering across his lips in quick invitation before pressing down, lightly, without demand. Somehow their noses didn't collide. Somehow, Mal's lips were parting before a swipe of Brian's tongue.

Brian didn't invade, though. He teased. He waited.

Understanding flashing inside his head like a cracked blind at dawn, Mal leaned in and kissed back. Offered up his mouth. Tasted. Hummed at the delicious flavor of whiskey and man. The persistent hint of orange. The prickle of stubble as their mouths moved and realigned. He touched his tongue to Brian's and opened his mouth. Brian swept inside and the warmth at the back of Mal's neck now must be Brian's hand. Oh God, it felt good.

So warm.

So necessary.

Then Brian was shifting back, blinking slowly, and noise crashed into the perfect bubble of their kiss, breaking the moment apart with cheers of "Happy New Year" and the lambent strains of "Auld Lang Syne."

Mal breathed. Quaked. Ignored the near pain behind the fly of his jeans. Took another breath. "That was . . ."

"Some kiss." Brian's grin had that lazy aspect again. His eyes were hooded. Shifting on the stool, he pulled his wallet from his back pocket. "Did you drive?"

"Yeah." They were at that part of the evening already?

Could he?

Just this once?

Brian was flipping through his wallet, examining cards, peering inside the billfold, poking his thumb under the flap holding his driver's license. Mal glanced down at the picture and it was, unsurprisingly, a good one. While everyone else managed to resemble a death-row candidate on their license, Brian wore a sunny and handsome smile. Mal checked the date of birth and discovered Brian was two years younger than him.

When he looked back up, Brian's expression had lost all traces of lazy intimacy. "I need to go," he said.

"Huh."

Brian tapped the bar. "Leo."

"What's up?"

"Can I settle with you tomorrow?"

"Sure. Leave your wallet at home?"

Brian held up the well-worn fold of black leather. "No, my credit cards. All of them. I can stop by with some cash in a little bit—"

"Don't worry about it. You can pay next time you're in."

Mal reached for his wallet. "I can cover it."

"That's not necessary. Listen . . ." Brian's eyebrows crooked together. "Thank you for the kiss."

Mal swallowed, unsure if he was supposed to say *you're welcome* or *thank you* in return.

Brian seemed to hesitate for a second, and then he tapped the bar again. "I'll see you around." A quick smile, a flash of blue eyes and raised brows, and then he was gone, taking the scent of oranges and whiskey with him.

Mal stared after him for a moment, until Brian got to the door, and then he stopped, because staring at a closed door was kinda pathetic. He turned back to the bar and put his credit card next to the spreading puddle under his glass. "Why don't you ever give me a coaster?" he asked.

"I did. From now on, you only get one. Any more and you'd leave too much of a mess on the floor." Leo took the card. "Just the beers?"

Mal licked his lips. Tasted whiskey. Wanted to scowl. Wanted to go hide somewhere. "You can add Brian's tab."

"He won't thank you for it."

"I'm not doing it for thanks. It's . . . the holidays."

"Must have been some kiss."

The flush that had heated his back and shoulders, his neck, finally worked its way up Mal's face, heating his cheeks. He dipped his chin.

"I don't have to tell you—" Leo began.

"Anything. I can handle myself."

Shrugging, Leo turned away to run the card.

Mal gave in and looked toward the front door of the bar. It opened, and his heart jerked upward. Two guys, neither Brian, pushed inside, and the door swung closed. Mal leaned against the bar and exhaled slowly.

It was just a kiss.

Probably meant nothing to a man like Brian Kenway. He'd left as soon as it was done. Mal should be hurt by that, but he decided not to be. Even though he was.

Damn it. It was just a kiss!

Mal licked his lips again.

CHAPTER 8

B rian had never been cockblocked by an empty wallet before. Inconvenienced by one, spent too much of his youth trying to fill one, but not this.

God, what a mess.

What a kiss. That kiss had been . . .

Brian hadn't been planning to stop by the Colonial. It wasn't on the trendy side of Morristown Green, and the entire building had a derelict feel to it. Appearance aside, it wasn't his kind of place. Not that he had a kind of place. That would mean people knew where to find him.

He scanned South Park Place for traffic before crossing over to his cozy little neighborhood. Then he scowled and muttered because this was the third time he'd made this trek in a week.

The professor hadn't been there this past Thursday. Brian didn't think he'd ever seen Mal there on a Thursday. Yet Brian had gone and waited. He'd waited last night too. He hadn't meant to stop by tonight because it was New Year's Eve, and he could have had his pick of any number of flexible fucks at the Frog. And yet . . .

The kiss had been worth it. So worth it.

And Josh had some serious explaining to do.

Brian picked up his pace, the anger boiling off his skin pushing the cold night back. Turning onto King Street, he looked for flashing lights, half expecting to find his house up in flames. Not that he usually equated theft with arson, but his mood tied them together nicely enough. It'd be just his luck to have found out that Josh had left a bag of popcorn in the microwave too long, resulting in a fire.

The condos were intact, lit from within in and without, and all except his hung with Christmas lights and wreaths. Scowling, Brian stomped down his neat little path, up the steps, and to the front door, key already out.

He called for Josh as soon as he pushed the door open. "Josh! You up?"

Silence greeted him. Brian checked the time. Barely twelve twenty. Had he gone to bed already?

"Josh?"

Brian glanced into the dark family room, paced down the hall to the kitchen, knocked on the door to the hall bath, and checked out his den. All quiet. All *dark*. He jogged upstairs. Listened at the door to the spare bedroom where Josh had been staying, before opening it a crack.

"Josh?" he whispered. Then, "Josh!" He was supposed to be pissed off.

Nothing stirred. Brian flipped on the light. The bed was empty. Unmade, cold, and flat. The guest bath was empty. His own bedroom was dark . . . but not as neat as he'd left it. His closet door hung open and the light in his bathroom had been left on.

Brian checked inside his closet; his suits and shirts had been shoved aside, but none were missing. Frowning, he counted his shoes. All there. He checked the bathroom next, but couldn't figure out any *whats* or *whys*.

Anger giving way to concern, uncertainty fizzing beneath, he stepped back into the upstairs hallway. "Josh? You here?"

Silenced answered. Had Josh gone out? He hadn't said he might. And where would a fourteen-year-old go at midnight, anyway?

He has all your cash and your cards.

Pulling out his cell phone, Brian brought up his banking app and logged in. He could see a list of transactions that day. The grocery store. The bookstore. Transactions from earlier in the week: Clothing for Josh. Shoes for Josh.

A creeping sensation inched over the back of Brian's scalp. He returned to his bedroom and checked the closet again—focusing on the space between the disturbed suits and shirts. His gym bag was missing.

Josh had . . . left?

The next emotion to hit Brian made no sense: loss. He felt as though he'd failed a test. Tucking his phone into his pocket, Brian jogged back downstairs, pausing long enough to exchange his jacket for a heavier coat and hat, then headed outside.

Okay, if he was fourteen and had a bag of clothes and a pocket full of cash and cards, where would he go?

Brian checked King Street in both directions and saw nothing out of the ordinary. He looked back toward the Green. On a warm day, some of the town's nonresident population used the benches for a nap. But it was after midnight and *cold*. There were a few places in Morristown that provided overnight shelter, but they all locked their doors at ten. And why would Josh leave Brian's house for a shelter on New Year's Eve? Why not wait for morning, and then go?

Shoving his hands deep into his pockets, Brian walked back toward the center of town. Would Josh have gone home? If so, why take his new stuff? Maybe Ellen didn't buy him much. He pulled out his phone again and dialed Ellen's number. His call went to voice mail.

"Josh ran off tonight. I don't know where he is. Listen, he's recovering from a cold and shouldn't be out in this weather. If he turns up at your place, will you text me? I need two words: he's here. You don't need to talk to me. Just text me." He took a breath. "Have you listened to any of my messages? Do you even use this phone?" She must. The voice mail was still set up, so someone was paying the bill. "Text me, okay?"

He texted Josh next, at his old number and the new one they'd set up yesterday.

No answer.

Pocketing his phone, Brian checked where he was and took a right on South Park before stopping in front of Family Promise. As he'd known it would be, the big house was quiet and dark. Closed for the night. They might have had a party of their own inside, but now, this far after midnight, everyone was sleeping because who knew where they'd be tomorrow?

A sound caught his attention, and Brian turned southeast again, feeling as though he were in a dream. It was the train. The quiet shriek of its wheels attenuated by the distance and the cold. Even though it was louder at his place, he'd become used to the sound.

Josh had said he'd arrived by train. Would he try to leave the same way? How late did the trains run on New Year's Eve?

Though it was probably useless, Brian broke into a careful run. He was only a few blocks from the station. He should have gone there first. But if Josh had left his place early, then he'd already be gone.

Don't be gone. Don't be gone!

Brian ran down Morris Street, past the supermarket they'd been at only a few hours earlier, across the parking lot, and into the station. The train was gone. He'd heard it leave, heading toward Dover. Unless Josh planned to run away to the country, he wouldn't have been on it. How often did the trains run back to the city at night, though?

His shoes were not made for running and his shins ached by the time he reached the platform. The half-light was ghostly, old-style lanterns buzzing beneath larger, overhead lights that fell in regular spots along the length of the tracks.

"Josh?"

Brian strode from one end of the platform to the other. No figures huddled on the benches, and why would they? It was cold. He went back to the main building. The ticket office was closed. No surprises there, and according to the schedule, no trains ran back to the city after midnight. Last one had been at ten thirty. They kept running out to Dover until nearly two in the morning, though. He scanned the platform again, then tried the door to the commuter lounge. It opened with a soft creak and the scent of concrete dust, old wood, and disinfectant.

A shapeless bundle covered one of the benches at the back, the only clue to its identity a tuft of blue hair sticking out of the top.

Brian's phone buzzed in his pocket, and he dug it out, waking the screen. He had a text. Three words.

He's not here.

"No kidding." Brian kicked the bench in front of him and swore again as his toes cracked inside his black leather dress shoe. "Goddamn it!" He danced on one foot, hissing, and thought about throwing his phone. Again. Ellen wouldn't feel the crash, though. Instead, he tucked it inside his pocket and kicked the bench with the side of his sore foot, taking satisfaction in the loud *thwack* and the shock of pain rolling through his toes. In fact, he was having so much fun (not) that it took him a while to notice that the bundle had moved, a blue head emerging, blue eyes opening wide.

Brian limped toward his nephew. "What the actual fuck, Josh? I've been all over Morristown looking for you. Why are you here? You could have left anytime this week. Why tonight?"

Because he'd gone out?

He'd been out nearly every night this week.

"I couldn't pay my tab." Brian's hands flailed upward, following some weird urge to get all explain-y. "I actually thought you might have burned the house down. I was worried. You don't get to worry me, okay? Or take my stuff. Just what the fuck?"

Josh answered with a deep, hollow cough.

"Did you even pack the medicine I bought you?"

Josh shook his head, but coughed again, and damn, he was pale. And shivering. And sweaty.

"Shit." Brian got down on one knee, hissing as his sore toes protested, and put a palm to Josh's damp forehead. "How long have you been here?"

"I was going to catch the ten thirty train."

"Well, you missed it."

Josh coughed and shivered.

"Goddamn it. You were nearly better, Josh. How could you do this?"

No answer.

"C'mon, you need another hot shower and bed."

"I want to go home."

Fuck. Half-standing, Brian swung his ass sideways and slid onto the bench next to Josh. "I can . . ." He shook his head, pushed his hands through his hair, and glanced at his nephew. "I don't think that's a good idea."

"I can't stay here."

"Why not?"

Josh managed an eye roll before he had to lean forward and cough again. "You made it pretty clear you don't want me around."

Not having a wall close enough to hit his head against, Brian mentally slapped himself. "Listen, I've been checking out options for you, but it's hard over the holidays . . ."

"Then I'll go home."

Brian winced. "And live in the shed?"

"Maybe she'll let me in if I'm sick."

A burn crept up the back of Brian's sinuses. "I . . ." Should he lie? Would it be kinder to lie? He pulled out his phone. "I don't think so."

Josh stared at him, eyes still wide and a lot red. He wasn't well enough to be out in the cold.

"Maybe we should wait until we get back to my place."

The kid didn't move.

Brian accessed his call log. He showed the screen to Josh, scrolling through the twenty-some calls he'd made to Ellen since Christmas Eve. "That's how many times I've called your mom. I got a text back tonight. One. To tell me you weren't there."

"You called her?"

"I was worried when I couldn't find you." Irritated, angry, seriously pissed off. "I needed to know you were somewhere safe."

"Like you care."

"Josh, I'm forty-eight. I've never been with someone who was interested in having kids and never figured it was something I wanted for myself. I'm not warm and fuzzy. I'm sometimes not very nice. I told you I was an asshole. But that doesn't mean I don't care." He paused to let that sink in for a second before delivering the bad news. "I really don't think your mom does. I don't know what her deal is." *Yes, you do.* "But I do think going back there is a bad idea."

Coughing, Josh frowned down at his hands.

"Come home with me."

Josh shook his head, but Brian could see his resistance was crumbling.

"You can stay as long as you want. I'll stop looking for another place. You can stay either until we work something out with your mom or . . . until whenever." Brian drew in a not-so-deep and somewhat shaky breath. "You're family, okay? Probably the only family that wants anything to do with me. So, let's stick together. See how it goes."

"You sure?" The hope in Josh's eyes was painful.

Brian nodded. "But there'll be rules."

"Like what?"

"No stealing my stuff. You need something, you ask for it."

Josh nodded.

"And school. You need to go to school."

Not a suggestion met with excitement. Then again, who would be excited about school? Professors might be.

Warmth briefly tickled Brian's cheeks. He felt the touch of an all-too-brief kiss against his lips. Reluctantly, he shoved the memory aside.

"And I need to know where you are. I'm not going to put you under house arrest, but if you disappear on me again, shit will come down, okay?"

That apparently warranted a cough. A deep, dragging sound that rocked Josh's thin frame. But he didn't say no.

Brian stood and held out a hand. "C'mon. Let's get you home and warmed up."

Josh hesitated before standing, and the hand he slid inside Brian's was too warm and too cold at the same time. Brian nearly pulled him into a hug. Instead, he picked up Josh's bag and slung it over his shoulder. "How long did it take you to find the station?"

Josh shot him a quizzical frown. "It's at the end of your street."

Brian's smile felt weak. "See, you're settling in already."

CHAPTER 9

"Mal, there you are. Come in, have a seat." Rachel stood up behind her desk, gesturing toward the small arrangement on the other side of the office, the cozy circle she kept for the students she counseled.

Mal knew, firsthand, that *his* students preferred to sit on the other side of the desk from her. They found the "cozy circle" intimidating—as though they were expected to divulge all their secrets.

Rachel was a smart woman.

Mal leaned his crutches against the wall and hobbled over to the circle.

"How're the legs holding up?" Rachel asked.

"Just." Mal answered with a grimace that tried to be a grin.

It was his second week back at work. The first had been exhausting and exhilarating as he'd pushed himself to limits he hadn't outside of physical therapy. The long halls were less daunting this week, but his whole body ached with the effort of keeping pace with his students. Today he'd reluctantly brought both crutches, knowing he'd need them by the afternoon.

He got himself settled and stretched both legs out with a relieved sigh. "I should be back to one crutch next week. Under my own power the week after." God willing.

"Whenever you're ready," Rachel said.

Mal forced his instinctive bristle to retreat. If there was one thing he'd become good at over the past several months—aside from using crutches in ice and snow—it was forcing himself not to react to people who meant well, even when they didn't know what they were talking about.

"So, I'm guessing you know why I wanted this meeting?" Rachel continued.

"If it's to talk about the fact I won't be coaching the track team this semester, save your breath. I knew that coming back. I can hardly walk."

Rachel smiled. "I'm not your guidance counselor, but I am your sister-in-law. We can talk about it if you want."

"I don't want." Talking about it would only remind him of what he was missing out on.

Having to give up football had always stung less when he ran. Then running had become his thing. Jogging at first, to simply feel physical again. Then competing. Running faster and farther. Training for marathons. They'd asked if he'd like to coach football when he came back to Morristown High. He'd asked for the track team. Mal wasn't ready to dwell on what losing another direction meant, yet.

"I wanted to talk about the Gay Straight Alliance," Rachel said.

Mal leaned forward in his seat. "How so? You aren't going to cut funding for the club, are you?" It was vital, especially now.

"We're not cutting it. You know the club has always had the school's full support."

He let out a breath. "Then what's the issue?"

"I want you to lead it."

"But it's Cheryl's thing. She started it."

"Cheryl's leaving us next week. Moving out of state."

"Huh." Why hadn't she said anything? Then again, when would she have? Mal hadn't extended his crutch practice far beyond his classroom at lunchtime. Still, she could have called. "I don't know, Rach. I'm not a group leader. I'm always happy to help out, but I'm not sure I'm the right one to lead a group. Some of the kids need a lot of guidance. Someone to look up to. Someone who has fought the good fight and won."

"Someone like you, you mean."

"What? No. I've had it easy. My parents have always loved me, so I've never really had to think about my sexuality." The falseness of that statement swirled around his gut even as it left his lips. He did think about it. Often. The current political climate made sure of that. But he'd never been in a position where he had to fight for something he wanted—not really. His life might have been very different if he'd continued to play football, but Mal had always assumed he'd find a way around whatever stood in his path. That was what a wide receiver did, after all.

While he asked himself why he didn't remember that fact more often—like when he was asking his cat to cheer him up, Rachel demonstrated that she felt differently.

"Mal, you know I tell it like I see it, and I'm telling you that you are an asset to this school. We love having you here. You're every principal's dream. Returning sports hero, and a good teacher who is well-liked by his students. You've always been open about who you are in a manner that's perceived as healthy. The students and staff respect you. Sure, we've had the odd parent who has other opinions, but you've always had the support of this administration because you're good at what you do."

"And I don't make waves."

"If you had a sideline as Miss Bacon, things might be different."

"You're not going to tell me—"

"You know I'm an advocate and an ally. Before that, I'm your friend, our relationship to Donny aside. And I'm asking if you'll consider heading up the GSA club. We need it, especially now. Our young people need you. And, with coaching being out of the question at the moment, you'll have the time."

Thanks for the reminder. But what else was he going to do—stand on the sidelines and tell the kids to keep running?

Mal blew out a sigh. "I don't know. I always kinda liked that our GSA was led by a straight white married lady. It felt safe. I think the parents and kids felt safe. It's one thing for them to support gay rights, but to picture their kids alone in a classroom with a gay man—a lot of them aren't going to like it."

"The club isn't for parents, it's for the teens. These are kids who are already out there having conversations about identity and sexuality. They're already *having* sex, Mal. And you know some of them are being bullied and abused. Disrespected. Not treated well at home. They need this club. The straight kids need this club too."

Mal closed his eyes over a slow exhale. He had other reasons for not doing this, his being gay still chief among them. But Rachel was right

"Okay, I'll do it. But I want an assistant. Another teacher or parent in the room with me. I don't want any possibility of inappropriate rumors. I like being here as much as you like having me."

"I'll see what I can do. Ask your students too. In the group. One might have a parent who'd like to be more involved."

Mal nodded. "Does the club still meet on Mondays?"

"Yes."

"That's today." Giving him no time to panic.

"Yes."

"You couldn't have asked me last week?"

Rachel smiled. "I was busy. New Year, new semester. You know how it is."

"Mm-hmm."

Her smile widened. "You're going to be great."

Shaking his head, Mal got ready to stand. "Next time, give me a chance to think things over."

"You spend altogether too much time thinking, Mal. Anyway, Cheryl will be there this afternoon, so you only have to introduce yourself and observe." Rachel squeezed his shoulder. "This is going to be good for you. You'll see."

"Heh."

Mal crutched slowly back to his classroom. He had a PT session scheduled for later that afternoon but wasn't all that sure he was going to make it. His legs already ached. His shoulders hurt. A steady throb poked the back of his skull, and his mind was tired. And he was pretty sure he was going to fail the kids in the GSA. He loved that the school had a club—and had had one for years. But all he knew about being gay was . . . that he was gay.

Things might have been different if he hadn't wrecked his shoulder in college. He'd been aware, even before then, that he was attracted to guys. It had made being an athlete interesting and being on the football team difficult at times. He'd been able to keep a lid on his sexuality, though. Had been so focused on his career, so into the game, he hadn't cared. He'd served the game first, himself second.

Tearing his rotator cuff had rearranged a lot of his priorities.

What about his life was going to change following two broken legs, and how did that qualify him to advise a group of kids? The GSA club didn't feel like an issue he could find his way around, wide-receiver fashion. He was going to have to go through this one headfirst.

The bell rang, indicating the end of the lunch period. Students trickled into the end of the hall, subdued voices echoing off the closed lockers and scuffed linoleum. Mal pushed open the door to his classroom and leaned heavily on his crutches as he moved toward his desk. He had one class that afternoon with the final period free, giving him eighty extra minutes to figure out how to run a GSA club. Or eighty minutes to fret.

But first, the Tokugawa shogunate. Pity he couldn't involve his kids in a game of *Total War*.

Students pushed through the door in pairs and threes, the idea of entering one at a time apparently not occurring. Mal watched, bemused, as they jostled and cajoled, many of them sharing the easy camaraderie of kids who'd grown up together. Another advantage of living in a small town. The flow ended right before the second bell.

"Ethan, could you close the door for me?"

"Sure, Mr. M." Mal's elected helper hopped up to do as bid, and paused in the doorway as a final student stepped through. No . . . slunk through, as though by angling his shoulders and chin down and pressing himself close to one side of the door, he could escape notice. Unfortunately, his choice of hair color gave him away.

The bright blue—almost aqua—highlighted the pallor of his skin and drew attention to his small stature. When he glanced up, his delicate features, including large eyes nearly the same color as his hair, also gave him away. No one with a face like that could hide. Or should hide.

Even Ethan, who'd had the same girlfriend since third grade, seemed affected. He stuck out a hand. "Haven't seen you around. I'm Ethan."

The blue-haired kid eyed the hand skeptically before accepting the shake. "Josh."

Ethan shuffled his feet, obviously waiting for his cue, and Mal thanked every deity for good and helpful kids he could rely on to do the right thing, even if it was just to close a door. Mal nodded and Ethan closed the door. Idly Mal wondered if he could get Ethan to volunteer for the GSA. He would be a welcoming face. Then Mal turned his attention to the new student, standing stiff and still near the doorway. His clothes were new and expensive. His backpack stiff and suspiciously clean. Newness emanated from him like a shiny wave, and he clearly hated it.

Was that a row of metal around the edge of his ear? Mal was tempted to let the kid go and find a seat. Let him blend. But he wouldn't be doing him any favors by leaving him unchallenged on his first day.

Mal nodded Ethan back toward his place and beckoned Josh forward, extending a hand. Josh slid a hand into his, quickly and quietly.

"Welcome to Morristown, Josh. Can I see your schedule?" Might as well make sure he was supposed to be here. Most of Mal's students were juniors and seniors, but he did get the odd freshman and sophomore who was ahead.

Josh dug into his pocket and withdrew a much-creased piece of paper. He didn't smooth it out before handing it to Mal, so Mal had to spread it on his desk so he could read it. He glanced at the class list first, confirming Josh was supposed to be in this room at this time, then checked his morning classes. Honors French, Chemistry, and art. *Interesting combination.* He was only in tenth grade, but he was at least a year ahead of his age. And his name was Joshua Kenway.

Kenway?

Mal studied the boy's face again, specifically the eyes, and felt his own widen in response. Then he swallowed, immediately feeling guilty for staring. He tapped the schedule. "Any relation to Brian Kenway?"

Josh's pale-blonde eyebrows rose. "He's my uncle."

Oh really? "I'm going to guess you've done the introduction thing three times over already today, so why don't you take a seat so we can get started."

Josh fairly wilted with relief. Mal pointed out the chair next to Ethan. "How about there? Ethan is good people. He'll look after you."

Another wilt.

Mal didn't dare touch a student, especially uninvited, but he made his expression as calm as he could—striving for that balance between friendliness and not-taking-shit. Students needed to know they could approach him without feeling like they could then walk over the top of him. "I'm here all day if you need anything."

Josh gave him a quick nod and fled for the desk where, as Mal had expected, Ethan immediately welcomed him.

Mal took a breath that did not calm the racing of his heart, or the burn of his curiosity. He turned a smile toward his class. "Okay, let's get started."

CHAPTER 10

The Colonial had a suitably dive quality during the day. All taverns did, as though night were required to hide the stickiness of the carpet and the tackiness of the décor. Daylight seemed to intensify the odor of spilled beer too, though the bar didn't smell as bad as some places he'd been. Leo obviously cleaned his floors now and again—and the windows, judging by the amount of light streaming through the tessellated panes.

Monday afternoon didn't seem to invite a lot of drinking, or maybe it was too cold to be out. A few patrons gathered around one large table, all with silver or thinning hair. They were watching one of the TV screens in total silence—which they could be doing at home?

Another guy slumped at the end of the bar in what Brian had come to think of as Mal's spot, and his pulse quickened for the thirty seconds it took to figure out the guy wasn't Mal. That Mal was probably at work, professoring or whatever it was he did. And why didn't he know that yet? They'd talked twice now.

Leo took a break from the glass-polishing bartenders always seemed to do when they weren't pouring drinks. "Brian." He cut loose a cheeky smile. "Not really your crowd today."

"No kidding." Brian jerked his head toward the TV-watching group. "This a regular thing?"

"Mm-hmm. Bowling club today. Ladies day tomorrow. They all come in around lunch and watch *The Price is Right*."

"Okay." What else did you say to that? Brian dug in his pocket for his wallet. "I wanted to settle my bill. Sorry I haven't been in sooner."

He'd spent all of last week and most of the weekend shepherding Josh from appointment to appointment, making sure he wasn't going to die on him and that his shots were up-to-date. Then he'd needed a tooth filled and something for a rash. How complicated were children supposed to be?

"No worries," Leo said. "I know where you live."

"You do?" Had he ever taken Leo home? Guy was attractive enough, though not Brian's type. He was too . . . friendly? *What the fuck?* And married. He was married. "I don't do married."

"And I like that about you."

"But not much else," Brian guessed, remembering why he never would have approached Leo. He was Simon's friend and Simon's friends had always been across a really thick line.

Leo put down his glass. "What does it matter what I think?"

"It doesn't." A stack of papers rested atop the bar, and though Brian wasn't the overly curious sort, he recognized the letterhead for the company that owned the hotel across the street. He nodded toward the stack. "Doing business with the Billings Group?"

Leo's expression darkened. "No. They want to knock this building down. Put up a row of boutiques or something."

"What? This building should be registered, not bulldozed." Good lord, one stray thought and now he sounded like Simon.

"'Registered'?"

"It's probably been here for over a hundred years." Brian's inner-Simon waved toward the windows. "Possibly longer, judging by the refit on the windows and the roof. Do you know the history of the place? The bar has been here for a while, yeah?"

"My grandfather started the original tavern. Not sure what it was before, but he wanted a place for men to drink and talk about sports. His son, my father, was a hometown football hero."

Damn, both Simon and his annoying friend Frank ate this sort of shit for breakfast. Not only did the building have history, it had a story. Brian looked around again, using a different eye—not the one that evaluated a drinking establishment, but one that decided whether a building could be saved, or would be better out of the way. The interior, while relatively clean, was shabby, but that was a bar during the daylight hours. He could see where one corner sank slightly, meaning an issue with the foundation, and he vaguely remembered seeing cracks in the plaster of the hall. The building didn't feel ready to fall, though. It was solid. It just needed some work.

"I have a friend in a historical society. I could call him and find out what it takes to get a building registered. Find out if that could save it. Do you have the funds to renovate? That might be something you could work out with the Billings Group. When did they buy the building?"

"Why are you so interested?" Leo asked.

Brian shrugged. "Why not? It's what I do. Building and renovation. Usually on a larger scale. I can at least check a few things for you."

"That'd be . . . Thanks, Brian."

"Don't mention it. Now, what do I owe you?"

Leo waved a hand. "It's taken care of."

"I don't even know if I can help you yet."

"No, it's already paid. Mal picked up your tab after you left."

"Mal did."

"That's what I said." Leo's expression indicated that he wanted to say more, but he didn't.

Brian put his wallet away. "Okay, then. Ah . . . Do you know where he works?"

"You going to harass him?"

"No. I want to thank him. Can you give me his number?"

Leo nodded toward the framed prints. "He teaches at the high school."

Well, that made sense. Brian glanced over at one of the prints. A footballer being lifted up by his teammates. The headline beneath proclaimed the Morristown Colonials the 1985 State Champions. "The place is named after the high school football team?" he asked.

"Yep." Leo nodded toward the picture. "Guess who number twelve is."

Number twelve was the player being celebrated. "Your dad?"

"Fuck no. About twenty years too late for him."

"You?"

"Wrong again."

"Mal?"

Leo grinned.

Brian narrowed his eyes. "You two went to school together, didn't you?"

"Yep, and I'm not going to give you any hints," Leo said. "You want in, you gotta earn it. And if you mess with him like you did Simon, you gotta deal with me and half the guys in this bar. Got that?"

"Maybe I'll just mail him a check."

Leo was still laughing as Brian left the tavern. On the street, he pulled out his phone and dialed Simon Lynley, ex-lover, former business partner, and most talented architect he knew.

Simon answered after the second ring. "Hello, Brian."

An odd pang dove through Brian's center, from somewhere below his throat to somewhere above his gut. He recognized the pain; it often accompanied thoughts of Simon. What he couldn't figure out was what it was, exactly. Not loss, but like that. Not sadness, but almost.

"Happy New Year," he said.

"And to you. How's things?"

"Um, fine." Straight to business. "You're in the Bethlehem Historical Society, right?"

After a pause, Simon answered, "Historic Bethlehem, yes."

"How do you go about getting a building registered?"

"That's something you could google."

"Sure, but then I wouldn't be able to tell you about this building." Brian noticed, for perhaps the first time, the collegiate font used to spell out the tavern's name on the sign hanging over the door. He'd hazard a guess that maroon and white were the school's colors too. "Remember the Colonial?"

"Your Thursday-night venue?"

"The Billings Group bought the building and wants to knock it down."

"Sounds more like your area. You can help them design a sleek and modern replacement."

"Maybe I want to help save this place. It's ..." Brian grimaced at the small, nondescript windows on the second floor. "It's got character."

"Leo is married, Brian."

"Why are you being such an ass? I went and looked at Frank's place when you asked. I put together a great proposal for it. That project is nearly halfway done with phase one. I helped make it happen. Now I'm asking for a favor in return and you're . . ." Brian ran out of steam. He thought about ending the call. Instead, he breathed into his end, waiting for his temper to settle. Hating that Simon could still get him so riled up.

"I'm sorry," Simon said.

"Whatever."

"No. Really, I am. I'm just . . . You always have an angle, and I'm in the habit of skipping ahead so I don't get left behind the turn."

"I'll google it. Don't worry about it."

After a pause, Simon said, "I'll get my partner to send you some links. He loves this kind of stuff." Simon's business partner was about as old as the Colonial Tavern and was supposed to have retired about a year ago. "Send me some pictures too."

"Okay."

"Brian?"

"Mmm?" Brian answered, striving for as neutral a tone as possible.

"Take care."

Shaking off melancholy he absolutely shouldn't be feeling, Brian ended the call and used his phone to take pictures of the outside of the building, including the alley down one side and the back. He texted a couple to Simon with a note that he'd upload the rest later, then tucked his phone into his pocket and pulled out his car keys.

A few minutes later, he was turning into the parking lot of Morristown High School and that weird pang was back. He'd hated school. The paperwork involved with getting Josh transferred and registered last week had been enough of a reminder for a lifetime, and he'd seriously considered letting Josh do the homeschool thing. Except that he would suck as a teacher.

Josh needed to have a future. After he finished high school, he could do what he wanted. But he needed this taken care of. Also, according to the transcript from his old school, Josh was ridiculously smart. Made Brian feel like he'd quit around third grade.

Sighing, he parked in the visitor lot and made the icy trek to the front doors. Buses were already lining up in the bus lot, but the doors remained sealed. Someone buzzed him through and he prepared to show his driver's license to the front desk, marveling at the security put in place since the last time he'd been inside a high school.

"I'm here to see Mal . . ." What was Mal's last name?"

"Mr. Montgomery?"

"Yes."

"In relation to?"

"Ah, my nephew. He's just been enrolled as a student here. Joshua Kenway." And Josh probably didn't have a class with Mal, so this was going to be super weird.

The secretary smiled. "Josh with the blue hair?"

"That would be him."

"I hope he's settling in okay. This was his first full day of classes, wasn't it?"

"Yeah."

She'd been pushing buttons all the while, now she spoke into the phone. "Mal? Parent here to see you. About Joshua Kenway?" Before Brian could explain that he wasn't there about Josh, she hung up the phone and said, "He'll be right out."

Right out meant about ten minutes, and a rhythmic *click* preceded Mal through the office door. Then he appeared, dressed in a rust-colored sweater, rumpled khakis, and a big ugly brace that covered his right leg from thigh to ankle. He had his arms hooked over a pair of crutches and looked pained and exhausted.

"Holy—" Remembering he was in a school, Brian swallowed the rest of his curse. "What the hell happened? Sorry, I could have come to see you. Well, I did. But I mean your classroom." Oh God, since when did he ramble? Brian stuck out a hand, retracting it when he realized Mal would have to juggle crutches to shake. "Ah, er, hey."

Mal's smile had a well-worn quality to it. "Hey. You're here to talk about Josh?" Brian glanced at the secretary. Following his gaze, Mal said, "I think the staff lounge is free. Want to step in there for a minute?"

"Sure. Is it close?"

"Right behind me."

Thank God.

Brian hurried to get the door as the secretary asked, "Will you be taking Josh with you this afternoon, Mr. Kenway?"

"Ah, yeah. Can I do that?"

"Of course. I'll sign him out for you and send him in after the bell. There's only a handful of minutes left in last period."

"Thanks."

Mal had already gone inside the small lounge and was easing himself down onto one of the chairs.

"Can I—"

"I've got it," Mal said. "I normally only need one crutch, but it's been a long day. My good leg, which is an entirely relative description right now, hates me, and I have no idea how I'm supposed to do PT this afternoon."

"Should you even be working?"

"I had to take all of last semester off. Just got back."

"What happened?"

"It's a long story. You wanted to talk about Josh?"

"Ah, no, actually. I came to thank you for paying my tab the other night and to apologize for leaving so abruptly."

Mal's expression closed a little. He gazed down at the braced leg he had extended in front of him. Spoke to the Velcro tabs as he adjusted a couple of them. "No big deal. As you can see, I was hardly in a position to follow up."

Brian felt his eyebrows drawing together. "Wait, you were wearing that brace at the bar?"

"It's dark in there and you were on my left side."

"Both times?" Now he felt like a totally unobservant ass.

Mal smiled.

"Well, thanks for covering my tab. How much do I owe you?"

Mal waved him down. "Don't worry about it."

"I don't usually bail like that."

He didn't normally go searching dive bars for men like Mal either. Not that he could explain why—except that Mal didn't come across as easy, which was Brian's preferred flavor. Nor did he seem simple or uncomplicated. He was altogether too quiet, and quite a bit older than the guys Brian usually went for. But even now, sitting in a teacher's lounge of all places, Brian could feel the indefinable spark that drew him to this man.

It wasn't some weird professor fantasy, though he loved the scholarly look—Mal's glasses, the intelligent glint in his gray-blue eyes. The sweater that didn't quite match his pants. God, his shoes . . . He didn't love the shoes. But those shy smiles. The way Mal had fallen into flirting, then made it awkward. The sense Mal needed someone to chase him.

Probably shouldn't be me.

Mal was watching him, expression not exactly bored, but definitely patient. Brian felt like a student again, coming up with an excuse as to why he hadn't done his homework.

"Your students like you, don't they?"

Mal smiled. "Most of them, yeah. History isn't math or English. It's not so much a matter of skill, as interest. And I like to think I make it interesting."

"And Josh is in your class?"

"I met him this afternoon. He has—" Mal stopped. Fiddled with the Velcro tabs on his brace.

"Blue hair?"

Mal glanced up with a more rueful smile. "He looks a bit like you." *Oh.* "He seems like a nice kid."

"When he's not cleaning out my wallet, credit cards and all, and disappearing with a packed bag on New Year's Eve."

Eyes widening, Mal echoed Brian's earlier thought. "Oh, wow."

"Yeah. Took me until nearly one in the morning to find him. He was at the train station. He . . ." Brian pushed a hand through his hair. "He's been having a rough time."

"I'm sorry to hear that. He seemed to have an okay day here. I sat him next to a kid who'd make him a good friend."

"Good, that's great. I don't think—" Brian clamped his lips shut. Josh wouldn't thank him for expressing several thoughts: that he didn't seem to have any friends, that he could use a friend, that he needed someone more qualified to care for him, that he needed a father, damn it, and that Brian didn't feel up to any of it.

"Kids can be complicated," Mal said as though he'd guessed at Brian's thoughts. All of them.

"Yeah." Brilliant repartee . . . not. Why had he come here again? Brian leaned forward, putting a hand to Mal's good knee. "Listen—"

The door to the lounge opened, and Josh walked in, eyes widening. "Why are you here?"

Brian withdrew his hand. "I, ah, came to pick you up." He could hear Mal shifting beside him and immediately cursed himself for lying—even though that could have been his intent all along. Mal would be the sort of guy who preferred the truth, though, and not only because he wanted to set a good example for his students.

"I would have been fine on the bus."

"I know, I just thought you might like to see a friendly face."

"More like you wanted to hit on my teacher."

Brian pushed to his feet and immediately regretted it as blood swirled behind his ears. This had been a terrible idea. "I, ah . . ."

"I've only been here one day and you're already fucking it up for me. God, why do you have to be so gay?"

The sound of Mal clearing his throat drew both of their attention, and when Brian turned, he understood what it was that kept drawing him to this man. He hadn't seen this expression before, but he'd known it was possible. Authority. Command. But also a gentleness that impelled a frightening amount of respect.

"We do not tolerate that kind of language in this school, Josh. Morristown High School is a safe place for all students, regardless of their gender, race, or sexuality. I'll ask you once to remember that. Next time, I'll be handing you a note for detention."

Josh didn't exactly sag, but he did seem to curve backward. His shoulders drew down and his chin dipped. Nodding toward the floor, he mumbled something like "Yes, sir."

Brian produced the keys to his car. "Why don't you go wait for me? I'll be out in a minute."

Without looking up, Josh snatched the keys and fled.

CHAPTER 11

"You need a minute?" Mal reached for his crutches. Josh had left the door open and Brian appeared to be in no mood to close it. The moment, the hand on Mal's knee, had been utterly shredded anyway.

Brian glanced up, frowning, as though he'd forgotten Mal was there. His expression cleared immediately. Or tried to. The smile he seemed to seek eluded him, though he recovered quickly. "No. I should get going in case he decides to steal my car."

"Do you mind if I ask how long you've been Josh's guardian?"

"Two weeks. Two very long weeks."

"Trouble at home?"

"You could say that."

Mal licked his lips and immediately wished that hadn't become a habit around Brian. "Listen, I'm . . ." He pushed out a sigh. "I—"

"Do you ever wonder what it might have been like to have all of this?" Brian asked sweeping his hands out to gesture the walls around him.

"What do you mean?"

"A safe place, even if it was just words."

"Words have power."

"You'd really give a kid detention for being inappropriate?"

"Yes. I would." Now Mal understood what Brian was getting at. "And I do wonder, sometimes. It's why I like being a teacher so much. I'm here, where it . . . not begins, but . . ."

"Where it begins." Brian's expression was haunted, and it did not suit him. Again, he shook it off quickly, returning to the smile that didn't quite work. Something had rattled this man; something more than his nephew's behavior.

"It is easier now, I think," Mal continued. "There will always be people who don't understand and a lot of folk are frightened by what they don't understand. And there will always be the kids who will do anything for their parents' approval. But, deep down, I do feel like there's a shift. Kids are coming out earlier and earlier, and they're being supported by their friends if no one else. And I—*we* fight hard to make sure this school is a safe space. Me and my sister-in-law, especially."

Brian's face brightened. "Rachel Montgomery, of course. I knew your name was familiar."

"She mentioned you at Christmas." Oh, no. Why had he said that?

"You were talking about me at Christmas?"

"Donny was complaining about you, actually. Something about a kitchen contractor."

Brian's brow furrowed. "Kitchen contractor?"

"He called you for a recommendation and you gave him the number of a guy who took eight months to renovate his kitchen."

"Eight months!"

Mal grinned. "Is there an echo in here?"

Brian blushed and it was . . . amazing. He'd shaved that morning, but even if he hadn't, the flush creeping across his skin would have stood out—if only because it didn't belong there. Men like Brian Kenway did not blush. They weren't uncertain or left off-balance, and they were never lost for words. And yet, Brian was currently standing there, cheeks heated, lips moving soundlessly.

"Score another one for me, I think," Mal murmured.

Brian smiled. "I think that was more than one point. So, tell me about this kitchen contractor."

"I don't recall the name, only that he seemed rather useless."

Brian pulled out his wallet and extracted a card. "Get his details for me. I'll look into it. At the very least get him reviewed. He shouldn't be on our list if he's not reliable."

Smiling, Mal took the card. "I'll do that, thanks. I'm sure Donny will appreciate it."

"So what did Rachel have to say about me?"

"She mentioned some letters you write to the scholarship kids."

Brian's recovered humor dipped again. The haunted look returned. "Education is important."

"I can only agree. Listen . . ." Mal cut a glance toward the door, wondering if Josh actually would steal Brian's car. "I'm heading up the GSA this semester."

"GSA?"

"Gay-Straight Alliance."

"Okay, yeah. Rachel has mentioned it, or I've seen it on a few transcripts. Another wonder of the modern age, huh?"

"Indeed. Um . . . I don't want to presume . . ." Mal hesitated as the color in Brian's cheeks returned. "But it's a welcoming place, if Josh needs, ah, support." *Way to sound like a leader, Malcolm.*

"I'll mention it to him, maybe in a decade or so, when we're talking again."

Mal laughed. "Teenagers are masters in the art of grudge holding."

"Please don't say that."

Right, it had only been a couple of weeks. "I'd like some adult volunteers as well. Parents, guardians. The more the merrier." Had he actually said that out loud?

"You don't want me talking with kids, trust me. I suck at it."

"It's not about talking. Just being there . . . being gay and successful is what they need to see. You're a businessman. Put together and charming. You're succeeding at life and a lot of my kids need to see that."

"Charming, hmm?" Brian's blue eyes twinkled, and it was wrong that they were the same color as Josh's—that looking at a troubled boy would remind Mal of his uncle, every single time.

"You know you are," Mal stuttered.

"Well, of course *I* know. I did wonder if you did, though."

"Is this where I roll my eyes?"

"If you like."

Mal tried hard not to roll his eyes. "Stop smiling like that."

"Is it too charming?"

"Yes! We might have a policy regarding bullying, but we also have one regarding harassment."

Brian lifted his chin and laughed, the sound warm and rich. Then he tapped the card Mal still held in his hand. "Call me. We'll have coffee and talk about this club of yours."

"We could talk about it over the phone."

"But talking in person is so much more fun."

"Brian, I don't think—"

"Don't think. Just do."

God, was everyone going to tell him that? "The meetings are on Monday afternoons."

"Today? I—"

"I know. They sprang it on me too. How about next week?"

"Hmm. We should meet for coffee this week, then."

"We don't have to—"

"What are you doing tomorrow?"

With a strange joy, Mal answered, "PT, probably, if I skip this afternoon."

Brian took in his crutches again, as though he'd forgotten. "What happened?"

"Why don't we save some conversation for our coffee d—" Do not call it a date. "For coffee."

Brian had heard the *D*. He grinned. "Let's do that." A wrinkle of concern crossed his brow. "Tell me, this GSA. Are straight kids actually involved?"

"Yes. Not as many as I'd like, but enough to give the title credence."

"Times have changed, haven't they?"

"They really have."

CHAPTER 12

Simon emailed on Thursday, wanting to come out and see the Colonial. He was interested in the job—as Brian had known he would be. What Brian hadn't known was how much he didn't want Simon to come back to Morristown . . . and that was new.

If he were honest with himself, he'd been manufacturing excuses to stay in touch with Simon for over a year, starting shortly after Simon had moved to Bethlehem. And now Simon had been the first person he called when confronted with an old building that needed work.

Was Vanessa right? If so, why didn't he want to see Simon now?

Brian averted his gaze from the picture wall before he could find the photo of them together. Damn it, he was over Simon. He had been the one to leave! After nearly twelve years of not understanding why he couldn't make it work, despite knowing he loved Simon and wanted to be loved by him—exclusively—he'd packed a bag and moved into the house where he now lived. The one of four that had always remained vacant for reasons he'd never examined too closely, because admitting that he'd liked having somewhere to go when things didn't work out was too much like sharing that he had once needed somewhere to go.

"Not the same."

Sort of the same.

Opening a reply message, Brian checked his calendar. His business always slowed in winter. Foundations couldn't be dug and no one wanted to work outside when it was snowing, sleeting, or twenty-something below freezing with the wind chill—had it always been this cold in the northeast? This time of year, he did a lot of consulting and planning for when the ground thawed. In between, he dealt with emergencies and told Vanessa, over and again, why he was too busy to appear personally at any of the Smart Foundation board meetings.

He smiled as he saw the bright-purple bar on his calendar denoting a social appointment that afternoon: coffee with Mal. Since when did he look forward to a coffee date—that wasn't a date? Mal wasn't going to sleep with him, he knew that. He'd known that on New Year's Eve. Mal wasn't the hookup type, his lack of attendance Thursday nights at the Colonial aside. But, God, the idea of getting under the professor's skin. Or under one of his button collar shirts.

Mal would have hair on his chest, Brian decided. Not a thick pelt. The hair on his head was a silky, flyaway texture that seemed to defy all styling aid. Brian could easily imagine it longer and supposed it was easier to tame with a little length. More weight would help. Longer hair would suit Mal's face too. He had an interesting manner: not as intense as his job might demand, but not as relaxed as he could be. He was a thinker, but also a dreamer. The breadth of his shoulders and leanness of frame indicated he was athletic.

He'd played football in high school, right? What position?

They'd agreed to meet at Olive's, a café two doors down from the Colonial, in the adjacent building. As Brian studied the façade, he wondered what the Billings Group would replace this row with if they tore everything down. He checked the next building along, and then looked across the street at the still-new hotel. Getting the large chain here had been a triumph for downtown, especially as they'd constructed one of their flagship, upmarket models. The conference space was sorely needed, and Brian was a member of the gym on the ground floor.

Returning his attention to the older buildings on his side of the street, he tried to picture how the row of tired brick in several different colors and mismatched windows would appear to someone from out of town.

They could seem charming, to use a word that had been applied to him. But was *charming* a term people used when they saw something that was supposed to be appealing, and yet . . . wasn't?

"You could have waited inside," said Mal, appearing next to him. He was using only one crutch today and looked a lot less tired than on Monday, and all warm and cozy in his dark felted wool coat, gray hat, and matching gray scarf.

"How's the leg?" Brian asked, nodding toward the big black brace.

"Numb, mostly. Hopefully they'll have a chair I can prop it up on."

"We could try the Colonial instead."

"I love Leo like a brother, but I don't like visiting his place during the afternoon. It's usually full of old men and women watching talk shows and curling."

"Curling?"

"It's like hockey with broomsticks."

"You're making that up."

Mal smiled. "So totally not. Google it."

Brian felt a laugh tickle his throat. "Jesus, you're like the third person to tell me to google something this week."

Shrugging, Mal tipped his head toward the café door. "We heading in?"

"Yeah, let me get that." Brian pulled the door open and held it until Mal made his way through. The server took one look at Mal's leg and crutch and ushered them to a table near the back that had plenty of space around it, and an extra chair he could use to prop up his foot.

Brian draped his coat over the back of his chair and then fidgeted next to Mal, who was working the buttons at the front of his own coat.

"Need a hand?" Brian asked.

"I think I can undress myself." Mal's cheeks flushed a little over an easy laugh.

Grinning, Brian took Mal's coat anyway, and hung it over the back of his chair. Then he angled the extra one so Mal could get his leg up there.

"How long have you been dealing with the brace?"

"Since the surgery, which was about seven weeks ago. I've just had it unlocked, meaning I'm allowed to bend my knee a few degrees when I walk. And I don't have to sleep with the damn thing anymore."

"You had to sleep with that on your leg?"

"And shower."

"Damn."

"It's been easier to deal with than the cast."

"Cast?"

Mal tapped his other leg. "This one was broken. In three places. I have enough metal in there to set off an alert at Newark Airport from about a mile away. I've had three surgeries on that leg and a combination of casts and braces. I'd just gotten them off when we decided to do the surgery on this one." He tapped his right knee.

"What the hell happened?"

"What can I get you guys?" The server was back, pencil poised over her pad.

Brian picked up one of the menus she'd left on the table, then glanced over his shoulder at the glass cases facing the front and side of the shop. "Coffee, black, and one of those fruit tart things. Have they got custard under the fruit?"

"Uh-huh."

Mal ordered a complicated confection of coffee and cream, and a slice of pound cake, with cream and strawberries.

"You like cream," Brian observed after the server had left.

"I do. And if I have to endure the torture of physical therapy for another three months, I'm going to eat it every day."

Brian indulged in a quick fantasy of Mal licking cream from his lips. Licking cream from his skin. Licking something creamy from his lips.

"You have to stop looking at my mouth like that."

Brian flicked his gaze upward to Mal's smiling eyes. "Ahh, but I know what those lips taste like. It's only natural that I would want to look at them." He did remember Mal's taste, too. Hops, peanuts, and man. Mal. He'd tasted warm and altogether too cozy—like long mornings tangled in down comforters.

"I was hit by a car," Mal said.

"What?"

"You asked what happened." Mal glanced at the table, under which his knee was propped on a chair.

"Oh, right. Jesus. Also, that's a hell of a subject change."

"Not really. Just reminding you why we're here."

"You think that because this is coffee and it's still light outside"—barely—"that you're safe from any advance?"

Mal shifted in his seat.

Brian grinned. Leaning forward, he murmured, "Do you remember what I taste like?"

Cheeks flushing a deeper shade of pink, one that couldn't be hidden with a smile, Mal muttered inaudibly.

"What was that?"

Their server arrived back with coffee and cake.

Brian considered pressing for an answer, but decided to let Mal enjoy his coffee and cream and cake and cream until Mal rolled his eyes and put down his fork. He licked his lips, which were not coated with cream, and reached into the satchel-type bag he'd put on the side of their table. "So, the GSA."

Inwardly, Brian groaned. He hadn't mentioned the group to Josh, and he hadn't given any thought to joining himself. What would be the point if his nephew wasn't there?

"Basically, the aim of the club is to provide a safe space for kids to express themselves. The teacher who started the club is moving, and I'll be heading it up from now on. I'd like more parents and teachers to get involved, but this late in the school year, most teachers already have full schedules. So I'm asking parents. I've talked to the mother of one of my students, and she said she'll try to make it. She'll be encouraging her son to join too, which is great, as he's well-liked by the other students. He'll probably bring his girlfriend. Did you ask Josh about it?"

"Ah..."

Mal put his folder down. "Is he gay?"

Brian felt his brow furrow. "Are you allowed to ask that?"

"Technically, no. Not to Josh, anyway. But I'm asking you. Is that why he's living with you?"

"For the time being." Brian tried to appear happier about it, or at least content. Mal's eyebrows lifted in question, but before Mal could voice whatever he was thinking, Brian returned to their earlier conversation. "What happened with the car?"

"What car?"

"The one that hit you?"

Mal swallowed. Licked his lips. Shuffled his papers. He leaned forward, as though preparing to ask a question, then leaned back again.

"I was out running," he said. "It was late, I'd gotten a late start, and it was dark by the time I turned back toward home, but most of the path is in parkland, except where it crosses roads. The car caught me on Lake Road, just as I tried to jump out of the way, hitting both of my legs and throwing me nearly twenty feet. I broke my collarbone, wrenched my shoulder, hit my head, vomited everywhere, broke one leg, and tore all the ligaments in the other. I had a severe concussion and couldn't hear out of one ear for three months. It still fuzzes now and again. One of my bones was poking through my skin. That's what they tell me." Mal's gaze had taken on a faraway aspect as he added, "They also tell me that I nearly died. On the operating table. I lost a lot of blood and my brain was swollen."

Brian's tongue was dry. He closed his mouth, rewetting it. "Holy crap, are you freaking kidding me?"

"No."

"And this was when?"

"August last year."

"And you're already walking?"

Mal's jaw tightened. "Not well enough, but . . . yeah. I . . ."

Brian could see it then, the pain beneath the more rested expression, and that not all of Mal's hurt was physical.

"What happened with the driver of the car?" he asked.

Mal shook his head, his eyebrows bunched together. "He left the scene."

CHAPTER 13

The date that wasn't a date wasn't going as planned. Brian wore a pinched expression and Mal felt sick. His four or five mouthfuls of cake and cream swirled in his stomach. Why on this good Earth had he given so much detail? Fewer facts would have been better, judging by the pallor of Brian's face. And the "I could have died" bit? What the ever loving—

"Do they know anything? Are there any suspicions?" Brian asked.

"What do you mean?"

"About the car and the driver."

"Probably someone from out of town."

"On Lake Road?"

"You could cut through there from 202 to Sussex."

Brian shook his head. "It doesn't make any sense. Were they speeding?"

Swallowing, Mal pushed his plate away. "Can we talk about something else?"

To his surprise, Brian immediately nodded. "Of course. I'm sorry. And I'm sorry you were in such a terrible accident."

Mal shrugged. Brian wasn't the first person to apologize for things that weren't his fault. Mal had received a lot of the same attention back in college, and understood that it was reflex to offer an apology when you couldn't think of anything else to say.

Brian reached across the table then, suddenly enough to catch Mal by surprise. He grasped Mal's wrist. "I saw the photo of you next door. I can't imagine how hard it must be to be so limited right now."

"Photo?" Brian's hand was warm.

"The football one. You winning some award."

"Oh, that picture at the Colonial." Cue another gut swirl. God, why had he ordered everything with cream? "Yeah, football isn't exactly my thing anymore. I wrecked that in college. Another spectacular accident."

"Sounds like you need a guardian angel."

Are you applying for the job?

Even though Mal didn't say the words, Brian obviously heard them. Smiling, he stroked Mal's wrist. "I've seen you at the Pig. Why haven't you ever introduced yourself?"

"Why haven't you?"

Brian frowned. "That's . . . a good question."

Mal withdrew his hand. "Listen, Brian—"

"Hmm?"

"What are we doing here? No, don't answer that. What are you doing here?"

"In Morristown or in this café?"

"Sitting across the table from me pretending you're interested in my life story."

"Ouch."

Mal shrugged.

Brian leaned back and folded his arms. "You asked me if I wanted to help out with this GSC—"

"GSA."

"Right, that. So I'm here."

"You don't really want to help, though. Do you?"

Discomfort tugged at Brian's easy smile. "Are you always this direct?"

"No, actually. But . . . I'm tired and in pain and . . . I don't know where you think this is going, but it's probably not where you think it is."

"But you don't know where I think this is going."

"Brian."

"I do like the way you say my name."

"Brian!"

Brian held up his hands. "Okay. I'll state the obvious. I want to get to know you."

"In a biblical sense."

"In every sense."

Heat suffused Mal's cheeks before shooting southward. "I'm not a Thursday night kinda guy."

"I know."

"Then . . ."

Brian's throat moved as he swallowed, and the idea he seemed to be taking time to choose his next words filled Mal with a combination of excitement and consternation. Uncrossing his arms, Brian leaned forward, lips quirking up on one side. "When was the last time you let go, Mal? Just went with a feeling and did something you really wanted to do?"

"Seconds before the car hit me."

"Not what I'm talking about and you know it."

"So, what, you think my love life needs a little shaking up and you're offering to do the shaking?" A combination of *yes* and *no* rolled through Mal's middle. Hadn't he been thinking this exact thing?

"Why not?"

"Putting aside the fact that I can barely walk, you could choose any of a dozen other guys." Mal tapped his wrist. "It's Thursday. You could go next door tonight and get what you need."

"You're not there on Thursday nights."

"Are you always this direct?" Mal asked, echoing Brian's earlier question.

Brian smiled. "When I see something I want, yes."

Mal gave in to the urge to tug at his shorter hair. He had about an inch all over now, which was enough to push his fingers through, but he missed having it longer. Being able to hide behind it. Heck, even the warmth of it. Letting his hand drift back to the table, he aimed for the folder and pushed it forward. "Help me with this and I'll think about it."

"That's not much of an offer. You could think and say no."

"I could. I guess it depends on how much you"—he'd said want, hadn't he?—"want me."

Brian's smile was slow and it did awful and wonderful things to Mal's equilibrium. Competing urges stopped clashing and started aligning, making the warmth spreading through his middle and down his legs withdraw to a more central point. He could feel his cheeks flushing again and wanted to loosen his collar—though he wore no tie and the neckline of his sweater was not snug.

"What you're feeling right now?" Brian said. "That's why I'm going to say yes to your deal. I'll show up to this club of yours and then you'll show up to a date with me."

"I didn't say anything about a date."

"You'd rather meet up and fuck?"

Oh God. Mal tapped his folder. "Meeting first."

"Of course." Brian's grin said he knew Mal was only making that point for himself.

"And now we need to change the subject."

"Did you know the hotel across the road was planning to knock down this entire row of buildings?"

Mal felt as though someone had opened a window and let a blizzard swirl into the center of the coffee shop. "What?"

"I was chatting with Leo on Monday, and he showed me the notice. I did a little research and discovered it's not just his building, but this one and the one next door."

"But the Colonial has been in Leo's family forever!"

"Fifty-seven years. Before then, it was a café. Before then, a soda shop. I'm still digging into before then."

"Wow."

"I've been poking about in city records."

"Why are you telling me this?"

"You wanted to change the subject."

Mal glanced at the wall separating the café from the building next door and frowned. He couldn't imagine the Colonial not being there. Here. It was his place. His bar. "My dad used to drink at the Colonial."

"It's a landmark and a tradition."

"What can we do? Can you do anything? You have access to those sorts of records, so . . ."

"Anyone can look at public records. But I have a few connections in city hall, so . . . yeah, I'd like to do something. The Billings Group is citing age and bad repair as reasons to knock down the row."

"Let me guess. Whatever they put here will probably be too expensive for the current tenants."

"Probably."

"Leo must be going crazy."

"I imagine he is."

An odd impulse had Mal stretching his hand across the table toward Brian's. He patted the back of Brian's fingers. "Thanks for telling me. The school principal is involved with the city council, I think. I'll see what he knows and maybe between all of us, we'll figure something out."

"Maybe talk to your father as well. And encourage Leo to do the same. If we could get some history on the buildings, the Billings Group might be convinced to renovate instead of knocking them down."

Mal nodded. "Okay. Done."

Smiling, Brian angled his hand so that his fingers slid over the top of Mal's. "Can we talk about our date now?"

It would be childish and somewhat ridiculous to extract his hand. Also, the stroke of Brian's fingers was traveling up his arm and down his side and back to his middle. *Yes* and *no* were doing their thing in his gut again. Hope against fear. He missed being with someone, but a sumptuous feast was not the recommended way to end a starvation diet. "If I invite you to my house, are you going to immediately assume that means sex?"

"Of course."

Inwardly, Mal groaned. In a good way. "Do you have any friends, Brian?"

"What kind of a question is that?"

"What if I said I wanted to be friends?"

"You don't." Brian continued to stroke his hand. "Right now you're imagining my fingers elsewhere. Friends don't think like that."

Their server appeared then. She didn't frown at their joined hands, or the snippet of conversation she'd obviously overheard, but her cheeks flamed nonetheless. "Can I get you guys anything else?"

Extracting his hand—leaving Mal's cold and alone—Brian opened his wallet and pulled out a card. "Can you give this to the owner? My associate and I are researching the history of these buildings in an effort to save them from the hotel's refurbishment plan."

Shrugging, the server took the card. "Sure."

"Have them call me."

"Okay."

"And we'll take the check, thanks."

She peeled off a ticket and laid it on the table. "Up the front, when you're ready."

Brian glanced back at Mal and caught him staring. He raised his brows. "What?"

"You're serious about this. About saving these buildings."

"Yes. Why wouldn't I be?"

"I looked you up." Mal's last blush hadn't faded yet. It was too warm in the café. "I know your business is mostly residential and that you're more about building new than restoration. What's your interest in this particular row of buildings? You could put in a bid for whatever they wanted to build next."

"I could."

"Then why try to save the row?"

Mal had a feeling Brian's answer would be the key to unlocking a man who, on the surface, didn't appear to have much mystery at all. Brian Kenway was as advertised. A flirt, a player. Someone who went after what he wanted and rarely took no for an answer. But something deeper lurked below the surface. Beneath that handsome façade lay a man who was currently acting as the guardian of a disaffected teenager, and perhaps a man who wanted something more.

He had done more.

Brian picked up the check. "This one's on me. I never paid you back for the other night."

Waving a hand, Mal waited for *more*. For the answer to his question.

Brian let out a soft sigh. "I've spent the past two years waiting for an opportunity to leave Morristown. I don't hate this city, I just . . ." Was that sorrow reflected in his eyes? "Maybe this will be my last project. The first thing I did here was build a collection of condos near where I live. Maybe the last thing I do here will be to save something old." His smile was small and secretive. "It would be fitting, in a way."

"You're not planning to stay?"

"I'm not planning anything, Mal. I'm following my instincts, as I have always done. It's an attitude that usually does well for me."

"I can imagine," Mal said, his tone dry. "And me?"

Brian's smile widened. "See above."

"Not sure if I like being categorized as a project."

Brian laughed, and it wasn't his usual laugh—short and sharp. This was more a chuckle. Soft, gentle, rueful. "Then stop thinking of yourself that way," he said. "Simple as that."

CHAPTER 14

B rian nearly jumped off the couch as something exploded on the TV.

"How could you not see that coming?" Josh asked.

Tuning into the show, Brian tried to make sense of everything on the screen. "What?"

"Are you even watching?"

"Sure."

Josh turned back to the blazing inferno, and Brian thought back over his knowledge of the plot that was about as confusing as the wreckage littering the . . . Were those zombies?

"What's this called again?"

"*The Walking Dead.*"

"Right." They'd elected not to watch a movie because jumping into a show at the beginning of the fifth season had made so much more sense. "You promised to catch me up. What exploded?"

"A gas tank. She shot a hole in it and then sent a Roman candle over there."

"Uh-huh."

Brian watched as the people he supposed were the good guys shot at the people he supposed were the bad guys, and why were they all shooting each other when there were zombies to kill? Then his mind wandered back toward the Colonial Tavern.

Would Mal be there tonight?

Would Brian be breaking their agreement if he stopped by for a drink and happened to flirt and maybe coax (gently, oh so gently) Mal into another kiss and then saw where the night went? Their last kiss had been going places. *Oh, yeah.*

Someone screamed and Brian startled back to reality.

Then the screen went black.

Josh tossed the remote onto the table and stood up. "I can watch upstairs."

"What? Why? I was watching."

"No, you weren't."

"What does it matter, anyway? I don't even know what's happening, Josh."

An angry pout pinched his nephew's small mouth. "Why don't you just go out and do your thing?"

Because he was trying to accomplish something here, even if it didn't make sense. He and Mal weren't together or anything, so heading out to the Frog or the Pig (and why were so many bars in Morristown named after animals? Must be a farm thing) wouldn't be cheating. So why did it feel like it might be?

Going to the Colonial tonight *would* be cheating, though—on his deal with Mal. Why was that important?

Then there was Josh. Between New Year's and getting him into Morristown High, they'd spent a lot of time together and it hadn't been terrible. And he couldn't help feeling that being here for Josh was more important than anything else he had going on right now.

"The only plans I have for tonight are watching whatever this is with you. So can we—"

"Why?"

Brian pushed his fingers into his hair. "Because—"

"You don't need to watch me. I'm not going to run away."

Brian peeked up at his nephew, dropped his hands, and sighed. "I figured if we spent more time together, you'd be more comfortable here." Would now be the right time to bring up the GSA? "What other things do you like to do? Have you thought about joining any of the clubs at school?"

"I dunno."

"Help me out here, Josh. I'm trying."

"I like art."

An idea materialized out of the tattered remnants of their Friday night. "How about if we head up to Newark for the day tomorrow?"

"I do not want to visit my mom."

"We won't go near your neighborhood." Though maybe a drive-by could be worked into the schedule. "I've got a friend living up there and she's an artist. Really talented. We could check out her stuff, hang around her studio. She's putting together a new exhibit, so we could be the first ones to see some of her new paintings."

"What's her name?"

"Vanessa Smart."

"You know Vanessa Smart?"

"You've heard of her?"

"She's, like, amazing." Josh's face animated, making him look not so much alive as actually engaged with the act of living. "Her work is so intricate. It's, like, deconstructed but not. Like putting a microscope to reality."

What? "You mean that series where she painted the inner workings of mechanical things?"

"All her work is like that. It's all inner workings."

"Huh."

"Do you even like art?" Josh asked, his tone full of teenage skepticism.

"I don't know a lot about it, to be honest. But I really like Vanessa's stuff. So, listen, ah, how about if we get away around ten? I'll text Ness, make sure she'll be around. We can do lunch and visit with her."

Josh's expression brightened, and Brian decided that even if it was more due to the mention of Vanessa than the prospect of spending a day with his uncle, he'd take it.

Tension shot down Brian's legs, pointing his toes as he fisted his cock and squeezed, pausing in the lazy stroke he'd been idling with for some time—from sleepiness to wakefulness. He'd brought himself off last night, trying not to think about Mal. This morning's session would likely feature the same blend of non-thought and restraint that often made things . . . harder.

Since when was denial his kink?

Loosening his grip, he stroked the length of his shaft before running his fingers over the tip, letting skin drag against damp skin—enjoying the tease. Collecting a bead of pre-come, he slicked his fingers and glided back down, squeezed, and stroked back up. Down, squeeze, up, pull, twist, drag, down, squeeze. He established a rhythm, thought about how he hadn't had Mal yet—had yet to feel Mal's lips around his cock, though he could imagine them. There was something sensual about Mal. The way he enjoyed cream in his coffee and rich, dark beers. He'd savor a blowjob. Lick and suck and make a meal of it.

Oh God.

Positioning might be difficult. Mal could hardly get to his knees. He'd have to lie on his back, as Brian currently was, propped up on a couple of pillows, face at the right height for Brian to straddle his torso. To thrust forward and meet Mal's mouth. To fuck his face— gently and sweetly at first, teasing Mal's lips with his cockhead, painting them with desire. Then to press forward, easing himself inside that envelope of warmth. Feeling the touch of Mal's teeth as he tucked them out of the way. Filling his mouth, touching the back of his throat. Nudging that constriction and gasping at the flutter and close.

Forgoing the twist at the top, Brian opted for a simple squeeze, imitating the imagined pressure of Mal's throat. The suction of his mouth and lips. The quick slide in and out. His balls tightened, his legs strained again. His toes curled. Then his hips rose up off the bed, and he came, jetting through the crosshatch of his fingers, his yell muffled by the press of his forearm. He bit his arm, sucking at sleep-warm flesh until several quakes had moved through him. Until his hips stopped jerking and the delicious torpor of a good orgasm stilled his legs.

He hoped his date with Mal led to sex. If it didn't, he was going to wear the skin off his cock with twice-daily pulls.

Half an hour later, showered, dressed, and nibbling on a slice of toast, he greeted a sleepy Josh, who gave him a side-eye as he leaned into the fridge to grab a prepackaged soy something.

"You sure jerk off a lot," Josh said. Might have said to the interior of the refrigerator.

"What?"

"You could bring someone back, you know. I wouldn't freak out."

"I . . ." Too embarrassed to blush, Brian furrowed his brow. "Do you— Has someone talked to you about sex?"

"Yeah."

"Listen, what you said at school on Monday, when you walked in on me and Mal?" How to phrase this? "That's not what being gay is about. I'm not a walking hit machine."

"A what?" Josh closed the fridge, soy smoothie in hand.

"A testosterone factory."

"Uh—"

"I know everyone thinks gay men are always having sex, but this gay man is not, okay?"

"You're making me uncomfortable."

"I'm sorry. I just . . . I want to answer questions if you have them." *And to talk you into going to this GSA thing with me.*

"Okay."

"Okay." Subject closed. "So, when will you be ready to leave?"

Another half hour saw them on the road, along with the rest of New Jersey. Where the heck was everyone going on a cold Saturday morning in January? Brian had a mental list of topics to discuss on the drive, which could take up to an hour if everyone kept slowing down to rubberneck at accidents on the other side of the interstate. He might try 280 on the way home.

"So . . ." God, he'd become one of those people who started every sentence with *so*. Clearing his throat, Brian continued, "So, how was your first week at Morristown High?" He stopped short of asking if Josh had made any friends because he remembered how such questions felt. Even asking about Josh's week might border on intrusive.

When Josh didn't answer, Brian glanced over to find him plugged into his new cell phone. Above the sound of traffic, he could hear the thin beat of whatever Josh was listening to. Sighing, Brian indicated a lane change and navigated around another slowdown.

"I was chatting with Mal—Mr. Montgomery. Do you call him Mr. M. or something? I wonder if he ever compares himself to M in the Bond movies? Though, his profession is completely different, so that'd be stupid. Jesus, my brain is weird. So, anyway, he's heading up this club for gay kids. And straight kids. And I sort of volunteered to help out. You want to come along? It's Monday afternoon."

As Brian had supposed, Josh heard none of what he'd said. Josh did glance over once, frowned at Brian's moving lips, and turned back to his phone.

Great. Terrific. Why did people have kids?

The urge to call Simon was short-lived, even if his ex did currently have the experience of living with a teenager. Charlie had a daughter, and their house often harbored a cluster of young people. Brian liked Charlie's daughter. She had a lot of personality. She also made him feel somewhat inadequate, however, and because he couldn't explain that, he pretty much avoided thinking about it. And if he did call Simon, Simon would probably tell him to google it. Or link him to articles he could have found himself.

Maybe he could ask Mal. Mal spent all day, every day with kids Josh's age.

Duh. Why didn't you think of that before?

Brian banged his hands on the wheel.

"What?"

He glanced over at Josh. "Now you listen?"

"You're banging the wheel."

"I was struck with inspiration."

"Okay."

"We'll be there in a few minutes." *Don't ask if he's excited.* "So . . ." Jesus fucking Christ. "Have you been to one of Vanessa's shows before? How did you hear about her?"

"She visited our school a couple years ago." In went the earbuds. "Nice chat."

Ten minutes later, Vanessa opened the door and greeted Brian with her customary smile and smacking kiss to his lips. Brian hugged her tight, inhaling the familiar scent of perfume and Vanessa, his oldest friend. He loved this woman. Would marry her if she wasn't always getting married to someone else. Also, he'd suck as a husband. He had no interest in sex with Vanessa and a lot of interest in sex with other people. Men. Mal, currently.

"You must be Josh," Vanessa was saying to his pink-cheeked nephew. "The color of your hair is fantastic! How long ago did you dye it?"

Josh did a little gaping.

"And I cannot get over how much like Brian you are. It's like being transported back a hundred years."

"Which would make you as old as I am," Brian put in.

Vanessa, of course, looked amazing and ten years younger than he did.

Putting her hand around Josh's shoulder, she guided him up the stairs and into her studio, a light-filled space that encompassed nearly the entire top floor of the house. Brian followed.

They were across Elizabeth Avenue from Weequahic Park, light-years from where he'd grown up, but only a few miles in actual fact. Brian didn't visit Vanessa often—he found the reminder of where he'd come from both nostalgic and painful. Mostly painful. After he'd been kicked out, he'd lived in this house with Vanessa and her uncle Tristan for a handful of years before college. They'd been good years, despite the fact that Tristan had been slowly dying the whole time. But Tristan had done his best to convince Brian that life was worth living, and now, some thirty years later, Brian had to agree. Still, returning to Elizabeth Avenue was always hard—even more so than simply being in Newark—and Brian often wondered why Vanessa had remained. Of course, she hadn't had his start. And she'd always had Tristan. Maybe she'd dulled pain of his loss by continuing to live here, even after Tristan's death.

Brian was unaware he'd made a sound until Vanessa touched his arm. Had he sighed? Hopefully it had only been a sigh. As though she sensed his thoughts, she squeezed his arm and gave him the special smile that had made and kept their friendship. "Wait here."

Vanessa abandoned them in the middle of the large attic room, where two couches faced each other over a coffee table piled high with books and magazines. All of the walls were hung with her paintings. One also had a row of low counters and cabinets, which was where she stored her tools. Adjacent to her work space were the windows overlooking the park, and the source of most of the light. Large skylights opened up the sloping ceiling so that even on the darkest days, Vanessa barely needed to turn on a light. She had lights, though, clustered over the half of the attic devoted to her easels and tables.

She'd disappeared into one of the two rooms at the back that she used to store her work.

While Brian worked to steady his breathing—no more sighing!—Josh wandered toward the half-finished painting on the closest easel.

"I can't believe I'm actually here. Do you think she'd let me take a couple of pictures?" He had his phone in his hand.

"Probably. Maybe not the unfinished stuff, but I don't know. I've never asked."

"How come you don't have any of her paintings at your place if you're such good friends?"

"I do. I just haven't hung them up. I've only been in that house for . . ." Two years. "I had them hanging in my old place."

"My art is in a box? For shame, Brian." Vanessa popped out of the storage room, carrying two small canvases.

Brian recognized the frames. "Oh, no. Ness. Don't show him those."

Grinning evilly, Vanessa held out the two portraits for Josh to see. "Me and Brian, age . . ." She glanced over her shoulder. "God, were we seventeen? Eighteen?"

Brian reached out to snatch the portrait he'd done, the crime against art he'd painted so long ago. "I cannot believe you kept these."

"I kept all your art."

"What do you mean 'all'?"

"I have your sketchbooks too."

"You are no longer my best friend."

Vanessa laughed. "So you keep trying to tell me. Find someone else who will put up with you for as long as I have and we'll visit that topic again." She hadn't let go of his painting, and Josh was studying it and comparing it to Vanessa's portrait of Brian, which even then showed what would become her style: messy blocks of color that could look like nothing so much as a cut-up picture pasted back together again. Badly. But also showed exactly what it was meant to be: a face. An impossibly young face framed by dark-purple hair and big blue eyes.

"You had purple hair?" Josh asked, glancing up at Brian.

Cheeks heating, Brian reached for his picture again. "For a while."

"And green and blue, something like yours. Orange. Black. Do you remember your black phase?" Vanessa asked.

"Unfortunately, yes."

Josh turned his attention back to Brian's painting. Brian's style was much more realistic than Vanessa's—something he'd struggled with and probably the reason he'd given up on art. He'd never been able to get anything to look exactly as it should and had never grasped why you would paint a scene other than realistically, even though he could appreciate Vanessa's style for what it was. But he'd never had any real talent. His lines were timid and his perspective off. He had an easier time with buildings. Plans. Square things.

Josh's lips pressed together and apart. Then he glanced up. "You were good."

Snorting, Brian pointed toward Vanessa's latest canvas. "If you want good, check out Vanessa's stuff."

An hour passed with Vanessa allowing Josh to take pictures of whatever he wanted. Apparently she posted regular updates of her works in progress online. They chatted art and music and food while Brian made affirmative noises when called upon. He envied the ease with which Vanessa bonded with his nephew, and was grateful for it at the same time. Josh was obviously having a good day, and that meant Brian was having a good day.

When Josh excused himself to use the bathroom, Vanessa sidled up next to Brian and put her arm around his waist, snuggling in close as she always did. "He's adorable."

"Today he is."

"Have you stopped looking for somewhere to send him?" Vanessa arched her eyebrows in question, while eyes dared him to say no.

Brian shrugged and she smiled.

"I like seeing you like this," she said.

"Like what?"

"With family. With Josh. He likes you."

"I'm sure he does"

"No. He . . . Be nice to him, Bri. I get the feeling you're the only thing standing between him and you know what."

Brian grimaced lightly. "That's because I am."

"So you know how important what you're doing is."

"That's why I brought him here today."

Her smile widened. "I'm glad you did. You don't visit me often enough."

"Yeah, well."

Sobering slightly, Vanessa gave him another hug. "It's okay to let go, Brian. You know that, right? You can't hold on to everything forever."

He wanted to tell her he had let go—of a lot. This house, for instance. But as quickly as the thought occurred, a second replaced it. He'd never encouraged a friendship between Vanessa and Simon, and this was why. Just as he'd always kept one condo empty, he liked to keep spaces between the compartments of his life. Vanessa here, with his past, Simon . . . There was no Simon. Not anymore. Was it because of this . . . this feeling welling up inside him now? The memory of himself at Josh's age? A younger version of himself. The self he had only ever shared with one person, the woman hugging him so tightly right now?

And if he was going to be doing all this thinking—it must be Vanessa's perfume. She always smelled like a fresh spring morning after the rain . . . If he was going to keep thinking along these lines, examining the rights and wrongs, then which part of himself was he going to share with Mal?

Or was that something else he should let go of?

Once again sensing his thoughts, Vanessa pressed a kiss to his cheek. Brian sighed—purposefully this time—and rested his forehead against hers.

CHAPTER 15

Mal surveyed the nearly empty classroom and wondered again, for the fifty-seventh time, if he and Ethan would be the only people attending the GSA meeting that afternoon.

"Maybe they didn't get the room change," Ethan suggested.

Where is your mom? Mal wanted to ask, but didn't. Brian would be here. Brian was late, but he struck Mal as the sort of guy who didn't leave someone hanging. Not intentionally, anyway.

The door opened and a familiar blond head poked through. Mal let out a sigh of relief. So they'd have a GSA meeting with one straight kid. At least Brian hadn't let him down.

Brian lifted a hand. "Hey." He surveyed the room, one eyebrow arching more elegantly than the lack of people required, and stepped inside. He was dressed in a gray suit, cut to fit Brian Kenway and only Brian Kenway, complimented by a teal shirt that nearly matched Josh's hair. Fluttering from one lapel was the visitor badge required by the school office, after school hours included, and that small imperfection in an otherwise flawless picture made Mal smile.

"Big crowd," Brian said.

He turned in, and Josh slipped quickly through the doorway as though he'd rather be anywhere else, even if anywhere was an airless moon on the other side of the galaxy.

Ethan hopped off the desk he'd been sitting. "Josh!"

Why couldn't Ethan be gay? He was so damn confident and nice and . . . by the blush staining Josh's cheeks, definitely crush-worthy.

Well, damn. Maybe Mal shouldn't have encouraged that friendship.

The scent of oranges and cardamom drifted toward him as Brian moved into Mal's sphere and leaned in slightly. "This would have been an easier sell for both me and Josh if you'd told us no one would be here."

"There's supposed to be nearly thirty-five kids. I think they're in the wrong room."

"Why's that?"

"I changed the meeting to here because I didn't want to walk all the way to Cheryl's old classroom and then back to mine. The door at the end of this hall is the closest exit to the staff lot."

Brian's gaze flicked down, taking in the brace covering Mal's right leg. "How's the knee? Both legs? Getting enough rest?" Genuine concern creased his brow. "Can I get you anything? Is there a soda machine around?"

"In the cafeteria, but I'm fine. Unless you need something?"

"Nope, I'm good."

So.

Brian smiled.

Josh and Ethan hovered in one another's periphery.

The last bell chimed through the empty hallway outside the nearly empty classroom.

"I told Rachel I was the wrong choice for this group," Mal said.

Brian began to put a hand out, then cut the gesture short, shifting so that he pushed his fingers through his own hair. "I'm sure it's just the classroom mix-up. Let's use the time to go over your notes."

"You think I made notes?"

"You're a professor. Of course you made notes."

Mal extracted his notes from beneath a stack of homework.

The classroom door banged open and students started filing in. *Phew.* Mal recalled most of the faces. He'd stopped by the meeting last week, late, sweaty, and exhausted from the trek to Cheryl's classroom, had briefly introduced himself, and then quickly left for the PT appointment he hadn't made. *Coward.* Now, he studied the faces more intently and realized that he knew most of them. Some surprised him, others not at all. The arrival of one student in particular had him smiling. She always kept to herself in class and had a face that rarely looked happy in repose. But when she pushed through the door with two other girls, she was obviously comfortable and friendly with both.

For a couple of minutes, the sound of scraping chairs, shifting desks, and chatter filled the room, and it wasn't unlike the beginning of class, except a really nice smelling man stood next to his desk, crumpling the piece of paper Mal had handed him. Mal snatched it back before Brian could render the agenda completely illegible, and glanced up to meet what could almost be described as a "deer in the headlights" expression.

He couldn't touch the back of Brian's hand. Not here. He smiled instead. Dipped his chin. *You're going to be fine.*

After much dragging and resettling, the desks had been converted from neat rows into a loose circle and everyone was sitting comfortably and chatting. Resisting the urge to call for attention in an official capacity, Mal simply cleared his throat. Most of the kids stopped talking and turned to the front.

"Hi," he said.

A few murmurs and giggles answered him.

"Most of you probably know me. I popped in to the meeting last week. But, anyway, I'm Malcolm Montgomery. In here, you can call me Mal or Mr. M. I don't mind which. I've taught history here at Morristown High for just over twenty years and will hopefully teach it for another twenty years. I'll be that creepy old teacher people tell stories about, because I also went to school here and played football here. I'm like a part of the furniture."

A few students snickered at that.

"What I'm trying to say is that I've been around for a while and I'm not planning on going anywhere soon. I'm not going to tell you all I hope we can be friends, because as a teacher, that's not my job. But I am here to support you and guide you, and while I'm anxious about having this club handed over to me, I believe in the importance of it. I want to reiterate that this classroom is a safe space, even outside Monday afternoons.

"I also want this to be an honest space. You can be yourselves in here, whoever that is, okay?"

A few more nods, a couple of shy smiles, a collection of *yeah, yeah, we've heard it all before* grumblings, and a whole lot of silence from Brian. Mal glanced his way and instantly regretted it. Brian maintained his confident stance, his easy smile, but the back of his neck was damp, and the line of his jaw had tightened, his skin a little pale beneath his tan. He was obviously uncomfortable. Maybe even . . . afraid? What was he scared of? Surely men like Brian feared nothing.

"So, that's my introduction. We're all going to miss Cheryl. She was a good teacher, and as I understand it, a valuable mentor to many of you. But she's moving on to the next phase of her life and we can only wish her the best. Now comes the part you all hate. I know some of you, but not all of you, so let's rectify that. Going around the room, names and something about yourself. Can be anything, silly or serious." Mal held up his hands. "You don't need to tell me why you're here, but if you ever do want to talk, my door is always open."

God, he was already exhausted and only five minutes had passed. How long was an hour anyway?

The kids started rattling off their names and facts, the few names he didn't quite have to hand quickly attaching to the faces he'd recognized, most of the facts making him smile and laugh. Pamela was addicted to Mallomars. Anna Marie wanted to be an astronaut. Geraldo had moved recently from Puerto Rico and was living with his aunt and uncle. Kat boldly proclaimed they preferred nongendered pronouns, and Daria shot them an envious look. Ethan surprised everyone by saying he'd been thinking about attending the group for a while because he was questioning a lot of things about himself. Briefly, Mal wondered if that included his relationship with his girlfriend, who was conspicuously absent. Josh finished the circle by stating his name and adding that his favorite color was blue. He spoke softly, but everyone heard him and everyone laughed. Flushing, he dipped his head.

Mal risked another glance at Brian. The fear from before was still there, but somewhat dimmed by a mixture of fondness and pride that looked good on him. Mal nudged his elbow. "How about you?"

Brian opened his mouth, faltered slightly, then seemed to reset, as though he remembered who he was and what he was capable of. "I'm Brian Kenway. Not a teacher. Just a volunteer."

Not just *anything*, Mal thought.

"We need a fun fact," Kat called out.

Brian's smile tightened. "I build things."

"That's what you do," Josh pointed out. "Tell us something else."

"I wish there'd been a club like this when I was in high school."

Still not a fact, not really, but enough of a statement to quiet everyone. Approving nods rippled around the room and once again Mal had to resist the urge to touch Brian intimately—to wrap his hand around Brian's arm and squeeze. It was the lingering tightness in Brian's expression and more. He'd been leading Brian on for a while—and it wasn't quite fair. Mal couldn't lay the blame entirely at the feet of his ex, though. He'd been waiting for something, for this. A kindred soul. A man who understood what it was like—not only to be gay, and not only gay and fifty or nearly so, but someone who'd taken the same journey to this place. Someone who'd watched the world change, often for the worse but sometimes for the better.

He didn't know what Brian was so afraid of, but had a feeling it was because he understood on a personal level why this club was so damn necessary.

Swallowing, Mal flattened out his agenda and peered down at the loops of his far-from-neat handwriting. "So, from what I understand, aside from making time to talk, you all are working on a couple of fund-raisers. One for Vernon Williams." Who had recently been the victim of a hate crime—right here in Morristown—and was still recovering from his injuries.

Mal knew about the case and had been shocked and dismayed. Knowing Vernon was a part of this group made his situation all the more personal. This was why Mal hadn't wanted to get involved. Because now Vernon was one of his kids, and while he'd cared before, now he felt responsible.

He cleared his throat. "And for a drop-in center."

Brian glanced over. "A drop-in center?"

"There's one in Morris Township," Daria said, "but it's a bus ride or car ride away. It's not here, in our neighborhood. This club is one afternoon a week. Sometimes we met with Cheryl for coffee on other days, or at lunch"—there went his entire schedule—"but some of us need a safe space after school and on weekends."

Eyebrows lowering, Brian dug his phone out of his pocket. "Is there anything even remotely like that in Morristown right now?" he asked, opening an app and tapping at the display.

"Nothing," Daria replied. "There are a couple of places for women and children and three shelters, but nothing specifically for us."

Mal glanced at his notes. "I see you've already raised a considerable sum." The club had a couple of corporate sponsors—local businesses— but that money would be withheld until they were fully funded and had a site. "Okay, Brian and I will get up to speed on that side of things later. When's the next fund-raiser?"

"Winterfest."

"That's just a few weeks away. What are our plans?"

The meeting continued in that vein for another couple of minutes, Mal and Brian both making notes, then they opened up the session to more personal issues. Mal discovered that this was when some of the students liked to break off into smaller groups where they would offer support to each other. It was heartening to see. A couple of students approached him for a brief chat and one group called him over for a consult. Brian was also called upon and seemed to get along well with the group he chatted with.

Finally, after an approximate hundred hours, it was time to go and the shuffling began in reverse—desks being pushed back into line, backpacks swinging up off the floor, the rustle of coats and hats and scarves. The chatter of folks celebrating the end of their day. Then they were gone, except for Josh, who lingered by the door with Ethan a moment, before Ethan ducked out.

Josh pulled out his phone and plugged in, as kids seemed to do when left alone for more than three seconds, and Brian glanced up from straightening the last desk. His smile was a strained and weary thing.

"I'm so sorry," Mal said. "I had no idea."

"Neither did I."

"Thank you for coming. I'd understand if you didn't come back. That was heavy."

"It was. But also . . ." Brian pushed his fingers through his hair and gripped the nape of his neck. "I dunno. I don't want to say 'affirming,' though that word keeps popping up in the front of my verbal center. It was enlightening. And sad, but also positive. That these kids have each other. I had no idea there were groups like this."

"But the foundation you're involved with is all about kids. That's how I got you signed off as a volunteer for this thing."

"I'm the money man, Mal. I write the checks. And those letters..."
His eyebrows crooked together. "I always meant to get more involved.
The Smart Foundation is important to me. Tristan, the man we named
it for, was the uncle of one of my best friends. I knew him. I..." Brian
drew in a quick breath. "We're probably on your list of donors for the
drop-in center, or we would be if someone had approached us." He
gazed back out at the empty classroom, attention lingering on Josh a
moment. "But this is more real."

"Is it too much real?"

"What do you mean?"

"Are you going to come back?" Mal raised his hands. "Before you
answer, just let me say"—*you look amazing in that suit*—"I understand
this is the middle of a workday for you, and I appreciate you making
time and doing whatever it was the office needed you to do to get your
visitor badge." The list got longer every year.

"They're not strip-searching yet, but that might be coming." Brian
offered a thin smile.

"Really. I can't thank you enough for being here this afternoon.
Was Josh..."

"Pretty much dragged here, but I'm beginning to realize that kids
will only let you drag them to places they actually want to go."

"That's... Yeah."

Brian gave him a serious look. "You were amazing, Mal. I can see
why you've been at this school for twenty years and will be here for
twenty more. You've got that perfect combination of 'trust me, but
don't play me' down. It's impressive."

"Teaching 101."

"You didn't need me here."

"I didn't say I did. But the kids do."

Brian took in the empty classroom. "Yeah. I can see that."

"So will you come again?"

Lips quirking up on one side, Brian murmured, "I haven't come
once yet. Not with you actually in the bed with me, anyway."

"Did you just admit to fantasizing about me while you jerk off?"

"I did."

Mal patted his cheeks, which were quite hot. "You can't say that
here."

"Why, is there an inappropriate language button on your desk?"

"Ha ha. Very funny. And, yes, there is. Me."

"Going to report me?"

"How do you do that? Go from zero to one hundred in less than sixty seconds."

"A lot of practice. So, do I get my date?"

Yes. "Are you going to come again?"

"Are you changing the rules on me, Professor?"

"No." *I'm stalling because I've already changed them in your favor.*

Brian's smile cooled by a degree or two. It was still flirty, but also more serious, and only a combo he could have managed. "How about this? Whether or not you keep our bargain, I'll be here again. I can't say this was the most fun afternoon I've spent, ever. It was, frankly, terrifying. But you're right." The fear made a brief and dark reappearance. "These kids need us. So, yes. I'll be back."

"I'd have given you your date even if you weren't going to come back."

Brian's lips twitched. "I know."

A sigh gusted out of Mal, along with words he probably shouldn't say. "What are we doing?"

"Getting to know each other, the way you planned. How's Friday night? Am I picking you up or are you cooking for me?"

"I'll cook."

"Am I allowed to kiss you?"

"Quickly."

"No pressing any buttons now," Brian breathed as he leaned in. Then his lips were against Mal's, touching, tasting, moving oh-so-delicately. Teasing.

"Seriously?" Josh's mild bellow held little censure, and when Mal glanced over, Josh's scowl had a wistful angle to it.

CHAPTER 16

After extracting fourteen separate promises from Josh—one for each year he'd been alive—that he'd stay home, not steal anything, and not run away, Brian spent the short drive to Mal's place paying close attention to his GPS. He knew where Walker Street was in a vague, "it's over by the park" kind of way. He could find it without directions, but focusing on the turn by turn allowed little time for other thoughts.

He'd been doing the *other thoughts* thing all day—reaching inbox zero at eleven in the morning before hassling every contractor currently under his watch for project updates. If it wouldn't have made him late for his date, he'd have driven out to the Poconos to check on the roof of Franklin Tern's lodge. An hour in Frank's company—particularly when the subject of Simon came up—always made him feel like an asshole. And that would have given him something else to focus on.

Mal's split-level ranch was attractive in the same understated manner as the man: neat, tidy, a little shopworn, but obviously well tended. No one's garden looked good in winter and Mal's was no exception. The low bushes lining the front walk were trimmed and bagged, though, so he knew what he was doing. Fresh snow covered what was probably a terraced lawn, and dripped from dark holly bushes clustered on both sides of the front door. Circles of light over the garage door and to the left of the front stoop illuminated dark siding. The windows were not picked out in a contrasting color, which only made Brian like Mal more. A house could say a lot about a person, as could the colors they chose to paint it. There was nothing charming or cute about Mal's place. But neither was it completely staid.

The path and drive were swept of snow, prompting thoughts of Mal struggling with a shovel. Did he have a blower? Maybe he used a service.

Why the hell was Brian sitting in his car wondering who shoveled Mal's walk?

Brian grabbed the bag of stuff he'd spent thirty minutes dithering over and got out of his car. The wind chose that moment to whistle down the street. Drawing his shoulders up to protect his ears, Brian made short work of the front walk and prodded the buzzer. Mal opened the door a second later.

"Were you sitting on the stairs or something?" Brian asked.

"Pretty much. If I got all comfortable on the couch, your ass would be frozen by the time I got to the door."

"Fair enough."

Brian hustled inside and started removing his shoes.

"You don't have to do that," Mal protested.

Brian gave him a quick grin. "Just making myself comfortable."

Like the outside, the inside of the house said a lot about Mal. Or rather confirmed several details. The main level—a handful of steps up—spread out in an open and inviting manner. Brian could see into the kitchen, but not the sink, thankfully. No one wanted to see a stack of dirty dishes from the front door. Instead, arresting his attention from the kitchen was the seemingly endless expanse of wide plank flooring that made the space feel larger than it was. Mal had a good-sized living area, a dining area separated by a couple of columns, and beyond that, another small seating arrangement that obviously took advantage of the tall windows lining the back of the house, and the morning sun that probably streamed through them. The color scheme was light and bright; the rugs outlining each space muted but not boring. The furniture didn't all match, but nor did it clash. It had the look of being collected over the years and, like the house, was well cared for.

"I love your house," Brian said.

Mal smiled. "Thanks. I do too."

"How long have you lived here?"

"Nearly as long as I've been teaching. My parents helped me with the down payment and I got a good rate."

He'd have had to. Real estate in Morristown wasn't cheap. Twenty years ago, though . . .

"Is the basement finished?" A handful of stairs led down from the front door as well.

"It's a half basement, rest is garage, and yeah. I only use it for storage and workout space, though."

Nodding, Brian held out his bag. "Where can I put this?"

"You didn't need to bring anything."

"Of course I brought something." Brian stepped forward, and whether unsteady on his legs or simply slow off the mark, Mal didn't step back. "Hi." Brian smiled, knowing the breath carrying that single word would have touched Mal's lips.

Mal returned his smile. "Hi." He leaned in.

Brian met him in the middle, and what he'd intended as a tease, a quick peck, a kiss that said *hello, I'm here,* turned into, *wow, I am so happy to see you.* Any anxiety Brian had felt about coming here tonight, about their date, fell in a heap around his feet. He set his bag on the floor, ignoring the rustle and clink, and framed Mal's face with his hands. Kissed him soundly. Took his mouth and possessed it—committing the curve of each lip to memory, the taste of him, the warmth, and the fact that Mal was not a passive kisser.

With a rumble in his throat, Mal leaned in a little more, shifting his face so that the not-quite-smooth skin of his cheek rubbed over Brian's palm. He hooked fingers into Brian's belt and pulled him closer and deepened the kiss, his tongue being the one to make the first official move, inviting Brian inside, toying and playing.

"Mmph." Brian fell into sensation, as his body heated and chilled, and the thrill of kissing someone he wanted raced from lips to dick, before curling around his balls. "Want you so bad."

"Been thinking about this all day," Mal returned, pausing to nip at Brian's lips.

"Why did you make me wait so long?"

"Had to make sure you wanted it."

Brian put his hand to the growing bulge at Mal's crotch and squeezed. "Oh, I want it."

Mal shuddered and moaned, his hips rocking forward, his shoulders back, as though his body was dealing with mixed signals.

Chuckling, Brian slid a hand around Mal's back and reeled him in again, snatching his mouth into another kiss. With his fingers, he molded the outline of Mal's cock, straining behind denim, and grinned into the kiss as Mal bucked and swore and breathed. Knowing Mal wanted this as much as he did was such a turn-on.

"Hold up." Mal gripped Brian's arms, holding him in place.

Brian's heart tried to push through the front of his chest. Surely Mal didn't mean to—

"If we keep on like this, I'm going to do something awkward with my leg and ruin the moment."

"Oh crap, your leg."

"I know. Mood killer extraordinaire."

Brian pressed a quick kiss to Mal's lips. "Never." Figuring out how to get off—if that was where this was leading—around the leg brace was going to be interesting, though. "Couch?"

"Couch."

Mal led the way to the generous living area, walking without crutches, his gait stiff-legged and almost painful to watch. Brian guessed that offering a hand, an arm, or a shoulder would kill the mood, though. In Mal's position, he'd be insulted by the gesture.

"Where's your crutch?" he asked instead.

"I'm supposed to be trying to walk without it. Short distances. It'll be easier when the doc unlocks the brace all the way so I can actually bend my knee."

"No kidding."

"Right now, the idea of bending it makes me break out in a cold sweat."

"Then don't think about it."

"I'm killing our vibe, aren't I?" Mal was standing in front of his couch, hands on hips, surveying the terrain as though planning an entrenchment.

Brian grinned. "Not at all. Get yourself set up so we can get back to showing each other what want feels like."

Mal chuckled. "So, ah, in the name of expediency, what are we talking here? If we're going to do something with pants off, I kinda need to get them off now."

Unable to help himself, Brian started laughing. "Wow."

The color stinging Mal's cheeks took off ten years. His glasses flashed as he dipped his chin. "I know. Maybe we should just eat?"

Brian made a show of sniffing the air. "I don't smell any food."

"That's because I haven't cooked it yet."

"What are we having?"

"Tuna steaks and this bok choy mushroom thing my brother makes that will blow your mind. That is if you like mushrooms. Do you like mushrooms?"

"I love mushrooms. I also love that you planned sex food."

"How so?"

"No lasagna."

Mal joined him in the laughter. "Yeah, I think we're both old enough to figure out what not to eat on a date, heh?"

Sobering, slightly, Brian put himself between Mal and the couch, and cupped Mal's cheek again. "I'm still turned on. Even more so knowing you figured we'd be getting busy tonight."

Mal made a soft sound. "Want you so bad."

The echo of his own need lit a fire in Brian's veins. Leaning in, he captured Mal's mouth again and kissed him with a heated languor that was theirs alone. A balance between the desire thrumming through his veins and the need to take care of Mal, to let him set the pace.

Shifting his lips to Mal's jaw, Brian kissed his way out to one ear before trailing his tongue down the side of Mal's neck. There, he nipped the cord of muscle and exhaled into the warm hollow of the throat. Mal was mouthing his hairline, kisses that missed their mark, but still meant something. The grip of Mal's fingers at his shoulders held them together.

Brian flattened his palm to Mal's chest and took a moment to appreciate the heat radiating through Mal's simple long-sleeve T-shirt. Skin was less than a millimeter of cotton away. Pressing his mouth to Mal's shoulder, he breathed. Mal kissed his neck. After sliding his hand downward over taut abs, Brian tugged on Mal's belt, and slipped his fingers behind the waistband of the jeans. Another pull and he got busy with the belt. Then the button, then the fly.

Mal quickly proved he wasn't the kind of guy to stand there and be pleasured—though Brian wouldn't care if he was. Brian knew that sometimes it was hard to reciprocate, and sometimes you just wanted to feel. To be worshipped. On a good night, everyone got their turn.

Mal was pushing Brian's coat from his shoulders, and Brian paused to let it fall to his elbows, then flicked the coat toward the chair alongside the couch. His sweater joined the coat, and then Mal started in on his shirt buttons.

"This color suits you," Mal said as he dragged the russet shirt away from Brian's shoulders.

"Hmm," was all Brian managed in return as he helped remove Mal's shirt, adding that to the pile they were creating. He cupped the hard ridge at Mal's crotch again. His own dick pulsed in response, and the urge to press his groin to Mal's became overwhelming. Grabbing Mal's ass, Brian crushed their hips together and groaned as the pressure he'd sought ground against his erection.

Mal huffed at his ear. "I need to sit."

Brian sidled out from between man and couch and let Mal turn around and ease himself down. Once settled, Mal started ripping Velcro and unbuckling black plastic.

"Are you going to be okay without the brace?" Brian asked. "I could suck you off."

"You can do that anyway, and I'll be . . ." Mal winced. "Damn it. I hate this."

Brian knelt in front of him. "Don't. This is temporary. Yeah, it's going to make this interesting, but . . ." Okay, reminding him that he had two functioning legs, even if they weren't the steadiest right now probably wasn't going to improve the mood.

Mal read the thought in his eyes. "My brother tells me the same thing all the time. I'm just frustrated. And horny."

Putting on his most charming grin, Brian leaned in. "Me too. Here's what we're going to do: I'm going to blow you. Then we can relax and figure out whatever we want to do later."

Mal crooked his eyebrows together, his expression gathering toward something negative, and then he relaxed and nodded. Pressed his palm to the side of Brian's face. "Having you here, kneeling in front of me, is blowing my mind."

God, he was sweet.

Smiling, Brian turned to kiss Mal's palm. "Give me a few minutes, then I'll really blow your mind."

Groaning, Mal settled back on the couch, legs spread. Brian pushed Mal's jeans down and pulled out the hard length of his cock. Mal fisted his shaft, pointing it toward Brian's mouth, and Brian swallowed. He could already smell Mal's skin and that whiff of sweat that always clung to testicles. The scent of arousal hung thickly between them, and Mal's lap was warm and inviting, the erection bobbing before Brian's lips the cherry on top of a sundae.

"I rubbed one out thinking about exactly this last week," he said, making sure his words ghosted over the dark-pink head of Mal's dick.

"Fu-uck. I want to feel your mouth on me before I come."

"Tell me you jerked off thinking about me." Leaning in, Brian flicked his tongue out to catch the bead of pre-come collecting in Mal's slit.

"I did. I did!"

Brian opened his mouth and swallowed Mal down.

Mal hissed as his hips bucked. "Oh, Jesus."

Brian lifted his gaze, knowing what the sight of a man on his knees, lips stretched around the girth of your cock, could do. How it made you feel. Mal didn't disappoint. His mouth opened in a soft O and his head fell back, exposing the column of his throat.

Mal was well-built. Lean and rangy like a runner, with the shoulders of a wide receiver. His pecks were dusted with hair a shade lighter than his head. The gray creeping in only made him sexier. His nipples were small and hard, and he had freckles, damn him. Clustered and spread, pale against his winter skin. Brian wanted to do so much more than suck Mal's cock. He wanted to lick those nipples and count the freckles. Find out if Mal was ticklish. Taste him. Make him whine.

The pulse of Mal's cock against his tongue indicated he was close, and Brian stopped plotting what they'd get up to next. *One orgasm at a time.*

Tightening the ring of his lips, Brian eased his way back up Mal's shaft, pressing his tongue to the prominent vein on the underside, and then sucked his way back down, opening his throat to take it all, again. Mal couldn't fuck his face, not like this. Brian could make sure he felt as though he had, though. He dug one hand under Mal's hip and wrapped the other around the base of Mal's cock, and put everything he had into making sure Mal would remember him and his mouth.

It didn't take long. Mal was so beautifully responsive, even with the limitations of his braced leg. He panted and gasped. Every deeply guttural moan seemed to echo through his skin, because Brian felt all of them. Mal gripped Brian's hair and stroked his ears. Whispered words of encouragement and called him "baby" more than once.

Then he managed a hip spasm and came, flooding Brian's mouth with the bittersweet taste of pleasure—sweeter in this instance, because Brian had wanted it so much. Dropping a hand to his own cock, Brian swallowed, stroked, and then followed Mal half a minute later, spilling into his palm.

He hadn't counted the strokes, but it barely mattered. He hadn't come this fast in twenty years. With this little effort. Panting softly, he put his cheek to Mal's left thigh and looked up. Mal had his eyes closed, but he still found Brian's face, fingers drifting over Brian's cheek in a light caress.

"That was amazin'," Mal slurred.

"Mm-hmm." Brian smiled, the curve of his lips widening as he felt the pull and tingle of a mouth that had worked pretty hard. "So, if you have a PhD, why don't you go by Dr. Montgomery instead of Mr. Montgomery?"

Mal's laughter jerked through his body. "So not what I figured you were going to ask."

"We can talk about what you taste like if you want."

"Jesus Christ."

Brian grinned. "So . . ."

"I did for a while. When the letters were all fresh and shiny. Then I got sick of explaining that no, I'm not a brain surgeon, and no, I don't earn a brain surgeon's salary, and I decided I preferred being a mister."

"Makes sense."

Mal was quiet.

Brian kissed his knee. "What are you thinking about?"

"Nothing."

"Mal."

"You're still staying for dinner, right?"

Brian sat up and lifted a hand to Mal's shoulder. Touched his neck and turned his face downward. "Look at me."

Mal complied, his expression abashed.

"Yeah, you should feel like that," Brian said.

"Like what?"

"Like you're embarrassed by what you asked me."

"I'm sorry. I'm just . . ."

"Endearingly awkward. Kinda shy. Sweet. And the man I plan on spending the night with. Got it?"

"Because I owe you a blowjob?"

"Maybe I want to call you doctor and act out a long-held fantasy."

Mal looked vaguely horrified for a second, and then he laughed.

CHAPTER 17

M al stopped mid-hum when Brian leaned in behind him. The fragrance of the soap Brian had used to wash up didn't quite mix with the lingering scent of orange and sex, but the combination had Mal smiling. Brian was here, in his house. In his kitchen.

Brian kissed his cheek from behind, lips brushing Mal's ear more than his face. "Only me," he murmured. "Though if I lived with a tiger, I'd be jumpy too."

"A tiger . . . Oh. You've met Lois."

"You call that thing Lois?" Brian's weight left Mal's back as he stepped away.

Mal shifted his own weight and turned from the cutting board where he'd been getting a start on dinner. "Did you call my cat 'a thing'?"

"It . . . She? Your cat is huge. Like the size of a dog."

"A small dog."

"I was scared to leave the bathroom."

Mal laughed. "You were scared of my cat?"

"I did say huge, right?"

Shaking his head, Mal returned to his fish preparation. "The only time you need fear for your safety is when she decides to start kneading your lap. And maybe when she thinks your chest is a good sleeping place. Or your back. She *is* heavy. Has nearly smothered me a time or two."

"And yet you continue to share your house with her."

"She lets me stay. It's a cat thing. Someone needs to organize her meals."

Brian's laughter was soft. "So, what can I do to— Ah!"

Mal glanced down, already knowing what he'd see: Lois testing the steadfastness of Brian's leg as she leaned against it, purring. His leg would be next, and then she'd have her paws (and claws) stretched upward, nearly reaching the counter because she *was* a large cat, as she demanded her piece of tuna.

"Hold still and she won't knock you down," he advised.

"Tell me the cat is the one who broke your legs."

"Ha! No. Shh, Lois. Give me a sec." Lois's purr had deepened into a rumbling yowl. "Want to feed her?"

"No. I do not. Where was this beast when I arrived?"

"Probably hiding. She can be shy."

"I refuse to believe it."

Grinning, Mal put Lois's portion of tuna on a plate and handed it to Brian. "Can you put this on the floor for her? Beside the fridge there. It's either that or invite her up onto the counter, and I think you've been traumatized enough for one night."

Brian took the plate and crouched to put it on the floor by the side of the refrigerator. He snatched his hand away and danced back a step as Lois practically threw herself at the tuna.

"I nearly got eaten!"

"You're more dramatic than I'd have guessed," Mal said.

Looking somewhat sheepish, Brian dusted ginger hair from one leg. "As need requires. So, before I was so rudely interrupted, I was going to ask what I can do to help?"

Mal indicated the bag he'd rescued from the floor near the front door. "Unpack your bag?"

"Oh, right. Forgot about that." A light flush still highlighted Brian's cheeks—the glow of a good orgasm. Beneath that, he seemed slightly surprised, as though he wasn't used to being forgetful. "I brought red and white wine because I didn't know which you liked. Or what we were eating. I'd drink anything with whatever, but Si—I have friends who put a lot of stock in that sort of thing."

"Snobs."

"Exactly."

Brian set the bottles on the counter beside the bag and reached in for a cardboard box. "I do know that chocolate goes with everything."

Mal's grin felt a little strange until he realized it'd been a while since he'd smiled so often and so wide. "You went to all the trouble of buying me wine and chocolate and then got lucky the minute you stepped through the door."

Brian kissed his lips softly before whispering, "I know. I should put my bag of tricks back in the trunk of my car."

"Don't you dare."

Brian moved his lips to the top of Mal's ear and nipped it. "Okay, what's next?"

Take these kisses to the bedroom?

Mal would not have guessed Brian could be so sweet, but it fit. And he liked it. He directed Brian toward plates and silverware and let him set the table. Either that, or he was going to cut or burn himself. Brian's lips anywhere near his . . . anything was way too distracting. Brian also carried out the dinner when it was done, leaving Mal to make the walk unencumbered—which was nice. In fact, the past half hour had been nice, and different to what he'd imagined. He'd prepared for awkwardness, because Malcolm Montgomery was awkwardness personified. But somehow they'd got through that part.

Brian ate with apparently genuine hunger and savor. It was always fun to watch someone who enjoyed food, especially when the meal had been prepared with them in mind. He didn't seem to mind the simplicity of their dinner and defiantly washed down his tuna steak with a glass of red wine. Under the table, his foot rested casually next to Mal's. As they talked, he'd apply subtle pressure now and again, as though to emphasize a point.

Their conversation was quiet and limited to food and drink. Favorites, things they each encouraged the other to try. Brian poured them both another glass of wine and touched Mal's hand gently after setting the bottle back down on the table.

Why had the idea of this date been so daunting? Brian was as congenial as a bobbing starling. Bright, happy, and interested.

"Thanks again for coming to the meeting on Monday," Mal said.

"I didn't just come along to snag this date. I want you to know that. I'd have wrangled a date out of you another way if I'd had to miss the meeting. But—" Brian licked his lips "—I felt like Josh needed me to be there, and it's the weirdest thing because I am not that guy. I'm selfish as fuck."

"An asshole. Yes, you've explained that a couple of times." Mal had to wonder who'd planted that idea so firmly in Brian's head.

Brian gave him a weary grin. "And I have no idea how to look after a kid. But when I think about myself at that age? At fourteen, without the blue hair and all the"—he waved a hand around his ear—"stuff, I know I'd never go to a meeting like that. I mean, hell, when I was fourteen . . ." A wrinkle appeared between Brian's eyebrows and something of the haunted look he'd worn during the GSA meeting passed through his eyes. He shook both off with a version of his rascal smile. "That'd have invited a beating, right?"

Mal offered a cautious nod. "Yep."

"I don't get people."

"What do you mean?"

Brian drew in a tight breath. "Josh is staying with me because his mom kicked him out."

Mal could feel his jaw unhinging. "For being gay?"

"Not for having blue hair. At least, I don't think that was part of it." His expression hardened. "He told me. The morning after he arrived. She called him perverted, a crime against God and nature, and told him to leave and never come back. Gave him fifty bucks and pushed him out the front door."

"What . . . How . . . Why?"

"Because he decided to trust her and tell her he was gay."

"Oh God."

"I knew it still happened. But . . ." Brian rubbed a hand over his face, pausing to massage his forehead, and Mal couldn't help thinking the gesture had been made in part to cover the dark look in his eyes. "Sorry. Not the best dinner or date conversation."

"So, the rest of your family . . .?"

Brian shook his head.

What did that mean? That they were gay-friendly, or . . . *Not, Mal. Decidedly not. Otherwise Josh would be staying with them, wouldn't he?*

Should he change the subject or ask Brian about his own experience? With a flash of insight, Mal figured he probably didn't have to ask. The pain in Brian's posture told part of the story. Would Brian ever tell him the rest?

Brian interrupted the broody silence by asking, "Yours?"

"Huh?"

"Your family?"

"Oh, they're great. I told them when I was in college. That's when I figured it out for myself, mostly. At the time, I thought . . . Heck, I don't know what I was thinking." Mal gestured toward his braced leg. "I was feeling like this, I guess. Down about life. I went to college on a football scholarship and got injured toward the end of my first season. Tore my rotator cuff and broke my other wrist. Accident on the field. A bad play, an even worse takedown. The other guy . . . God, I think I ruined his career as well. Anyway, Donny deferred the rest of his first year of college to come babysit me. I was pretty morose and couldn't use my hands."

He shot Brian a wry smile and Brian returned a smaller grin.

"He stayed with me for three months and all he could talk about was his girlfriend."

"Rachel?"

"No, his first wife." Mal waved a hand. "Another long story. Anyway, he kept pressing me about who I liked and what I'd gotten up to while I was away, and when I told him I liked guys, it was like I was telling myself at the same time. Admitting it. I remember feeling like the weight of the universe shifted in that moment. I was floating but also afraid of falling. I was so damn scared, but also exhilarated. Does that make any sense?"

Brian nodded, but his eyes continued to tell a different story.

"Anyway, Donny hugged me and thanked me for telling him."

"He knew," Brian guessed.

Mal nodded. "He knew."

"And your parents were cool."

"Yeah. They were confused at first, like the idea had never occurred to them, but then they literally shrugged and said, 'Okay.' Then my mom started trying to fix me up with guys." He smiled. "They don't always get it right. They're not members of PFLAG or even politically active. None of us are. But they've never denied me. Not to my face and not to their friends. I think that . . ." Mal swallowed over an unexpected bubble of emotion. "That's always meant more, you know?"

"Because they didn't make a big deal out of it."

"Yeah. Exactly that."

Brian's smile took on a grim aspect, and Mal knew he was correct in his guess that Brian's experience had been something like that of his nephew. Rather than allow the conversation to go there tonight— they had time, didn't they?—he pushed back from the table, wincing slightly as the action sent a pain through his right knee. "Time for chocolate?"

"Would you be more comfortable on the couch?"

"You don't have to—"

Brian held his hands up. "That's my way of asking if we can get cozy again. I'm having a nice time, Mal. Heavy conversation aside."

"It's like a rite of passage, isn't it? How you come out."

"I wonder what straight people talk about on first dates."

"According to Donny, nothing so exciting, unless they've just broken up with someone. Then it's that. On loop. All night."

"Sounds awesome."

"Right?" Mal glanced up.

Brian had moved in close, supposedly to help him stand and hobble to the couch. Instead he leaned in with the same smile he'd worn at the front door and kissed Mal lightly on the lips. "I don't think straight people invite each other over for first dates, either."

"More fool them," Mal murmured.

"Can we take the chocolate to the bedroom? Or are you a 'no cookie crumbs on the sheets' kind of person?"

"I'm a 'sheets can be washed' kind of person."

"I knew I liked you." Brian kissed his top lip, teased his bottom lip, and licked into Mal's mouth. He tasted of wine and sesame seeds. He tasted good. And somehow, he managed to kiss Mal all the way to the bedroom, practically carrying him up the short flight of stairs, pausing at the top to ask, "Which door?"

Mal pointed out his bedroom, the largest of three, and they shuffled over there, slow enough for him to keep upright on his braced leg—slow enough to have their shirts and pants undone again by the time they got in there.

"Forgot the chocolates," Mal muttered before nibbling the side of Brian's neck.

"I'll get them later. Want you first."

Brian's kisses became urgent, touching down and lifting off like dancing birds, and it felt good to be this desired. To have Brian sucking at the skin over his collarbone, and pushing at his jeans. Cupping the bulge under Mal's fly and whispering all the things he wanted to do, the most enticing of which was, "I want to ride you."

Oh God.

Mal hadn't hooked up with so many guys that he had a line for discussing preference. A trusted conversational opener. He usually left it to the other party. Being flexible was good for that. The idea of fucking Brian, though . . .

Oh God.

Brian was chuckling against his lips. He squeezed Mal's cock. "I can tell you like that idea. You got even harder."

"I really, really like that idea." Also, logistically, it worked. He could . . . "Be careful putting weight on my right leg."

"Gonna take such good care of you, baby."

Clothes seemed to flee their bodies, the rush paused only for the puzzle of Mal's leg brace, which Mal removed as carefully as he could with his hard cock objecting to every movement not designed to bring him off. Brian hovered close and took the brace away after Mal lifted his leg, and stashed it close to the bed. Then Mal pushed his jeans down and Brian took those too, dropping them with a lot less ceremony than the brace.

Brian didn't wince at the scar tracing the swollen knot of Mal's knee, or at the fading staple marks. No comment on the bruising, or the slightly twisted appearance. He did glance at Mal's other leg, his gaze darkening as he took in more surgery scars. His hand hovered over one. Then he looked up and smiled. "Up you get," he said, indicating the pile of pillows he'd made.

"You're . . ." Mal bit his tongue, sure what he wanted to say would be interpreted incorrectly.

"Not always a selfish prick? I'm getting fucked here. I've got pretty good motivation to help you get comfortable first."

Still standing, Mal put a hand to Brian's shoulder. "You need to stop doing that."

"What?"

"Putting yourself down. I don't know who gave you the idea you weren't a nice guy, but you should let it go." Mal moved his hand over Brian's bare shoulder, enjoying the feel of his skin. Stretching his fingers out, he cupped the back of Brian's neck and drew him closer. Kissed his mouth. "It's okay to want things."

Brian's eyes widened. His breath hitched. Then the grin arrived, the one Mal now recognized as a defensive maneuver. "And you need to stop thinking so hard. All the time. Let stuff happen."

Closing in for another kiss, Mal murmured, "I think I can do that."

Brian's laugh rumbled through his skin, stirring Mal's fingers and touching his lips. They kissed, braced against the side of the bed. With one hand, he learned the shape of Brian, from his shoulders to his arms, the space between his pecs and hips, tracing goose bumps across his ribs, discovering soft chest hair—all pale gold—and the trail leading south to a neatly trimmed nest and jutting cock. Brian gasped into his mouth. He had his hands at the back of Mal's hips. One smoothed upward, the other down to cup his ass. Mal nudged their hips together and moaned as their cocks collided with flesh, pressing into each other's hip bones, his tracing the crinklier hair at the top of Brian's thigh.

His knee twinged and instead of feeling inadequate, Mal said, "Need to get off my feet."

"Best idea yet," Brian returned.

Mal eased himself back onto the bed, careful of his leg until he was settled up against the pillows. Brian knelt across his hips and leaned in for another kiss before grasping Mal's upright and very needy cock.

"You're nearly slick enough without lube," Brian said, dragging his thumb across Mal's slit and spreading the moisture over the head. Mal's cock jerked in Brian's hand. "But I'm still going to ask where you keep your supplies."

"Drawer. Right there."

Brian found the lube and condoms and got back into position. When Mal reached for the stuff, Brian smacked his hand away. "Let me."

"Is this a control thing?"

Brian's eyelids fluttered. "No, just me wanting to take care of you." He peeked upward. "We can make it about control, if you like."

"You mean like this?" Mal grasped Brian's wrist, arresting his movement, and said, "I want to watch you prep yourself."

A low groan left Brian's throat. "Yes."

Mal took the condom and put it aside for the moment, then picked up the bottle of lube. "Hold out your fingers."

He applied a generous amount to Brian's hand and put the bottle aside so he could watch. Brian was on his knees already, straddling Mal's thighs. Lifting up a little higher, he reached behind his hip, eyelids lowering right at the moment he touched himself.

Mal could come from this—from watching Brian finger his own ass. Watching Brian's cock harden and knowing how much Brian got off on his own touch, and showing that to Mal. It was hard to move his own hand, grab the condom and get ready. Brian was mesmerizing.

"We ready to do this?" Brian asked, wiping his fingers on a small towel he'd also pulled out of the drawer.

"God, yes. I nearly came watching you."

"Good."

"Line me up," Mal ordered, knowing it was exactly the right thing to say.

Brian did as bid, shuffling forward, grasping Mal's sheathed cock, rising over it, and pressing the tip to the hot center of his being. He kept his gaze locked to Mal's as he lowered down—not too fast, but with an ease Mal envied. Brian's expression didn't change as he came to rest with Mal's cock tucked deep inside him, but he looked different. Not . . . full, though that was the obvious descriptor. More . . . replete.

"You like this," Mal whispered, lifting his chin for a kiss.

Brian leaned in to touch his lips to Mal's. "I love this."

He shifted his hips, rolling forward and back. Mal groaned. "So, so good."

Brian squeezed next, and Mal put his hands to Brian's hips. "Stop. Do that again and I'll come."

"Oh, I don't think so. I think you want to watch me ride you for a while first."

"Fuck, yes. I want that. Ride me, baby. Nice and slow." Mal didn't know where he'd found the wherewithal to issue instructions, to ask for what he wanted so plainly, but Brian's reaction—the quickening of his breath, the hooding of his eyes—had made it worth the effort to try. To be more bold.

Brian raised himself up—slowly. Then lowered himself down. Rocked his hips forward and back, gently, and did it again. His eyes fluttered closed on the second go 'round. His head tipped back and his mouth dropped open.

"Look at me," Mal said.

Brian opened his eyes. He grasped the headboard, bracing his hands, and moved up and down, lifting until Mal thought his dick would pop out, then lowering, welcoming him back into that wonderful place of intense pressure and heat.

"You feel so good," he said into a moan.

"So do you." Brian was clearly trying hard not to close his eyes, not to bliss out. He was beautiful in his struggle and so much more real than he had been previously—out at the bar, tonight between Mal's knees, then beside him at the dinner table. He was here and now and having absolutely no trouble taking what he wanted.

"Faster," Mal urged. "Eyes open. I love watching your eyes."

"God, you're making me so hard."

"Want me to touch you?"

"Yes . . ." Brian was working harder now, rising and falling in an easy rhythm and obviously moving toward his peak.

"Ask me," Mal said, still not sure where the small demands were coming from. Brian's reaction to each, though . . . He could get used to this.

"Please touch me."

Mal ghosted his hand over Brian's straining cock, touching but not. "Again."

"Oh . . . Hmm." Brian's eyes fluttered closed. His lips compressed. "Please, Mal. Touch me, jerk me."

Mal was having a hard time concentrating. His balls had tucked the minute Brian had lowered himself onto his cock. The steady rhythm was working for him too. He was so close. So damn close. "Slower," he panted as he grasped Brian's cock and squeezed.

"Oh, God."

The strain of the decreased speed showed in every line of Brian's face—nearly every line. His mouth was curved.

Mal's cock pulsed. His earlier orgasm seemed to count for nothing. His balls felt as though he hadn't come in a month. Desperately he searched for something that would hold his climax at bay. His lips started moving, forming a familiar cadence: *1413, 1417...*

"Are you counting?" Brian asked.

"Dates, God, I'm listing dates. Don't want to come yet." Mal switched his thoughts from history to the present and stroked Brian's cock. "How close are you?"

"So close."

"Don't come."

Brian actually whined, though the sound was low and sexy.

"Slow down again." Somewhere in between 1452 and 1456, Brian had sped up.

"You're killing me," Brian gasped.

"You're loving it."

"I am."

He rocked his hips again, circled them, squeezed. Mal reciprocated, stroking Brian's cock in a similar pattern, taking advantage of the pause. The end would come quickly now. If only he could get onto his knees and drive into Brian from behind. Drill him into the mattress.

Brian leaned forward. "You're not supposed to be thinking."

"Sorry, I just wish—"

Brian clenched around him.

"Ungh..."

"You were saying?"

"Faster. Fuck yourself on me. Ride me to the end."

Brian's grin spread wide. "At your command."

Time ceased to have meaning about a second after that. Brian rose and fell at an ever-increasing pace—the movement jarring Mal's knee now and again. He was so beyond caring. Sex like this was worth another week in the evil black brace. Worth being laid out and all but helpless, worth...

Brian's cock jerked in his hand right as Brian shouted and came, hot semen hitting Mal in the chest before coating his fingers. He kept stroking, Brian's cock almost becoming his as he eased his partner through his climax, and then he was coming too, pumping into Brian, his hips bucking up off the mattress, the back of his head whacking the headboard.

"Oh fuck, oh fuck, oh fuck . . ."

Was that him? His lips formed another *F* and yep, it was him, yelling. Shy Malcolm shouting as he came and came and came.

Later, he'd be embarrassed. Or maybe he'd simply acknowledge that he'd been as loud as Brian, that Brian's cries had demanded he reciprocate, and that sex was already messy and noisy and why shouldn't it be and . . . Oh God, why wasn't sex always like this? He couldn't even remember the date Vasco da Gama discovered . . . What *had* he discovered? And who was he, anyway?

"Are you counting again?"

"Fourteen ninety-eight."

"What?"

"I have no idea."

After lifting off him—pulling another gasp and moan from both of them—Brian knelt by his side and brushed a quick kiss over his lips. "You're adorable when you're well fucked."

"Good to know."

"Stay there. I'll get us cleaned up."

"I could get to really liking you," Mal murmured, knowing he was already well past that point.

Brian's grin was light and bright and so much more than simply replete. "Good," he said. "Because I could get to really liking you too."

CHAPTER 18

Twin pains across his sternum wrested Brian from a dream where he'd stabbed himself in the chest with rusty nails for some inexplicable reason. One minute he was trying to decide which wound he should apply pressure to, the next he was staring into deep-orange eyes and wondering why everything smelled like fish. And if the bed was shaking.

But no, it was that damn cat, standing on his chest—pinning him with a thousand-yard stare at a distance of less than a foot, and the weight . . . God, it hurt. How heavy was this beast? Vaguely, he remembered Mal's warning about suffocation. He should be thankful he was face up, right?

Brian nudged the cat, hoping merely touching its fur wouldn't a) set off a vicious attack or b) increase the weight on his chest.

The cat didn't move.

Brian lifted one shoulder, intending to roll over, and claws with the tensile strength and edge of Ginsu knives dug into the previously thick and cuddly quilt—now nothing but shifting layers of down, easily pierced. Hissing, Brian lay flat. The weight on his chest seemed to increase.

"This is ridiculous."

He nudged the cat again, more firmly this time, already prepared for any flesh ripping that might follow. Lois resisted, claws flashing then seemed to launch sideways, bearing down first so that her weight increased exponentially. Breath exploded out of Brian as she left, and he immediately pushed the quilt back to inspect his chest. He was actually surprised not to find rusty nails embedded in his flesh, or a circle of bloody pinpricks. He'd be further surprised if twin bruises didn't develop later on. That cat weighed a ton.

And Mal hadn't stirred.

Brian grabbed his phone from the nightstand and checked the time. Just before six. Still early. He checked his messages next, scrolling past the quick exchange of texts with Josh last night. Should he feel guilty about leaving him alone? Was it okay to leave a fourteen-nearly-fifteen-year-old alone overnight?

He was only a mile and a half away . . .

Brian tapped out another quick text, feeling like an idiot, but also unable to settle the underlying conflict between guilt and concern: *Hey, checking in. Everything okay?*

Five minutes later, he hadn't received an answer, Mal was still snoring beside him, also on his back, and the damn cat had settled in between them and was involved in some complicated licking exercise.

Brian decided to indulge in a mini crisis. He'd nearly been mauled to death by a cat, he'd abandoned his ward and, most importantly, he'd stayed over—something he hadn't done since . . . since Simon. Without quantifying and qualifying, he hadn't had a lot of hookups since then, either. Not recently. Nothing like arriving newly single to the desert, but if he were honest with himself—and why not? He'd just suffered a near-death experience—he hadn't really been trying. The game hadn't been as fun, lately. Then he'd met Mal.

He glanced past the huge cat at the man sleeping next to him. Mal had a great nose and a strong profile. He resembled the all-American football player he'd apparently been. Everything about him was square and firm, from his broad shoulders to his well-muscled thighs. He had big hands and feet. But he didn't move like a large man did. It might be the injuries, but Mal had probably always been the sort of guy who didn't know his own strength. Who had no idea he was powerful. It was sexy and endearing. Something Brian wanted to explore.

His phone vibrated. Brian woke the screen.

House still here. Me too. [crazy eye emoji]

Brian smiled at the message. He was slowly becoming used to Josh's sense of humor. No surprise that it was sometimes as terse as his. *I'll be home before lunch*, he texted back.

He'd happily spend the weekend in bed with Mal—fucking, cuddling, and doing the simple conversation thing. But it was early days, yet, and he wanted to spend a part of his weekend with Josh too. Maybe he was projecting, but at Josh's age, he'd have given anything to have some secure adult company.

Melancholy seeped across the edges of his thoughts. Memories of himself at that age and a little older, when he'd finally found someone to confide in. First Vanessa and then Tristan, the man who'd believed in him, championed him, and turned his life around. A man he'd loved like a father, and then lost too soon.

Stop.

Brian rolled over, slid his phone back onto the nightstand, and tested the air outside the comfort of Mal's bed. Cold. But his bladder was becoming insistent, so he'd have to brave the floor sooner rather than later. The lingering ache in his ass made him smile as he padded around the end of the bed toward the bathroom. Sex with Mal had been good. Better than good. He cast a glance over his shoulder before stepping through the door and warm, fuzzy feelings surrounded his heart with a gentle squeeze.

After taking care of business, Brian checked his reflection in the mirror, taking a minute to smooth his hair—which was, of course, sticking up in every direction but normal—and then he noticed the window behind him. A curve of white clung to the lower pane. He crossed to the window and peeked through the upper portion, out into a world freshly blanketed by snow. Another four to six inches, judging by the layer of white along the top of the fence.

Mal was still sleeping—and still looking like a cuddly lion of a man next to his feral cat—when Brian returned to the bedroom. Without disturbing him, Brian collected his clothes and tiptoed out into the hall. After dressing in the hall bath, he tiptoed downstairs where a quick exploratory mission turned up a snow shovel in the garage, and a door that opened onto the driveway. He snagged a coat from the peg right there, tried on a pair of gloves and ducked out into the crisp, white morning.

He'd have to shovel some to get his car out, anyway, he reasoned as he started with the walk to the front door. He was half done with the driveway when a car stopped at the curb and idled for a minute. Then a man dressed for similar exercise jumped out and strode up to meet him. With a wool hat pulled down low and jacket zipped up high, it took Brian a handful of seconds to recognize him.

Mal's brother spoke first. "What are you doing?"

"What does it look like I'm doing?"

"That's what I'm trying to figure out." Donny reached for the shovel. "I can take it from here."

Riddle of who'd been shoveling Mal's walk and drive: solved.

Brian held on to the shovel. "It's okay, I've got it."

Donny took note of Brian's snow-shrouded car. "You've been here all night?"

"What business is that of yours?"

Donny glanced between the car and the house a few times, and then back at Brian. "He's not your type."

"And what is Mal's type?"

"He needs someone dependable. Someone quiet, like him."

"What makes you the expert on what Mal needs?"

"I'm his brother."

"And I'm the guy who shared his bed last night. I think I've got a handle on it."

Donny's already red cheeks burned redder. "Listen, I don't . . . I'm sure you're . . ." He chewed on a sigh for a second before letting it go. "I got a letter from some lawyer."

"Huh?"

"About the kitchen contractor. Someone lodged a formal complaint, and they're forming a class-action thing. Your name was on it."

"Mal told me what happened. I'd never have recommended them if I'd known they were that bad. I don't even remember why I had their card. I must have gotten them confused with someone else. I'm sorry."

"No, it's all good. I just . . . Damn it. I don't want you to be decent."

Brian jerked back. "What the hell does that mean?"

"I asked around about you."

"And?"

"Everyone says you're a player."

"I'm single, Donny. And have been for a couple of years. So I like to hook up on occasion. That does not make me a player."

"Mal needs—"

"I think Mal is well old enough to know what he needs."

"You don't understand. His accident, this thing with his legs. He nearly died. And he's been—" Donny broke off and fidgeted in place.

Knowing, or guessing what Donny had been about to say, Brian offered him a respectful nod. "Worst case, he'll get bored of me or figure out I'm not his type. Until then, maybe I'm the distraction he needs."

Donny shrugged, then turned toward the shovel. "He's not that easily impressed."

"Okay."

"And don't think you can get to him through me. I appreciate what you did with the contractor and all, but I'm not his gatekeeper."

"Could have fooled me."

Donny said nothing for a minute. Then he ducked into the side door and grabbed another shovel. "I'll start on the sidewalk."

"Thanks."

Between them, they had the drive and sidewalk cleared fifteen minutes later. By then, Mal was at the front door, all cozy-looking in sweats. "C'mon in. I've got breakfast started," he called.

It wasn't the breakfast Brian had hoped for. Donny's presence pretty much precluded another round of sex. But it was interesting to measure the closeness of the brothers. They had similar builds and their eyes were the same muted shade of gray. But they didn't look like twins. After observing them together for longer than a few minutes, however, Brian conceded they were intensely connected. As close as he'd imagined twins might be. He knew Donny had given up a semester of college to care for Mal, and suspected Mal had probably made several similar sacrifices for Donny.

If Brian wanted more, Donny would be a permanent part of the equation. Was he prepared for that?

Mal walked him to the door a short while later.

"How's the leg holding up?" Brian asked.

"A little sore." Mal grinned. "Last night was worth it."

Brian smiled, and when Mal leaned in, he met him halfway in an altogether too sweet kiss.

"Thanks for last night. All of it."

Mal kissed him again. "Thank you."

"See you soon?"

Mal's grin was adorable. "Yes."

Josh was in the kitchen when Brian got home, something turning endless circles in the microwave.

"What are you making?" Brian asked.

"Lunch."

"I should teach you how to actually cook."

Josh replied with one of his habitual shrugs. "How was your date?"

"Good. Mal's brother showed up this morning, which was all kinds of awkward."

A grin flashed across Josh's face, spreading when he glanced down at his phone. His thumbs raced across the keyboard for a couple of seconds before he looked back up. "So weird you're dating my teacher."

"Does it bother you?'

Shrug.

"You seemed a little put out by it on the first day of school," Brian added.

"Everything's weird on the first day of school. And I was still getting used to the idea of being here and stuff. But I can see you guys together."

"Yeah?"

"You're both, like, old and stuff."

"Gee, thanks." Should he ask for a definitive definition of *stuff*?

Josh's phone grabbed his attention again. Grinning, he tapped out another text.

"Who are you chatting with?"

"Ethan."

The microwave *ding*ed and the sound replaced the warning bells already tolling in the back of Brian's psyche. "Be careful, Josh. I know he's probably got a lot of questions right now, and he'll need friends like you to talk to, but don't fall for him, okay?"

Josh frowned. "Who said anything about falling for him?"

The clearing of his frown as he checked his phone screen and the smile edging his lips as he moved his thumbs across the keyboard, that's who.

"He has a girlfriend," Brian pointed out.

"They broke up."

The microwave repeated its call to duty.

"Josh, look at me for a sec?"

Josh glanced at him. "What?"

"You know I got kicked out of home like you did, right?"

"Yeah."

"Did you know it was over some straight guy who was experimenting?"

The wrinkling of Josh's brow indicated he'd finally started paying attention.

Leaning past the renewed frown, Brian opened the microwave and retrieved the steaming tray of vegetarian gunk. "Here." He put the tray on the counter. "Ethan seems like a nice guy, but you don't want to be the one he experiments with, okay? Because it never ends well. Not for him and not for you."

"Easy for you to say. You had one bad experience."

"Not just one. I've been around for a while."

"Bisexuality is a valid orientation."

"I'm not trying to argue that it's not. I know a bunch of bisexual guys. Hell, Simon's new partner was married to a woman and has a kid." Brian tried not to shudder.

"Who's Simon?"

"My ex, and not who we're talking about."

"What do you care who I hook up with? You're getting some. Why shouldn't I?"

"Josh . . ." Brian dug his fingers into his scalp. "Okay, you said we don't need to have the sex conversation, but . . ." *God, forgive me.* "Have you ever—"

"I'm not answering that."

So that was a no, then.

Brian thought back to his first time and blew out a tight breath. "I'm going to sound like a freaking Hallmark ad here, but your first time should be with someone you like and trust, okay? It's a big deal

It's scary and exciting and not a little life changing. Especially if you're doing more than fool around."

Josh's skin took on the shade of an overripe tomato. He opened his mouth.

Brian waved him off.

Josh's situation was different. He'd already been kicked out, based only on a confession. He hadn't been caught by . . . He hadn't . . . His first time wasn't yet a permanent scar. But Brian couldn't think of a way to share that sentiment without spilling a story he'd never told anyone, or without ruining what had, so far, been a pretty decent Saturday. So he let it go, for now.

CHAPTER 19

"Rachel isn't coming?" Mal frowned over his brother's shoulder at the car parked in his driveway. The suspiciously empty car. "We always watch the Pro Bowl together."

It'd been a week since his first official date with Brian. They'd seen each other twice in the intervening days, outside of the GSA meeting at school, and each date had been better than the last. Mal could feel himself getting used to Brian's attention. His kisses, his taste, the intensity of his orgasms. And his company—to counting on it. Which was why he wanted to spend today with his brother and sister-in-law. Before he forgot what it was like to be simply Mal.

Of course, the fact that he'd be meeting Brian and Brian's friends at the Colonial this afternoon as well had nothing to do with him needing company of his own to walk through the door.

Nothing. Nope. *All's good here.*

"Hayley was running a fever, so Rachel decided to stay home with her," Donny said.

"And miss the game." Rachel rarely missed a game at the Colonial, not with Grandma and Grandpa ready to babysit anytime, anywhere.

"We do have a TV at our house," Donny pointed out. "Three of them, in fact."

Mal delved beneath the glib humor in Donny's expression. "Why is she really staying home?"

Donny sighed. "C'mon, get in the car. It's cold. I'll tell you on the way. Where's your crutch?"

"I'm only walking as far as your car and then as far as the front door of the Colonial. I'll be fine."

"Are you sure?"

"Why couldn't you have been the one to stay home?"

Snorting, Donny stepped off the walk and waited for him to pass before following him.

"I can feel you waiting for me to slip," Mal said.

"And I can feel you trying damn hard not to," Donny returned.

Mal continued his slow progress toward the car. His left leg, the one that was supposed to be good, ached in a bone-deep way, and his right knee was still swollen. He was finding it hard to remember what it had looked like before his accident and, at the moment, the act of walking felt mentally taxing—weighing thoughts of not slipping against more dire fantasies of wrecking his new knee so badly that walking with a brace would become a full-time sport.

Once in the car and belted in, he turned to Donny. "Okay, spill." They only had a mile to travel and probably ten miles of conversation to get through.

Donny didn't talk until he'd turned onto Speedwell. "I asked if I could have this time with you."

"Damn it, Donny. You know Brian's going to be there this afternoon. At the bar."

Uncharacteristically, Donny flushed.

"Stop the car," Mal ordered.

"What? No."

"We'll watch the game at home."

"Why?"

Mal touched the door handle. "Donny, I'm serious. You stop this car or I'm going to roll out and screw up my legs."

Donny slowed, indicated, and turned onto a side street before pulling to the curb. "What?"

"You know what."

Sighing, Donny held up his hands. "Just hear me out, bro. You've been with him every night for the past week."

"Not true. Not even close." Though, given the chance . . .

"He's not who you think he is."

"What do you have against Brian? So he recommended a crap contractor. He's already made an effort to fix that situation, though he wasn't obligated to."

"And I appreciate it, but you're not a contract situation. You're my brother. And you're in a shitty place right now. You're vulnerable And there's something about him I can't quite make work. It's like he has a secret."

Mal briefly recalled Brian's sometimes haunted look, then just as quickly brushed the memory aside. Everyone had secrets and not all of them were fit for sharing. "You need to stop."

Donny gripped the wheel. "That's the thing. I can't." Shoulders bunched up tight, eyes squeezed shut, he made as if to shake the wheel. "I . . ."

"What is it?" Twin connection or not, Mal could feel Donny's distress. Heck, it was visible. Anyone would feel it. He put a hand to his brother's shoulder. "What's going on? Is something up with you and Rachel?"

"No." Donny glanced over at him, eyes brimming. "It's you, Mal. Fuck, man. The night you got hit." He gave the wheel another shake. "I felt you die in surgery, okay? I *felt* you go. And I never want to feel anything like that ever again."

Mal swallowed over the lump forming in his throat. "How is preventing me from seeing a man I really, really like going to accomplish that?"

"He's not from here. He's not a hometown boy. No one knows where he grew up."

"You could say that about half of everyone in Morristown."

"I don't want to see you hurt." Donny turned to face him fully. "Both of us had rough ends to our last relationships." The end of Donny's first marriage had been a lot messier than the end of Mal's only long-term relationship, but Donny always acted as though Mal's split with Noah had somehow been worse.

Maybe because no one had expected him to be with someone like Noah, and at first glance, Noah and Brian were similar—but not in the respect that mattered to Mal. Yes, Brian shone with confidence. He was outgoing. But he'd yet to put Mal down. In fact, he went out of his way to be positive and encouraging.

Mal gripped his brother's shoulder. "You can't spend your whole life looking out for me."

"Watch me."

Shaking his head, Mal squeezed harder, digging his fingers into Donny's triceps. "No. I want you to watch me. Watch me live, Donny. Watch me learn to walk again. Learn to love again. I'm not going to say I needed my legs broken, but look at what's come my way since. This new club at school and a chance to make a difference with these kids, and a man I might never have tried anything with if I hadn't been brooding alone at the bar on Christmas Eve. And Brian isn't Noah, isn't like him at all. He isn't a condescending prick for a start."

"God, Noah was a bastard."

"No, he wasn't. He—" Mal closed his mouth. Why was he trying to think of an excuse for a man who'd left him feeling as though he had even less worth than he had when they met? He'd always had a problem with self-esteem and wasn't sure why. Maybe because Donny seemed more solid somehow. He was definitely louder and more assertive. Donny had been the one to stand up to their bullies in school, and Donny had been the one who made him feel safe in his sexuality.

When Noah's dismissive attitude had become less an occasional poke and more a habit, though, Donny had been the one to notice— and Mal had ignored his brother's advice. He'd assumed Donny's bitter suspicion came from his divorce, but . . .

Mal sighed. All of that was in the past. They'd both learned something from the experience, hadn't they? "Listen, I know you've all been worried about me, but I'm coming back, okay? I'm getting out there and trying new things. Don't stand in the way of that."

Donny held his gaze for a long minute before nodding. "Okay."

"I *am* the older brother." Mal offered a quick smile.

Conflict played across Donny's face as he obviously wrestled with his need to assert himself. Then he sighed and nodded. "Order doesn't matter. Never has. We watch out for each other, right?"

Mal squeezed Donny's shoulder. "Always. So can you do that today while being nice?"

Donny managed a half smile. "Probably."

"Then let's go. Game's starting soon."

Brian was already at the bar when they arrived, seated at a table with two other men, his back to the door. A sense of awkwardness and elation gripped Mal's lungs as he limped through the entryway.

His chest wanted to expand and contract at the same time. He'd been looking forward to seeing Brian and meeting his friends, but he'd also hoped to have some time to settle in first.

"Want your usual?" Donny asked, nodding toward the bar.

"Sure."

Mal gazed longingly at the stool in the corner he'd claimed as his own. There'd be no bar propping today. He'd have to sit at a table with people and be sociable. He started toward Brian's group.

The two men opposite Brian were obviously a couple. It was evident in the way they sat with their shoulders almost touching, an invisible thread of connection between. When they glanced toward each other, they communicated with intimate smiles. A pang of jealousy poked Mal in the sternum before ending up as a burn somewhere near his navel. Had he ever had that close a relationship with a person who hadn't shared a womb with him for nearly nine months?

The taller of the two, dark haired with impossibly blue eyes, looked up as Mal approached. Brian turned around and smiled. His eyes brightened. His entire countenance lit with pleasure as he pushed his chair back and stood.

"Hey!" He stepped around the other table between them. "You're here."

"Game's about to start, so . . . yeah." Mal sought a grin he hoped wasn't too odd. "How are you?" Was that a stupid question? It'd only been about thirty hours since they'd last seen each other. Since he'd had Brian's cock in his mouth.

God, he was bad at this flirting, dating thing. Dating thing? Jesus. What if Brian didn't think they were dating?

"I'm glad you're here, that's how I am," Brian said more quietly, his words clearly meant not only for Mal's ears alone, but to settle and soothe, judging by the tone.

"Did I forget to mention, at some point, how awkward I can be?" Mal asked.

"You might have, but you demonstrate it pretty regularly, so I'm all up to speed."

"Stop grinning like that."

"You're kind of adorable. Also, yay, no crutch. How's the knee?" Brian's eyebrows lifted. "No particular complaints?"

Mal felt the blush sweep in.

Donny also chose that moment to reappear at his side, holding two glasses of beer. He offered Brian a stiff nod. "Hey."

"My partner in crime." Brian gave him a rogue grin.

Donny returned a not-too-cool smile. "So, where are we sitting?"

They spent a minute nudging another table closer and rearranging chairs so that Mal had enough room to extend his leg or lift it onto a seat if he needed to. At the same time, Brian introduced his friends. "Mal, this is Simon and Charlie."

Simon was the tall, dark, even-more-handsome-up-close guy, and Charlie had friendly brown eyes. Mal shook hands with them both. "Nice to meet you." They murmured nice things in return and everyone sat down.

And stared at each other.

Well, Simon and Brian and Mal did. Charlie and Donny were already discussing the upcoming match.

Simon broke the silence with a smile. "Brian says you teach history at Morristown High. What period?"

Okay. Good. Mal could do this. "Early modern, so the latter part of what we call the Middle Ages."

Simon's expression brightened. "The Renaissance and the Age of Discovery, right? So much to cover. And you fit all of that into a year of study for high school students?"

"Not hardly." Mal allowed a slight smirk. "I get two years to cover the highlights."

Simon was nodding. "How do you choose what to highlight?"

"Between board-mandated curriculum and standardized testing, I generally don't." This conversation was going to die fairly quickly if he didn't say something more positive. "But I slip in extra material when I can. Luckily, most of my students find the period as fascinating as I do," Mal finished with a smile. "What about you?"

"Simon's an architect," Brian answered. "He oversaw the restoration of the Kinney Building on South Park."

"Oh, cool. That was a nice job. I can see why Brian wanted you to visit the Colonial."

Simon glanced around at the gloomy interior of the pub. "Yes." He didn't sound enthused. "It would be an interesting project. Saving the entire row from demolition would be a good first step."

"Exactly," Brian said. "We should talk to Leo. He was supposed to chat with his father, get what information he could." Brian produced a short stack of cards from his pocket. "And I've been talking to the other business owners in the strip. I have their numbers here."

Simon glanced at the cards. "You could have emailed this information to me."

Brian's jaw tightened. "I could have, but I know you like paper." He nudged the cards across the table. "So here's your stack of paper."

Donny interrupted the odd moment of tension between the two "friends" by turning around to tug Mal's sleeve. "Guess who this is!" he said, pointing to Charlie.

Mal studied Charlie's friendly face. "Um . . ."

"C.R. King."

"Who?" The letters fell into place, and Mal opened his mouth again, only to manage no words at all. He gaped for a minute before finding, "Holy crap. Really?"

Charlie showed a perfectly self-effacing grin. "Really. You're a fan?"

"He has all your books," Donny said, with the authority of a proud father.

Mal did. All six volumes of Kaze Rider, kicking ass and taking names, in space. He loved the series and not only because the lead character was queer.

Mal turned in his seat, ignoring the pull against his knee. "I do. Wow. Um, sorry, is this weird?" It was weird, right?

Charlie chuckled. "Not at all."

Brian and Simon and historical restoration completely forgotten, Mal got up and repositioned his chair, not caring how awkward it was. He was sitting next to C.R. King! "So, the Norma Device."

Charlie rolled his eyes dramatically. "If I had a dollar for every person who asked about the Norma Device, I'd never have to write another book."

"But you could! About the Carina Fleet. Any plans for a spin-off series?"

"Maybe. I do have a sort of outline for how it could work, but I always liked leaving that end loose, you know? So people could imagine their own outcome to it."

"I get that, definitely. Like the end of book six. I really liked how you left things with Kaze and Jory. And the plot was all wrapped up, but there was still the question of— Oh man, is this, I dunno, annoying? Do you hate talking about your books?"

"I love talking about my books. Seriously. I don't get time to do more than nod and smile at cons and signings and so on."

The theme music announcing the beginning of the actual game floated through the bar. Mal glanced at the screen. "Thank God it's only the Pro Bowl. If this was the Super Bowl, I'd have to pay attention—though my money's on the Steelers over the Eagles." He then noted Charlie's distinctive green jersey. "Crap. You're an Eagles fan."

"Born and raised."

"Think they can win another one?"

Charlie raised his glass. "No doubt." After taking a healthy swig of beer, he glanced at the man next to him, smile softening.

Simon raised his glass. "What are we drinking to? It's the green team, right?" Mischief married his eyes.

"Next week, yes." Laughing, Charlie clinked glasses with his partner.

Mal noted Brian's expression and didn't like what he saw. He understood the jealousy—he felt it himself. But there was something mournful about the downward curve of Brian's lips. Something lost in his gaze. He glanced at Mal and made an attempt to smile. A mostly successful attempt. Then the game started and Mal turned to watch the kickoff—more out of habit than anything else, but also because he didn't want to see what he thought he'd seen. Didn't want to wonder whether it was Simon or Charlie who was making Brian look so sad.

After a few minutes—not being able to leave well enough alone—he asked Charlie, "How long have you and Simon been together?"

"Just over a year. He's not as serious as he seems, by the way. Except when he is."

Donny chuckled. "Sounds like Mal."

Mal rolled his eyes.

"He's not much of a football fan, either," Charlie continued. "And he totally sucks at *Assassin's Creed*, which I thought he'd rock. But he has other charms."

"You play *Assassin's Creed*? Which one?"

The next hour passed in a comfortable blur of football and gaming talk. Mal remembered to check in with Brian on occasion, but Brian always seemed involved with Simon, touching his arm, making sure his glass was full. They were obviously close . . . but how close? Presumably, they moved in the same circles—both being involved with building and architecture, both being stupidly handsome, and the whole gay thing. Had they ever been involved? Mal distracted himself for a good twenty minutes deciding they had, and suffered a near debilitating burn of envy over it. Of course, they weren't together now, and Simon and Charlie exchanged glances often enough to ensure everyone in the bar knew they were tightly coupled.

So what was Brian's deal?

It wasn't until the game was nearly done that Mal realized he and Brian hadn't actually exchanged more than a few words throughout the course of the afternoon. Feeling Donny's curious gaze, Mal turned back to the game and the sporadic conversation he and Charlie were having about Bujold's Vorkosigan Saga. He was having a good time. A great time. And he really needed to take a leak.

Levering to his feet, Mal pushed back his chair. He managed the walk to the men's room without too much hassle. His physical therapist said he needed to bend his knee more—get used to walking without a limp—but without overdoing it. As always, the contradictory instructions proved frustrating. He was grateful to be on his feet, though.

He stopped at the bar on his way back. "Hey, Leo."

Leo offered a brusque nod. Frowning, Mal glanced at the closest TV screen and back down. The NFC were holding on to their seven-point lead. "Do you have money on this game?"

"What? No." His gaze narrowed on the table where Brian and Simon sat.

"What?" Mal asked. "Are you going to warn me off Brian as well? Has Donny been talking to you? You know, I only broke my legs. Not my head. Or my dick."

Leo's mouth worked a little, as if he were fighting between a smile and a grimace. "It's not that, it's . . . Simon, Brian's ex? He was a good friend of mine."

So they *had* been together.

"You didn't know?" Leo asked.

"About Brian and Simon? I sort of assumed." They were a matched set, after all. Dark and Light. As compatible as salt and pepper.

"Twelve years. And Brian didn't treat him well."

Twelve . . . "Did you say twelve years?"

"I did."

"They were together for over a decade?"

"On and off."

"On and off?"

"You should ask Brian about it. No, better ask Simon. He's more likely to tell you the truth."

Brian glanced up then, meeting Mal's gaze, and even from a distance, he seemed to read whatever expression Mal had managed—though Mal had no idea what he currently looked like. He was too surprised. And so was Brian, if Mal was interpreting the shape of his mouth correctly. Mal was no lip-reader, but he could practically hear Brian's "Oh shit" from across the bar.

Ducking back into the hallway leading to the men's room was a cowardly move, but Mal needed a minute to work on his reaction. To put away the surprise and find some logic. Brian was forty-eight years old. Of course he had exes. Probably a dozen of them, on top of his dozen years with one particularly good-looking man.

A shadow darkened the top end of the hallway. One familiar enough that Mal's heart rate picked up.

"What lies was Leo telling you about me?" Brian asked.

"He actually suggested you'd be the one with the lies." Wait, that sounded bad. "I mean . . ." A pulse of anger pushed through the confusion twisting Mal's tongue. "Twelve years, Brian? You couldn't have said something?"

"How is my past relationship with Simon in any way relevant?"

"Oh, I don't know. Maybe because you've hardly left his side all afternoon."

"We've had business to discuss."

"Right, business I guess that's the excuse you used during the on-and-off phases too."

Brian rocked back. "I see."

Mal sucked in a breath . . . and let it go with an apology. "I'm sorry. It's none of my business. I've just got Leo and Donny all up in mine and— Jesus, Brian. Why didn't you tell me you guys had been together? This is awkward, and I don't know how to react."

"How about cutting me some slack?"

"What do you mean?"

"You and me, we re really new and we're still getting to know each other."

"Twelve years, Brian. It's not insignificant." Mal couldn't figure out why it felt so important, either, except that Brian had been paying so much attention to Simon that afternoon.

Brian dipped his chin in a bobbing nod. "Okay." He took a step back. "Fine. Next time I ask you out, I'll remember to bring my résumé."

"That's not . . ." Mal sighed. "You're right. It's not relevant." And it wasn't the relationship that bothered him. Not completely. It was more that if eight years with Noah had left Mal with a lingering sadness, all these years later, then Brian had to be carrying something from his relationship with Simon. Was that why he looked so sad sometimes? Was this his secret? Was he missing his best friend and confidant?

And what did that mean for Mal?

Mal cleared his throat. "I'm . . . I think I'm going to head out, okay? My legs are killing me, and I need to get ready for school tomorrow."

Expressionless, Brian backed out of the hall and gave him room to pass.

Donny hopped up as Mal reached their table and tugged his coat off the back of the chair. "We're leaving?" he asked.

Mal flicked a hand toward the screen. "I think we all know how this one's going to end." He made himself shake Charlie's hand.

offered a polite nod to Simon, and even managed to exchange a look with Brian. One that accomplished nothing more than to add to the weirdness that had started . . . when? The moment he'd started thinking that maybe he wasn't good enough.

Donny was going to love this.

But in the car, Donny didn't say a word, and an hour later, installed on the couch with his cat, his sandwich, his whiskey, his TV remote, and PlayStation controller, Mal couldn't decide whether that had been better or worse than an "I told you so."

CHAPTER 20

Mal's empty chair felt a lot like the space he'd left inside Brian's chest.

A part of Brian roiled with contempt for the man who'd walked out of the bar, head not exactly held high, but obviously fueled by self-righteousness. Mal had probably never fucked up a thing in his life. He was the saint life tested instead. His past relationships had obviously ended on a note of perfect fucking harmony.

Another part of Brian simply wanted to leave. Go home. He didn't want to care as much as he did. His past was his past and should have no bearing on his future, and if Mal was going to get his panties in a knot over stuff not mentioned, then he could sit on that knot and spin around for a bit.

Okay, so both parts of him felt pretty much the same.

Brian picked up the glass in front of him only to discover it was empty.

"Hey."

Glancing over at Simon, he arched a single eyebrow. "What?" *Had* he been paying too much attention to Simon over the course of the afternoon?

"What happened?" Simon tipped his head toward the bar.

"Leo happened. And you. And . . . I might not have told Mal we used to be together."

"So?"

"Leo is your number-one fan, Simon. You know he told Mal everything he didn't need to hear about you and me. I'm sure he made it sound as if I'd been a lying, cheating son of a bitch as well."

While Charlie glanced over before studiously turning his attention back to the game, Simon did Brian the courtesy of remaining silent, though the accusation . . . No, it wasn't in his eyes.

Brian sat back. "Why aren't you pointing out the obvious?"

"Because it's done. It was done a long time ago."

"So we're just friends now?"

Simon let out a soft sigh. "I guess. It's what you want, isn't it?"

"I thought . . ." Brian did exactly that, again. Ran back over what he'd been doing with Simon over the past two years, since they'd broken up. Since Brian had left, apparently shredding the last of Simon's patience, and breaking his own heart.

He gazed at Simon, at a face so familiar, he couldn't even begin to explain the emotional twist working inside of him, and thought about the questions he'd wanted to ask for two years now, and knew he never could.

Instead, he gathered up the business cards he'd put out on the table and shuffled them into a slim stack. "Listen, I'll take care of this. I appreciate you coming all the way out here, but I've got it covered." He chanced a sideways glance. "This is going to be my last project here. Then I'm going to get out of Hicksville."

"Oh, are you thinking about New York?" They'd talked about it sometimes. Together.

"Or maybe the West Coast." Because they hadn't talked about that.

"It's a—"

"Different market out there, I know. But I've got a few connections."

"Why are you telling me this?" Simon asked.

"Because it means I won't be . . ." Brian swallowed. God, why was this so hard? "I think it's time I walked away for good. Don't you?"

Simon's perfect eyebrows moved together. "Brian—"

"It's okay. I realize I've been making a pain of myself for some time now. That I never let go, and it's fucking stupid, because I'm the one who walked out."

"You are."

"So why can't I let go, Simon? Why did you let me go?"

Simon's already pale features lost a little more color, and he glanced at Charlie, who was still watching the game with dogged determination, and then around the bar. "Can we do this somewhere else?"

Brian got to his feet. "We don't have to do it at all." He might have vowed not to ask his questions, but now that the first, the biggest, had slipped out of the bag, his mood had begun to dip dangerously. He yanked his coat and scarf from the back of his chair, tugged the scarf around his neck, and began wrestling with sleeves.

Simon stood next to him. "Brian, please don't go like this."

"This is the perfect exit, don't you think? Everything has always been so cool and controlled between us. Even the day I left, you just stood there with your face like stone and let me go. So get your look on, Simon, because this time I'm disappearing for good. Wouldn't want to disappoint your fans."

Rather than harden, Simon's face fell apart, his mouth dropping open, his eyes growing wide. Then anger swept across his features. Anger thick and dark, like Brian had never seen before. Grabbing Brian's upper arm, Simon turned toward Charlie. "Brian and I are going outside for a conversation. We'll be back shortly."

Charlie gave a quick nod.

Brian allowed himself to be led outside, head caught in a dizzy whirl between Simon, Josh, and Mal, and the thought that he was letting them all down. His relationship to each, and the fact that none of them really knew him. Not the real Brian. Not the scared little boy who'd come back to haunt him in the form of a gawky teenager with blue hair and too many earrings.

Outside, the cold evening pinched Brian's cheeks. Simon's face flushed pink under the bright light outside the bar. He looked as though he wanted to shake Brian. He let go instead, so he could finish putting his coat on, then shoved his hands into his pockets and turned square toward Brian. "Okay, let's do this."

"Do what?"

"Have the conversation you've wanted to have for two years."

"Fuck you." Brian started away. "I'm done."

"You don't get to do that. Not this time." Simon caught his arm again, yanking him to a stop. "You want to know why I let you go? Huh? Because I couldn't do it anymore. I couldn't keep pretending I knew you. That I loved you."

Brian's knees lost a few ball bearings. Straightening them, he turned to face Simon, wrenching his arm out of Simon's grip. Again. "You . . . What?"

"I loved you for so long that I didn't know how to not love you when the time came. I stayed because . . . I don't know. Because I was waiting for you to tell me why I wasn't enough. But also because it was easier. Because you were familiar. Because I was too scared to try doing it on my own."

Simon was killing him. Tearing out the Scotch-taped pieces of his heart and shredding them into even finer pieces.

"Hurts, doesn't it?" Simon said, fabulous blue eyes blazing. "Feels like someone tore you into tiny little bits."

"Yes."

"That's why I let you go."

Brian tried to swallow and got stuck halfway, his throat aching and his vision misting. He forced the issue, working his throat over a razor-edged lump. "Why didn't you tell me?"

"Because I didn't want you to know how much you'd hurt me."

Brian's knees lost a few more essential parts. Moving toward the wall of the bar, he braced one hand on the distressed brick and let his head drop forward. Exhaled and then struggled to pull air back into his lungs. "Fuck."

He'd waited two years for this? Why?

He studied the toes of Simon's shoes—deep brown and well-worn. Obviously polished and weatherproofed. Practical and handsome and . . . not a pair he recognized. Nor were the neat denim cuffs hiding the rest of the shoes from his view.

He glanced up. "You're wearing jeans. I didn't even know you knew jeans existed."

A tight smile tugged at one side of Simon's mouth.

"Simon—"

"I know you're sorry. You always were."

"No, that's not what I was going to say." Actually, it was, but not for the reasons Simon might think. "I wish we'd had this conversation back then. Then I might not have been such a pain in your ass these past couple of years."

"You haven't been a pain in my ass. We've been working together, and I've enjoyed the projects. We always worked well together."

"Maybe we should never have tried for more."

Simon took a step closer. "Did you not hear what I said?"

Brian shook his head.

"I loved you. I wanted more. For a long, long time, I wanted more. I'm not sure you knew what you wanted, though."

"You. I wanted you."

"Then why wasn't I enough?"

Brian shook his head again. Truth danced across his tongue until he swallowed it down. It was too late to tell Simon why. To share what he'd always held back. A great sigh left him and his chin dipped. "I never meant to cheat."

"I know that too. You were always so goddamn sorry."

"I . . ." The itch was back. "Does it make sense for me to say I wanted more too?"

"More . . ."

"I was always so afraid of losing you. And after every time I apologized, we'd go away or spend a weekend together, just us, and it'd be so damn good. Not at first. We'd be all careful with one another. But then we'd make love and our connection was there, it had always been there, and . . ." Brian scrubbed at an itch on his cheek, not even surprised when his glove came away damp. "We'd be so close for a while, and I'd really believe you loved me."

"I don't even know how to tell you how fucked up that is." The words were harsh, but the tone Simon delivered them in was gentle.

"It's okay. I get it." Brian half turned. It was time to go. Delving deeper wouldn't expose anything he wanted to talk about. Not with Simon. "So, ah, good talk." Brian sniffed. Squinted his eyes a little, hoping his lashes would deal with the couple of tears gathering there. Maybe if he pointed his face into the wind, he could get some icicles going.

"Brian?"

"Mm?"

"I'm glad we're still friends."

Brian studied Simon, the sincerity written all over his face. "Even though I'm an asshole and cheat?"

"You're good to your friends. You always have been. And I do like working with you, but I've been conscious of not inviting more."

"Because you're with Charlie and you two are it. I know. I get it. I'm sorry if I . . ." Brian pushed his gloved palms to his eyes. "I'm sorry."

"Apology accepted."

Brian peeked through his fingers to find Simon wearing one of his favorite expressions: quiet composure. Simon's ability to remain placid, or apparently unmoved, had often annoyed him when they'd been together. But now he could reflect back on that steadfastness with affection, and realized—with a sense of levity that nearly pulled him up off the pavement—that any lingering feelings he had for this man were just that. A deep affection born of years of friendship. The struggle to put their business together and the struggle to make their relationship work. Of knowing someone so well, you could tell even the most nuanced expressions apart. Knew the definition of each smile.

Tucking one hand in his pocket, Brian extended the other. "Thank you."

Simon studied his hand for a second, then stepped in and drew Brian into a close embrace. Simon Lynley was . . . hugging him. It was weird. And nice.

"Charlie's good for you," Brian murmured as he hugged back.

"I know." Simon let him go, then took his hand in a solid shake. "You should go find Mal. I like him, Brian."

Brian swallowed. "I'm actually going to let him do his own thing for a while, I think. I'm sick of chasing people who might not want to be run down."

Simon offered him a sad smile. "Maybe he's the one you'll . . ."

"The one I'll what?"

"The one you'll let in. Be wholly Brian with."

"I—"

Simon held up a gloved hand. "Don't let him brood for too long, hmm?"

Shoving his own hands into his pockets, Brian put his head down. He was done with the weepy business now and the wind was cold on his face. After acknowledging Simon's final words of advice with a brief nod, he set off in the direction of home. He'd think about it, about being *wholly Brian* with Mal. Maybe. But first he needed to chill for a while, both metaphorically and physically.

CHAPTER 21

Mal checked the hallway one last time before conceding defeat. Brian wasn't coming. Blowing out a short sigh, he pushed the door closed. Behind him, the GSA club continued rearranging desks, filling his classroom with the scrape of chair and table legs, and directionless chatter. It was a good sound, one he was used to and one he welcomed. It was the sound of industry and organization and of kids getting along.

The door pulled away from his hand, and Mal turned, already knowing his expression was all wrong. Ethan and Josh recoiled slightly from whatever he showed them—joy, need, everything utterly ridiculous—and sidled into the classroom to join the throng.

His disappointment was sharper this time. It hurt more. Yes, he'd been the one to limp away yesterday afternoon, but he'd hoped Brian would prove to be the bigger man. Then again, why should he be? Mal had acted like a fool. An insecure ass.

And he should be used to this by now.

After closing the door again, Mal made his way to the spot they'd made for him at the top of the circle and took a deep breath. "Hey."

Murmurs and smiles.

He studied the assembled group, testing his recall of faces and names. Noting who'd been there last week and the week before and checking them off against his mental list of facts and assumptions. Two new faces, a couple of missing faces. After the two new kids introduced themselves, Mal asked after the missing faces and learned that one was home ill. The other hadn't been seen since last Thursday.

"Should we be concerned?" God, he hated asking that, but this was his job now. These, even more than those he taught, were his kids.

He'd had a bond with a couple of his students before. Those who performed well and made him proud, and those who'd asked for extra help. One of his favorites had been a girl four years ago who greeted every lecture with the attitude of the extremely bored, only to prove she secretly loved history but didn't want to seem like a nerd or geek or whatever they called it now.

These kids were different. They needed more.

Pamela Kee spoke up. "I think they're okay. Pretty sure they'd text me if they needed anything. Probably just sick as well."

"I'll check with the office later," Mal said. "This brings up something I wanted to talk about today. I know not all of you are friends outside this classroom and that's okay. You don't need to be. I'm not going to be the one to tell any of you what to do. But I think a part of being in a club is networking with your people, whether we're here to talk about music, art, sports, language, or gender and sexuality. I guess what I'm trying to say is that you have an opportunity to make a difference. That's why you're here. So I hope you'll be friends to each other inside and outside of this classroom."

The students exchanged varying nods. Some enthusiastic, others more reserved, but Mal got a sense that the bond he hoped for existed. None of these kids wanted to be heroes, but they were already keeping tabs on each other. Even quietly.

"Anyone got anything they want to add?"

A few students spoke, the first two basically confirming that they were there for everyone. Ethan looked as though he'd like to stand up, and Mal wondered why he didn't. He was a natural born leader. Instead, he just fiddled with his phone, mouth twisted to one side. Next to him, Josh fiddled with his phone.

Were they texting each other? Sitting side by side?

A third student spoke up. "A few of us have been meeting at the boathouse. It's pretty casual and kinda cold right now, but—"

"The boathouse?"

"It's on the side of the lake. About half a mile up Speedwell."

"You mean at the end of Elliott?" Mal had passed the place every time he did the Patriots' Path. "That building is closed."

"There's a window into the cellar on the lake side."

Mal held up a hand. "I can't condone this. I'm sorry. I know you all need more than one afternoon a week, but Winterfest is coming up fast. Rachel—Mrs. Montgomery and I have reached out to a few additional sponsors. We're going to get this drop-in center funded and open. Our biggest challenge will be finding the right place." And it wouldn't be an abandoned building in the park. "Any suggestions on that front are welcome. Until then . . ." Should he do this? What the heck, why not? Wasn't like he had the life he'd been bragging to Donny about. "How about if I keep this classroom open after school Every day. Would that help?"

A few of them exchanged nods. Others appeared totally disinterested. Still others hid what they were thinking. Mal had seen it all before. What he did get, though, was that his offer would be appreciated by those who needed it.

He could do his grading and lesson plans here instead of at home. Lois would be fine on her own for a couple more hours every day. Maybe Rachel could help out on occasion. She'd definitely be an asset when it came to figuring out if he was even allowed to offer such a thing. Then again . . .

Think later. Do now.

"Okay, speaking of Winterfest, where are we at?"

"We need an ice sculpture."

Mal wrote that down. Where the heck was he supposed to get an ice sculpture? He tapped his pen against the pad. Maybe Leo's husband could be persuaded to donate something? Could painters sculpt?

"Okay, what else?"

Satan's helper was back. Amanda of the casual indifference to pain. If she ever decided to quit being a physical therapist, she could take a job with the CIA in interrogation. State secrets could be gained at the bending of every knee.

"Stop!"

She stopped trying to break his knee and let him stretch it to the almost flat he'd managed to achieve about a week ago. At least he hadn't lost that.

"Did you feel something tear? Snap?" Her expression didn't hold the concern her questions warranted.

"No, it just hurt. A lot."

"Are you still experiencing a lot of pain? On a scale of one to ten—"

"Seven." Not quite put-me-out-of-my-misery, but talking wasn't his favorite thing right now.

"According to my notes, you had an eighty-seven-degree flex last week."

"It didn't feel like it was going to snap last week."

"Have you been on your feet a lot?"

"Yeah, I guess. I've been trying to walk without the crutches."

"Let's see you walk."

Oh, sure. Break my leg and then make me walk on it.

Mal reached for the brace, but Amanda waved him off. "Let's do a walk without it, then one with. You need to be working on your gait. You don't want to develop a limp."

Develop a limp? Hadn't that happened the minute a car hit his legs?

Mal got down from the table and stood on two legs. Pain shot through the left, the same ache he'd been dealing with for a while now without being able to tell if it was a new pain or just more of the same. He pushed off the edge of the bench and walked the line Amanda indicated.

Her brow creased as she watched him. "You're favoring your left leg."

"It's been aching."

"On a scale—"

"It's a three, if that. It doesn't hurt if I don't think about it. I figured it was the cold or the weather." It was one of those not-cold, not-warm days, where damp air hovered over old snow, turning the world an indistinct shade of gray. It made his left leg ache.

"You suffered a pretty catastrophic break," Amanda murmured, studying her notes. "Let's see if we can get in an X-ray."

"Now?"

"If you have the time."

Unease slithered through Mal's middle. "Okay."

The X-ray was about as uncomfortable as trying to walk, arranging his legs at varying angles while the machine burped overhead. Then came the wait. Mal pulled out his phone and surfed Facebook, not taking in anything until the receptionist called his name. He looked up to find his surgeon standing near the desk wearing a serious expression.

The unease snapped rather than slithered as Mal struggled up out of his chair and followed Dr. Chimo to his office.

Once they were comfortable, Mal perched atop another bench, Chimo in a chair in front of him, the surgeon angled his laptop screen toward Mal. It was one of his X-rays and the sight of his bones bristling with pins had his stomach clenching. Chimo traced a faint line high on his left thigh. "This is a hairline fracture."

"A . . . what?"

"It's not uncommon in your situation. We knew your left leg was going to be vulnerable during this recovery. It could have been a knock, or simply you spending too much time on your feet."

Mal thought about the long walk to his classroom and the fact he'd actually taken pride in being able to complete it without crutches this week, despite the nagging pain. "What does this mean?"

"Well, a few things." As the surgeon began to detail those few things, a buzz started up somewhere around the back of Mal's skull. He wanted to interrupt with questions, but he also didn't want to ask anything in case he didn't like the answers he got.

What he really wanted to know was: *Am I going to run again?* He figured marathons were out. Participating competitively in any sort of fun run was out. He could maybe walk or jog a 5K in a couple of years. But would he ever get back to running the Path? To being able to run in the evening—every step distancing him from the stress of his day, settling his thoughts, insulating him against . . .

"Am I going to run again?" he asked, wincing as his voice cracked.

Chimo arranged his features into an expression of professional sympathy. "You were fit before this happened. Strong. For older folks, injuries like this can mean the loss of a lot of mobility, a lot of what they had, because . . ." He worked one hand through the air in a vaguely circular motion. "They didn't have much to begin with. You're, what? Forty?"

"Fifty."

"You're doing great for fifty. We're not going to recommend contact sports, or stressful activities like skiing—"

"I just want to run."

"It's going to be some time and even then . . . It's too early to tell, Mal. I'd like to do some bone-density tests."

"What about hiking? Can I hike? I've been sectioning the Appalachian for about fifteen years."

The surgeon shrugged.

"And my knee?"

"First, you need a day or two off your feet. Elevate your legs and use some ice packs. They'll help more with pain relief than anything I can prescribe. Then, we need to adjust your physical therapy regime. I'm also going to give you something for the swelling around your knee. It should have subsided by now." Chimo leveled a considering look in his direction. "I'm going to be honest with you. You might not be able to run and you might not regain an even gait, but there will be a lot you can do. Hiking canes could get you onto a trail, and for longer walks around town and such, a sturdier cane. It will take some of the weight off your left leg and extend your upright time. Help you build strength in your new knee."

"A . . . a cane? Like a walking stick?"

"You're strong, Mal. Strong, fit, and you're committed. Let's do what we can, okay?"

Mal wasn't listening. All he could think was: A walking stick. Like the elderly used. He felt feeble and old and useless, and for the first time in a long time, very, very alone.

CHAPTER 22

I t had been an odd week. Brian's research had turned up exciting possibilities regarding the Colonial. Leo's betrayal hadn't dampened his enthusiasm for the project. Instead, it'd made him work harder. Delve deeper. Morristown might not want him, but before he left, he'd save this damn building. Having no one to share the project with got him down, though, and it wasn't because he liked to talk about his work. He missed having someone to talk with, about the interesting and the mundane. He missed Mal.

Wednesday night tired, lonely, and wondering if winter would ever end, he parked outside his condo and sat in the cooling car. Spending the evening with Josh required another sort of energy, and he wasn't sure he had enough of it. Seriously, how did people parent 24/7? Most folks started at the beginning, he supposed. Broke themselves in slowly. He'd always assumed babies meant sleepless nights and that the teenage years would be a vacation in comparison.

His phone buzzed. Brian extracted it from the inside pocket of his coat and nearly dropped it. Ellen had texted him. Hallelu— What?

Getting calls from truant officer. Need Josh back.

Brian woke the screen to tap out a reply. *I filed transfer paperwork with both districts. What's your email addy?*

A horrible swirl of uncertainty toured his midsection. Send Josh back? No, he wasn't going to do that. Josh wore him out, but he did like having his nephew around. He liked the idea of seeing Josh settled and happy and cared for. Loved even. Yeah, he could love the kid. They were blood, after all.

Tucking his phone back into his pocket, Brian exited the car and stomped his way through the cold evening toward the kitchen door, where the replaced pane always caught his attention because it was shinier than the others. Inside, the kitchen smelled like popcorn. Smiling, Brian called out. "Josh!"

"Here."

The answer had floated from somewhere else in the house. Probably the living room. Sure enough, he found Josh sprawled across half the sofa, phone in one hand, TV remote in the other. A messy pile of school books and notebook paper littered the coffee table.

"Homework all done?" Brian asked.

"Mostly. I'm trying to find this documentary on bees for my anatomy homework."

And that made no sense.

"Need to use my laptop?"

"Maybe." Josh glanced up. "You look rough."

Brian scrubbed the stubble he'd let grow across his face all week. Sometimes he didn't feel like shaving. "It's winter. Beard season."

Josh flashed him a quick grin before glancing at his phone where he replied to a text. Absently, Brian noted his own phone had yet to buzz with a return text from Ellen. "Have you heard from your mom?" he asked.

"Nope."

"Who are you texting with?"

"Just a friend."

"Is it Ethan?"

"What's up with you and Mr. M.? He kept watching the door on Monday. Yesterday and today, too."

Brian frowned. "Which door?"

Josh finally glanced up from his phone. "The classroom. He's doing extended hours now, so some of us in the club have somewhere to hang out after school."

"Huh."

"You didn't know? I thought you were helping organize the club."

Brian scraped his palm over his scratchy cheek again. "I've been busy this week. Monday and Tuesday I was chasing down leads on the Colonial. I have nearly everything I need to put together a proposal for the new owners." And he was telling the wrong person. Josh didn't care about a divey old bar.

Josh shrugged. "Okay. You coming to the meeting next week?"

"I dunno. Maybe."

"What happened with you and Mal?"

What happened to calling him Mr. M.? Though, Mal had invited the GSA kids to use his first name. "He, ah, I . . . It's complicated."

"Adults always say that when they can't figure out a way to explain something they think kids shouldn't know." With a look of studied nonchalance, Josh added, "You two not sexually compatible?"

Brian gaped. "We . . ." What was the right thing to say here? "We were very compatible."

"'Were'?"

"It's—"

A hurt expression creased Josh's forehead.

Brian breathed out a sigh. "Fine. He found out I'd been in a long-term relationship with someone, which, you know, is stupid because I'm forty-eight years old. I've had time to do a couple of relationships. But I wasn't good to Simon. My ex." He scratched his face again. "And you know what? He wasn't good to me, either. I don't know why I'm only figuring that out now. I mean, I'm the one who cheated, but there had to be a reason for it, right?" Rather than think about Simon's quiet words about not having had all of Brian, he focused on the extended advertisement for a set of copper pans currently playing on the TV. "I probably shouldn't get into details."

"You already told me you cheated. Does it get worse?"

"No. Maybe. I don't know. I never understood why I felt compelled to go after other guys, you know? It was dumb. Stupid. I liked the rush of being with someone new, but I always knew I'd go back to Simon. That I wanted to be with Simon. But . . . He's pretty spare with the affection. An animal in the sack, but outside the bedroom?"

For someone who didn't want to talk about his own sex life, Josh was all fascination, now.

Brian swallowed. "He could be so cold. No, not cold. Just . . . implacable." Which Brian had recently decided he liked. His emotions were all over the place. "Sometimes the only way I could get him worked up was . . . Well." Should he be discussing this with his nephew?

"How does Mal fit into all of this?"

"He thinks I was a lying, cheating bastard."

"Weren't you?"

"That's the complicated part. I was, but I'm also starting to realize I was in a relationship that didn't fit." Maybe it was this *wholly Brian* thing.

Josh allowed a sober nod.

"I wasn't trying to put you off before, when I said it was complicated," Brian continued. "It really was . . . complex. A relationship takes a lot of work and not everyone is cut out for it. For the commitment and for the emotional involvement."

"Is this your way of telling me I'm too young to know what I want?"

Brian shrugged. "Maybe. Or maybe it's my way of telling myself that I'm not a relationship guy."

Josh nodded again, and a quiet space opened up between them, broken only by the quiet oohs and ahs on the TV as an entirely too happy couple cooked all manner of things in their copper pans.

Right as Brian was trying to figure out if he could adapt the berry cobbler recipe to one of his own pans, Josh said, "I think you are a relationship guy."

Brian glanced over to find his nephew studying him with a serious expression. "What makes you say that?"

"You wouldn't have spent as much time trying to get into Mr. M.'s pants if you didn't want to date him."

"I could have just wanted to fu— Ah, get into his pants."

"Easier ways to scratch an itch. Are you on Grindr?"

Brian made himself shudder. "No."

"Why not? I figured your lying, cheating ass would be all over that." Josh's smile took any sting out of his words.

"It's not the same. I know you kids think the whole world happens online, but I much prefer meeting someone in person. A dick pic doesn't tell me how they smell, or what their smile looks like. If they've got any sensuality about them. If they can carry on a conversation past the opening line. What they like to drink. What makes them tick. Who they voted for and if they're out, proud, or not. If they're funny or boring. What sort of house they live in. What they do for a living and whether they enjoy it or not."

Josh was blinking at him.

"What?" Brian asked.

"And you think you're not a relationship guy."

Brian's phone buzzed, and he shrugged out of his coat while extracting it from his pocket. When he checked the screen, the warm fuzzy feeling he'd gained over the past half hour seeped in toward his soul and took hold, fingers digging in deep.

Ellen's email address. Josh was his to keep.

He placed his phone on the coffee table and picked the remote up off the couch. "Let's find that documentary. What did you say it was about?"

"Bees."

"And how does that relate to anatomy?"

"It doesn't, but there's this theory . . ."

Brian didn't get half of what Josh said, but he figured that didn't matter. He listened and he asked questions. Josh had listened to him, after all. Had given him some valuable advice too. There was more to parenting than paperwork and truancy officers. So much more. And if he had to watch bees do their thing for an hour before working out what Josh wouldn't eat that night, then that's what he'd do.

Fuck you, Ellen . . .

"Stop, I think that was it."

Brian pressed Play.

CHAPTER 23

M al tucked his new cane into the shadow of Brian's kitchen island and sat on the closest stool. As instructed, he'd taken yesterday off to elevate his leg and pack the affected area with ice. It had helped. Using the cane helped. He still wasn't used to being the sort of guy who carried a walking stick, though. Or the sort of guy who showed up at someone's house unannounced. But Josh had asked for a ride home and Mal and Brian really needed to talk. Well, Mal did.

"Want me to make some coffee or something?" Josh asked.

"No. I, ah—"

Keys jangled outside before the kitchen door whooshed open with a rush of cold air. Brian stepped inside, gaze pointed down toward his shoes. Mal swallowed thickly, wondering if he'd made the right decision in stopping by.

Brian looked up.

"Hi." Mal levered himself off the stool.

"What are you doing here?"

Not an auspicious beginning.

"I gave Josh a ride home from school. I can go."

Brian's brow wrinkled. "Can you stay a minute? I wanted to talk to you about Mondays."

"What about Mondays?"

"The meetings. I think you should find another volunteer."

Oh. So that was how this conversation was going to go.

"You're quitting the GSA?" Josh asked.

"Josh—"

"No. You spent a whole weekend telling me how important that damn club was. Practically forced me to go. You can't quit. I only went because you wanted me to."

"I wanted to go for you," Brian said.

Mal raised his hands. "Maybe I should—"

"Wait. Please?" Brian stepped fully into the kitchen and braced his hand on the center island. "Josh, I talked you into it because I wish we'd had stuff like that when I was in school, and I genuinely thought it could be a good thing for you. Also, I didn't want to go alone."

"Also, you wanted to get into Mr. M.'s pants," Josh said.

"And I wanted to get into Mal's pants. Yes."

Mal gaped. "Um . . ."

Brian shot him a grin, which died an oddly quick death. "But, hey, mission accomplished. Now we're all off the hook."

"Seriously?" Josh spoke up, taking the words out of Mal's mouth. "This is not the conversation we had last night."

Mal started edging toward the hallway. So he was a coward. Brian made it easy.

Josh looked from Mal to Brian and back again. "I'm going to go upstairs and listen to music. Loud music. So, um, maybe you two can talk."

Brian waved a hand, either acknowledging or giving permission, and Josh left.

Mal made to follow him down the hall until Brian blocked the doorway.

"I really think I should go," Mal said.

"I wish you wouldn't."

"Then why would you make a remark like that?"

"Because I'm an—"

"You're not an asshole, Brian. And if we're ever going to make something out of this, whatever this thing is we've got going, then you need to stop pretending you are."

Brian caught his gaze and held it, his soft blue eyes shaded with sadness. "I think I'm finally beginning to understand that."

"Good."

"I didn't tell you about Simon because it felt like it was this huge big deal. Usually guys don't want to hear about exes. That was in the past, right? Shouldn't be relevant. But even I know a relationship of that length is kind of relevant, especially when I'm the one who messed it up."

"How do you know that? It takes two to tangle."

"Tango."

"Whatever."

"Because I cheated on him. A lot. And I lied about it. A lot. That's why I think I'm an asshole, okay? Because I spent twelve years breaking another man's heart."

Not what he'd expected—not that he'd had a specific expectation for this conversation. Mal wasn't sure what he'd hoped to accomplish by giving Josh a lift home, except to put himself in close proximity to Brian. Because he missed him. Because he hadn't treated him fairly. And because he wanted Brian's side of the story.

"Leo said I should ask Simon about it because he'd tell the truth," Mal said.

"Yeah, well, there it is."

Mal gestured toward the hall. "Mind if I sit down and prop my legs for a while?"

"Oh, sure." Brian visibly shook himself. "Want me to get some ice or a heating pad?"

Mal felt himself smiling. "No. I just need to sit."

"Why are you smiling?"

"Because I really like you, Brian Kenway."

Brian's forehead wrinkled. "I am so confused."

"I like that too."

Brian followed Mal down the hall, a hand at the small of his back, and spent considerable time arranging cushions on the couch until Mal was propped, his legs stretched out in front of him, feet up on another stack of cushions.

Finally, Brian sat down on the love seat and leaned forward, elbows to his knees. "So, did you miss the part about me cheating and lying?"

"No."

"Why are you here, then?"

"Because I'm not Simon."

"Then why did you leave the bar?"

"Because I was hurt and confused and . . . I don't know. Confused. It's not like I haven't had a long-term relationship before, or thought you hadn't, but I had this picture of you in my head, and it didn't include a guy who looks like he was made by God's hands alone. A guy you spent all afternoon talking to and touching and gazing at as though you could see the marks of His craftsmanship."

Brian leaned back with a long sigh.

"Do you still have feelings for him?" Mal asked.

"No." Brian sought his gaze and held it, his expression solemn. "I miss him sometimes. That's the truth. But . . . we talked after you left, and I think I figured out what I've been trying to hold on to."

Mal's stomach twisted. "What's that?"

"That version of me, maybe? Of a guy who could do things right."

"Sounds like you did everything wrong. If you don't mind me saying so."

"The mind is a funny thing, isn't it?" Brian had his hands in his hair now, massaging back and forth. "I thought I was trying to hang on to something good because the most I ever did with my life was with Simon. But now I realize what I was hanging on to was . . . not rotten. But a corpse, nonetheless. I've been stuck in place." He moved his hands back to his lap, squeezing his knees. "Or I was, until I met you."

"I am so not crafted by a god."

"Funny you should say that."

"Why?"

"I was trying to tell Josh the other day that he's as God made him. I'm not big on religion, but that was one of the excuses Ellen threw out along with her son. Ellen's his mother. My sister. Can't remember if I told you that. But I got to thinking that we're all as we were made, aren't we?"

Mal considered that for a moment because clearly Brian needed him to think about it. To not give a glib answer. "Do you think that means we can't change?" he finally asked, wondering if this was the point of their conversation. If this was where Brian would tell him he'd always be a lying, cheating asshole and that they shouldn't continue to see each other.

And that made him more than merely sad. It hadn't been long, but losing Brian would hurt. He'd never been with a man like this. Someone so complicated, yet bright. A man with so much goodness inside, and who needed help exposing it. Help to be who he really was.

Brian glanced over. "I don't know. Have you changed? Are you the same guy who lost his football scholarship?"

"I didn't lose it. I had the grades to keep it."

"Jesus Christ. I found myself another Simon, didn't I?"

"What do you mean?"

"You were born perfect."

Mal wished he could push up off the couch without disturbing a hundred pillows and maybe tripping over the coffee table in the process. "No one is perfect, Brian. Not me, not Simon, not Charlie, not you. Not even Josh, though the blue hair is probably a step closer than we'll ever get."

"What do you mean?"

"Because he's trying to find his perfect, isn't he? While we're sitting here feeling old and mortal and maybe a little bit broken."

Brian's brow creased. "Is that how you feel?"

"Yes." And the weight of it was heavy and not at all supported by his ridiculous castle of cushions. "I was told this week I should use a cane. I've developed a fracture in one of the bones of my left leg. Too much standing or maybe not enough pins or just . . . I don't know. I'm feeling very mortal right now."

Brian got up and sat next to him. "I'm so sorry, Mal. I wish you could see yourself as I see you."

"I could say the same to you."

"You are such a complete person. You have this amazing career that you love. You're so great with the kids. You're part of a community. People like and respect you. You have a gorgeous house that you obviously take care of. Houses . . . they say so much about a person. It's like a structure. Your house is solid and dependable, but it's also well-kept. It's nice to look at, and dependable doesn't mean it isn't fun. There's so much of you there. All your weird little statues."

"My gaming miniatures. You saw those?"

"And your books and the colors you put on the walls, the plank you chose for your flooring. It was when I saw the inside of your house that I really wanted to get to know you better. I already wanted to fuck you . . . but that house, Mal. It's you."

"Wow."

Brian leaned in close. "I was going to let you cool off for a couple of days. Then try to explain the Simon thing."

"What sort of house does Simon live in?"

Brian grinned. "He lives at Charlie's place and Charlie's place is Charlie all over and . . ." His smile faded, but not in a bitter way. "And it's the sort of house Simon always wanted to live in."

"Oh God, is it messy?"

"Like you wouldn't believe."

Mal laughed. "I think this could be the oddest conversation I've ever had."

"You and me both. Can I kiss you yet?"

"Why?"

"Because that's why you're here, isn't it? So we can kiss and make up?"

"Yeah. But before we get to that part, I need to apologize."

Brian leaned back. "What for?"

"For overreacting." Mal held up a hand. "It's none of my business. You're right. The past is the past and . . . I should have left it there. I'm sorry."

Brian put his palm to Mal's and folded their fingers together. "I think it was a conversation we needed to have."

"Maybe." Mal swallowed. "You're new territory for me. I'm a look-don't-touch guy. I always have been. I daydream about being with men like you. About doing something other than go home to my cat and paint a battlefield with sixteen-year-old blood."

Brian blinked.

"Virtual blood. PlayStation? I'm not, um, very good at real life."

"Did you miss the part where I told you how great your life is? I've seen you around, Mal, and you want to know what's funny?"

"Always."

"You're new territory for me too. Took me a while to figure out how to approach you."

"Me? Why?"

"Because you're not a one-night thing. You're . . . I don't know what I'm trying to say."

Mal got it anyway, and beneath a searing blush, he was enormously flattered and somewhat humbled. But he believed Brian meant what he said, or rather couldn't find the words to say. Because if it had only been about the sex, then they wouldn't be sitting here with their fingers tangled together, staring at each other like this meant something. As though this moment had been foretold or some such literary wonderfulness.

"I wasn't sure if I should do this. Come here this afternoon," he said.

Brian smiled. "I'm glad you came."

"Haven't come yet."

Groaning, Brian leaned in and captured his lips in a soft, sweet kiss. "That joke is forevermore banished. Done. Never to be used again." He brought up a hand to cup Mal's cheek, his thumb hooking around Mal's ear, and the gesture, combined with the renewed kiss, plucked a chord inside him. Near his heart. This was the real Brian, the man underneath the brash exterior. This sweet and gentle being, perched next to him, careful not to put any weight on Mal's bad knee.

Mal lifted his chin to join the kiss fully, and brought his own weight to bear. His reality. His need. All he'd missed over the past four days.

CHAPTER 24

B rian hummed into the kiss, enjoying the flavor of coffee and brownies. Mal always had a different and decadent taste, as though he were a buffet of samples. Beneath, however, was the essence of the man Brian knew lurked inside the quiet exterior. The glasses, the book collections, and the weird little gaming things. The cat fur that clung to his clothes.

Pulling back, he plucked Mal's glasses from his nose, waiting for Mal to turn one ear toward him so he could unhook that arm. He set the glasses on the coffee table and put both hands to the sides of Mal's face before leaning in to kiss him again. Still softly. He wanted to devour this man, but he also wanted to worship him. Dot his face with small kisses. Touch his own tongue to the prickly line of Mal's jaw. Taste his full lips again. Kiss each eye closed.

"This would be easier upstairs," he murmured over the perfect shell of Mal's ear. "We could lie side by side and play."

"We could." Mal's breath was hot on his cheek. "How loud does Josh play his music?"

Brian laughed. "Loud enough. He heard me jerking off one morning and has kept his earbuds in since."

"Were you thinking about me?"

This was one of the things he liked most about Mal. His quick imagination. The fact he had such sexy thoughts and rarely appeared abashed by them. Brian dropped a kiss to Mal's lips. "Mm-hmm. You were in my bed, propped up against the headboard. I was straddling you, hips level with your face—"

"Fucking my mouth. God, yes. Let's do that."

"Really?"

"Can't believe you fantazied about me."

"Are you kidding?" Brian kissed him again. "Give me one of yours."

"You on your knees in front of the couch. You pretty much made all my dreams come true that night."

Grinning, Brian backed off the couch and held up a hand. "Then let's start on some fresh material." Mal tried to play off his awkwardness in getting upright and ascending the stairs, and Brian put a quick stop to it. "Not always going to be like this, and even if it was, the leg brace isn't you, Mal. Just be you, okay?"

They got to the top of the stairs, where the door to the spare bedroom was already shut tight. Brian paused for a brief moment, under the guise of letting Mal find his feet, and wondered if he was setting a bad example for his nephew. Then decided that Josh already knew he and Mal were sleeping together and that knowledge meant he was getting a better idea of what a healthy, adult relationship was all about. So long as he and Mal kept it healthy.

Okay, enough thinking for now.

Brian got Mal into his room and started undressing him. "You need to be anywhere tonight?" he asked.

"Nope."

"Good, because even though my dick is all 'Let's get busy,' I want to take my time with you."

Mal groaned. "Jesus, don't say things like that or it'll all be over before we get my pants off."

"Could work for us. A quick detour, then a long, leisurely drive?"

"I'm fifty, Brian. Did you know that?"

Brian kissed the self-deprecating smirk off of Mal's lips. "You're not dead, and I'm only a year and a half behind you."

He'd managed to get Mal's sweater and shirt off and took a moment to smooth his palms over Mal's shoulders, letting his thumbs trail through the fuzz of hair at the top of Mal's pecs. Bending, he flicked his tongue over one nipple, then the other. Mal's shudder answered the question of whether he liked that. Brian spent some time there, sucking and plucking, until Mal gripped his hair and pulled him back.

"You need to stop."

"Like that, hmm?"

"A little too much. And you're still dressed."

So he was. Brian remedied that situation, kicking his clothes into a pile just clear of the door, and then helped Mal with shoes, leg brace, and pants. Then came the stacking of pillows.

"Before we get to Fantasy A, can we lie together for a bit?" Mal asked. "Facing each other."

"We can do that"

Mal got on his right side, bad knee braced against the bed.

Brian slid in next to him so their bodies touched all the way down. "Oh, that's nice."

"Mmm," Mal agreed.

Brian leaned in for a kiss, and Mal met him halfway, their lips coming into contact only briefly before seeming to melt away as they fell into a deeper kiss. Mal wrapped one arm around Brian's shoulders and pushed his other hand to Brian's chest, fingers digging in at intervals as he explored, kneaded, touched. Brian looped his own arm lower, bringing their hips together, and their cocks clashed, hard flesh to hard flesh. Mal moaned into his mouth. Brian felt his ass clench. He liked the idea of thrusting into Mal's mouth, but having Mal inside him again was suddenly infinitely more appealing.

Grabbing Mal's hand, Brian moved it down between them, to their dueling erections. Mal immediately wrapped his fingers around both of them and tugged. "Hmm, so good."

"How long until you can put weight on your knee?" Brian asked.

"Too long. Want to fuck you so bad."

"Want that too."

"We could try side to side. Save the face-fuck for later." Mal paused. "Or the morning."

Brian grinned. "Morning. Yeah. Want to send you to school in the same clothes you wore yesterday."

Mal laughed. "You think you're clever, but I've got you on this one. I am the world's most boring dresser. All my pants and shirts look the same."

"Damn it." Brian squeezed a nipple. "Going to have to make you wear one of my shirts, then."

Mal pushed him away. "Go get your stuff and then give me that ass."

God, yes. "You're a hidden gem."

"What do you mean?"

"That quiet, reserved thing you've got going. The fact you don't mind topping. I had no idea how much you'd be into that."

Mal's smile was quiet. "You didn't consider the angles before approaching me?"

"Briefly? I wanted to get to know you, and I figured the sex stuff would either sort itself out or it wouldn't, but it never hurts to try."

A brief nod. "Just so you know, I'm flexible."

Brian felt his forehead crease even before he'd thought to frown. "Are you really, or is that what you decided you need to be?"

Disquiet flashed through Mal's eyes, there and gone. Then he gave another nod. This one firmer. "It's what I am."

"Good." Brian dropped another kiss to his lips before rolling away to find condoms and lube. When he rolled back, Mal was flexing his legs. "We good to go?" he asked.

"Yep." Mal made a beckoning motion with his fingers. "Gimme. I want to slick you up." He met Brian's gaze. "That okay? Want to feel you."

"God, yes."

Brian tossed the supplies over and lined himself up facing away from Mal, smiling as Mal molded himself to his back and kissed his neck. "You always smell like oranges. Why is that?"

"It's my shampoo."

Mal nibbled his neck. "Love it."

It was a casual remark, but Brian tucked it away as something to take out and cherish later. Sentimentality be damned. If Mal could love his shampoo, then—

"Ah!" A slick finger slid between his buttocks. Brian arched, giving Mal better access, and held in a needy whimper as Mal circled his hole, teasing and exploring.

"Feel so good," Mal said. "Hot."

Brian let all thought subside, then, even though his brain wanted to examine these words as well. Compare them to who he'd thought Mal might be and who he'd hoped for. Hold them up against the curiosity that had had him approaching this particular man with his broad, footballing shoulders and quiet, professorial manner.

Mal didn't tease for long. He seemed to assume, correctly, that Brian didn't require excessive prep. That he liked the burn. Brian held his breath until Mal touched his sheathed cockhead right there, pressing at his entrance, then let go and let him in. Mal slid forward slowly, giving them both time to adjust to the angle of being side to side, and managed to hit that magic spot on the first try.

"Ungh." Shuddering, Brian grabbed the pillow from beneath his head and dragged it toward his chest, bundling it into his arms.

The sensation of Mal withdrawing pulled Brian's hips backward, as though he was reluctant to let go. He was, but also needed to arch further. Wanted to further open himself.

"So beautiful." Mal touched his hip, curling his fingers into Brian's flesh. He kissed the back of Brian's shoulder. "You're so goddamn beautiful." He licked Brian's neck and drove forward. "So hot, so smooth."

Brian managed another inarticulate sound as he absorbed the thrust.

With every forward movement of his hips, Mal seemed to close around him. He wasn't measurably taller, but he was broader, and the feeling of him wrapping Brian from behind, holding him close as he drove deep, was almost more intimate than if they'd been face to face. He sucked and bit at Brian's shoulder, traced a hand up and down Brian's torso, pushing the pillow forward. Played with his nipples and stroked his hips. Ignored his cock until Brian thought to beg.

He could take himself in hand, but asking Mal for what he wanted held so much more appeal. "Touch me."

"Here?" Mal caressed Brian's upper thigh.

"My cock."

"Say please."

"Please, Mal. Please."

Mal stroked down as he thrust, curling his fingers around Brian's balls before withdrawing both his hand and cock at the same time, leaving Brian to float in some in-between place where he craved pressure from both sides. There it was again, Mal balls-deep in his ass, fingers wrapped tightly around his cock, and then away. It was almost like having two lovers, and Brian gave himself over to the sensation of both, jerking his hips forward and back, letting his body and need dictate the pace.

Arching, begging Mal to fuck him, pushing into Mal's hand.

Behind him, Mal let out a keen. His chest, tickling Brian's skin, was damp with sweat. Brian pictured Mal's nipples sliding against him. Reveled in the slight friction of body hair and skin. Groaned as his balls drew up tight. As Mal squeezed his sac, his cock, his hip. Bit his shoulder again. Thrust deeper, harder, faster. Panted, sweated, called out, and came, jerking against Brian's hips with bruising force.

The grip Mal had on Brian's cock slackened as he gave way to the tide of his orgasm. Close and wanting to be there, coming with Mal, Brian wrapped his fingers around Mal's hand and stroked harder and faster. Mal hugged him from behind, panting noisily against the nape of Brian's neck, and the combination of his pants, murmurs, and skin—the tightening of his fingers again—his very presence there in the bed—worked to bring Brian to the edge of the cliff and toss him over the other side.

He came so hard it felt like he'd fallen off the bed, and facing away from his lover felt odd all of a sudden, as though he were in this alone. Then he jerked back against Mal, felt their connection once more, the slide of Mal's cock in his ass, and he almost started coming again.

Brian lay with his thoughts shifting between the cool air at his front and the warm man at his back until Mal withdrew, eliciting gasps from both of them. Mal rolled away, and Brian heard the condom snap and hit the floor and wondered, vaguely, if Mal had tied it off before he tossed it aside. He probably had. Would it matter if he hadn't?

Rolling onto his back, so they were lying side by side, Brian let his head flop toward Mal, who wore a lazy and contented smile. "How's the knee?" he asked.

"Still there, trying to hurt, but so far down the scale of importance, it's barely registering."

"Know what the best part about getting together while you're recovering is?"

"Finding a position that works?"

"That." Definitely. "And knowing that we might still be getting to the good stuff."

Mal seemed about to take offense. For a second. Then he laughed. "The good stuff might actually kill us."

Brian managed a quiet chuckle. "But what a way to go."

Sobering, Mal simply gazed at him for a while before showing a smile that could be called shy. "So, about Josh's headphone situation. If we're going to continue looking for accommodating positions, you might want to get something noise canceling."

Was this Mal's way of asking if they were going to continue seeing each other? If so, it was cute and awkward and very, very Mal. Also damn practical, which for some inexplicable reason, warmed Brian right at the center of his chest. Where his heart was. God, he could fall for this guy. Fall hard. Had maybe already started on the headlong slide.

"You're looking kinda thoughtful over there," Mal said, his expression sliding in a direction Brian would not allow him to go in.

Rolling toward him, Brian put a hand to Mal's cheek and leaned in to kiss him. Sweetly, because that was their thing, and because he loved the feel of Mal's lips against his. "You were pretty loud," he whispered.

"Me? I think the neighbors know, to the second, when you came."

A memory of his yell echoed not so softly in Brian's ears. "Noise-canceling headphones it is, then."

CHAPTER 25

The morning of the Winterfest dawned cold and lonely. Mal poked at the snow with his cane, waiting for Brian's car to turn into the end of the street. His cell phone rang, and he had to take his glove off before extracting it from his pocket. Organizing his hands and gloves and cane and phone was frustrating. He was going to miss the call. Hurriedly, he swiped the screen before checking the number, and pressed it to his ear.

"Hello?"

"Brian still picking you up?"

"Yes, Donny. Jesus. He'll be here any minute."

"Are you outside?"

"Yes."

"Why are you outside? It's freezing."

"I'm fine, Donny. See you soon." Mal hung up, returned the phone to his pocket, and was fiddling with his glove when Brian's car pulled up alongside. Then Brian was out of the car, hands to either side of Mal's face, gloved palms warm against Mal's skin as he leaned in for a hello kiss.

"Oh my God, you're cold. Why are you waiting outside?"

Mal smiled into the kiss and wondered how long it took to develop an ache in the happy muscles.

"Someone's sunny this morning," Brian observed.

"What's this thing you needed to tell me?"

Brian had been keeping a secret for the past week. Mal guessed it was the good kind of secret, because Brian smiled every time he mentioned it. Still, Mal didn't like not knowing something.

"Soon." Brian tweaked his nose. "I like it when you're this happy."

"Doesn't take much. No snow is a good start." Having his nose tweaked by Brian shouldn't be an excellent follow-up, but what the heck. "C'mon, I've got the tables and chairs ready to load up."

"Snow would make the theme, though, right?" Brian said, smacking the roof of the car. "C'mon, Josh, there's stuff to carry and you're younger and fitter than we are.

Mal led the way up the driveway. "Do you remember last year's festival?"

Brian blinked. "Not sure I've ever been to a Winterfest."

"Never been to a— How long have you lived here?"

"Hmm, maybe ten years?"

"Tourist."

Brian laughed. "Whatever." He cocked his head. "Wait, last year it snowed, didn't it?"

"Yep. It was a freaking blizzard. We got about an hour in before everyone packed up to go home and mostly ended up getting stuck on 202."

"Good times."

"Speak for yourself."

Brian slung his arm around Mal's shoulder. "And this year, we've got Mr. Sunshine warming the day."

Scoffing, Mal pushed him off. "Enjoy it. Supposed to snow again by the end of next week."

"I so regret thinking that you guys being together was in any way good," Josh said, holding a hand to his stomach.

Brian tackled his nephew, putting him in a headlock, and Mal watched them tussle for a moment, thinking this much happiness should be a warning. Or maybe it was their reward. Brian hadn't had an easy time of it lately and neither had he. Maybe it was their turn.

Together they hauled the table and a couple of chairs to the car. The short drive to Morristown Green passed in companionable silence. Then they hauled the same table and chairs (Brian and Josh on the table, Mal limping along behind with a folding chair under each arm, cane dangling from his wrist, legs sore, always sore, but doing their job) down Speedwell to N. Park and Morristown Green, which already had the appearance of a half-dressed circus. Pavilions filled half the festival space, the rest of them being assembled. The smell of coffee bit at the cold air, and every time Mal walked past someone clutching a grease-stained bag of hot donuts, his mouth watered. The food end of the festival would be warmed by barrel fires and gas lamps. The opposite side already glittered with assembled ice sculptures, many sponsored by local organizations, a handful still being crafted by local artists.

The last snow had melted earlier in the week, leaving the ground an off shade of browny-green that didn't complement anything. But by the time all the pavilions were set up, the tables arrayed in front of the food trucks, the makeshift stage erected and strung with pennants, and the sound of conversation and ice picks filled the air, the color of the ground faded to insignificance. The Green felt full of life and a bit like a party, despite the chill.

By ten o'clock, Mal had eaten three donuts and was finishing his second cup of coffee. His kids had signed up to work their table in shifts, and the first two groups were already there, red cheeked and bright-eyed. Optimism radiated from their faces. Donny and Rachel had visited and given the stall a halting stamp of approval, even though a vital component was missing.

Mal let out a relieved sigh as Leo and Kelsey arrived, each behind the handle of a wheelbarrow. Their ice sculpture was here, and obviously not grand if the huddle beneath the small tarp wasn't supposed to click together like ice-Legos. But it was here.

Leo put down his barrow handle and whipped back the tarp. "Ta-da!"

A grinning Kelsey blew on his hands.

Brian started laughing. Donny was clearly trying not to laugh, probably because Brian was, but soon gave in, clapping his hands to his sides.

Mal couldn't figure out what the lumps in the barrow were until Rachel asked, "Is that two frogs kissing?"

Kelsey was pulling something out of his coat pocket. "Here are their crowns."

"I think you should stick to painting," Mal muttered.

Kelsey seemed to be trying, unsuccessfully, for a hurt expression. "You're right there."

"They are sort of frog-like," Brian put in.

And they were, once you knew they were supposed to be frogs. Maybe the crowns would help.

Mal squeezed Kelsey's arm and gave him a smile. "Thank you. Kissing frogs is perfect. We'll be memorable!"

They got their ice sculpture set up, crowns in place. Now they just needed the flyers that Brian was having printed. The idea for their stand was two-fold: people would come to see . . . two frogs kissing . . . and make a donation to fund the LGBT drop-in center. Which still had no location.

Pamela pushed her way through the crowed, her arms loaded with wrapped bundles of flyers.

"Hooray, the day is saved!" Ethan said.

Josh and Brian exchanged a look that might have been secretive.

Frowning, Mal extracted a bundle from Pamela's arms and studied the top flyer. "This is a sketch of the Colonial." More than a sketch, actually. It was a complete drawing, with a vague, architectural style about it. The inked lines had been shaded here and there with hints of color. Mal glanced at Josh. "Did you do this?"

Josh answered with a shy smile.

"It's great, but why do our flyers have a picture of a bar on them?"

"Read it," Brian prompted.

Judging by the not-shy smiles on Leo's and Kelsey's faces, they already knew what it said. Mal read the flyer.

"Oh my God!" He looked up. "Is this true?"

"Yep." Brian rubbed his hands together. "It's perfect, right? We get to save the bar, the whole row, and the second floor will make a great drop-in center. It's a good location, close to the school. Olive from the café has already indicated she'd be interested in catering for it."

Brian had it all planned out except for one detail: who would be staffing the place. But that was a worry for later. First, they had to save the building.

Mal looked back down at the flyer, reading the first paragraph: *The Wheelhouse Building, erected in 1837, served as part of the Underground Railroad network between 1847 and 1852.*

A brief history of the other uses of the building followed, ending with the Colonial Tavern, described as an institution close to the heart of Morristown High School and Football alumni. Reading it over again, he had to blink mist from his eyes. The pitch was perfect. He doubted anyone reading this would fail to be moved. Brian might just have found a way to save the building . . . and to add to its history.

"This is amazing." The uneven ground jostled his knee as he stepped up to give Brian a hug. Wincing, he leaned against Brian's chest. "I wish you'd told me, but it's a great surprise." He watched as his students crowded in close, many of them reading their own copy of the flyer.

Ethan was grinning. "This is going to be great." He exchanged another look with Josh, then, and it was less secretive than before.

Someone bumped Ethan from behind, and he tripped forward before falling to his knees, exposing two boys behind him, both snickering into their hands. Josh whirled on them, and one of the boys held up his hands in mock dismay. "Oh no, Ethan. Your new girlfriend is growling at me."

Josh was growling . . . and advancing.

Brian put a restraining hand on Josh's shoulder, and Leo loomed over the boys, both of whom were probably larger than him, but so damn young.

"You got a problem?" Leo snapped. He had disgruntled pared down to an art form. Even his dreads were more crooked than usual.

One of the boys backed up, but the other sneered. "Yeah. With you. What are you going to do about it?"

Leo held up a hand, causing both boys to flinch. He extended a finger and tapped it as though preparing to make his first point. "Nothing. Because I'm an adult. Now grow up."

The boys stood there for a minute, probably waiting for the second point.

Leo waved them off with a growl, and they backed away, obviously confused.

Josh had wriggled free of Brian's hold and was trying to talk to Ethan. They'd moved off to the side, their conversation low but heated until Ethan shoved past Josh saying, "Just leave it."

Josh acquired a kicked-puppy expression as Ethan strode away. When he started after Ethan, Brian grabbed his shoulder. "Give him some space, okay?"

Mal stepped up to Josh's other side. "Text him. Let him know you're here. But don't crowd him. He's probably got a lot to think about right now."

Mal could feel Brian nodding next to him.

Josh nodded as well, and stalked off in the opposite direction.

Brian let out a sigh. "I warned him not to get involved with that kid."

"Ethan is good people. He won't leave Josh hanging."

"You sure about that?" A dark shadow lurked behind the blue of Brian's eyes.

Mal inspected the ground, now churned up by the passage of many feet. It'd be a total mess by the end of the afternoon. He glanced up and shrugged. "Either way, Josh will be okay. He has you, Brian. Support begins at home, right?"

Brian's answering smile was as grim as the cloud in his eyes.

Mal jostled his arm. "How about another donut?"

Brian's smile softened. "Fine, I'll get us another bag. But if you vomit red jelly all over the ground, I'm not holding back your hair."

Mal widened his eyes. "You wouldn't? We might need to talk about where this relationship is going."

"Don't make me say rude things about donuts. There are juveniles present."

And said juveniles needed the adults to stop flirting and step up to the table.

CHAPTER 26

B rian was returning from the food vans again—this time with a wrapped cheesesteak for Mal, who seemed to have a bottomless appetite for festival fare—when someone called his name.

He glanced toward the sound, the movement almost furtive. People didn't often recognize him for good reasons. Picking the distinctive figure of Franklin Tern out of the crowd, Brian couldn't decide whether having Simon's best friend track him down in the middle of a street fair was good or bad. Probably bad.

What had he done now?

Rather than drag trouble back to the GSA setup, Brian stepped out of the flow of traffic and waited for Frank to catch up to him. Belatedly, he noticed Frank's sidekick had come along for whatever this was. Thomas Benjamin could be intense. Brian liked his energy, particularly when it came to the resort renovation Brian was overseeing for them. It was a big job and Tom wanted it done right. Tom had a dark aspect, though. Something Brian recognized and never wanted to discuss. But the effort of keeping their conversation light always came at a cost. Every time he walked away from Frank and Tom, he felt even more like an asshole than he had waking up that morning.

Frank pulled up in front of him. In comparison to Tom, who was small and dark—almost elfin—Frank was a large man. And sunny. His hair was bright, his hazel eyes always seemed to shine with humor, and his lips crooked in a perpetual smile.

Brian greeted him warily. "Frank." He added a nod for Tom. "Hey." He looked around for Simon, didn't see him, and glanced back at the pair standing in front of him. "What can I do for you?"

"If you could see your face," Frank said.

Brian lowered his eyebrows. "Not in the mood for games."

"Well, that'd be a first. But we're not actually here to mess with you. We came to help."

"Help?"

"Simon said you were raising funds for a drop-in center for LGBT youth. It's a worthy cause. I won't say I'm surprised, but . . ." Frank's small mouth made a convincing grin. "Okay, I'm surprised."

"Did you come all this way to mock me? You couldn't have waited until next time I came by the site?"

"Oh, I'll mock you then too."

Brian glanced at Tom, wondering if he planned to jump in at some point, but Tom was too busy pointing one of his ever-present cameras at the crowd. As a photographer, he quite often viewed life through one of his lenses.

Brian returned his attention to Frank. Held up his foil-wrapped bundle. "Let me drop this off, and then we can go argue somewhere else."

Frank moved to follow him, and Brian practically barked, "Stay here."

Expression softening, Frank put a hand on his arm. "I know we're not friends, but we really are here to help."

"How?"

"Tom's doing what Tom does." Tom's camera clicked several times in agreement. "And I want to write about your club."

"It's not my club."

"Your boyfriend's club, then."

"He's not . . ." A horrifying prickle seared a path across Brian's forehead. His cheeks heated.

"Brian Kenway. Are you blushing?"

Yes. Because he didn't want to jinx things. Nor did he want to define what made him happy. Not yet. He wanted to keep doing whatever he and Mal were doing and hoped everything worked out the way he'd like it to work out—which he should figure out at some point.

"Why do you want to write about the Morristown GSA?" Brian asked. "Don't you have one in Stroudsburg?"

"I'm sure we do. Probably several given that our school district is chopped up into pieces. None of those clubs are trying to raise funds for an LGBT youth center, however."

"Maybe they should."

"Definitely. And me writing about this one may prompt them to try."

Tom glanced up from his camera at that, giving a quick nod. Brian took them both in, their serious-yet-calm expressions, and realized they were telling the truth. They hadn't come to mess with him. They'd come to . . . help.

"Did Simon put you up to this?"

Frank scoffed. "He mentioned what you were doing and we put the rest together ourselves. Satisfied? Now, can we meet Malcolm?"

"Um, sure."

Frank patted his arm again. "Uncertainty becomes you, my dear."

Tom snickered, but his smile was good-natured. Wide and friendly. He held up his camera. "I'd love to get some shots of the bar as well. Simon said you were involved in another project?"

"They've become one project. I found evidence to suggest the building the bar is in used to be a part of the Underground Railroad, which might be enough to save it from demolition. And the upper floor could be used for the youth center."

Frank beamed. "Brilliant! Well done." He elbowed Tom, jostling him back a little. Tom recovered quickly, as though used to amiable shoves from his outsized lover. "See, I told you this would be worth the trip."

"Actually, you said—"

"Never mind what I said." Frank made an imperious gesture. "Shall we?"

Swallowing a sigh, Brian led the pair to the GSA table. Mal seemed to be saying goodbye to a couple, half of whom was putting her checkbook back in her purse. *Excellent.* Mal turned, wincing slightly, and grabbed one of the pavilion poles to steady himself.

Brian quickened his stride. "Sit. Jesus. Before you fall down. How're your legs?"

"Fine." Mal's scowl said otherwise. Light flashed from his glasses as he turned toward Frank and Tom. He waved one of the kids toward them. "Can you—"

Pamela stepped up, brandishing a flyer. Frank listened to the whole spiel with the sort of attention that made him a good journalist. For the entire time she spoke, Pamela was obviously everything to him. Then he started asking questions.

Tom was photographing the melting ice sculpture. Frowning at it, he asked, "Frogs?"

"Frogs," Brian confirmed.

Snickering, Tom resumed his clicking.

"Friends of yours?" Mal asked.

"Not exactly. I'll introduce you in a sec. Here, let's get you a seat—" a quick cutting motion stopped Mal's protest "—so you can eat your lunch." Brian dropped the cooling cheesesteak into Mal's cupped hands and then, because Mal looked so damn adorable staring at his lunch as though he'd discovered a chest of treasure, Brian dropped a kiss on top of his head as well.

Mal glanced up with a smile. "Hi."

"Hi."

Frank finished his interview and stepped under the pavilion. He tucked away the flyer and held out a hand. "I'm Frank. A friend of—"

"Simon's," Brian provided.

Mal's eyebrows twitched together. He shook Frank's hand. "Mal."

"We've heard all about you," Frank said.

"You have?" Mal darted a glance toward Brian.

Brian shrugged. "Simon has become a gossip in his old age."

"Hasn't he, though?" Frank chuckled. "The idea of him even being talkative is hard enough to deal with. But having to watch what we say around him? Ridiculous."

"Frank's here to do a story on the GSA and the drop-in center," Brian said.

Mal's expression brightened. "Oh, that's great. Wow. Thank you."

"Of course. Anything for a *friend*."

Brian shook his head.

Chuckling, Frank patted his arm. Again. "Why are you so touchy, Brian?"

Brushing Frank's fingers away, Brian said, "I could ask the same of you."

"I'd forgotten how much fun you are to tease."

"Brian?"

Brian turned to find Vanessa standing on the other side of the table, wearing one of her perfect outfits and a bemused smile. Damn, he was glad to see her

"Ness." He rounded the table to kiss her and pull her into a hug. Then it was time to do the introduction thing. Everyone shook hands, except Mal, who was up to his elbows in onions and grease and looking for a napkin. Then everyone stared politely at one another, as though figuring out who should speak first.

Then Josh wandered in from the side, face lighting up as he spied his favorite artist. "Vanessa! Uncle Brian didn't say you were coming today!"

"That's because he didn't know," Vanessa said.

While Vanessa was exchanging hugs with Josh, Frank sidled up close enough to whisper, "'Uncle'?"

Brian flicked a glare in his direction. "Not a part of your article Got it?"

Frank gave a quick nod. "Got it."

One of the bands that had surreptitiously wrapped itself around Brian's chest eased a little, until he spied Vanessa handing Josh an envelope. "What's that?"

"Our check for the center. I thought I'd drop it off in person. Gave me a reason to visit my two favorite people."

Frank leaned in a little closer to Brian. "You're someone's favorite person?"

A return insult hovered on the tip of Brian's tongue for about a second before he decided to let it go. Prove he could be nice. "Is it so hard to believe?"

Frank was looking at Mal as he said, "No. Not really."

Josh opened the envelope and bugged at the check inside. "Oh my God." He blinked and peered again. "Um, is this for real?"

Brian knew it was. He'd discussed the figure with Vanessa. It was generous. Half of the amount they needed to fund the drop-in center generous. More than the Smart Foundation could actually afford, but an "anonymous" donor had made up the difference.

Mal touched his hand and Brian glanced down. "Thank you," Mal said, his voice barely carrying beneath the shouts of the other kids.

Frank and Tom angled their way into the quickly growing crowd, gathering material for their story, no doubt. Frank waved over the heads of the students. "Vanessa. Could we get a picture of you handing the check to one of the students?"

"Sure."

Brian took the opportunity to drop into the chair next to Mal's. Their hands were still touching, so he curled his fingers around Mal's and squeezed. A ghostly hand did the same to his heart as he watched the students yell and squeal with happiness and the reaction of the onlookers. Vanessa's gesture would make the day for them. People would pull their checkbooks out twice as fast now. The GSA would get the funding they needed for a drop-in center.

The only obstacle remaining was saving the Wheelhouse Building.

Brian couldn't say it felt good, but . . . Fuck it, he could. To think, a few weeks ago, he was ready to pack up and leave this town. Now, he was kind of— No, he *was* enjoying being a part of it. Squeezing Mal's hand again, he leaned over to brush a kiss over Mal's cheek.

Frank wanted to interview Mal next. Brian gave up his seat and moved with Vanessa to a position behind the table, giving the kids room to hand out their flyers and chat with the folks attracted by the hubbub.

"So when were you going to tell me about Mal?" Vanessa asked.

Brian said nothing.

Her coy smile widened. "So it's like that, is it?"

"I don't know what you mean."

"Oh, yes, you do. It means you can't be upset about my engagement anymore."

"Still no idea what you're talking about." And damn the smile that wanted to creep across his mouth.

With a touch less humor, Vanessa said, "I like him for you. I really do. He's . . ." She bit her lips. "He's the sort of guy I always pictured you with, to be honest."

"Keep your voice down."

Vanessa narrowed her eyes. "He looks like he knows you. The real you."

"We're just getting started, Ness. It's only been a few weeks. And you know me. I like to—"

"You can't bullshit me, Brian. You think you can, but you can't. I've known you for far too long. Mal is so your type. You like to pretend that you like young, pretty men, but how long has it been since you hit a bathroom stall with one of them?"

"Goddamn it, Ness. Stop. You're not my fairy godmother."

Uncharacteristically, her eyes glistened. Her voice softened. "I am, though, Bri. I was the one who found you on the streets of Newark, remember?" Vanessa pressed the back of her hand to one eye, and then the other. Then, clearing her throat, she asked, "So does this mean you're maybe not interested in opportunities on the West Coast?"

He'd put out a feeler or two after his conversation with Simon that Sunday afternoon. Hadn't followed up on any of them, though.

Swallowing, Brian turned to Vanessa and let the one person who really knew him see how he felt. First came the happiness he'd been carrying around like a delicate glass bauble. How much he liked Mal. How much this one man had changed his life—and not because Brian had changed what he wanted. He'd simply met it, *him*, finally.

Then came the fear. Of loss, that he'd screw it up, that Mal wasn't invested as he was—which was stupid, because he could see Mal was. Felt it in every brush of fingers, every searching look. Outside of good sex and warm camaraderie, Mal made Morristown feel like home.

Beneath the fear was terror, because Mal didn't know where he'd come from, and Brian didn't know if it was something he could share. If it would be too much for his gently broken history professor. Maybe after they finished putting Mal back together. After Mal began to believe he still had a lot to offer, a lot to do, whether he needed a cane for the rest of his life or not. That he was a completely worthwhile human being, and that anyone could see it. Even someone who didn't think they themselves were worthwhile at all.

Vanessa took his hand and brought it to her cheek. Brian drew her into a hug and absorbed the strength he needed from her quiet understanding. And he thanked God Vanessa *had* been the one to find him, and had been the only person thereafter to never let him go.

CHAPTER 27

The Billings Group offices in Jersey City were housed in a shining pillar overlooking the Hudson River and Lower Manhattan. As they navigated the tight, one-way streets to the underground parking, Mal tried not to read too much into the fact they'd had to come here rather than entertain the hotel execs at Brian's offices in Morristown. He couldn't help feeling somewhat displaced. And he couldn't stop thinking about what he'd overheard between Brian and Vanessa. The first part, about Vanessa liking him for Brian, made him smile. Lit him up inside. The other part not so much—Vanessa asking Brian about the West Coast, and Brian's lack of answer.

He remembered Brian mentioning that the Colonial might be his last project, but had tucked that away beneath the cozy layer of togetherness they'd knitted since.

When the black pit of the parking lot swallowed the gray February day, Mal decided it wasn't some sort of omen. Parking lots were a thing; they had them in Morristown.

He also decided their pitch was going to succeed. Too many people were counting on them for it to be otherwise.

"I think this is the farthest I've been from home in about eight months," he murmured, tucking his phone into his pocket. "I feel like I've been locked up in a monastery or something."

"We're not going to comment on that until later." Brian flashed a leer at him.

Mal returned a smile.

Visitor parking was located close to the bank of elevators. A small mercy. Brian took care of the large portfolio he'd brought along while Mal got his legs organized. Inside the elevator, they tweaked one another's clothes. Brian had opted for a suit, and Mal had gone "full professor," hoping his position as a teacher would lend weight to their proposal.

Brian rubbed a thumb over the sleeve of Mal's wool blazer. "The elbow patches on this coat are like the sexiest—"

Mal cut him off with a fast kiss. "Later." He rocked back with a grin.

"Thanks for coming with me today," Brian said.

"Of course. This project is important to both of us. To our friends. The kids. I have to be here."

"You're not going to play with your phone when we're—"

Mal looked down to find his phone in his hands. When had he pulled it back out? "You're cute when you're anxious," he said, squeezing the familiar shape of his cell once before putting it back away.

Brian's eyebrows drew together. "I'm not anxious."

"Says the sweat on your upper lip."

Brian pressed the back of his hand there, caught Mal's eye, and pushed his curving lips closed.

"We've got this." Only one of them was allowed to be anxious, and that was Mal's job.

Brian returned a sober nod.

The elevator dinged, and they exited into the lobby of the chain's corporate headquarters, a wide, spacious area with wall-to-wall windows showing off the views. Brian approached the reception desk and waited for the young man there to offer a greeting before stating their purpose.

"Good afternoon. I'm Brian Kenway. My partner and I have an appointment with Xavier Billings."

What a tool of a name.

Brian kept his smile short and professional, though from the appraising glint in the receptionist's eyes, he could have added a little sugar and maybe ended up with a date for later that afternoon.

The receptionist pecked at a recessed keyboard with one manicured finger. "What did you say your name was?"

"Kenway."

"And you had an appointment?"

"Yes. For 1 p.m. this afternoon."

"I'm not seeing you on his schedule."

Brian extracted a card from his jacket pocket and pushed it across the counter. "I called a week ago. It's regarding property in Morristown."

All business now, the receptionist glanced at the card, but made no move to take it. "I'm sorry. I'm not seeing anything here. Can I schedule another appointment for you?"

A different brand of insecurity rose through Mal's middle.

"No, you cannot. Our meeting is today." To anyone else, Brian probably sounded formal and in control. Mal could hear the exasperation, though.

"The building we're trying to save is marked for demolition," Mal explained in his quiet teacher voice. "It's important we speak with Mr. Billings today." He fumbled for his pocket. "I can show you the email with the appointment reminder."

Brian spread a hand over the top of the reception desk. "We don't need much time. Obviously there's been a mix-up, but we're here now—" he lifted his portfolio "—and we have all the details with us. Ten minutes will be enough."

The receptionist made a call and asked them to take a seat. Mal edged toward one of the low bench-style arrangements, wondering if they'd be left there long enough to fuse with the leather. Brian wandered over to the closest bank of windows, and Mal joined him there instead.

"Receptionist looked as though he'd like to make a completely different appointment with you," Mal murmured.

A flash of hurt crossed Brian's blue eyes.

Crap. Mal touched his sleeve. "I'm sorry. He's just—"

"If you say 'young,' you'll do yourself out of a good fucking tonight." Brian glanced over to meet Mal's eyes.

"Sorry. Now's not the time."

"No, it's not."

"Mr. Kenway?"

A man stood by a glass doorway. He had what Mal would term a dumpy shape, barely held in check by a dark wool suit. His fleshy face carried an unhealthy pallor, and his expression indicated he hadn't particularly enjoyed the walk to reception.

Brian extended a hand. "Brian Kenway." He gestured toward Mal. "My associate, Malcolm Montgomery."

"Xavier Billings. If you'll follow me?"

Billings led the way to a conference room right behind the lobby, another wide space with views, and held the door before following them into the room to hover by a chair at the head of a long table. That he didn't sit indicated he didn't have a lot of time for them. Mentally, Mal cut their presentation in half and then spent a full thirty seconds panicking about whether or not Brian would understand that they didn't have time to start at the beginning.

He's a professional.

This job is as important to him as it is to you.

Stop panicking.

Brian laid out the portfolio and reached for a picture of the Wheelhouse Building.

"We're here on behalf of the current tenants of the Wheelhouse Building in Morristown." He handed Billings a photo that showed the building to good effect. There was no hiding the age or neglect, but the afternoon light picked out the glorious red of the brickwork and the faded lines of old renovations. The period windows and doors. The bar and café signs were lined up in an aesthetically pleasing way and didn't seem quite as tattered as they did from the front.

Nostalgia rose up inside of Mal as he took in the details. This was his town. His home. His bar. A place he wanted to make for his kids.

"I'm familiar with the building," Billings said.

"We believe it would be a mistake to tear it down," Brian continued, "and have a proposal for renovation that would add value to the community. Are you aware of the building's history?"

Billings looked up from the photo. "The Underground Railroad connection? It's been mentioned, yes. It's not verified."

Mal nudged a packet forward. "We have verification."

Billings raised one eyebrow. "Do you know how many buildings in the northeast were supposedly a part of the Railroad? It's barely noteworthy."

Sensing they were losing control of the meeting, Mal said, "The historical implications tie well into the proposed use of the upper floor. A local organization has raised the funds necessary to create a drop-in center for disadvantaged youth—"

Billings held up a hand. "I appreciate you gentlemen coming all this way, but a center for homeless kids isn't the sort of property we want across the street from our hotel. Nor a rundown bar and café. Morristown has a vibrant city center. There are dozens of other eating and drinking establishments, many with a history all their own. The fact is, neither of these businesses is necessary—"

"We're not talking about homeless kids," Mal said. Brian put a warning hand on his arm, but Mal pressed on. "The LGBT community has little to no support, and those kids need this center. They need a place to go when they feel threatened or uncomfortable. A safe space. They just want the same opportunities as everyone else."

"I'm sure you have a YMCA."

Brian's expression hardened. "I think you misunderstand—"

"No, I think you do, Mr. Kenway. There is nothing special about this building. It's not performing a unique—"

"This is an opportunity for the Billings Group to give back to a community that welcomed it," Brian said.

Mal jumped in. "Outside any past history, the bar and café have a lot of recent history. Did you know the bar is named for the high school . . ."

Billings was checking his watch.

"Morristown doesn't need another soulless glass building. There is no view, there, Mr. Billings," Brian said. "There's local flavor and pride."

"Pride." Billings sighed. "Yes, that word gets thrown around by you people a lot, doesn't it?"

"'You people'?" Mal felt a flush rise across his cheeks. "Did you really just—"

Brian put a hand on his arm. "I think we're done here."

"No, we're not. We're not close to done. They're going to—"

"Mr. Billings's mind was made up when he got out of bed this morning."

Billings affected a weary expression that clashed with the snap and burn in Mal's chest. How had this meeting gone so badly? How had they failed? He couldn't even process the idea they'd had no chance of winning. That their trip to the city had been for naught.

Brian started gathering their papers, stuffing them into the portfolio.

Mal grabbed one and slapped it down onto the conference table. "No. We're leaving one here because this is a damn good proposal, put together by a community, including the kids who will one day look at your hotel, your name, and either regard it with respect or bitterness. A community you came into, that accepted you, that was excited by the prospect of hosting your business. Think about that and about what 'pride' means when you're asking someone to throw it away for you."

He turned and stalked out on stiff legs.

Mal thought he was going to be sick. "How did that go so badly?"

Brian shook his head before glancing over his shoulder to check traffic on the interstate.

"I mean . . . I . . ." *Don't have words, apparently.* Thoughts swimming, Mal tried to figure out where they'd gone wrong. "Should we have gone through the whole presentation?"

"I read the situation, saw we had maybe five minutes, and went with the most compelling image."

"Maybe Simon's sketch would have been better."

After a few seconds of tense quiet, Brian nodded. "Maybe."

Intellectually, Mal knew Brian's choice of presentation matter hadn't made a lick of difference. As he'd said, Billings had woken up that morning knowing the answer to their question. Heck, he hadn't even had to consider it, which was probably why their appointment had mysteriously disappeared off the company schedule.

Mal studied Brian's profile. His jaw was tight, a muscle flicking below his ear. His posture straight and square. But he had a lazy grip on the steering wheel and his expression didn't register the same turmoil Mal felt in his gut. He hadn't sabotaged the meeting on purpose, had he? Set them up for the wrong date?

"Are you not upset about this?"

Brian gripped the wheel a little harder. "Of course I'm upset."

"You don't look it." *Stop, Mal. This isn't the time.*

"And you're an expert on how I look now?"

"No, I didn't mean . . ." Mal rubbed at his forehead, then removed his glasses and let the traffic outside the car blur. His eyes ached. "I feel like I lost a race and you're . . ." He gestured with his glasses.

"I'm what? Not torn up enough?"

"This is stupid. I'm sorry."

Brian blew out a breath but kept his gaze straight ahead.

Mal pulled out his phone and scrolled aimlessly through Facebook, not really seeing anything, even with his glasses perched back on the end of his nose. The longer he bent forward, the sicker his stomach seemed to get. He sighed. "I'd have thought with a gay receptionist, they'd be more open to our pitch."

"That was rather naïve of you, then."

Mal snatched another glance at Brian. "I heard Vanessa asking you about the West Coast. Is that why you, we . . . Does this mean you're done?"

Brian jerked his head in Mal's direction. "What?"

"At Winterfest."

Brian turned back toward the road. "Can we talk about this later? I need to concentrate on driving."

Swallowing, Mal leaned back in his seat and fiddled with his phone again, turning it over and over in his hands. His thoughts tumbled along with the steel and plastic, reaching no useful conclusion by the time Brian merged with Route 24.

Then he took a breath and a chance. "I just need to know if this means—"

"It means the Billings Group is going to knock down the Colonial. That's what it means, Mal. That, and only that."

Not quite the answer Mal had been looking for, but Brian's refusal to address the other issue had to mean something, didn't it?

"So what do we do now?"

Brian didn't respond for a while, leaving Mal to wonder if he'd actually spoken. Then, quietly, Brian said, "I don't know."

"You inquired about other property for the youth center, didn't you?"

"Yeah, I did. There are a couple of alternatives, but none of them are as central as the Wheelhouse Building."

"None have the history, either."

A shrug.

"Brian, I'm sorry about the West Coast thing. I know it's probably none of my business and I shouldn't have brought it up now. I . . ." *Like you.* Which shouldn't be relevant, except that it felt like it was.

"Is that what the quip about the receptionist was all about?"

"No. Yes. I . . ." Time for another forehead massage. "I'm working on my confidence. I am. It's been . . . I'm sorry."

Brian glanced over at him. "I did look. But do you want to know what I saw?"

A young face, lightly tanned with impossible cheekbones and warm brown eyes. Black hair showing no hint of gray, and gelled away from a nice, square forehead. Lips that would—

"I saw you, Mal. Your face. I saw the face of the man I am with. The man I like being with. The man I went to Jersey City for. The reason I started on this project."

Ouch.

Not knowing how to answer that, Mal let an uncomfortable quiet blossom between them for the remainder of the drive. He didn't fiddle with his phone. He didn't adjust his glasses. He sat there, feeling like stone. Dry and sort of achy. Guilty. Still a little ill. And wrapped around it all like a heavy cloak, a sense of failure was weighing him down. By the time Brian turned into Mal's street, Mal had nearly convinced himself the entire venture had failed because of something *he'd* done. Maybe he hadn't been pushy enough. Had he let Brian do most of the talking? If he'd spoken up earlier, could he have saved the proposal? Had his lack of confidence sabotaged their efforts from the start?

He didn't notice the car had stopped until Brian touched his hand. Glancing through the window, Mal saw his house. "Thanks." His voice creaked over that single word.

"Mal?"

Mal met Brian's calm blue gaze.

Brian didn't say anything for a while. The radio hummed softly, and a light wind buffeted the sides of the car. The afternoon faded beneath a low-hanging crochet of soft gray clouds. *Looks like it might snow.* The urge to check his phone for a weather update tickled Mal's fingers. But he kept his eyes locked to Brian's until Brian spoke again.

"What was your longest relationship?"

Brow wrinkling, Mal shook his head. "What?"

"You know all about my most significant ex, but I know nothing about yours."

"Oh." Mal went to turn away, and Brian caught his chin. Gently.

"What did he do that made you feel like you weren't worth the effort? Did he..." Brian's swallow was audible. "Did he cheat on you?"

"No." Mal curled his fingers into his palms and squeezed. "We broke up about seven years ago."

Brian let go of his face, but Mal didn't try to turn away again Quietly, he ordered his thoughts. "It ended because he wanted kids and I didn't. Not... not with him."

"Why?"

"Because I couldn't imagine spending the rest of my life tied to someone who thought I was less." But hadn't that always been his story? "Noah was... is a money-market guy. A trader I don't know what he did, really, except make money. I don't even know what he saw in me, except an easy lay. Convenient? I was always home. Because I'm boring. But I'm reliable and I guess he figured I'd be happy to raise his family because he knew I liked doing things for him."

God, he sounded like he was twelve, and thinking back, he must have seemed...

Mal moved one of his hands through the air, before curling his fingers inward. "He was the gorgeous one, the confident one, the guy everyone liked, and I was the awkward one, cute and sometimes adorable, but not... I don't know. I was okay with that because I thought we were in love. But literally the second he mentioned kids I knew it was a lie. That I didn't love him, that I hadn't for a while, and that we weren't right. So I left, which was damn awkward as we were living in my house. I went to live with my brother until Noah moved out, and then I redid everything. Kitchen, bathroom, painted the outside blue."

Tears misting his vision, Mal peered through the gloom at his house. At the place he'd made his and his alone. Beside him, Brian maintained one of those silences he was so good at.

Finally, Brian asked, "How long were you together?"

"Eight years."

"Fuck."

The gray afternoon made Brian's profile granite. Mal resisted the urge to touch the side of his face, to try to warm one of his cheeks.

When Brian turned to face him again, his expression seemed deliberately blank. "I'm not planning a move to the West Coast. I'd thought about it, briefly, when it seemed like this town might be getting ready to chew me up and spit me back out. But then you and I did what we've been doing and I forgot all about it." He drew in a quiet breath. "I don't want to spend the next however many years reassuring you that you're worth it, though. That might be a selfish thing to say, and it's not that I don't want to do it; I just wish there was a way to let you know now, once and for all, that you're . . . you. And that's exactly who you should be. I chose you because you're you. I chased *you*."

Mal bobbed his chin in tacit agreement and allowed his thoughts to take a further step. Would now be the right time to tackle Brian's asshole complex? That'd make this conversation feel more even. But then he wondered if they were having a conversation at all.

"I'm going to head home," Brian said.

Mal's heart dropped through his chest. His stomach pushed upward.

"I'm tired and I want a drink. I want not to think for a while," Brian continued, apparently oblivious to the organs shifting around inside Mal's torso.

Mal swallowed dryly. "Okay."

Brian took Mal's hand again, cupped his fingers around the palm and squeezed. "We'll talk tomorrow. The next day. Let's chill for a bit. Then we'll figure out what we're going to do."

"About us?"

"About everything."

Mal got out of the car, watched Brian's taillights disappear into the gathering gloom, and then continued to stand beside the curb, wrapped in a weird bubble of unreality. Outside his skin, snow had started to fall. Inside, his heart was moving in a different direction. Up and out, as though the top of his head had split open and his self was flowing over the sides of his skull, spilling out and getting lost. He didn't understand the feeling, but could guess at what lay behind it.

The day's failure loomed large. Felt unreal. Surely he'd wake up tomorrow with good news to share with the school, the students in his club, with Leo. *Shit, Leo.* But the fact Brian wasn't running felt larger. For once, Mal didn't feel quite so alone. Yes, he had Donny. He always had Donny. But contrary to twin theory—which as often encompassed fraternals as identicals—they were separate people and had been for most of their lives.

Brian was . . .

Brian had gone home alone to brood. He'd given Mal something to think about and then taken off to go wallow—and as suddenly as Mal felt the cold seeping through his insubstantial layers, he understood what was wrong with that picture. Why he continued to stand on the side of the road, looking after taillights that were long gone.

Now wasn't the time for him to be awkward. Now was the time for him to show Brian he was here. Could be and would be. That their partnership was more than a failed business venture. That he was committed to this.

That fear wasn't going to hold him back.

Mind made up, Mal hefted the keys in his hand and approached the garage instead of the front door.

CHAPTER 28

Brian sat in the car for a while after pulling into his driveway, watching the first snowflakes melt against the windshield. The failure of the meeting nibbled at the edges of his thoughts, and his conversation with Mal prickled, but he let the icy frame forming on the cooling glass take precedence, drawing his mind into an ever-narrowing circle of coldness. Not that he was packing his emotions away. He was saving them for later.

When he couldn't see anything through the windshield, Brian got out of the car. He thought he heard voices from his house. Tucking the folio under his arm, he strode toward the kitchen door, ears tuning in along the way. Had Josh mentioned having someone over this afternoon? Maybe Josh and Ethan had sorted themselves out. God, he hoped so. Mopey teenagers were particularly unfun.

Brian had his hand on the door handle when one of the voices shrieked, "Now."

A shiver pinched his shoulder blades together. It couldn't be . . .

Brian pushed open the door, and sure enough, there in his kitchen stood a tall woman, hair the same color as his had been before he'd realized his highlights were actually silver, not gold, and eyes a similar shade of blue. Her profile was familiar but not quite how he remembered. Older. Harder. More attractive in an odd and startling way. But she looked like him. She looked like her son.

"Ellen."

His sister turned to face him and the years fell away. It was her expression—fury and disgust. "You." Spittle flew from her lips with the single word. Tucking her hands onto her hips, she said it again. "You . . ."

Apparent anger sliced through the rest of the sentence, rolling across the space of the kitchen to nearly knock Brian back out of the door . . . and for a second, he nearly let it.

Nearly let the string of time—knotted at such a similar moment—unravel, yanking him back toward the single most painful incident of his past. The day he'd been told he was an abomination, unnatural, deviant, not wanted. The day his father had . . .

A throb of pain piercing the middle of his skull, Brian pushed back against the cord of memory. This was *his* house. "What do you want?" He kept his voice quiet, but couldn't do anything about the venom cutting each word short and sharp.

"I want my son back."

What? This wasn't part of the pattern. His parents had never asked him to come home.

Of course, they'd have had to find him first.

Brian found a word. "Why?"

"Because he's my son?" Ellen's answer was rich with sarcasm.

In the darkest corner of the kitchen, Josh had become a ghost of himself, much as he had been the night he'd broken in: pale, cold, and lost.

"Josh," Brian said. "You okay?"

Josh shook his head.

"Do you want to go home?"

Without looking up, Josh shook his head again.

Brian lifted his chin toward Ellen. "I think you have your answer."

But it wouldn't be as easy as that. Ellen advanced, her beautiful face made ugly by contempt. "Why can't he speak for himself? What lies are you pushing into his head? How did he know where you lived, huh? How long have you been tainting my son?"

"I didn't even know I had a nephew until he showed up the night before Christmas."

"Uh-huh. Likely story. Maybe he'd not have got the notion to be a deviant if he hadn't known you."

"Do you really think I'm the only gay person he knows? Or that you know? You probably passed a couple on the highway, Ellen. You might have touched one when you were paying for your coffee yesterday."

Her eyes narrowed.

"At least one of Josh's teachers is gay. Several of his friends. More than one of his relatives."

"You need to stop spouting your filthy agenda and tell my son it's time to come home."

"His home is here. Josh is happy here."

Ellen leaned forward. "You diddlin' him?"

Brian staggered back a step. "Am I . . ." He could feel his mouth opening and closing as he grappled for the right response. To understand what his sister had just asked. Implied. "You . . ." Brian let his horror show. "No, Ellen. I have never behaved inappropriately toward my nephew. I think you're the only one here who has that honor."

"You think I—"

"I think you kicked your son out of your house with nothing but the clothes on his back and then let him blow in the wind for nearly two months. I'd call that pretty damn inappropriate. Wouldn't you?"

"I knew he was here."

"What if he hadn't been?"

"What do you mean?"

"Did you even stop to wonder what might happen to Josh out there?"

"He'd learn to take care of himself. Stop being precious and soft. Learn to be a goddamn man." Ellen looked him up and down. "Not that it worked for you."

Oh boy. So not going there. Not if he could help it.

"And now that Josh has apparently learned to be a man," Brian asked, "what do you expect of him?"

"What do you mean?"

"Do you think he's going to come home and suddenly not be gay?"

"That's his choice, isn't it?"

"Which part? The home part? Because you should know his sexuality isn't a choice."

"Of course it is. Like the color of his hair."

"No. It's not."

Ellen gestured sharply. "I didn't come all this way to argue with you. I want my son back."

"Why?"

"What business is it of yours?"

"Why do you want Josh to come home? Is it because you've realized he's your boy, no matter who he is, no matter who he loves?"

Eyes narrowing again, Ellen turned toward the corner where Josh continued to hide. Brian would say he'd never seen such a miserable boy, but he had. In the mirror, some thirty-three years previously.

Focusing back on Brian, she spoke in a low hiss. "Because I am not going to let you take something else away from me and pervert it, Brian. You wrecked everything with your filthy behavior. Stole something from me. I'm not about to let you do that again."

Brian grabbed the kitchen island and held on until he could get a stool under himself. He didn't know what he found more shocking: that Ellen still hated him, after all this time, or that she didn't get it. Had no idea what she'd done.

Yes, he'd taken something from her, but it had been someone she'd probably have been better off without. He'd received no thanks for that. Then again, he'd never expected it. Ellen had always, always disliked him. And he'd always wanted something more from her than anger and spite. She was his sister. Closest to him in age. They'd looked so much alike when they were kids that they could have been twins. He'd loved her. Adored her. Worshipped her.

His head stopped swimming. Maintaining his grip on the counter, Brian stared straight into Ellen's eyes. "Would you like to know what you stole from me?"

Ellen replied with a derisive sound.

Brian directed his next comment toward Josh, whose own Kenway gaze, blue as a spring sky, flicked back and forth between his mother and his uncle. Should he do this? Should he kill any last spark of love Josh might have for his mother? Was it right? "Josh." His voice was hoarse. "Do you love your mother? Do you want to go home?"

The kid's face crumpled like a used tissue. He shook his head and blubbered. Managed a word, "No."

Ellen shrieked. "I found him in bed with my boyfriend, Josh. That's the kind of man he is. All naked and tangled up with the boy

I loved. You can't trust him. Brian is a lying cheat and an asshole. He deserves everything he got."

Josh's eyes widened.

Brian felt sick. Swallowing, he said, "Why don't you share the rest of the story?"

"We kicked you out. Mom and Dad wouldn't stand for that sort of behavior in the house and neither will I. Josh can be gay if he wants—"

"It's not a matter of 'want'!"

"But while he's under my roof, he'll live by my rules. He can do whatever he wants when he's an adult."

"So, what, he has to come home and not be who he is for how many years . . . three, four? And then you can tell the world you were a good mother. Is that how this works, Ellen?"

Her eyebrows dipped. Her chin wobbled.

Brian would never have taken a show of vulnerability to be the cue he'd need to eviscerate someone, but apparently he was that person: cruel and spiteful. Or maybe he was done with words that had no real meaning. Rules that only applied to one half of an equation.

He started out low. "Did you ever wonder what happened to me after Dad finished beating me to within an inch of my life and Mom showed me the back door?"

Ellen shook her head.

"I hid in the shed at the back of the O'Malley's yard. For four days until I could walk without feeling like I had a knife poking in my side. I'd sneak into the house when everyone went out and get something to eat. Change my clothes. Mom caught me one day and I thought that was it. That she'd call Dad and he would finish me off. Kill me. Do you know what that feels like?"

He'd lost the low and was heading toward the high.

"She gave me twenty bucks. Twenty fucking dollars and told me to get so far lost, no one would ever find me. I figured it was because she cared. Because she didn't want my father to kill me. But, no, she just wanted me gone. So . . . I got lost. For eighteen months, I got so lost that by the time Vanessa found me, I barely remembered my name."

Ellen's face was hard, but her eyes flashed with emotion Brian didn't want to acknowledge.

"Want to know why that was, dear sister? Do you want to know what happened to me because you found me with a boy who only pretended to love you because it gave him access to me? Because you decided your heart was broken and that it was all my fault?"

She shook her head, but Brian hadn't been waiting for her answer. He couldn't have stopped now, even if someone had put a red sign in front of his face.

"I lived on the street. Under bridges, in abandoned buildings, deep doorways, and sometimes, if I was lucky, I scored a bench at the park. You'd think that in summer, it wouldn't be so bad, but that's when it was the worst because you couldn't sleep at night. Nighttime was when the boogeymen roamed the streets, looking for kids like me. Homeless, hungry, and willing to do anything to feel real for half an hour. That's how I fed myself, when I wasn't waiting out the back of restaurants for scraps or digging in dumpsters. That's how I got the money for aspirin when I was sick."

Ellen looked about ready to pass out, but still Brian couldn't stop. "Suck a cock, eat for a day. Let someone fuck me and I'd maybe have enough money to live through whatever fever had me that week." Every word that spilled from his lips left a mark behind, as though he were ripping pieces of himself away and offering them up toward some twisted ritual. But if he stopped now, he'd fail at something important. So that he might as well have gone back home and let his father grind him into little bits.

"I was so ill when Vanessa found me that I thought I had actually died. I'll spare you the details of how sick and how long it took me to recover, except to say that if not for the kindness of her uncle, a man who died three years later because no one cared enough about him, either. Because he had AIDS, he was a terrible person, right? Deviant, filthy, wrong." Brian squeezed his eyes shut. "Tristan Smart was the most beautiful man I've ever known. He saved me. When everyone else either wanted to kick me along the street, or use me like a cum rag, Tristan encouraged me to be more. He was dying the whole time I stayed with him, and still he made sure I lived."

The kitchen swayed around him. Brian readjusted his grip on the counter and struggled for breath. His throat felt raw, as though he'd been shouting. Maybe he had. Swallowing, he worked to modulate his tone. To be reasonable. To give a conclusion to the most impassioned speech of his life. Make all his pain worthwhile. "So don't tell me you know what being a parent is. It's not giving birth, that's for sure. And it's not kicking your son out of the house for something he can't help. Hell, it's not even kicking him out for something he can help. It's about loving him." His voice broke. "It's about loving whoever he is. Not because you have to, but because he's there and you're all he has."

Josh ran from the room, and Ellen stumbled away from the counter with a hiccupping sob. Brian opened and closed his eyes, willing his pulse to settle and the kitchen to stop moving. It almost felt as though he were having a heart attack, except for the lightness of his skin. The self he'd peeled away and flung at Ellen like strips of carrion.

Maybe it'd been wrong to lay it all out like this, but he couldn't let Josh go home knowing where he'd come from. Knowing what love was not.

Clearing his throat, he found his sister by the window and said, "I made all of this out of that. I lived, Ellen. I made it and I'm damn proud of what I am. But I had to do it all on my own and it hurt. Every birthday, every Christmas. Not having my family with me. Not even knowing if they cared if I'd lived or died. Don't do that to him. Please. Either love him for who he is, or let me love him. I'm begging you. Don't hate him because of what I did. I paid for it, a thousand times over."

Ellen shook her head—not in denial, maybe not denial. Shock simmered in her eyes, backlit by guilt. She wasn't going to give in though. Not for him and not for her son. He'd said too much, had revealed too much. He'd broken her when all he'd wanted to do was to somehow stitch the wound he'd left behind all those years ago.

Or maybe he hadn't wanted that.

Maybe he had wanted this.

Feeling his shoulders pull down as though the weight of a house had settled across his back, Brian turned his gaze toward the kitchen island and the myriad colors threading the granite countertop. His throat harbored a sob, but he was determined not to let it free.

Then he heard it, that whisper of agony, and it hadn't come from him.

Looking up, he turned and there, framed by the half-open kitchen door, was Mal, his face almost pink against the snow falling behind him, his forehead pinched, mouth open.

CHAPTER 29

Mal stumbled, his legs finally giving out, and hit his shoulder against the doorframe. He'd been trying to keep still for about ten minutes now, but his cane didn't want to grip the icy edge of the path. As he slithered down the frame, landing in snow not yet deep enough to cushion his fall, it wasn't the cold that came as a shock. Or the awkward jarring of his right knee. It was that Brian hadn't leaped up to help him. Brian, who always had a hand at his shoulder, his back, his hip—who hovered as he climbed in and out of cars, chairs, doorways.

After scrambling into a sitting position, Mal gripped the doorframe with one hand and the handle of his cane with the other. By the time he regained his feet, he was panting . . . and Brian was gone.

Mal opened the kitchen door fully and limped through. To the right stood a woman he took to be Ellen. She looked like Brian. Like Josh. Blond and blue-eyed. But she wasn't pretty. Not at that moment. She might have been once, before life had hardened her.

She stared at Mal for a handful of seconds, gaze unfocused. Then she gathered her belongings, the coat slung across one of the high stools, a purse, and pushed past him and out the door. Turning to watch her go, Mal wondered if he should hobble after her. Ask her to wait.

He went to look for Brian instead, and found him in the hallway, crouching in a shadow.

"Bri?"

Brian didn't respond. He didn't seem to be all there, either.

Steeling himself for yet another trip to the ground, Mal put one hand against the wall and started down. His right knee creaked in protest. His left leg ached dully. Once on his knees, he canted forward, resting his hands on Brian's folded legs. "Brian."

Brian met his gaze.

"Hey," Mal said.

"I shouldn't have—"

"Don't say anything. Just listen, okay?"

No response.

"I'm sorry. For all of it. I know that sounds stupid. I couldn't have known. There was nothing I could have done."

And would he have, even if he and Brian had known each other back then? Probably not. How many kids drifted off the edge of the map every year, unnoticed by classmates and friends? Teenagers were selfish creatures and adolescence was freaking hard.

Shaking his head, Brian pushed at Mal's hands, edging them back toward his knees.

Mal found it hard to grab a single thought out of the maelstrom pounding against his temples. He imagined Brian felt much the same. Something huge and terrible had happened and like all huge and terrible things, it could not be undone. Rocking back, Mal reached for the wall again and pushed up to his feet.

He extended a hand toward Brian. "Come on. I'll, um, make coffee."

Jesus.

When Brian failed to move, Mal was tempted to give in to panic. What was he supposed to do in a situation like this? How did one help a man who . . . what? Mal didn't even have words for what had happened. Gazing down at Brian crouched in a dark corner of his own hallway, however, he couldn't help but imagine the boy Brian must have been, picture him huddled somewhere else. Somewhere dark and unkind. It was such a different perspective on the man who always seemed to have a smile, who was outgoing and easy in any company, that Mal had a hard time marrying the two personalities.

Except that he could, couldn't he? This was what lurked behind Brian's sometimes dark looks. This was the undefinable thing Brian hated about himself.

Damn it, I don't know what to do.

Should he call his brother? Rachel? Emergency services?

"I was so ill when Vanessa found me . . ."

"Do you . . ." Mal's throat closed. "Should I call Vanessa?"

Brian's head snapped up. "No." He sort of climbed the wall then, pulling himself up hand by hand until he stood next to Mal. "I'll . . . be . . . fine."

"Go sit down."

Without waiting to see if Brian complied, Mal escaped to the kitchen. He braced his hands against the island in the middle and breathed into the ticking quiet. Cold air swirled around his legs and wrists and a quick check of the kitchen door showed it still hung open. The effort required to close it felt like all too much, but Mal did it anyway, shutting out the snow, imagining he was also shutting out the world.

He got coffee started and searched through Brian's pantry for snack food. Brian was obviously in shock. He needed something to eat and drink. Some quiet time—probably alone.

Damn it, he'd come here to cut through that step. To tell Brian he was done being awkward, and here he was interrupting something more than awkward.

Should he go?

No. God, no. Brian had been trying to take care of him for weeks now. It was way past time for him to do the same.

Mal pulled cold cuts and cheese out of the fridge and slapped together a sandwich. Filled a mug with coffee, collected both, and made his way back down the hall. Brian was in the living room, perched on the edge of the leather sofa, head tipped into his hands.

Mal set the mug and plate down on the coffee table and lowered himself onto the love seat. Silence opened between them like a dark and ghostly flower, marred only by creaking floorboards upstairs as Josh moved across his bedroom, and the scrape of a plow down the street outside. After a minute, the footsteps overhead stopped and the plow moved on and the silence became a loud and impenetrable thing.

Mal was trying to figure out how to break it when Brian finally spoke. "You should go."

"I don't think so," Mal said.

"I need you to go."

"You need me to stay. We don't have to talk about what just happened." Mal didn't even want to talk about it. Wanted to forget what he'd heard and didn't care if Brian never talked about it. Deep down, though, he knew he'd listen when the time came because that was what friends did, and he and Brian were friends. Lovers, but also friends.

Why had it taken him so long to realize that?

"I came over to talk about before, about how I was being an ass. But we don't have to talk about that, either."

Brian was shaking his head. "Please, Mal. I need to be alone."

"Eat your sandwich and I'll go."

"I don't want the fucking sandwich."

"Drink—"

Brian looked up, his hands falling by the wayside as he uncurled and . . . snarled. "Go. Just go."

Mal lurched back in his seat, face stinging as though he'd been slapped. "Listen—"

"Do you understand what I did?"

Mal licked his lips. Swallowed. Shook his head. There was an answer here, but he didn't have it. Not the right one.

"I broke everything I've worked so hard to build. Tore it all down. I've worked so hard to get over what she did, what my sister made happen. I'd even convinced myself it was maybe my fault."

"Not your fault."

"It doesn't matter, does it? I . . ." Brian scrubbed palms over his face and covered his eyes. "I didn't want to be that person. This person. God, Mal. Please, can you just . . . I need to—"

Brian broke off with a quiet sob, which pulled Mal up off the love seat and over to the couch. He sat awkwardly next to Brian and put his arm around Brian's shoulders, wincing as Brian tensed.

"I wish you'd go," Brian said again, his words wet.

"I can't."

Brian scrubbed at his face again, wicking moisture away from his eyes. "I'll call you tomorrow."

"Brian . . ."

"I'm asking nicely. Please don't make me angry. I'm not a good person when I'm angry."

"I don't care."

"Mal, please."

Mal stood up. While he searched for something to say, he twitched his sweater into place and plucked at a crease in his pants. He looked down at the top of Brian's head, a view he hadn't had very often, and wondered if Brian had always been smaller than him. They were of a similar height, but right now, Brian seemed shrunken. Broken. His hair wasn't perfect, his eyes were red.

Leaving would be wrong, on so many levels, but Brian's need for him to not be here was almost stronger than Mal's conviction. Leaving wouldn't be giving in to his awkwardness. It would be . . .

"No."

Brian looked up. Opened his mouth.

Mal held up a hand. "I'm not walking away. Not this time. You can hate me for staying, but I'd hate myself more for going. You need me here. And if you want to talk about being selfish, I need to be here."

Brian tried to talk again and Mal quickly overrode him. "I'm going to leave you alone for a while, okay? Give you some space. I'm going to check on Josh, and then I'm going to head home and feed Lois. Pick up a clean shirt and maybe a bottle of whiskey. But I'm coming back, okay? I am coming back."

A soft sound emerged from Brian's still-parted lips. His expression indicated he wanted to argue, but then he nodded.

"Right." Mal backed up stiffly on his sore legs. He made it up the stairs and tapped on Josh's door. No one answered, but he could hear movement inside. He'd check in again later. When he got back downstairs, Brian was right where he'd left him, sitting on the couch. He didn't seem to notice Mal passing by the hall.

Outside the snow had tapered off, but not by much. The wind had simply died, letting the snow drift straight down in wide, fat flakes. A few melted on his cheeks as he poked his way back along the path toward his car, and they felt a little like tears. His throat was too dry to cry, though, and Brian's pain wasn't his.

He'd save his sorrow for when Brian didn't let him back in.

CHAPTER 30

Brian ate the sandwich, drank the coffee, and cried over both because he had no idea why he'd wanted Mal to leave. And now that Mal was gone, he wanted nothing more than Mal's quiet implacable presence at his side . . . He'd be back, right?

Swallowing over gathering heartburn—he'd eaten too fast—Brian let his body unfold so that he lay sprawled on the couch. Pain festered along his limbs. The truth always hurt. Would Mal be able to put aside what he'd heard? Could they pretend it was a movie they'd watched together, one they'd silently agreed not to talk about?

Not likely.

Sighing, Brian closed his eyes. God, he was tired. But the inside of his lids brought no comfort. He kept seeing Mal's face. Ellen's and Josh's. Kept hearing himself reveal aspects of a story he'd never told anyone. Vanessa hadn't asked, and Tristan hadn't had to.

The world lurched, and Brian gripped the couch cushions opening his eyes. He looked around the bland space of his living room the neat and tidy house he lived in but didn't think of as home. The sandwich pushed back up his throat. Swallowing convulsively, Brian launched himself off the couch and made it to the hall bath in time to lose huge, undigested chunks of bread and meat and cheese.

Without examining himself in the mirror, he rinsed his mouth and washed his face and hands, then stood facing the towel, watching his hands tremble against the fibers. Shit and shit and shit. He had to pull himself together. Figure out why he felt so sick. Why he was reacting so badly to a truth that had lived inside him for so long Maybe he really needed the day he'd asked Mal for. The oblivion of sleep. Maybe the world would have righted itself by the morning.

Brian made for the stairs. He'd have a bath—and not drown himself in it. Then he'd go to bed and watch something mindless until he fell asleep. He'd resist the temptation to drink. He'd think about how not to think. Tomorrow would be a new day. A better day. He'd fix everything tomorrow.

He paused by Josh's door and cocked his head to listen for the faint echo of music. Silence, not quite as profound as the space that had stretched between him and Mal downstairs, pushed through the painted wood. Brian knocked. Josh didn't answer.

Brian opened the door and knew Josh was gone. The room felt empty, and the quiet of the house was suddenly just as profound as the space between him and Mal. No, worse. With trembling hands, he opened the closet. Josh hadn't had a lot of clothes and most of them were missing. His school bag was gone, books dumped out on the desk by the window. He'd taken the phone charger from beside the bed.

Hands still quavering, Brian dug into his pocket for his phone, even as his brain informed him it was downstairs in his coat pocket. He took the stairs two at a time, checking the front door as he passed. Chain slipped. Josh must have gone that way. While Brian was in the bathroom? Or while he'd been sprawled on the couch in a funk?

Brian yanked the door open and rushed outside, catching himself on the rail at the top of the steps as his shoes slid through three inches of snow. A trail led down the front walk and into the street, turning left toward town. The shallow indents were already filling with fresh snow.

"Josh!" He couldn't see anyone at either end of the street, but called out anyway. The falling snow cloaked his voice, making it too soft. Slipping and sliding, Brian ran toward the corner, but saw no one around the bend. He patted his pocket again, swearing, and turned back to the house. He needed his phone. He could call Josh. Text him. Tell him to come back.

Tracking snow down the hall, Brian pushed through the kitchen and snatched his coat from the back of a stool. He didn't even remember putting it there, or setting the folio on the island. He found his phone, woke the screen, and dialed. Josh didn't answer.

He tapped out a text: *Please come home.*

He might not think of his house as any place special, but for Josh, it could be a home.

After waiting another few minutes for an answer, Brian pulled on his coat and grabbed a hat and scarf from the pegs in the hall. He looked up Mal's number and stared at his phone. Mal would answer, wouldn't he?

Of course he will!

Mal answered with a cautious "Hey."

"Do you have Ethan's number?"

"What?"

"Josh is gone. He packed a bag. I don't know where he is."

"But I just checked on him. Are you sure?"

"His room is empty and his backpack is gone. He took his phone."

"Jesus. Hang on." After much rustling and cursing, Mal returned to the line. "I'll text it to you. Listen, I know Ethan's mom. I'll call her now, maybe head over there."

"You don't have to—"

"Yes, I do. Think about Josh, Brian. Nothing but Josh. We'll find him and we'll bring him home."

"Okay."

Brian ended the call and checked the text, tapped the number on his screen, and sent a quick note to Ethan, then followed it up with a call. Ethan didn't pick up and the text remained unread. Fucking kids. Weren't they all supposed to be glued to their phones?

Tucking his phone away, Brian slammed through the front door and out into the snow. He turned right instead of left, instinct drawing him toward the place he'd found Josh the first time he'd run away. Briefly, he thought about going back for his car, but with the snow still falling, he was probably safer on foot. Besides, Josh was on foot, meaning he could only go so far—unless the trains were running on schedule.

Brian picked up the pace, jogging toward the end of the street, ducking across Morris, and cutting through the parking lot outside the station. It was after six, already dark, and commuters were pouring into the lot. Brian hadn't even registered the hum and shriek of a train on the line. Thankfully, it was headed west. He dodged one car, then another, before reaching the sidewalk, and had to push against the tide of humanity until he broke through to the platform.

He checked the commuter lounge first, scanning the almost familiar benches for a bright shock of blue hair. A figure with a hoodie hunched in the far corner, looking down at a phone.

Words of anger and recrimination both tore at Brian's tongue as he yanked the hood backward to reveal a young woman with black hair and dark-brown eyes. No piercings, just a scowl.

"Hey!" She leaned back, away from him, holding her phone up in front of her face as if it were a shield.

Brian stepped away, holding his hands out in a placating gesture. "Sorry. I thought you were someone else."

"Well, I'm not."

"Have you seen a boy with blue hair?"

"What are you on?"

"My nephew, he's missing. Has blue hair. Piercings. High school student."

Mouth hanging open, she shook her head.

"Okay, sorry."

Brian checked the men's room and then returned to the woman. "Can you check the ladies' room for me? Please?"

She gave him an incredulous look. Brian pulled out his wallet and she waved him away.

"I don't want your money. Wait here."

She emerged from the ladies' room a minute later, shaking her head. "Not there, sorry."

The stationmaster announced the arrival of the next train, bound for New York, Penn Station. Brian followed the woman trackside and scanned up and down. The platform was nearly deserted, and if the snow kept up like this, the trains wouldn't be running for much longer.

The train slowed to a halt and the doors swished open. Nearly howling with frustration, Brian strode to the far end, peering through the train windows, checking every shadow, calling for Josh. A part of him felt as though his nephew was on the train, somehow, some way. Another part of him mocked. Told him he was chasing a loose end.

Yet another part of him wanted to sink onto the platform and let the snow cover him.

A garbled announcement urged passengers to stand clear, and the doors banged shut.

Brian stood there and watched the train as it rushed past him, certain he should be on it, every passing door hissing out the worst kind of failure, the silver-lined windows surely carrying his nephew away from him forever.

CHAPTER 31

"I haven't seen Josh since the weekend," Ethan's mother said. "I think he and Ethan had a falling out of sorts."

"Can I talk to Ethan? Ask if he's heard from Josh?" Mal asked. Quiet rolled over the line. Mal checked his phone to see if he'd lost the call, then put it back to his ear. "Are you there?"

"Ethan is with his girlfriend tonight."

"Oh."

"His ex-girlfriend. They're not together anymore, but—"

"It's a confusing age. Even more so when you've got so much to figure out."

"You're telling me. Listen, I'm sorry I haven't been at any of the GSA meetings. I should have called. But I got the idea if I was there, Ethan might be uncomfortable. I support him, but I don't want to stifle him."

"I understand."

"Let me know when you catch up with Josh, okay? He's a good kid."

"I will. And if you hear from Ethan—"

"Of course. Do you have his number?"

"I do. I already texted him, but didn't get an answer."

"Keep trying."

Mal hung up and put the phone to his forehead. *Think. If I was Josh and my mom came to get me and my uncle shared a harrowing story, where would I go?*

If his mind could produce a series of dots to indicate a complete lack of answer, it would.

Waking the phone again, Mal dialed the one person who had always been there for him. A bitter feeling lodged in his gut as the call went through. Not guilt. Luck and love had given him a brother like no other, and a family who accepted him. It wasn't his fault that Brian and Josh did not have the same.

But still.

"What's up?" Donny answered.

"Brian's nephew is missing. He might have run away. Stuff happened. His mom came to get him, and, Jesus, what a—" *Do not call someone you barely know a bitch.* "It wasn't good. I only caught the tail end of things, but let's just say Josh going home is probably not an option. So he took off, and I don't know what to do. Brian's out there searching and I want to help."

"Okay. Okay." Donny's exhale fuzzed across the line. "Who does Josh know around here? Who are his friends?"

"He's close to one of the boys in the GSA. I called there. Mom says he's out. He's not answering texts."

"Keep texting. Kids are never far from their phones. Is there a place they hang out?"

"My classroom, after school."

"Can they get into the school after dark?"

"No. If it was a Friday, there might be a game. Every other day, the school is pretty much dead after the last activity bus leaves."

"What about the Colonial?"

"They're teenagers. Leo wouldn't serve—"

"No, I mean upstairs. It's empty up there, isn't it? And that's where you're planning to put the center?"

A sick feeling settled across Mal's gut. *Not anymore*, he wanted to say. Instead, he forced out a less than enthusiastic, "Good thinking. I'll head over there now."

"I'll meet you there."

"You don't have to come out."

"Damn right I do. Can't have Josh wandering around lost or thinking he's lost. Me and Brian might not get along. He's— I don't know. But whatever it was I saw in him, whatever he's hiding, I don't think it's as important as what he's doing for the kids. The school, the town. For you. Fuck, I sound like a damn Hallmark card."

The urge to tell Donny he'd been right, that Brian had had a secret, pulled at Mal. He opened his mouth and closed it. Not his story to tell . . . and even if it was, even if he had the feeling Brian wouldn't mind what he shared—which he most definitely did not— some things were better left alone.

Telling Donny that Brian had been homeless for nearly two years, had been used and abused, might lend credence to the goodness that obviously charged all Brian did for the community, whether he owned up to it or not. But if Brian wanted to play that card, he would have. He was a businessman and he was very careful with his professional reputation.

"You still there?" Donny asked.

Mal swallowed. "Right now, the most important thing to Brian is finding Josh."

"Then let's do it."

Donny insisted on picking him up and Mal didn't argue. Two of them in the car meant one could drive while the other kept a lookout— not that there was much to see through the curtain of falling snow.

"How many inches are we supposed to get?" Mal asked, eyeing the four already piled up on the ground.

"Six to ten, so we're maybe halfway done?"

"Not a good night to be out."

Answering with a distracted hum, Donny pulled into the small lot behind the Colonial and killed the engine. "Why don't you head inside, ask Leo if he's seen anyone with blue hair skulking around, and I'll check the back of the building?"

"Right."

Mal made his way toward the front of the bar, pushing through the snow with little effort. Tonight it would settle and become harder and more brittle. Walking through it would be more difficult.

Was there a metaphor in there?

He ducked inside, brushing flakes from his shoulders, and nearly bumped into Leo.

"What are you doing here?" Leo asked. "I'm about to close."

Mal gaped for a second, torn between telling Leo about the meeting, and stating his real purpose. Josh won out. "Looking for Josh."

"Who?"

"Brian's nephew. Blue hair?"

"Haven't seen him. What's up?"

"Have you got keys for the upstairs?"

"No."

"Donny's checking around the back."

Leo's forehead wrinkled. "Why is everyone looking for Brian's nephew?"

"Because he might not be in a good place right now. Did you know his mom kicked him out? That Brian's been taking care of him?"

"I did hear something about that. And he's missing?"

"Might have run away."

"Sure picked a good night for it."

Mal lifted his shoulders against the chill wind at his back. "You're telling me."

"Has anyone notified the police?"

"Probably the next step if we can't flush him out in a few hours."

Leo nodded. "Let me close up and I'll head down to the park, check the sports sheds and so on. Where we all used to hole up when we ditched."

"You don't have to—"

"Let's get him found so we can all go home and stay warm."

Mal retreated to the parking lot and found Donny pulling at a loose board in the fence running around the yard behind the bar. "Upstairs is locked up tight, but if I was smaller, I'd be able to get through the fence."

"And sit in a cold yard?" Mal put his eye to the gap and spied on the landscape of snow covered tables and chairs. He leaned away from the fence. "I don't think Josh is here. It's too open, too cold, too dark. Leo's going to check the park, the sports sheds at Cauldwell."

"I lost my virginity there."

"I don't think we're going to find Josh having— You know what? I don't care if we find him with his jeans around his ankles. So long as we know where he is."

"If we find him having sex in the snow, we're going to have to talk to him about several life choices."

Though Mal managed a grin, it didn't go all the way down. Inside, he was still cold and worried. "Wait!" The park, the park . . . "Remember the old boathouse?"

"At the top of Elliott, yeah. I—"

"No more sexual history. Some of the students in the GSA go there sometimes to hang out."

"I thought they knocked that place down after that girl drowned . . ." Even in the meager light behind the bar, Donny managed to lose color. "Get in the car."

"I'm getting, I'm getting."

Once Mal got in and belted, he pulled out his phone. He called Leo first. "We're going to check out the old boat ramp at the end of Elliott."

"The lake house? Good idea. I'll come up there if I miss at Cauldwell."

He dialed Brian next. "Hey."

"Heard anything?" Brian's voice stretched over a rushing sound.

"Where are you?"

"In my car. I was going to head toward Newark in case he caught the train."

"A couple of weeks ago, one of the students in the GSA mentioned that some of them hang out at this old boathouse at the park." A cold finger traced Mal's spine. "It's about two miles along the Patriots' Path, at the end of Elliott Street." About a quarter mile from where he'd had his legs knocked out from under him. To think he'd run past it nearly every day and not realized kids might be hiding inside. "We're going to check it out."

"Do you think Josh might be there?"

"I honestly don't know, but if he knows about the place and if he's been there with some of the kids from the club, then it's a strong possibility."

"I'm turning around. See you there."

CHAPTER 32

There were two other cars in the Elliott Street parking lot. Brian nearly sideswiped the closest as he swung into the next available spot—which was marked only by a smooth and uninterrupted swathe of snow. Of all the nights.

He jumped out of the car. The snow seemed to have eased a little. Only a few flakes drifted past the white halos of light surrounding the lampposts. Tugging his coat closed, Brian looked for tracks and found them leading away from the parking lot in a line past the lumpy white shapes of the playground and into the woods. There were a lot of tracks. More than a single teenager and one limping man would leave. Frowning, Brian pressed on.

Though the snow was tapering off, he shivered as he jogged through the trees, cold snaking down his spine, regardless of his coat. He'd left his scarf in the car. A sense of defeat made him colder. After watching the train depart, he'd stood on the platform for nearly ten minutes, rooted by indecision and memory, convinced that Josh leaving was his fault.

It was his fault, wasn't it? He shouldn't have shared his story. Had Ellen needed to know what had happened after he'd been kicked out? Was it really her fault?

Hunching his shoulders up under his coat, Brian tried not to think about it.

He heard voices before he emerged from the forest onto a wider path and found a cluster of tall figures pointing in three different directions, phone screens flashing. "I thought it was this way?"

"There are footsteps going this way."

"And that way."

"They're facing this direction, dip shit."

"The boathouse is this way!" That was Mal, recognizable by the sweep of his cane and his yell. He turned and spied Brian. "Hey. You caught up fast."

"I hadn't left town yet. What's all this?" He couldn't see who the others were. Whatever moonlight there might be was muted by clouds.

Someone flashed a lit phone past the blur of faces. "Leo, Kelsey, Mal, and Donny." It was Donny doing the flashing and talking. "We'll find your boy, Brian. C'mon. Mal says it's up here."

"I jog past it every day. Or I used to." Mal sounded rueful.

The group turned in the direction Mal had indicated and started off. Brian fell in behind, even though he wanted to run ahead. Actually, he just wanted to run. Somewhere. Hopefully in the same direction Josh had gone. Why were they all here?

Mal glanced over at him. "You doing okay?"

Rather than voice his questions and all the other bullshit rolling around inside his head, Brian nodded and put his chin down. Shoved his hands into his pockets and followed them through the snow and trees until a gray outline appeared out of the gloom.

Donny handed out directions. "Leo, Kelsey, take that side. Mal, you check the doors. Brian and I'll check the lake side."

Mal called out, "Josh!"

The other adults picked up the cry, and Josh's name echoed through the night. A sense of unreality plucked at Brian as he picked his way through the snow-covered mulch and hidden clumps of dead twigs and branches, following Donny toward the slope of ground between the house and the lake. Off the path, the trees were more numerous, but they opened up again, allowing more ambient light to filter through. The sound that had been pricking his consciousness for the past ten minutes swelled into a rush of water. Brian glanced at the lake, the quiet blackness that barely appeared to move, and frowned.

"What's that sound?" he asked.

"Run off. This is a catchment area. Part of the town water facility. There's a big pipe upstream. Interferes with the current, which is part of why they don't use this boat launch anymore."

Brian eyed the square shape looming over them. "And this building?"

"Closed up."

Brian couldn't see Donny's expression, but he could hear a note of concern in his tone. "Did something happen here?"

"Don't worry about it. If Josh is here, we'll find him."

The urgency in Donny's tone reflected the alarm pinging in Brian's middle. This was wrong. All wrong. Josh shouldn't be out here on his own. Not now, not ever. Brian started toward the slope, shoes slipping in the snow, and put a hand down to brace himself. Josh's name rang through the woods again, accompanied by banging as various folk pulled at boarded-up windows and shook doors.

Leo called out from halfway around the side. "Doors are all chained shut. If he's here, he didn't get in that way."

"Check the basement windows," Mal called from close by, before rounding the building and limping toward them. Brian paused to wait. Mal would regret the exertion tomorrow, no doubt, but Brian didn't send him back to the car.

He needed Mal here.

Was so damn grateful to have someone at his back.

A break in the clouds allowed moonlight to strike the ground, finally illuminating the scene. Spread out before them was the flat black surface of the lake, disturbed here and there by clumps of debris, piled with snow. Closer to the shore, the water churned, the current visible. The slope between them and the lake was too even to be just ground.

Right as Brian figured out it was a boat ramp, Donny said, "Are those tracks on the ramp?"

"Oh shit."

"Josh!" Brian jumped onto the slope and cursed as his feet flew one direction, the rest of his body another. He landed in a jarring heap, facedown in the snow.

"Brian!"

"Mal, don't!" Donny called.

Someone yanked at Brian's arm. "Up you get," said Mal.

Stunned by the landing and cold pressing across his face, Brian struggled to get upright. His shoes kept slipping away from him. "Fuck."

"Mal!"

"I'm fine, Donny. Give me a hand."

"You shouldn't be out here."

"None of us should be, but I'm not sitting on the sidelines while you all slide into the lake."

Brian had managed to push up to his knees. "Donny's right. You could wreck your knee again."

"Can we all stop worrying about me and concentrate on finding Josh?"

"We need to get closer to the water. He might not be able to hear us over the noise of the runoff." Donny got onto his butt and started scooting down the ramp.

Brian mimicked him until his shoes finally caught in a deep furrow beneath the snow. The old concrete was buckled and broken in places. He dug in and waited for the others to catch up.

"Josh!" Donny called.

"Crap." Mal slipped, and Brian grabbed him as he passed.

"Dig a foot in. The concrete is broken underneath."

Mal stopped his slide, grunting with either the pain or effort. Then another sound floated over the top. A soft cry.

"Josh!" Brian called.

A feeble voice answered. "Brian?"

Brian's heart pushed upward inside his chest. "Josh!" He got to his hands and knees and started back down the slope, crawling backward.

"Uncle Brian! I'm caught." A whimper cut through Josh's shaky words. "I fell and I'm caught on something. Help me, please."

Relief, anger, confusion, and outright panic warred for dominance as Brian pushed faster down the slope. "Josh!"

"Shit," Donny cursed. He started climbing back up the slope. "Guys! He's down here. Call 911. Let them know there's a kid in the lake at the old boathouse."

Brian didn't hear anyone reply as he slid forward toward Josh's voice.

"Brian!" Mal called out. "Wait up. You don't want to fall in as well."

"I need to get closer." The concrete furrow he'd been following down seemed to disappear. "Shit." Brian clutched at the snow.

"Hold up," Mal called from just above him. "We should wait for emergency services."

"I can't wait. Josh, how deep are you?" Brian could see where the ramp disappeared into the water, but not Josh. The sound of the runoff was much louder. He checked that direction, then downstream. There! A small shape bobbing against the shore, half hidden by a clump of low branches. "Josh!"

Brian let go of the ramp and slid. Snow burned his palms. His jacket snagged, yanking him backward, and then he was rolling, face slamming down into the snow again, smacking something colder and harder. His head spun, and he thought he could hear a scream. The world seemed to turn over and over, and then the dark water caught him, slicing up through his legs like sharpened blades. His teeth clacked together and he tasted blood. Then cold blackness swallowed him.

Breaking the surface of the water felt like pushing from one vacuum into the other. Brian bit back a yell as he reached for the side of the ramp and scrabbled against the current. He quickly discovered he couldn't reach the bottom, and the icy water was cutting through his clothing, knifing his legs and groin. Every moment seemed to make the water colder.

"Brian," a voice breathed next to him.

"I'm here." Brian grabbed the gnarled branches that had snagged his nephew, and Josh flailed through the dark, his arms knocking against Brian with enough force to push him back under the water. Fuck, it was cold. Brian managed to surface, though he was rapidly losing contact with his legs and wasn't sure how long he could keep treading water.

"What's caught?" he asked.

"My coat. I can't get the zip down."

Brian yanked Josh a few times before agreeing the coat was hopelessly caught. He had little hope that his fingers would work better than Josh's, but tried the zip anyway. He got it halfway down and then yanked, tearing the tab free of the sides. "Okay, one arm out."

"So cold." Josh's voice was thick now.

"Mal?" Brian called. "Other arm, Josh. Stay with me."

Mal was near the edge of the lake. "Right here, you . . . Jesus. Have you got Josh?"

"Yes. His coat is stuck. I'm going to get it off him and then pass him up. Are you secure?"

"Mal, get out of the way." Donny's voice.

"No, I want to help. I've still got two working arms."

"Barely."

Brian hoisted Josh up. He was damn heavy, and Brian imagined it was the weight of the black water, clinging to his clothes, running over Brian's hands. The coldness of it. Josh jerked in his arms and was then hauled upward, both Donny and Mal saying soothing things as they pulled his nephew out of his hands.

"Now you," Mal said, his face floating out of the darkness above.

"Get Josh warmed up, quickly. Did someone call 911?"

"Kelsey did. Donny's carrying Josh up the ramp."

Brian slumped against the tangle of branches. The pain in his legs had progressed from a burn to a weirdly numb ache. And he was tired. So tired. Heavy, like he wouldn't be able to pull his own weight back up the hill. How long had Josh been down here? He'd still been responsive, so—

"Brian!"

Brian shook off his fatigue. "What?"

"Grab my hands."

Brian reached up, and a warm hand closed around his.

"I got you," Mal said.

Donny's voice called out of the darkness. "Mal, let me do that. You can—"

"For fuck's sake, Donny. I'm not leaving him in the water. Either help me or stand back."

After more muttering, Mal's hands seem to creep down to Brian's wrists.

"This is such a bad idea," Donny said, closer now.

"Where's Josh?" Brian asked. Tried to ask. His tongue felt thick.

"Leo has him, they're wrapping him up in their coats."

"Hold on," Mal instructed.

Brian tightened his grip around Mal's wrists and started climbing up the ramp. At first it seemed like he was moving upward, and then he slid back, tugging Mal closer. Donny yelled. "Mal, no!"

"Pull me back, Donny. Drag us both up."

"Mal." Brian couldn't let him get injured. "Just wait for the emergency crew."

"No!" Emotion choked Mal's reply. "I'm not leaving you down here. You understand? I'm not going to be the guy who leaves you in the goddamn water. Dig your feet into something and climb out of there. Donny's got me. Now climb!"

Brian found a foothold, slipped, and heard Mal grunt as his full weight threatened to pull them both into the water. Thankfully, one hard yank from Donny got Brian back to the edge.

"Don't—"

Donny cut in. "Hold on."

"Donny!"

Dark splashing, and then another hand grabbed him.

Mal cried out once. Donny swore. Together, they pulled, and Brian felt himself being dragged out of the water. He wanted to lie down on the snow-covered concrete and rest, but they wouldn't let him. Someone yanked at his arm or shoulder or . . . God, thinking was hard.

"Nearly there . . ."

"Grab his other arm."

"Wasn't in the water that long."

"He hit his head."

"I've got him, Mal. Just get out of here."

"For fuck—"

"I know. I know."

The world dipped and splashed, and sight and sound blurred into one indecipherable entity. Then a big white orb bobbed in front of him. Was that the moon?

More voices, flashing lights, someone patting his cheeks.

It was all too confusing. And tiring.

Brian closed his eyes.

CHAPTER 33

Turned out letting yourself be used as a piece of rope left you feeling a lot like a piece of rope. Who knew? Mal scowled at the scrapes along the insides of his upper arms, not even remembering how they'd gotten there. From the edge of the concrete under the snow, probably. He had a similar set on his hip bones.

Pulling down the sleeves of the wonderfully warm and dry shirt Donny had brought to the hospital for him, Mal checked the double doors leading from the waiting part of the emergency room to the business part. His head wasn't high enough to peer through the small windows at the top of the doors, and his legs sent a sharp warning about standing. In a row beside him, Donny, Leo, and Kelsey all sat in a similar posture: legs spread out, arms folded across their laps, heads back against the wall. Eyes shut. Kelsey might even be snoring.

It was a quiet night at Morristown Medical Center. Only a few other people littered the waiting area, all pale and tired. The overhead TV was set to CNN, and the story unfolding in bad captioning across the screen felt farther away than two states down and to the left. Mal checked the doors again.

The important stuff was happening through those doors.

Pushing to his feet, legs wobbling and complaining, Mal grabbed his cane and tried to walk more than hobble over to the reception desk.

The nurse seated behind it greeted him with a tired smile. "I promise I'll let you know if there's any news."

"Can't you look on a screen or something?" Mal asked.

The double doors opened, disgorging another tired nurse. "Malcolm Montgomery?" she asked, gaze flicking among her variously reclined audience.

"Here," Mal said.

"You're here for Brian Kenway?"

"Yes. Is he okay?"

He heard the rest of his crew rise to their feet behind him.

"I can only take one of you back," the nurse explained.

"That's okay," Donny said. He gripped Mal's arm. "We'll wait here. Tell him we're all thinking of him and find out what's happening with Josh." He picked up a sodden backpack from the floor and pressed it into Mal's hand. "Here, take this with you."

"Will do."

"You seem a bit banged up yourself," the nurse observed as she led him through a labyrinth of identical corridors, the length of each marked with wide doors, some open, many closed.

Voices, moans, a quiet sob, the beep of equipment. The sounds of the hospital clogged his ears. The smell of it burned his sinuses. Dizzy, Mal gripped his cane more tightly. "I've been worse."

The nurse smiled. "Here we are, uncle and nephew side by side."

Josh was sitting on his bed, small and pale in the harsh light. He was wrapped in several blankets. He looked older than he had the day before. Sad. Eyes red and shadowed. Cheeks hollow. But he managed a smile when Mal appeared. A very tired smile.

Gauze covered half of Brian's face. He was dressed in a hospital gown and obviously displeased by it. He was plucking the material, talking to Josh.

Mal cleared his throat. "Hey."

Brian turned and scowled and it was kind of adorable.

Mal held up a hand. "Don't even. You asked for me."

A weak smile replacing the scowl, Brian sighed. "I did. Now I'm wondering why."

"Love you too, in all your scary glory." A hot prickle crept back across Mal's scalp. "So! How are you doing? When can you go home?" Surely a quick rush of words would cover the spill of words he hadn't quite meant to share. Not like this. Not yet. He liked Brian a lot. Respected and admired him. Valued the unlikely friendship they'd formed. Loved . . . God, that damn word. Liked having Brian in his bed and could easily imagine waking up to that scowl for a long time to come. But . . . "Leo already moved your car for you, and we're all waiting out front. So, um, whenever they're ready to let you go, we can get you home. Or if you want some dry clothes first, we can do that. I didn't want to—"

"Mal."

"Yes."

"Take a breath. I'm fine. I'm maybe concussed. Very mildly. As in, I'm allowed to sleep once I get home. Half of my face is sort of missing—"

Mal must have turned a greener shade of pale.

"I'm kidding. It's all banged up. I hit the ramp on the way down. But they did an X-ray and everything is where it should be."

"I'm sorry." Really? "I mean . . . Ah . . ." The dizziness was returning, and Mal wanted to weep with frustration. This wasn't the man he wanted to show Brian. Now wasn't the time for awkwardness or weakness.

"You okay, Mr. M.?" Josh asked.

Swallowing, Mal nodded. "I spent a lot of time here last year." That must be it. The weight dangling from his hand registered, and he lifted the backpack. "Hey, Kelsey found this behind the boathouse."

Surprise flickered across Josh's face as he took the backpack, holding it gingerly at first, then digging inside the front pocket. His expression brightened as he pulled out his phone. "Thank you!" Then his thumbs were working and the phone was dinging and Josh almost looked like a normal teenager again.

The nurse returned, then, holding out a sheaf of paper. "Okay, Mr. Kenway. Here's your paperwork and your prescription. You can get dressed and go home!"

"Thank Christ."

"What about Josh?" Mal asked.

Brian quickly filled him in. Apparently Josh hadn't been in the water for more than a few minutes before they'd arrived. Having come through the park, he'd only just beaten them to the lake house and had slid down the ramp while searching for a way into the basement.

"He's going to be fine," the nurse said. "You should keep him warm. Lay low a few days. Instructions in the packet." She patted Josh's shoulder. "You're one lucky kid, you know that?"

Josh's head bobbed up and down.

Mal helped Brian and Josh into dry clothes, and then they were walking back through those doors and being crowded through the next set, Leo and Donny arguing about who would drive Brian home. Mal trailed along, feeling as though he were having an out-of-body experience, until Josh appeared next to him.

Mal glanced over at the boy, who seemed to have shrunk even further in on himself over the past few minutes. "You okay?"

Josh looked up. "Yeah."

Mal nodded toward the phone clutched in Josh's pale fingers. "Have you talked to Ethan?"

A smile edged across his young face. "I did."

"I'm glad."

Josh nodded, chewed on a lip, then glanced at him. "Ah, Uncle Brian said . . ." He shook his head. Started again. "Thank you for coming to find me. I . . . We're going to talk about it, Uncle Brian and me. When he hasn't got a headache. He's told me if I leave the house before we talk, he'll do worse than call my mom and tell her to come get me. I don't know what would be worse, but . . ." Josh paused. Rubbed the sides of his face. "I wanted to . . . I didn't mean to . . ."

Leaving his cane to rest against his hip, Mal put a hand on each of Josh's shoulders. "I'm sorry I walked in on what should have been private, between you, your mom, and your uncle. If I could rewind time, I would. And I get it, why you ran out tonight. We could call it dumb, but we all do dumb things when we're upset." Briefly, he wondered if night and settling snow would always mean clarity. "He wouldn't do worse, okay? Not Brian. He'd do just what he did tonight: come find you. He loves you and wants the best for you."

Josh chewed on his lip a little more.

"And listen. We might not have a drop-in center yet. But you've got us, all right? You've got Brian and me and Donny and Leo and Kelsey. More, probably. You can call any of us, whenever, and we'll be there. Anytime."

Mal hadn't wanted this. He realized that with an internal click so loud, he figured the world must have heard it. When he'd taken over the GSA, this—almost exactly this—had been his greatest fear. That he'd start giving out promises he had no right to give. That he'd have to care for these kids. Make them his own. But the expression on Josh's face, the wrinkle between his fair eyebrows and the quiver of his chin made thoughts of any future trouble fade. It would keep. Whatever came next, it would keep.

Almost without thinking, Mal drew Josh into a quick hug, and the lanky teenager stepped in close. Said something soft against this chest.

From halfway into the parking lot, Donny called out. "Mal, you coming or what? We're taking Brian home."

Leo and Kelsey were hugging Brian. Taking turns. Hugging him twice each.

What a weird night.

Mal tucked his arm around Josh's shoulders. "C'mon. Donny's friendly meter is probably going to run out soon."

Donny didn't object when Mal told him to go on home and leave him at Brian's. Neither did Brian. So far, so good. Mal didn't want to force his company on anyone, but neither did he want to leave Brian alone tonight. For all two minutes remaining of it.

He waited by the car until Brian and Josh were halfway up the walk, then turned back to his brother.

Donny held up a hand. "Don't say it."

"You don't know what—"

"You were right."

"What?"

"He's worth everything you have to give him, Mal. And you deserve someone like Brian."

"I was going to—"

"But if you ever try to slide into a frozen lake again, I'm going to fucking kill you."

"The lake wasn't frozen."

Donny's mouth opened and closed a few times, and then he laughed. "Love you."

Mal reached through the open window and squeezed his brother's shoulder. "Love you too."

He trailed Brian and Josh inside and found them in the front hall, gazes bouncing off in different directions: Josh, from the door to the street, Brian the kitchen.

"Josh," Brian said. Josh glanced up. "Why don't you go take a hot bath and head to bed? Doctor said you need to take it easy for a day or so. You were pretty chilled when we pulled you out of the water. When I ..."

Josh bobbed his chin.

"We'll talk in the morning, okay?"

Another nod.

"I promise not to yell."

A twitch on one side of Josh's mouth.

"Good night."

Mumbling "night," Josh leaped for the stairs and disappeared. A moment later, the sound of the bath filling swished against the ceiling. When Mal looked down, Brian was watching him. Or maybe just staring in his general direction.

"I can—"

"Stay," Brian said.

"Are you sure? I can call Donny back, or get one of those Uber things."

"I'd really like you to stay."

"Okay."

Brian moved to perhaps scrub the side of his face, found the bandage, and touched that instead. "I don't know if I'm ever going to talk about what you heard in the kitchen—"

"Brian."

"What?"

Mal winced slightly as he let the words he'd been going to say bounce around his head a bit and heard how wrong they were. Not inadequate, but pretty much beside the point. "Whatever, whenever, and if that's nothing, ever, fine. This is us. Now. You and me at forty-eight and fifty. Neither of us is who we were at fourteen or nineteen or even two years ago. Does that make sense?"

"No."

Mal sighed.

Brian smiled with half his face. The un-bandaged half. "I heard what you said to Josh outside the hospital."

"Which part?"

"The bit about him having all of us. Places to go, people to rely on."

"I wasn't making it up."

"I know." Brian shifted a little. Sort of slumped. He put his shoulder to the wall, sighed, studied the floor, and blinked a couple of times. Something glinted in the air. His lashes were wet.

Mal shuffled in place for about a second before moving in. He half expected Brian to resist, but wasn't at all surprised by the ferocity with which Brian clung to him. It wasn't a hug. It was a hold that screamed, *Don't let me go. Please.* And so Mal held on and listened as Brian shook quietly against his shoulder. Mal patted his back and stroked his hair. Curled his fingers around the back of Brian's neck and held him close, the only sounds him whispering reassurances and Brian snuffling quietly. Then the quiet squall passed.

Brian inhaled deeply. "I'm so tired."

"It's late. Why don't we get you to bed?"

Finding one of Mal's hands, Brian threaded their fingers together. "You too."

Upstairs, the bathroom door creaked open. Another door closed soon after. Josh going to bed. Squeezing Brian's hand, Mal led him upstairs, past the heavy mist rolling out of the bathroom to Brian's bedroom. "Want a bath or anything?" he asked. "A shower?"

"Maybe in the morning. Right now I just want sleep."

Mal helped him with his clothes, moving his shirt out and over the bandage on the side of his face. "Do we need to check that before bed?"

"It can wait until tomorrow. It's only an abrasion. Some bruising. I'll be as handsome as always in a week or two." His rogue smile had a softness to it, as though he didn't care what he looked like in a week or two.

He helped Mal with his clothes. "How're the legs?"

Mal considered the burning embers extending from his hips, the coal that was his right knee and the deep ache that formed the bones of his left leg. Donny had brought some Advil to the hospital along with the dry clothes, but the dose was wearing off. He dug in the pocket of his pants for the small bottle of pills. "I'm not even sure why they're holding me up, to be perfectly honest."

"Force of will."

"That, yeah." Mal shook a couple of pills into his hand.

"You going to dry swallow those or wait for me to get you a glass of water?"

Even now, after all that had happened, Brian wanted to take care of him. Mal waited for him to return, and accepted the water with a grateful smile.

They slid into opposite sides of the bed and met in the middle. Face to face. Tucking away all thought, Mal angled his chin forward and dropped a light kiss to Brian's lips. Brian caught him around the back of the neck and pulled them closer, so they touched all the way down, chest to chest, hip to hip, toe to toe.

"Thank you for tonight," Brian said.

"Always."

"I'll have to thank the others too."

"They'll be there again, Brian. For you and for Josh."

Brian's smile wavered and with their faces so close together, his expression was a soft and blurry thing. "I know," he said. "That's why I . . ." He sniffed. "Might not make sense, but that's a part of why I was, um, upset before."

"Oh, Brian." Mal kissed him again. "Everything will be better in the morning."

It was something Mal's mother used to say, and the leading edge of the Montgomery family philosophy. Didn't always prove true. Sometimes the mornings were the hardest part. But they were always followed by other mornings. Days. Weeks and months. Time had a habit of flowing forward and eventually, a morning came where everything really did feel better.

Snuggling in close to Brian, Mal vowed to make it happen more immediately. Or, he thought as fatigue started blotting out the edges of his consciousness, he could just stay here until it happened.

CHAPTER 34

B rian stood outside Josh's door, trying to calm the hammering in his chest.

His face hurt. Earlier, he'd cautiously peeled the bandage back and was not pleased with the yellow and red mess underneath. Nor the bruise circling his right eye. He looked as though he'd been in a fight—which he supposed he had. Felt like he had. His whole damn body ached . . . but none of it compared with the pain in his chest. The poke and stab as he stood outside a plain white door, wondering if his nephew had packed a bag and left. Again.

Brian wouldn't blame him. He'd be upset, he decided. But he'd understand. Working his fingers into a complicated tangle in front of the doorknob, he added that to the process: upset, but understanding.

He pulled one hand free and raised it to knock. Figured it was his house and went for the knob. Then knocked anyway, because, damn it, Josh—if he was there, if he hadn't packed up and run away again—was a guest. Josh invited him in and Brian opened the door.

Noon sunshine filled the room. The day after a snowstorm was always unnaturally bright. The sun had half a foot of snow piled up on every surface to bounce and reflect from, and it seemed most of that light blazed into the spare bedroom. Josh was there, sitting cross-legged in the middle of the bed. He wore sweats, a pair of Brian's woolliest socks, and a long-sleeve T-shirt of unknown origin. In his hands, he held his phone, his thumbs working in tandem at the lower edge of the screen.

He glanced up at Brian hovering in the doorway and gave him a cautious smile.

"Can I come in?" Brian asked.

"Yeah." Josh put the phone aside.

Brian sat on the side of the bed. "How are you doing?"

"I'm okay. Still kinda tired."

"Good thing school is closed today, huh?"

"Yeah."

Brian nodded toward the phone. "Did you talk to Ethan? Is everything okay with you guys?"

"Why do you want to know?"

"Because he's your friend." Brian breathed out. "I know I didn't come across as his biggest fan, but, um, I think after yesterday you might have a clue where I was coming from."

"My mom's boyfriend?"

"Yeah."

"Ethan isn't like that. This whole thing isn't like that. He broke up with his girlfriend a while ago, before I got here."

"Okay."

"Are you going to send me back to Mom?"

"What? No. Why would you think that?"

Scowling lightly, Josh wrapped a hand around the back of his neck. "Because you were being all nice to me last night. Everyone was."

Brian held out a hand, hesitated, then gripped Josh's knee. "I'm not good at warm-and-fuzzy-type speeches, so I'm going to say this as plainly as possible. Any kid under my roof has my protection. Blood relation or not. It could have been Ethan out in the snow last night and I'd have come found him. But you are my blood. You're my nephew. You came to me for help and I'm here. For as long as you need me to be. So, no, I'm not going to send you home. In fact, I'm going to suggest a guardianship agreement to your mom. That means you'd be able to stay here for as long as you like. Through high school at least."

Josh opened and closed his mouth before finally letting out a single word. "Really?"

"Really."

"Why?"

"Were you listening to a word I just said?"

"Is it because I got tossed out?"

Brian sighed. Squeezed Josh's knee and let go. "Partly? I mean, we share a horrific sort of kinship in that respect. Also, you're my nephew. I can't ignore that. Mostly, though? I like you, Josh. I want to get to know you better and I want to make sure you have the same opportunities I was given."

"By the guy who took you in?"

"Yes."

"Will you tell me about him?"

Brian swallowed. "Maybe. I'd like to." As he said the words, they became true. He did want to share Tristan with his nephew, even if only to prove there were good and kind people in the world. "It's hard for me to talk about back then. Because it was painful, but also because I'm not that boy anymore."

Josh offered a sober nod. "I get that."

"Good."

A moment of silence passed, marked only by the minute swirl of dust near the bright windows. The flash of Josh's phone as he received a message. The sound of a snow blower somewhere outside.

"Josh?"

"Yeah?"

"Please don't run away again. If things get . . . bad, or if you're feeling overwhelmed, come talk to me. If you feel like you can't talk to me, talk to Mal. Or text one of your friends. Please. I want you to promise me that."

Josh's face wavered. His mouth and chin. His eyes. He sniffed and a single sob escaped. He rocked forward, and Brian performed the same service Mal had for him last night. He didn't say it was going to be all right. Nor did he try to quiet the tears. He held his nephew and let him cry it out. Fourteen was a rough age. Probably wouldn't be the last time he held this boy while he cried. This young man. And that was okay because even though he had little idea what being a parent entailed, Brian figured this was a good start.

A short while later, he stood outside another door, this time with less uncertainty. Mal would be inside. Mal wasn't the sort to run away. He was more . . .

He was Mal.

Brian cracked the door open. Mal was on the bed, curled on his side, glasses askew, phone in hand. He'd showered and might have combed his hair, but the pillow had pushed it around. He'd dressed in a pair of Brian's sleep pants and a T-shirt, and he had the throw from the end of the bed wrapped around his shoulders.

He was snoring.

The sight of his lover snoring on his bed warmed the middle of Brian's chest. He liked that Mal was comfortable enough in his home to let go.

He even liked the soft snore.

Toeing out of his slippers, Brian crawled onto the other side of the bed and arranged himself along Mal's back, putting an arm over his shoulder and snuggling in close. Mal smelled of oranges. Brian kissed the back of his neck.

Mumbling, Mal shifted and lifted his head. "Sorry. I was going to make breakfast."

"I figured." Brian kissed his neck again.

"Here, I'll—"

Brian nibbled the spot he'd kissed, and Mal melted against him before embarking on a shuffling turn that brought him directly into Brian's arms.

"Hi." Mal smiled.

"Hi." After kissing Mal's smile, Brian reached up to pull his glasses off.

Mal took them and leaned back to put them on the nightstand. When he rolled back toward Brian, he had a question in his eyes.

"What?" Brian asked.

"What are we going to do about the bar and the youth center?"

"You want to talk about that *now*?"

Color appeared in two spots over Mal's cheeks. "Sorry. I was thinking about it before I nodded off. I was going over the proposal on my phone and—"

Brian kissed him hard enough for their lips to make a smacking sound as they parted.

Mal's expression was sweet and a little unfocused, but as soon as his gaze sharpened, Brian knew there'd be no stopping him.

"If I hear you out, can we have sex?" he asked.

"Most definitely." Mal's smile dimmed. "So . . . it sucks that we can't save the Wheelhouse Building."

"It more than sucks. That's two businesses we're talking about, and Leo and Kelsey were a part of last night. They were there for us. I'm going to figure out how to turn this around, okay? I'll go back to the hotel people or start a petition. We'll chain ourselves to the bulldozers when they turn up."

"I thought you'd feel like that."

"So it's settled? We'll fight the good fight?"

"And if we lose, we get over it and move on. Find another building. Help Leo and Kelsey and Olive in other ways."

"Are you saying this for me, or yourself?"

Mal grinned briefly before offering a more sober expression. "For us both, I think. We had so much tied up in that meeting— God, was it only yesterday? And the talk we had afterward. I didn't like it. I'm sorry about my attitude and I'm going to work on my awkwardness."

"And my face will heal and I'll be handsome again."

Letting go a sharp laugh, Mal rolled on top of him. "You're so damned arrogant. It's pretty much my favorite thing about you."

Brian lifted his chin, inviting a kiss. Mal's lips met his in a sweet caress.

"I love your awkwardness," Brian said. "I know I gave you the impression you should let it go, but your vulnerability calls to me, Mal. Maybe that's a horrible thing to say, but I want to be the man you lean on. The one who makes you feel sure and steady. I want . . ." And there was that pain, worse this time. Not just an ache in his chest, but a digging pang, right over his heart. "I want you to need me the same way I need you."

Mal smiled.

"But that's not all. It's your strength I admire most. We come from very different places, but I feel like we've both had to struggle. Not just because we're gay, but because life is hard. But we're both still here."

Mal seemed about to say something, then clearly chose not to. He kissed Brian instead, all but fusing his mouth to Brian's, showing that underlying strength and secret passion and the goodness that shone through every smile, awkward or not. He tasted like sun-splashed mornings and fuzzy flannel. Toothpaste and pajamas. And he felt so damn right in Brian's arms. Big and strong despite his gentleness. Brian rolled him onto his back and kissed his face. Pressing each eye closed, nipping at the stubble along his jaw and brushing his lips there, delighting in the prickling tingle.

Brian traced his fingers down Mal's side, caressing him through the thin cotton of the T-shirt before slipping beneath it to wrap his hand around Mal's side and pull him closer. Mal reciprocated, his hand diving beneath Brian's sweatshirt before skimming upward to press over his heart. The kiss was sweetness, their caresses, light. Desire simmering until the stroke of fingers spread warmth and arousal, Brian brushing a thumb over Mal's hip. Mal reaching for Brian's cock.

"Want you," Mal said, nipping Brian's earlobe.

"I need no convincing whatsoever. How're your legs?"

Mal ceased kissing his way down Brian's neck. "I love that you always ask, but let's agree that unless I tell you otherwise, my legs are good."

"Last night—"

"Was stupid on so many levels. The scrapes on my hips and arms hurt worse than my knee, though."

"How about if I kiss them better for you?"

"That'd work."

Brian settled for kissing whatever of Mal he could skim his lips over while they dealt with their clothes, T-shirts, sweats, sleep pants, and shorts flying over the side of the bed until they could revel in each other's nakedness. Brian kissed Mal's nipples. Bit them both. Traced his tongue down the trail of hair leading to his navel. Found the abrasions over his hip bones and kissed them gently. Turned Mal's arms until he found the scrapes there. Kissed those too.

Mal put a hand to either side of his face after that and guided him up for another mouth-to-mouth kiss, long and languid. So damn sweet. Then he moved to whisper in Brian's ear, "Want you inside me."

Fear snaked along Brian's spine. He'd told Mal he didn't mind topping and he didn't . . . very occasionally. He didn't exactly know where his fear came from, but it probably had to do with control, which might sound weird to anyone else. People always assumed the top was the one in control, but for Brian it had always worked the other way.

But this was Mal and Brian didn't have to think too hard before deciding he wanted it. That what they had was a true partnership, and that being inside of Mal would be a gift. Special and something he really, really wanted to give.

"Okay."

Mal gripped his shoulders. "Are you sure?"

Brian brushed a kiss over Mal's lips. "For you? Anything."

"That's a dangerous thing to say."

"I trust you."

He let Mal arrange himself without asking about his legs. Mal chose to lie on his back—a pillow under his hips so he wouldn't have to shift too much, and when Brian was pressing into him, watching Mal's eyes for his cue to pause, advance, pause again, he knew he'd forever remember this moment. He planned to make love to Mal a hundred different ways before the end of the year, to maybe spend the rest of his life with this man. But this first opening, even more than prep, doing the thing with condoms and lube . . . This moment meant something.

Mal trusted him with this. With the most intimate of connections. Mal was okay with being beneath him. Mal was . . .

Mal was *here*.

Then Brian was all the way in and Mal's mouth was open, his head dropped back. He had his hands wrapped around his upraised knees, and his chest rose and fell in short pants. "Oh God, oh God," he said, his voice strained and beautiful.

Brian leaned forward to kiss his chest. "I know. You feel so . . ." There were no words, except maybe, "You were made for me."

"The way you feel inside me, I could totally believe that."

Mal lifted his head and Brian met him in a kiss. Then it was time to move. His balls were already high and tight, and pressure was building at the base of his spine. The feel of Mal around his cock was perfect, and them being here, together, was nearly enough. He could almost come just thinking about it. But moving would make it all so much better.

Mal cried out as Brian drew back. Huffed noisily as Brian drove forward again. Shifted his hands from his knees to Brian's waist "More. Don't stop."

Brian obeyed, pushing deeper, a little harder. When Mal made only sounds of pleasure, he did it again. Harder. The buzz at the back of his hips spread and intensified. Became a language of sensation, pitching higher every time he thrust.

Trusting Mal wouldn't break, that Mal was here with him, Brian let go. He gave in to the need to bury himself inside his lover, to rut, to grind his hips forward and thrust and thrust and thrust. He could hear himself grunting and panting. Mal sighed with pleasure between entreaties for more. His cock bounced between them, whacking Brian in the stomach until Mal wrapped a hand around his length and started stroking.

"God, you're sexy. Could come watching you."

"I'm close," Mal warned.

"Good, because I'm ... Ah, fuck." The first surge hit him, the leap before the fall. Brian jerked, rocked back, and then came, tumbling, maybe dying a little, and not caring if he never got to the bottom because this had to be the best part. He felt Mal come between them, the hot rush hitting his stomach. Heard his shout. Wondered, briefly, if Josh was wearing his earbuds. Gave up all thought as his orgasm swept through him, becoming his world.

When Brian opened his eyes, Mal was still beneath him, face slack with pleasure, smiling—no, giggling. Huffing and panting and making small laugh sounds.

"Why are you laughing?" Brian asked, bending down to kiss him.

"Because I feel fantastic."

Brian laughed. "Good enough for me."

Securing the condom, he bent into another kiss, swallowing Mal's hiss as he withdrew. He hopped off the bed, trashed the rubber, grabbed a towel from the bathroom, and went back to tend to his lover.

Mal caught him in another kiss, and Brian fell in beside him, exchanging kiss for kiss until he didn't know where he ended and Mal began.

Eons later, Mal flopped back and breathed out. "Every Sunday should be like this. I'm going to make it a rule or something."

"It's not Sunday." It was Friday. One day after what could be called the second-worst day of his life.

"Even better." Mal rolled to face him. "Means we get two this week."

"Perfect."

"So . . ." Mal's brow crinkled.

"Hmm?"

"We didn't talk about me sort of accidentally dropping the L word at the hospital last night."

"You did?" A fuse lit inside Brian's chest. "When?"

Mal laughed. "Oh my God. I've been stewing over this and you don't remember. It was, like, an offhand thing, but I was so embarrassed. Admitting that is embarrassing enough because it's not like we're sixteen and confessing to something we think is going to be it, forever and ever."

Brian moved his hand up Mal's side. They'd slipped back under the bed covers and were cozied up together as though it was a Sunday morning, and it was beyond nice. Mal was by far the cuddliest partner he'd had. Brian liked it. Loved it.

"I don't need a promise. What we have is perfect. Love is . . . It's so complicated."

Mal touched his face, pressing his palm to Brian's cheek. "But I do love you. It's small right now. Precious. Like a spark, you know? But it's there. It's the joy that spreads through me when I see you and when I hear your voice. When you make your scowly face or say things like, 'I'll be handsome again next week.' Feeling you inside me. Being here with you. It's a simple love and . . . damn it. It's what I've been waiting for. I didn't know it could be like this, but now that I do . . . God, sorry, I'm totally doing forever and ever, aren't I?"

His cheeks blazed and his eyebrows drew down, and Brian immediately felt the call. Something shifted in his chest, a rightness or a feeling of elation. A light being shone into a corner previously unrevealed. Forgotten.

Mal's words were beautiful, but it was the simplicity that made them so. And even as Brian prepared to give in, to see what was there, he realized he'd ducked into that corner a while ago and that the light was actually shining on him.

Mal said it so easily. Made it make sense.

Could he . . .

Mal brushed a thumb across his lips. "You don't have to say it back."

"I do love you, though. It terrifies me. We're so new and there's so much of us that came before." He stroked Mal's side. "But you deserve to know you're loved, Malcolm Montgomery. That there's someone here for you and only you."

Mal grinned. "Thank you."

"You're welcome. Can we be done with the talking part of the day?"

"As long as that means I get to stay here, cuddled up with you."

"Your house is cozier. Even with that cat."

"Then we'll move this afternoon. Josh can meet Lois."

Brian laughed. "What else are we going to do with our extra Sunday?"

"If you haven't bought Josh noise-canceling headphones yet, we should One-Click a set. Then maybe eat something. Watch a movie. Then more sex?"

Laughing, Brian rolled away to lie on his back. "Sounds perfect, and in two days we can do it all over again."

A hand slid into his, fingers curling tight. "We could call tomorrow Sunday as well. I mean, what use is a Saturday?"

"Sounds like a plan." Brian tipped his head toward Mal. "Then on Monday, we'll start figuring stuff out."

Mal nodded.

Brian leaned in, took in the sight of Mal's precious face, and felt the surge of emotion he now equated with his need to do anything for this man. "I really do love you."

Mal smiled. "Love you too."

EPILOGUE

Eight Months Later - October

Malcolm loved Morristown. His experience might be limited, but why should he seek to broaden his horizons when everything he needed was right here? His family, his job, his community, and a lover who had started wheezing into his pillow.

Mal shoved at the cat pinning Brian to the mattress. "Get off, you great lump."

With a querulous yowl, Lois allowed herself to be pushed sideways. Hopefully she hadn't—

"What the—" Brian jerked up and flailed, one arm flying backward, the other out over his side of the bed. "Jesus Christ, Mal."

"Hey, I wasn't the one perched on your back. I saved you."

"From your cat. One of these days she's going to suffocate me. Until then, she's just going to prick holes in me until I . . ." Brian had pushed up into a sitting position and was twisting his head this way and that, trying to inspect his back. "Did she draw blood?"

Mal leaned over to kiss the fading mark next to Brian's spine. "Not this time." He looked up. "I'm sorry. We'll start closing our door at night."

"You guys should be doing that already. Headphones to block out the sound of you two doing whatever haven't been invented yet," Josh said, leaning through the open bedroom door. He had a toothbrush in one hand and a towel in the other. "Can we get breakfast out, or are you guys going to—"

"Not discussing our sex life with you, Josh," Brian said, twitching the covers a little higher around his waist. "But unless you want to

KELLY JENSEN

be scarred for life, you need to go finish brushing your teeth in the bathroom. I'm naked and I need to take a leak."

Josh held up his hands. "Going, going!"

Brian turned around to find Mal looking very amused. "What are you grinning at?"

Mal flopped back into the nest of pillows behind him. "You and Josh and this." He indicated his house, which, with Brian and Josh permanently installed, felt more like home than ever. "I love this house. I love having you here. I love having Josh here."

"You obviously slept well."

"Actually, I didn't. I kept running my speech over and over in my head."

"Hold that thought."

Brian jumped out of bed and padded across the room to the bathroom, his ass disappearing from view all too quickly.

Mal got up and followed him. "We should start getting ready, anyway. Did you check that Vanessa remembered your tux?"

Brian flushed and washed his hands. "Yeah. I texted her last night. Told her my speech was going to be two words: stay married."

"So mean."

"This is her third wedding."

"Third time is the charm, right?"

"Humph."

Mal kissed Brian's frowny face. "Can't wait to see you all dressed up."

"Your suit is pretty slick as well. No elbow patches—I won't recognize you."

Laughing, Mal took his turn at the toilet while Brian started the shower.

Later—door-closed, voices-echoing-off-the-shower-walls sort of later—Mal donned his new suit and inspected himself in the mirror. Brian had helped him pick it out, and he had to admit, he looked sharp. Nothing could hide the fact he was more gray than his former dark blond. Even his eyebrows had begun to betray him. And he'd have to use his cane today, but no leg braces. He'd suffered another fracture at the end of March and had to wear braces on both legs for two months—when he was upright. But he'd made it to the end of the school year and had spent the bulk of summer on his backside watching Josh and Brian take care of the yard.

Next summer, he hoped to hit the trails again. He might never run, but he wasn't going to let that stop him from getting out there and doing what he loved.

Brian stepped up behind him and reached around Mal's shoulders to adjust his tie. "There."

"Thanks."

Brian was wearing a slightly less formal suit, seeing as he'd have to change later that afternoon. First up, though, they had the opening ceremony for the new LGBT youth center.

"Got your notes?" Brian asked.

"Nope."

"No? Where are they?"

Mal tapped his head. "In here."

Grinning, Brian kissed his temple. "All right, then. Ready to go?"

Mal checked his reflection again, this time with Brian standing at his shoulder, and smiled. "We should get a picture of us all dressed up." A blush burned an immediate path across his cheeks. "Ah—"

"I think that's a great idea. I'll make sure Tom gets some of us at the wedding this afternoon. A couple with Josh too. We can hang one in the hall. You know, one of those family portraits he'll have to lead his friends or boyfriends past to get to his room."

"You're evil."

Brian showed off one of his roguish grins.

They said goodbye to Lois, piled into the car, and drove the quarter mile to the Elliott Street parking lot. Not far, but with all the walking and standing he had to do today, Mal wasn't taking any chances. He did leave his cane in the car for the walk through the park, however.

A crowd was already gathered outside the new youth center, and Mal and Brian stopped a short distance away to admire seven months' hard work. The old boathouse had been completely renovated, inside and out. The ramp at the rear had been torn up and the slope leading to the lake was terraced with stairs joining each level so that even in winter, people could walk down to the new dock without worrying that they'd slide into the water. The dock extended out past the current, making it safer. A lifeguard would be on duty in the summer months.

Mal sucked in a breath. They'd done this. All of this. Would he ever stop feeling amazed?

By the time he and Brian made it through the crowd to the front of the center, shaking hands and accepting congratulations, he no longer felt amazed. He was exhausted and—

"Here." Josh handed him his cane.

Mal arched a brow in Brian's direction.

"Thought you might need it," Brian said with a smile.

"Thank you."

Then Ethan appeared and claimed Josh's hand, and the pair disappeared around the side of the building.

"Do we need to worry about what they're doing back there?" Mal asked.

"Nope, because it's time for you to do your thing."

Someone bumped into Mal from behind, and a flash of silver caught his eye.

"Please don't kill Mal with the giant scissors," Brian said.

Pamela giggled. "Sorry, Mr. M.!"

The mayor of Morristown stepped up to the microphone and the celebration started. The mayor began in the usual way, thanking everyone for coming to the opening and thanking everyone who'd made it possible. Her remarks were brief, and for that Mal was grateful. He didn't want his speech to duplicate hers. Then she moved aside and it was his turn.

Mal stepped up to the microphone and took a deep breath. When he exhaled, the sound system hissed. Leaning back a little, he smiled. "I wish I'd had a place like this to come to when I was a teenager. Not because I knew I was different, or because I felt alone. I didn't. I've been fortunate enough to have rarely felt alienated because of my sexuality. I've always had the support of my family and those closest to me. I've enjoyed a career many would have considered inappropriate at one time.

"But though I've rarely felt the need to hide an important part of myself, neither have I felt encouraged to share it. For nearly thirty years, who I chose to love has been something of an open secret.

Something people haven't encouraged me to talk about. I've been accepted as a member of this community because I'm not loud. I'm not proud."

Mal glanced over his shoulder at the newly restored building. "But I couldn't be more proud of what our community has accomplished with this venture."

Turning to the covered plaque mounted on the right to the side of the main entrance, Mal peeled away the adhesive covering. "Morristown, I give you the Kenway Center for LGBTQ Youth."

Beside him, Brian gasped. Mal didn't look over, because if he did, he'd probably start crying or laughing or something equally embarrassing.

"The Kenway Center is a project that we've all worked so hard for and the fact we were able to build it out of a place that was abandoned and almost forgotten feels meaningful. It's as though we as a town came together and said, 'You know what? Our kids need this. Our town needs this. Let's do it.'

"This was a place of tragedy. A young girl lost her life here ten years ago, and one of my students nearly drowned here last winter. His guardian also. But even then, this community pulled together to save them, and we've turned this building into a place of hope.

"The Kenway Center is open to all youth, regardless of gender and orientation. But in particular, it's a safe place for the kids who need it. Everyone is welcome here with the understanding that we are a community for the better."

Mal took Brian's hand. "If I'd had a place like this to come to when I was a kid, I might have lived more loudly. For me, now, that might not seem like it'd have made much of a difference. Like I said, I've had it easy. But if I'd been encouraged to be who I was at a younger age, then maybe I could have helped someone else who was having a difficult time. If I hadn't been afraid of who I was, I could have told someone else not to be afraid.

"So, I give to you a place where our kids can be themselves. Where they can be safe. Where they can learn to be proud of who they are and where they can learn to share that pride in helping others."

He dipped his chin toward Pamela, and she lifted the scissors toward the red ribbon being held at each end by Leo and Kelsey

She snipped the banner, and applause broke through the quiet fall morning.

Mal tapped the microphone. "I'm going to introduce our staff, and then we'll open the doors and everyone can head inside for coffee and some of Olive's fabulous treats." He beamed at the former café owner and gestured toward her. "Let's start there. Olive is our head of catering. She'll also be offering cooking classes." He gestured toward Leo. "Both Olive and Leo lost their businesses earlier this year when the Billings Group demolished the Wheelhouse Building. Though we were sad to lose a piece of our town's history, these two amazing people saw it as an opportunity to do something new. Leo is our daytime program director and is currently working on a second degree so that he can offer counseling services to those who need them."

Leo dipped his chin to acknowledge his role and moved to step back. Mal grasped his hand and squeezed. It had been difficult to tell Leo that they hadn't been able to save his bar, but Leo had taken the news better than expected. Turned out he'd only been holding on to the place to honor his father and felt he could do that just as well at the new youth center while actually using his psychology degree. Most of the Colonial memorabilia had been moved and now decorated the halls of the refurbished boathouse, making the place feel as though it had been a part of the community for longer than five minutes.

Mal introduced the rest of the employees and volunteers, detailing their roles and thanking them for being a part of the enterprise. His list included Rachel and Donny, of course, Kelsey, and Vanessa Smart, both of whom would be teaching art classes and running field trips.

Finally, Mal got to the last name on his list. "Donations from the community and generous grants from local businesses helped make this happen, but none of it would have been possible without the oversight of Brian Kenway. Like myself, he was not encouraged to be out and proud as a young man, and yet he has always been there for beneficiaries of the Smart Foundation scholarships and programs. With this center, he has stepped out from behind his substantial checkbook to do what he should have been doing all along. Work with the kids.

"Brian is more than our director of operations. He's the guy who saw a boarded-up hulk of a building and said, 'We can make this something special.' He's the guy who knew the right architects, the right builders, and the right people to staff our programs. He didn't want his name on the building, but we all decided he didn't have a say in that. He's running everything else, so we took that one thing away from him."

Laughter rippled through the crowd. Brian looked as though he'd welcome the Rapture at any moment.

Mal finished with another smile and, "Thank you, everyone."

Brian tugged on his hand, and Mal let himself be led around the corner. The students from the GSA were on hand to open the doors and invite everyone inside. This was their center, and they were ready to show it off. When Brian pressed him up against the cool brick wall on the shady side of the building and tried to melt him with a glare, Mal smiled.

"Not working."

"I hate you right now," Brian said.

"I know. I'm sorry."

Brian let his hands go and stepped back. "Can we change the name of the center? Put Vanessa's or Tristan's name on it? Yours? Hell, we could even call it the Colonial after Leo's bar."

"Let me think about it. Um. No."

Brian turned a broody circle. "Why me? All I did was sign a few checks."

Large checks. Mal had had no idea how much wealth Brian actually had because although he dressed well and drove an expensive car, he rarely spent any of it. Most of his wealth was tied in programs that benefited youth the money left to him by Tristan Smart and a good portion of what he earned. It had been the most surprising thing Mal had learned about Brian when they decided to move in together. That and the fact he really, really liked shoes. Like, needed an entire closet just for shoes.

"It's not only the money," Mal said. "It's everything else. Going to bat for us with the council, finding the right contractors. Organizing them. You did more than the rest of us."

"Maybe it meant more to me."

A lump rose in Mal's throat. Statements alluding to Brian's lack of family would always affect him this way. Ellen Kenway had signed the guardianship agreement without comment, as far as he'd heard. Mal wasn't sure whether her wordless acquiescence was a good thing or not, though. He couldn't imagine not being in contact with his mother and harbored hope that the relationship between brother and sister and mother and son might one day be repaired. But it was a slim hope. Ellen hadn't responded to the invite to today's opening.

Privately, though he grieved for Brian's lack of family—for Josh's situation—Mal was glad she wasn't here. This was Brian's day.

Brian tangled their fingers together again and squeezed. "Tristan would have loved this. Vanessa and Kelsey being involved, showing the kids art. Leo with his crazy hair and take-no-prisoners attitude. Everyone doing something not because it's right but because they care."

Mal smiled. "Still not putting his name on the front."

Brian returned a nod. "This has been the most meaningful project I've ever taken on. Vanessa and I started The Smart Foundation and Smart Kids to honor Tristan's memory. To try to duplicate what he'd done for me. Taking me in and helping me believe I was worthwhile. I went back to school because he convinced me it was important."

"I'm glad."

"But it took you to show me that I needed to do more."

Unable to speak, Mal simply nodded. They'd done that for each other.

"Love you," Brian said.

Mal's heart skipped a little. The fear that never quite departed. He knew Brian loved him. Knew they were making their relationship work and that it was a new and different thing for both of them. Open, honest, warm, and loving. But Awkward Mal wasn't laid to rest that easily.

Brian brushed a kiss across his lips. Mal leaned in, inviting a deeper kiss, and Brian delivered, as he always did. Their kisses were never casual. Brian kissed as though he meant each and every one. And that was how Mal knew Brian loved him.

Brian drew away to catch his breath and touched his palm to the side of Mal's face. "I wanted to ask you something before we went to Vanessa's."

"Okay."

"I know we've said we don't need to talk about forever and ever, but . . . I want that, with you. Not because we're going to a wedding this afternoon, or because we've already built so much together. But all of those things, on top of me finally feeling like I'm home. Every day. With you."

"Brian." Mal wanted to say more, but his throat felt too tight. He cleared it. "I . . ."

"You don't have to say anything—"

"Yeah, I do. I . . ." Mal had to pause for another throat clearing. "I want that too. You and me for always. I love you, and I want to be a part of your life for as long as it all lasts."

Brian's answering smile was radiant. He was a beautiful man, but in that moment, he was transformed. Lit from within. He pulled Mal into his arms and hugged him tight. "Thank you."

Mal circled his arms around Brian's middle, hugging him back just as hard. "Thank you."

"Going to be so good to you."

"I know."

"I mean it."

"I know you do, Brian. I have no doubts whatsoever."

Brian clutched him one impossible degree closer. "God, I love you."

"I love you too."

Explore more of the *This Time Forever* series:
riptidepublishing.com/collections/series-this-time-forever

Dear Reader,

Thank you for reading Kelly Jensen's *Chasing Forever*!

We know your time is precious and you have many, many entertainment options, so it means a lot that you've chosen to spend your time reading. We really hope you enjoyed it.

We'd be honored if you'd consider posting a review—good or bad—on sites like **Amazon, Barnes & Noble, Kobo, Goodreads, Twitter, Facebook, Tumblr,** and your blog or website. We'd also be honored if you told your friends and family about this book. Word of mouth is a book's lifeblood!

For more information on upcoming releases, author interviews, blog tours, contests, giveaways, and more, please sign up for our weekly, spam-free newsletter and visit us around the web:

Newsletter: riptidepublishing.com/newsletter
Twitter: twitter.com/RiptideBooks
Facebook: facebook.com/RiptidePublishing
Goodreads: tinyurl.com/RiptideOnGoodreads
Tumblr: riptidepublishing.tumblr.com

Thank you so much for Reading the Rainbow!

RiptidePublishing.com

Acknowledgments

Once is chance, twice is coincidence, third time is a pattern.

Fourth time means a story.

While writing Simon and Charlie's book, I realized that I had a habit of naming the not so lovely exes of my main characters "Brian." I don't really have an explanation for why. I know some very nice Brians! So I decided, then and there, even before I knew I was going write a series, that Brian needed a book. I wanted to know why he couldn't commit. I wanted to know his story. Then Frank got a book and Brian was the last of the three, meaning I actually had to figure him out.

I'm so glad I did.

Every book in this series has been meaningful in some way. The characters have been people I've always wanted to write. Charlie, my SF author, Simon, my quiet architect. Frank—loud and proud. Tom—too proud, and so true. Mal is my soldier. The man who never gives up. Then there's Brian, my enigma, my challenge. I loved figuring out what makes him tick and I love the book I've written for him.

Thank you to my first round readers: Eli, Lennan, Chris, and Skylar. Your feedback truly helped shape this story.

A bigger thank you to Caz, for helping me knit the two halves of this book together!

Thanks to the rest of the team at Riptide for their outstanding attention to detail.

Thank you to the readers who have followed the story this far; I hope you enjoyed the journey as much as I did.

As always, thanks to the Lady Writers for being excited about this book, and for all the help with the beginning chapters.

Thank you to my family, for standing by once again. Extra thanks to my daughter for answering all my questions about school and clubs and being a teenager!

Finally, thank you to all the people who strive to make a difference for our youth, regardless of gender, sexuality, or race. I've dedicated this book to Brian, because I wrote it for him, but it's for all of you too.

ALSO BY
Kelly Jensen

This Time Forever series
Building Forever
Renewing Forever

To See the Sun
Out in the Blue
Wrong Direction
When Was the Last Time
Best in Show
Block and Strike

The Counting series
Counting Fence Posts
Counting Down
Counting on You

The Chaos Station series, with Jenn Burke
Chaos Station
Lonely Shore
Skip Trace
Inversion Point
Phase Shift

The Aliens in New York series
Uncommon Ground
Purple Haze

ABOUT THE
Author

If aliens ever do land on Earth, Kelly will not be prepared, despite having read over a hundred stories of the apocalypse. Still, she will pack her precious books into a box and carry them with her as she strives to survive. It's what bibliophiles do.

Kelly is the author of a number of novels, novellas, and short stories, including the Chaos Station series, cowritten with Jenn Burke. Some of what she writes is speculative in nature, but mostly it's just about a guy losing his socks and/or burning dinner. Because life isn't all conquering aliens and mountain peaks. Sometimes finding a happy ever after is all the adventure we need.

Connect with Kelly:
Newsletter: eepurl.com/czGhYz
Website: kellyjensenwrites.com
Facebook: facebook.com/kellyjensenwrites
Twitter: twitter.com/kmkjensen

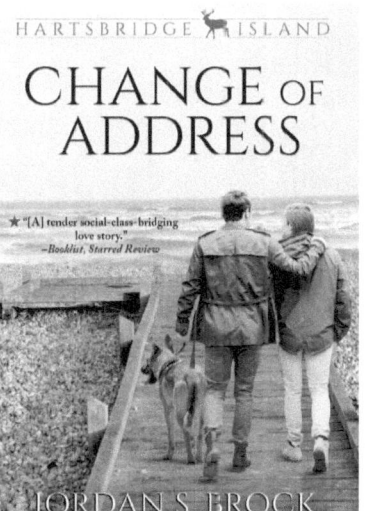